Julia Quinn started writing her first book one month after finishing university and has been tapping away at her keyboard ever since. The No. 1 *New York Times* bestselling author of more than two dozen novels, she is a graduate of Harvard and Radcliffe Colleges and is one of only sixteen authors ever to be inducted in the Romance Writers of America Hall of Fame. She lives in the Pacific Northwest with her family.

Please visit Julia Quinn online:

www.juliaquinn.com
www.facebook.com/AuthorJuliaQuinn
@JQAuthor

By Julia Quinn

The Rokesby Series:
Because of Miss Bridgerton
The Girl with the Make-
Believe Husband
The Other Miss Bridgerton
First Comes Scandal

The Smythe-Smith Quartet:
Just Like Heaven
A Night Like This
The Sum of All Kisses
The Secrets of Sir Richard
Kenworthy

The Bevelstoke Series:
The Secret Diaries of Miss
Miranda Cheever
What Happens in London
Ten Things I Love About You

**The Two Dukes of
Wyndham:**
The Lost Duke of Wyndham
Mr Cavendish, I Presume

Blydon Family Saga:
Splendid
Dancing at Midnight
Minx

Agents for the Crown:
To Catch an Heiress
How to Marry a Marquis

Bridgerton Series:
The Duke and I
The Viscount Who Loved Me
An Offer from a Gentleman
Romancing Mr Bridgerton
To Sir Phillip, With Love
When He Was Wicked
It's In His Kiss
On the Way to the Wedding
The Bridgertons: Happily
Ever After

The Lyndon Sisters:
Everything and the Moon
Brighter than the Sun

**The Ladies Most
(written with Eloisa James
and Connie Brockway):**
The Lady Most Likely
The Lady Most Willing

The Wit and Wisdom
of Bridgerton: Lady
Whistledown's Official Guide

Miss Butterworth and the
Mad Baron (graphic novel)

BRIDGERTON

TO SIR PHILLIP, WITH LOVE

JULIA QUINN

PIATKUS

PIATKUS

First published in the US in 2002 by Avon Books,
An imprint of HarperCollins, New York
First published in Great Britain in 2006 by Piatkus
This paperback edition published in 2021 by Piatkus
by agreement with Avon

15 17 19 20 18 16 14

Copyright © 2002 by Julie Cotler Pottinger

The moral right of the author has been asserted.

A CIP catalogue record for this book
is available from the British Library.

ISBN 978-0-349-42946-5

Printed and bound in Great Britain by Clays Ltd, Elcograf S.p.A.

Papers used by Piatkus are from well-managed forests
and other responsible sources.

Piatkus
An imprint of
Little, Brown Book Group
Carmelite House
50 Victoria Embankment
London EC4Y 0DZ

An Hachette UK Company
www.hachette.co.uk

www.littlebrown.co.uk

For Stefanie and Randall Hargreaves—
You opened your home,
you showed us your town,
you stored our stuff,
and when we arrived,
you had a care package waiting on the porch.

And when I really needed someone,
I knew exactly who to call.

And also for Paul,
this time Because.
It's always really Because.

. . . I know you say I shall someday like boys, but I say never! NEVER!!! With three exclamation points!!!

—from Eloise Bridgerton to her mother,
shoved under Violet Bridgerton's door
during Eloise's eighth year

. . . I never dreamed that a season could be so exciting! The men are so handsome and charming. I know I shall fall in love straightaway. How could I not?

—from Eloise Bridgerton to her brother Colin,
upon the occasion of her London debut

. . . I am quite certain I shall never marry. If there was someone out there for me, don't you think I should have found him by now?

—from Eloise Bridgerton to her
dear friend Penelope Featherington,
during her sixth season as a debutante

. . . this is my last chance. I am grabbing destiny with both my hands and throwing caution to the wind. Sir Phillip, please, *please,* be all that I have imagined you to be. Because if you are the man your letters portray you to be, I think I could love you. And if you felt the same . . .

—from Eloise Bridgerton, jotted on a scrap of paper,
on her way to meet Sir Phillip Crane
for the very first time

February 1823
Gloucestershire, England

It was ironic, really, that it had happened on such a sunny day.

The first sunny day in, what had it been—six straight weeks of gray skies, accompanied by the occasional sprinkling of light snow or rain? Even Phillip, who'd thought himself impervious to the vagaries of the weather, had felt his spirits lighten, his smile widen. He'd gone outside—he'd had to. No one could remain indoors during such a splendid display of sunshine.

Especially in the middle of such a gray winter.

Even now, more than a month after it had happened, he couldn't quite believe that the sun had had the temerity to tease him so.

And how was it that he'd been so blind that he'd not expected it? He'd lived with Marina since the day of their marriage. Eight long years to know the woman. He should have expected it. And in truth . . .

Well, in truth, he *had* expected it. He just hadn't wanted to admit to the expectation. Perhaps he was just trying to delude himself, protect himself, even. To hide from the obvious, hoping that if he didn't think about it, it would never happen.

But it did. And on a sunny day, to boot. God certainly had a sick sense of humor.

He looked down at his glass of whiskey, which was, quite inexplicably, empty. He must have drunk the damned thing, and yet he had no memory of doing so. He didn't feel woozy, at least not as woozy as he should have been. Or even as woozy as he wanted to be.

He stared out the window at the sun, which was slipping low on the horizon. It had been another sunny day today. That probably explained his exceptional melancholy. At least he hoped it did. He wanted an explanation, needed one, for this awful tiredness that seemed to be taking over.

Melancholy terrified him.

More than anything. More than fire, more than war, more than hell itself. The thought of sinking into sadness, of being like *her* . . .

Marina had been melancholy. Marina had spent her entire life, or at least the entire life he'd known, melancholy. He couldn't remember the sound of her laughter, and in truth, he wasn't sure that he'd ever known it.

It had been a sunny day, and—

He squeezed his eyes shut, not certain whether the motion was meant to urge the memory or dispel it.

It had been a sunny day, and . . .

* * *

"Never thought you'd feel the likes of that on your skin again, eh, Sir Phillip?"

Phillip Crane turned his face to the sun, closing his eyes as he let the warmth spread over his skin. "It's perfect," he murmured. "Or it would be, if it weren't so bloody cold."

Miles Carter, his secretary, chuckled. "It's not as cold as that. The lake hasn't frozen this year. Just a few patchy spots."

Reluctantly, Phillip turned away from the sun and opened his eyes. "It isn't spring, though."

"If you were wishing for spring, sir, perhaps you should have consulted a calendar."

Phillip regarded him with a sideways glance. "Do I pay you for such impertinence?"

"Indeed. And rather handsomely, too."

Phillip smiled to himself as both men paused to enjoy the sun for a few moments longer.

"I thought you didn't mind the gray," Miles said conversationally, once they'd resumed their trek to Phillip's greenhouse.

"I don't," Phillip said, striding along with the confidence of a natural athlete. "But just because I don't mind an overcast sky doesn't mean I don't prefer the sun." He paused, thought for a moment. "Be sure to tell Nurse Millsby to take the children outside today. They'll need warm coats, of course, and hats and mittens and the like, but they ought to get a little sun on their faces. They've been cooped up far too long."

"As have we all," Miles murmured.

Phillip chuckled. "Indeed." He glanced over his shoulder at his greenhouse. He probably ought to take care of his correspondence now, but he had some seeds he needed to sort through, and truly, there was no reason he couldn't conduct his business with Miles in an hour or so. "Go on," he said to Miles. "Find Nurse Millsby. You and I can deal later. You know you hate the greenhouse, anyway."

"Not this time of year," Miles said. "The heat is rather welcome."

Phillip arched a brow as he inclined his head toward Romney Hall. "Are you calling my ancestral home drafty?"

"All ancestral homes are drafty."

"True enough," Phillip said with a grin. He rather liked Miles. He'd hired him six months earlier to help with the mountains of paperwork and details that seemed to accumulate from the running of his small property. Miles was quite good. Young, but good. And his dry sense of humor was certainly welcome in a house where laughter was never in abundance. The servants would never dare joke with Phillip, and Marina . . . well, it went without saying that Marina did not laugh or tease.

The children sometimes made Phillip laugh, but that was a different sort of humor, and besides, most of the time he did not know what to say to them. He tried, but then he felt too awkward, too big, too strong, if such a thing were possible. And then he just found himself shooing them off, telling them to go back to their nurse.

It was easier that way.

"Go on, then," Phillip said, sending Miles off on a task he probably should have done himself. He hadn't seen his children yet today, and he supposed he ought to, but he didn't want to spoil the day by saying something stern, which he inevitably seemed to do.

He'd find them while they were off on their nature walk with Nurse Millsby. That would be a good idea. Then he could point out some sort of plant and tell them about it, and everything would remain perfectly simple and benign.

Phillip entered his greenhouse and shut the door behind him, taking a welcome breath of the moist air. He'd studied botany at Cambridge, taken a first, even, and in truth, he'd probably have taken up an academic life if his older brother had not died at Waterloo, thrusting the second-born Phillip into the role of landowner and country gentleman.

He supposed it could have been worse. He could have been landowner and city gentleman, after all. At least here he was able to pursue his botanical pursuits in relative serenity.

He bent over his workbench, examining his latest project—a strain of peas that he was trying to breed to grow fatter and plumper in the pod. No luck yet, though. This latest batch was not just shriveled but had even turned yellow, which had not been the expected result at all.

Phillip frowned, then allowed himself a small smile as he moved to the back of the greenhouse to gather his supplies. He never minded too terribly when his experiments did not produce the expected outcome. In his opinion, necessity had never been the mother of invention.

Accidents. It was all about accidents. No scientist would admit to it, of course, but most great invention occurred while one was attempting to solve some other problem entirely.

He chuckled as he swept the shriveled peas aside. At this rate, he'd cure gout by the end of the year.

Back to work. Back to work. He bent over his seed collection, smoothing them out so that he could examine them all. He needed just the right one for—

He looked up and out the freshly washed glass. A movement across the field caught his eye. A flash of red.

Red. Phillip smiled to himself as he shook his head. It must be Marina. Red was her favorite color, something that he'd always found odd. Anyone who spent any time with her would have surely thought she'd prefer something darker, more somber.

He watched as she disappeared into the wooded copse, then got back to work. It was rare for Marina to venture outside. These days she didn't often leave the confines of her bedchamber. Phillip was happy to see her out in the sun. Maybe it would restore her spirits. Not completely, of course. Phillip didn't think even the sun had the ability to do that. But maybe a bright, warm day would be enough to draw her out for a few hours, bring a small smile to her face.

Heaven knew the children could use that. They visited their mother in her room almost every evening, but it wasn't enough.

And Phillip knew that this lack was not made up for by him.

He sighed, a wave of guilt washing over him. He was not the sort of father they needed, he knew that. He tried to tell himself that he was doing his best, that he was succeeding in what was his only goal when it came to parenthood—that he *not* behave in the manner of his own father.

But still he knew it wasn't enough.

With resolute motions, he pushed himself away from his workbench. The seeds could wait. His children could probably wait, too, but that didn't mean they should. And he ought to take them on their nature walk, not Nurse Millsby, who didn't know a deciduous tree from a coniferous and would most likely tell them that a rose was a daisy and . . .

He glanced out the window again, reminding himself that it was February. Nurse Millsby wasn't likely to locate any sort of flower in this weather, but still, it didn't excuse the fact that *he* ought to take the children on their nature walk. It was the one sort of children's activity at which he truly excelled, and he ought not shirk the responsibility.

He strode out of the greenhouse but then stopped, not even a third of the way back to Romney Hall. If he was going to fetch the children, he ought to take them out to see their mother. They craved her company, even when she did nothing more than pat them on the head. Yes, they should find Marina. That would be even more beneficial than a nature walk.

But he knew from experience that he ought not make assumptions about Marina's state of mind. Just because she'd ventured outside did not mean that she was feeling well. And he hated when the children saw her in one of her moods.

Phillip turned around and headed out toward the copse where he'd seen Marina disappear just a few moments earlier. He walked with nearly twice the speed of Marina; it wouldn't take very long to catch up to her and ascertain her mood. He could be back at the nursery before the children set out with Nurse Millsby.

He walked through the woods, easily following Marina's path. The ground was moist, and Marina must have been wearing heavy boots, because her prints had sunk into the earth with clear definition. They led down the slight incline and out of the woods, then onto a grassy patch.

"Damn," Phillip muttered, the word barely audible as the wind picked up around him. It was impossible to see her footprints on the grass. He used his hand to shade his eyes from the sun and scanned the horizon, looking for a telltale scrap of red.

Not near the abandoned cottage, nor at Phillip's field of experimental grains, nor at the large boulder that Phillip had spent so many hours clambering upon when he was a child. He turned north, his eyes narrowing when he finally saw her. She was heading toward the lake.

The lake.

Phillip's lips parted as he stared down at her form, moving slowly toward the water's edge. He wasn't quite frozen; it was more that he was . . . suspended . . . as his mind took in the strange sight. Marina didn't swim. He didn't even know if she could. He supposed she was aware that there was a lake on the grounds, but in truth, he'd never known her to go there, not in the eight years they'd been married. He started walking toward her, his feet somehow recognizing what his mind refused to accept. As she stepped into the shallows, he picked up speed, still too far to do anything but call out her name.

But if she heard him, she made no indication, just continued her slow and steady progress into the depths.

"Marina!" he screamed, now breaking into a run. He was still a good minute away, even moving at top speed. "Marina!"

She reached the point where the bottom dropped off, and then she dropped off, too, disappearing under the gunmetal gray of the surface, her red cloak floating along the top for a few seconds before being sucked under after her.

He yelled her name again, even though she couldn't possibly hear. He skidded and stumbled down the hill leading to the lake, then had just enough presence of mind to yank off his coat and boots before diving into the freezing-cold water. She'd been under barely a minute; his mind recognized that that was probably not enough time to drown, but every second it took him to find her was one second toward her death.

He'd swum in the lake countless times, knew exactly where the bottom dropped off, and he reached that critical point with swift, even strokes, barely noticing the drag of the water against his heavy clothes.

He could find her. He *had* to find her.

Before it was too late.

He dove down, his eyes scanning the murky water. Marina must have kicked up some of the sand from the bottom, and he had surely done the same, because the fine silt was swirling around him, the puffy opaque clouds making it difficult to see.

But in the end, Marina was saved by her one colorful quirk, and Phillip pumped through the water, down to the bottom where he saw the red of her cloak floating through the water like a languorous kite. She did not fight him as he pulled her to the surface; indeed, she had already lost consciousness and was nothing more than a dead weight in his arms.

They broke out into the air, and he took great, big gasps to fill his burning lungs. For a moment he could do nothing but breathe, his body recognizing that it had to save itself before he could save anyone else. Then he pulled her along to the shore, careful to keep her face above water, even though she didn't seem to be breathing.

Finally, they reached the water's edge, and he dragged her upon the narrow strip of dirt and pebbles that separated the water from the grass. With frantic movements he felt in front of her face for air, but there was none emerging from her lips.

He didn't know what to do, hadn't thought he'd ever have to save someone from drowning, so he just did what seemed most sensible and heaved her over his lap, face down, whacking her on the back. Nothing happened at first, but after the fourth violent thrust, she coughed, and a stream of murky water erupted from her mouth.

He turned her over quickly. "Marina?" he asked urgently, lightly slapping her face. "Marina?"

She coughed again, her body wracked by spasmodic tremors. Then she began to suck in air, her lungs forcing her to live, even when her soul desired something else.

"Marina," Phillip said, his voice shaking with relief. "Thank God." He didn't love her, had never really loved her, but she was his wife, and she was the mother of his children, and she was, deep down, beneath her unshakable cloak of sorrow and despair, a good and fine person. He may not have loved her, but he did not want her death.

She blinked, her eyes unfocused. And then, finally, she seemed to realize where she was, who he was, and she whispered, "No."

"I've got to get you back to the house," he said gruffly, startled by how angry he was over that single word.

No.

How dare she refuse his rescue? Would she give up on life just because she was *sad*? Did her melancholy amount to more than their two children? In the balance of life, did a bad mood weigh more than their need for a mother?

"I'm taking you home," he bit out, heaving her none too gently into his arms. She was breathing now, and clearly in possession of her faculties, misguided though they may be. There was no need to treat her like a delicate flower.

"No," she sobbed quietly. "Please don't. I don't want . . . I don't . . ."

"You're going home," he stated, trudging up the hill, oblivious to the chill wind turning his sodden clothes to ice; oblivious, even, to the rocky soil pressing into his unshod feet.

"I can't," she whispered, with what seemed like her last ounce of energy.

And as Phillip carried his burden home, all he could think was how apt those words were.

I can't.

In a way, it seemed to sum up her entire life.

By nightfall, it became apparent that fever might succeed where the lake had failed.

Phillip had carried Marina home as quickly as he was able, and, with the aid of Mrs. Hurley, his house-keeper, had stripped her of her icy garments and tried to warm her beneath the goose-down quilt that had been the centerpiece of her trousseau eight years earlier.

"What happened?" Mrs. Hurley had gasped when he staggered through the kitchen door. He hadn't wanted to use the main entrance, where he might be seen by his children, and besides, the kitchen door was closer by a good twenty yards.

"She fell in the lake," he said gruffly.

Mrs. Hurley gave him a look that was somehow dubious and sympathetic all at the same time, and he knew that she knew the truth. She had worked for the Cranes since their marriage; she knew Marina's moods.

She had shooed him out of the room once they had Marina in bed, insisting that he change his own clothing before he caught his death as well. He had returned, though, to Marina's side. That was his place as her husband, he thought guiltily, a place he had avoided in recent years.

It was depressing to be with Marina. It was *hard*.

But now wasn't the time to shirk his duties, and so he sat at her bedside throughout the day and into the night. He mopped her brow when she began to perspire, tried to pour lukewarm broth down her throat when she was calm.

He told her to fight, even though he knew his words fell on deaf ears.

Three days later she was dead.

It was what she'd wanted, but that was little comfort as Phillip faced his children, twins, just turned seven years old, and tried to explain that their mother was gone. He sat in their nursery, his large frame too big for any of their tot-sized chairs. But he sat, anyway, twisted like a pretzel, and forced himself to meet their gazes as he wrenched out the words.

They said little, which was unlike them. But they didn't look surprised, which Phillip found disturbing.

"I—I'm sorry," he choked out, once he reached the end of his speech. He loved them so much, and he failed them in so many ways. He barely knew how to be a father to them; how in hell was he meant to take on the role of mother as well?

"It's not your fault," Oliver said, his brown eyes capturing his father's with an intensity that was unsettling. "She fell in the lake, didn't she? You didn't push her."

Phillip only nodded, unsure of how to respond.

"Is she happy now?" Amanda asked softly.

"I think so," Phillip said. "She gets to watch you all the time now from heaven, so she must be happy."

The twins seemed to consider that for quite some time. "I hope she's happy," Oliver finally said, his voice more resolute than his expression. "Maybe she won't cry anymore."

Phillip felt his breath catch in his throat. He hadn't realized that they had heard Marina's sobs. She only seemed to sink so low late at night; their room was directly above hers, but he'd always assumed they'd already fallen asleep when their mother started to cry.

Amanda nodded her agreement, her little blond

head bobbing up and down. "If she's happy now," she said, "then I'm glad she's gone."

"She's not gone," Oliver cut in. "She's dead."

"No, she's gone," Amanda persisted.

"It's the same thing," Phillip said flatly, wishing he had something to tell them other than the truth. "But I think she's happy now."

And in a way, that was the truth, too. It was what Marina had wanted, after all. Maybe it was all she had wanted all along.

Amanda and Oliver were quiet for a long while, both keeping their eyes on the floor as their legs swung from their perch on Oliver's bed. They looked so small, sitting there on a bed that was clearly too high for them. Phillip frowned. How was it that he'd never noticed this before? Shouldn't they be on lower beds? What if they fell off in the night?

Or maybe they were too big for all that. Maybe they didn't fall out of bed any longer. Maybe they never had.

Maybe he truly was an abominable father. Maybe he should know these things.

Maybe . . . maybe . . . He closed his eyes and sighed. Maybe he should stop thinking quite so much and simply try his best and be happy with that.

"Are you going to go away?" Amanda asked, raising her head.

He looked into her eyes, so blue, so like her mother's. "No," he whispered fiercely, kneeling before her and taking her tiny hands in his own. They looked so small in his grasp, so fragile.

"No," he repeated. "I'm not going away. I'm not ever going away. . . ."

* * *

Phillip looked down at his whiskey glass. It was empty again. Funny how a whiskey glass could go empty even after one filled it four times.

He hated remembering. He wasn't sure what was the worst. Was it the dive underwater or the moment Mrs. Hurley had turned to him and said, "She's gone"?

Or was it his children, the sorrow on their faces, the fear in their eyes?

He lifted the glass to his lips, letting the final drops slide into his mouth. The worst part was definitely his children. He'd told them he wouldn't ever leave them, and he hadn't—he wouldn't—but his simple presence wasn't enough. They needed more. They needed someone who knew how to be a parent, who knew how to speak to them and understand them and get them to mind and behave.

And since he couldn't very well get them another father, he supposed he ought to think about finding them a mother. It was too soon, of course. He couldn't marry anyone until his prescribed period of mourning was completed, but that didn't mean he couldn't look.

He sighed, slumping in his seat. He needed a wife. Almost any wife would do. He didn't care what she looked like. He didn't care if she had money. He didn't care if she could do sums in her head or speak French or even ride a horse.

She just had to be happy.

Was that so much to want in a wife? A smile, at least once a day. Maybe even the sound of her laughter?

And she had to love his children. Or at least pretend so well that they never knew the difference.

It wasn't so much to ask for, was it?

"Sir Phillip?"

Phillip looked up, cursing himself for having left his study door slightly ajar. Miles Carter, his secretary, was poking his head in.

"What is it?"

"A letter, sir," Miles said, walking forward to hand him an envelope. "From London."

Phillip looked down at the envelope in his hand, his brows rising at the obviously feminine slant to the handwriting. He dismissed Miles with a nod, then picked up his letter opener and slid it under the wax. A single sheet of paper slipped out. Phillip rubbed it between his fingers. High quality. Expensive. Heavy, too, a clear sign that the sender need not economize to reduce franking costs.

Then he turned it over and read:

No. 5, Bruton Street
London

Sir Phillip Crane—

I am writing to express my condolences on the loss of your wife, my dear cousin Marina. Although it has been many years since I last saw Marina, I remember her fondly and was deeply saddened to hear of her passing.

Please do not hesitate to write if there is anything I can do to ease your pain at this difficult time.

Yrs,
Miss Eloise Bridgerton

Phillip rubbed his eyes. Bridgerton . . . Bridgerton. Did Marina have Bridgerton cousins? She must have done, if one of them was sending him a letter.

He sighed, then surprised himself by reaching for his own stationery and quill. He'd received precious few condolence notes since Marina had died. It seemed most of her friends and family had forgotten her since her marriage. He supposed he shouldn't be upset, or even surprised. She'd rarely left her bedchamber; it was easy to forget about someone one never saw.

Miss Bridgerton deserved a reply. It was common courtesy, or even if it wasn't (and Phillip was quite certain he didn't know the full etiquette of one's wife dying), it still somehow seemed like the right thing to do.

And so, with a weary breath, he put his quill to paper.

Chapter 1

May 1824
Somewhere on the road from
London to Gloucestershire
The middle of the night

~

Dear Miss Bridgerton —

Thank you for your kind note at the loss of my wife.
It was thoughtful of you to take the time to write to
a gentleman you have never met. I offer you this
pressed flower as thanks. It is naught but the simple
red campion (Silene dioica), but it brightens the
fields here in Gloucestershire, and indeed seems to
have arrived early this year.
It was Marina's favorite wildflower.

Sincerely,
Sir Phillip Crane

Eloise Bridgerton smoothed the well-read sheet of
paper across her lap. There was little light by which

to see the words, even with the full moon shining through the windows of the coach, but that didn't really matter. She had the entire letter memorized, and the delicate pressed flower, which was actually more pink than red, was safely protected between the pages of a book she'd nipped from her brother's library.

She hadn't been too terribly surprised when she'd received a reply from Sir Phillip. Good manners dictated as much, although even Eloise's mother, surely the supreme arbiter of good behavior, said that Eloise took her correspondence a bit too seriously.

It was common, of course, for ladies of Eloise's station to spend several hours each week writing letters, but Eloise had long since fallen into the habit of taking that amount of time each day. She enjoyed writing notes, especially to people she hadn't seen in years (she'd always liked to imagine their surprise when they opened her envelope), and so she pulled out her pen and paper for most any occasion—births, deaths, any sort of achievement that deserved congratulations or condolences.

She wasn't sure why she kept sending her missives, just that she spent so much time writing letters to whichever of her siblings were not in residence in London at the time, and it seemed easy enough to pen a short note to some far-off relative while she was seated at her escritoire.

And although everyone penned a short note in reply—she was a Bridgerton, of course, and no one wanted to offend a Bridgerton—never had anyone enclosed a gift, even something so humble as a pressed flower.

Eloise closed her eyes, picturing the delicate pink

petals. It was hard to imagine a man handling such a fragile bloom. Her four brothers were all big, strong men, with broad shoulders and large hands that would surely mangle the poor thing in a heartbeat.

She had been intrigued by Sir Phillip's reply, especially his use of the Latin, and she had immediately penned her own response.

Dear Sir Phillip—

Thank you so very much for the charming pressed flower. It was such a lovely surprise when it floated out of the envelope. And such a precious memento of dear Marina, as well.

I could not help but notice your facility with the flower's scientific name. Are you a botanist?

Yours,
Miss Eloise Bridgerton

It was sneaky of her to end her letter with a question. Now the poor man would be forced to respond again.

He did not disappoint her. It had taken only ten days for Eloise to receive his reply.

Dear Miss Bridgerton—

Indeed I am a botanist, trained at Cambridge, although I am not currently connected with any university or scientific board. I conduct experiments here at Romney Hall, in my own greenhouse.

Are you of a scientific bent as well?

Yours,
Sir Phillip Crane

Something about the correspondence was thrilling; perhaps it was simply the excitement of finding someone not related to her who actually seemed eager to conduct a written dialogue. Whatever it was, Eloise wrote back immediately.

Dear Sir Phillip—

Heavens, no, I have not the scientific mind, I'm afraid, although I do have a fair head for sums. My interests lie more in the humanities; you may have noticed that I enjoy penning letters.

Yours in friendship,
Eloise Bridgerton

Eloise hadn't been certain about signing with such an informal salutation, but she decided to err on the side of daring. Sir Phillip was obviously enjoying the correspondence as much as she; surely he wouldn't have finished his missive with a question, otherwise?

Her answer came a fortnight later.

My dear Miss Bridgerton—

Ah, but it is a sort of friendship, isn't it? I confess to a certain measure of isolation here in the country, and if one cannot have a smiling face across one's breakfast table, then one might at least have an amiable letter, don't you agree?

I have enclosed another flower for you. This one is Geranium pratense, more commonly known as the meadow cranesbill.

With great regard,
Phillip Crane

Eloise remembered that day well. She had sat in her chair, the one by the window in her bedchamber, and stared at the carefully pressed purple flower for what seemed like an eternity. Was he attempting to *court* her? Through the post?

And then one day she received a note that was quite different from the rest.

My dear Miss Bridgerton—

We have been corresponding now for quite some time, and although we have never formally met, I feel as if I know you. I hope you feel the same.

Forgive me if I am too bold, but I am writing to invite you to visit me here at Romney Hall. It is my hope that after a suitable period of time, we might decide that we will suit, and you will consent to be my wife.

You will, of course, be properly chaperoned. If you accept my invitation, I will make immediate plans to bring my widowed aunt to Romney Hall.

I do hope you will consider my proposal.

Yours, as always,
Phillip Crane

Eloise had immediately tucked the letter away in a drawer, unable to even fathom his request. He wanted to marry someone he didn't even *know*?

No, to be fair, that wasn't entirely true. They did know one another. They'd said more in the course of a year's correspondence than many husbands and wives did during the entire course of a marriage.

But still, they'd never *met*.

Eloise thought about all of the marriage proposals she'd refused over the years. How many had there been? At least six. Now she couldn't even remember why she'd refused some of them. No reason, really, except that they weren't . . .

Perfect.

Was that so much to expect?

She shook her head, aware that she sounded silly and spoiled. No, she didn't need someone perfect. She just needed someone perfect for her.

She knew what the society matrons said about her. She was too demanding, worse than foolish. She'd end up a spinster—no, they didn't say that anymore. They said she already *was* a spinster, which was true. One didn't reach the age of eight and twenty without hearing that whispered behind one's back.

Or thrown in one's face.

But the funny truth was, Eloise didn't mind her situation. Or at least she hadn't, not until recently.

It had never occurred to her that she'd always be a spinster, and besides, she enjoyed her life quite well. She had the most marvelous family one could imagine—seven brothers and sisters in all, named alphabetically, which put her right in the middle at E, with four older and three younger. Her mother was a delight, and she'd even stopped nagging Eloise about getting married. Eloise still held a prominent place in society; the Bridgertons were universally adored and respected (and occasionally feared), and Eloise's sunny and irrepressible personality was such that everyone sought out her company, spinsterish age or no.

But lately . . .

She sighed, suddenly feeling quite a bit older than her twenty-eight years. Lately she hadn't been feeling so sunny. Lately she'd been starting to think that maybe those crotchety old matrons were right, and she *wasn't* going to find herself a husband. Maybe she had been too picky, too determined to follow the example of her older brothers and sister, all of whom had found a deep and passionate love with their spouses (even if it hadn't necessarily been there at the outset).

Maybe a marriage based on mutual respect and companionship was better than none at all.

But it was difficult to talk about these feelings with anyone. Her mother had spent so many years urging her to find a husband; as much as Eloise adored her, it would be difficult to eat crow and say that she should have listened. Her brothers would have been no help whatsoever. Anthony, the eldest, would probably have taken it upon himself to personally select a suitable mate and then browbeat the poor man into submission. Benedict was too much of a dreamer, and besides, he almost never came down to London anymore, preferring the quiet of the country. As for Colin—well, that was another story entirely, quite worthy of its own paragraph.

She supposed she should have talked to Daphne, but every time she went to see her, her elder sister was so bloody *happy*, so blissfully in love with her husband and her life as mother to her brood of four. How could someone like that possibly offer useful advice to one in Eloise's position? And Francesca seemed half a world away, off in Scotland. Besides, Eloise didn't think it fair to bother her with her silly woes. Francesca had been widowed at the age of twenty-three, for heaven's sake. Eloise's fears and worries seemed terribly inconsequential by comparison.

And maybe all this was why her correspondence with Sir Phillip had become such a guilty pleasure. The Bridgertons were a large family, loud and boisterous. It was nearly impossible to keep anything a secret, especially from her sisters, the youngest of whom—Hyacinth—could probably have won the war against Napoleon in half the time if His Majesty had only thought to draft her into the espionage service.

Sir Phillip was, in his own strange way, hers. The one thing she'd never had to share with anyone. His letters were bundled and tied with a purple ribbon, hidden at the bottom of her middle desk drawer, tucked underneath the piles of stationery she used for her many letters.

He was her secret. *Hers.*

And because she'd never actually met him, she'd been able to create him in her mind, using his letters as the bones and then fleshing him out as she saw fit. If ever there was a perfect man, surely it had to be the Sir Phillip Crane of her imagination.

And now he wanted to meet? *Meet?* Was he mad? And ruin what had to be the perfect courtship?

But then the impossible had occurred. Penelope Featherington, Eloise's closest friend for nearly a dozen years, had married. And what's more, she'd married *Colin.* Eloise's brother!

If the moon had suddenly dropped from the sky and landed in her back garden, Eloise could not have been more surprised.

Eloise was happy for Penelope. Truly, she was. And she was happy for Colin, too. They were quite possibly her two most favorite people in the entire world, and she was thrilled that they had found happiness. No one deserved it more.

But that didn't mean that their marriage hadn't left a hollow spot in her life.

She supposed that when she'd been considering her life as a spinster, and trying to convince herself that it was what she really wanted, Penelope had always been there in the image, spinster right beside her. It was acceptable—almost daring, even—to be twenty-eight and unmarried as long as Penelope was twenty-eight and unmarried, as well. It wasn't that she hadn't *wanted* Penelope to find a husband; it was just that it had never seemed even the least bit likely. *Eloise* knew that Penelope was wonderful and kind and smart and witty, but the gentlemen of the *ton* had never seemed to notice. In all her years in society—eleven in all—Penelope had not received one proposal of marriage. Nor even a whiff of interest.

In a way, Eloise had counted on her to remain where she was, what she was—first and foremost, Eloise's friend. Her companion in spinsterhood.

And the worst part—the part that left Eloise wracked with guilt—was that *she'd* never given a thought to how Penelope might feel if she married first, which, in truth, she'd always supposed she would do.

But now Penelope had Colin, and Eloise could see that the match was a splendid thing. And she was alone. Alone in the middle of crowded London, in the middle of a large and loving family.

It was hard to imagine a lonelier spot.

Suddenly Sir Phillip's bold proposal—tucked away at the very bottom of her bundle, at the bottom of the middle drawer, locked away in a newly purchased safebox, just so that Eloise wouldn't be tempted to look at it six times a day—well, it seemed a bit more intriguing.

More intriguing by the day, frankly, as she grew more and more restless, more dissatisfied with the lot in life that she had to admit she'd chosen.

And so one day, after she'd gone to visit Penelope, only to be informed by the butler that Mr. and Mrs. Bridgerton were not able to receive visitors (uttered in such a way that even Eloise knew what it meant), she made a decision. It was time to take her life into her own hands, time to control her destiny, rather than attending ball after ball in the vain hope that the perfect man would suddenly materialize before her, never mind that there was never anybody new in London, and after a full decade out in society, she'd already met everyone of the appropriate age and gender to marry.

She told herself that this did not mean she *had* to marry Sir Phillip; she was merely investigating what seemed like it might be an excellent possibility. If they did not suit, they would not have to marry; she'd made no promises to him, after all.

But if there was one thing about Eloise, it was that when she made a decision, she acted upon it quickly. No, she reflected with a rather impressive (in her opinion, at least) display of self-honesty, there were *two* things about her that colored her every action— she liked to act quickly and she was tenacious. Penelope had once described her as akin to a dog with a bone.

And Penelope had not been joking.

Once Eloise got her claws into an idea, not even the full force of the Bridgerton family could sway her from her intended goal. (And the Bridgertons constituted a mighty force, indeed.) It was probably just dumb luck that her goals and those of her family had never crossed purposes before, at least not over anything important.

Eloise knew that they would never countenance her going off blindly to meet a man she'd never met. Anthony would have probably demanded that Sir Phillip come to London to meet the entire family en masse, and Eloise couldn't imagine a single scenario more likely to scare off a prospective suitor. The men who'd previously sought her favor were at least familiar with the London scene and knew what they were getting into; poor Sir Phillip, who had—by his own admission in his letters—not set foot in London since his school days, and never participated in the social season, would be ambushed.

So the only option was for her to travel to Gloucestershire, and, as she came to realize after pondering the problem for a few days, she had to do it in secret. If her family knew of her plans, they might very well forbid her to go. Eloise was a worthy opponent, and she might prevail in the end, but it would be a long and painful battle. Not to mention that if they did allow her to go, whether after a protracted battle over the subject or not, they would insist upon sending at least two of their ranks to accompany her.

Eloise shuddered. Those two would most probably be her mother and Hyacinth.

Good gad, no one could fall in love with those two

around. No one could even form a mild but lasting attachment, which Eloise thought she might actually be willing to settle for this go-around.

She decided that she would make her escape during her sister Daphne's ball. It was to be a grand affair, with hordes of guests, and just the right amount of noise and confusion to allow her absence to go unnoticed for a good six hours, maybe more. Her mother had always insisted that they be punctual—early, even—when a family member was hosting a social event, so they would surely arrive at Daphne's no later than eight. If she slipped away early on, and the ball did not wind down until the wee hours of the morning . . . well, it would be nearly dawn before anyone realized she was gone, and she could be halfway to Gloucestershire.

And if not halfway, then far enough to ensure that they wouldn't find it too terribly easy to follow her trail.

In the end, it had all proven almost frighteningly easy. Her entire family had been distracted by some grand announcement Colin planned to make, and so all she'd had to do was excuse herself to the ladies' retiring room, slip out the back, and walk the short distance to her own home, where she'd hidden her bags in the back garden. From there, she needed only to walk to the corner, where she'd arranged to have a hired coach waiting.

Goodness, if she'd known it would be this easy to make her own way in the world, she would have done so years ago.

And now here she was, rolling toward Gloucestershire, rolling toward destiny, she supposed—or hoped, she wasn't sure which—with nothing but a few changes of clothing and a pile of letters written to her by a man she'd never met.

A man she hoped she could love.

It was thrilling.

No, it was terrifying.

It was, she reflected, quite possibly the most fool-hardy thing she'd done in her life, and she had to admit that she'd made a few foolish decisions in her day.

Or it might just be her only chance at happiness.

Eloise grimaced. She was growing fanciful. That was a bad sign. She needed to approach this adventure with all the practicality and pragmatism with which she always tried to make her decisions. There was still time to turn around. What did she know about this man, really? He'd said quite a lot over the course of a year's correspondence—

He was thirty years of age, two years her elder.

He had attended Cambridge and studied botany.

He had been married to her fourth cousin Marina for eight years, which meant that he'd been twenty-one at his wedding.

He had brown hair.

He had all of his teeth.

He was a baronet.

He lived at Romney Hall, a stone structure built in the eighteenth century near Tetbury, Gloucester-shire.

He liked to read scientific treatises and poetry but not novels and definitely not works of philosophy.

He liked the rain.

His favorite color was green.

He had never traveled outside of England.

He did not like fish.

Eloise fought a bubble of nervous laughter. He didn't like *fish*? That was what she knew about him?

"Surely a sound basis for marriage," she muttered to herself, trying to ignore the panic in her voice.

And what did he know about her? What could have possibly led him to propose marriage to a total stranger?

She tried to recall what she had included in her many letters—

She was twenty-eight.

She had brown hair (chestnut, really) and all of her teeth.

She had gray eyes.

She came from a large and loving family.

Her brother was a viscount.

Her father had died when she was but a child, incomprehensibly brought down by a humble bee sting.

She had a tendency to talk too much. (Good God, had she really put that into writing?)

She liked to read poetry and novels but certainly not scientific treatises or works of philosophy.

She had traveled to Scotland, but that was all.

Her favorite color was purple.

She did not like mutton and positively detested blood pudding.

Another little burst of panicked laughter passed over her lips. Put that way, she thought with no small bit of sarcasm, she seemed a fine catch indeed.

She glanced out the window, as if that might possibly give her an indication as to where they were on the road from London to Tetbury.

Rolling green hills looked like rolling green hills looked like rolling green hills, and she could be in Wales, for all she knew.

Frowning, she looked down at the paper in her lap and refolded Sir Phillip's letter. Fitting it back into the ribbon-tied bundle she kept in her valise, she then tapped her fingers against her thighs in a nervous gesture.

She had reason to be nervous.

She had left home and all that was familiar, after all.

She was traveling halfway across England, and no one knew.

No one.

Not even Sir Phillip.

Because in her haste to leave London, she'd neglected to tell him she was coming. It wasn't that she'd *forgotten*; rather, she'd sort of . . . pushed the task aside until it was too late.

If she told him, then she was committed to the plan. This way, she still had the chance to back out at any moment. She told herself it was because she liked to have choices and options, but the truth was, she was quite simply terrified, and she had feared a total loss of her courage.

Besides, he was the one who had requested the meeting. He would be happy to see her.

Wouldn't he?

Phillip rose from bed and pulled open the draperies in his bedchamber, revealing another perfect, sunny day.

Perfect.

He padded over to his dressing room to find some

clothes, having long since dismissed the servants who used to perform these duties. He couldn't explain it, but after Marina had died, he hadn't wanted anyone bustling into his bedroom in the morning, yanking open his curtains, and selecting his garments.

He'd even dismissed Miles Carter, who had tried so hard to be a friend after Marina's passing. But somehow the young secretary just made him feel worse, and so he'd sent him on his way, along with six months' pay and a superb letter of reference.

He'd spent his marriage with Marina looking for someone to talk to, since she was so often absent, but now that she was gone, all he wanted was his own company.

He supposed he must have alluded to this in one of his many letters to the mysterious Eloise Bridgerton, because he had sent off his proposal of not-quite-marriage-but-maybe-something-leading-up-to-it over a month ago, and the silence on her part had been deafening, especially since she usually responded to his letters with charming alacrity.

He frowned. The mysterious Eloise Bridgerton wasn't really *so* mysterious. In her letters she seemed quite open and honest and possessed of a positively *sunny* disposition, which, when it all came down to it, was all he really insisted upon in a wife this time around.

He yanked on a work shirt; he planned to spend most of the day in the greenhouse, up to his elbows in dirt. He was rather disappointed that Miss Bridgerton had obviously decided he was some sort of deranged lunatic to be avoided at all costs. She had seemed the perfect solution to his problems. He desperately needed a mother for Amanda and Oliver, but they'd grown so unmanageable that he couldn't imagine any woman willingly agreeing to cleave unto him in marriage and thus bind herself to those two little devils for life (or at least until they reached majority).

Miss Bridgerton was eight and twenty, however; quite obviously a spinster. And she'd been corresponding with a complete stranger for over a year; surely she was a little desperate? Wouldn't she appreciate the chance to find a husband? He had a home, a respectable fortune, and was only thirty years of age. What more could she want?

He muttered several annoyed phrases as he thrust his legs into his rough woolen trousers. Obviously she wanted *some*thing more, else she would have had the courtesy to at least write back and decline.

THUMP!

Phillip glanced up at the ceiling and grimaced. Romney Hall was old and solid and very well built, and if his ceiling was thumping, then his children had dropped (pushed? hurled?) something very large indeed.

THUMP!

He winced. That one sounded even worse. Still, their nurse was up there with them, and she always managed them better than he did. If he could just get his boots on in under a minute, he could be out of the house before they inflicted too much more damage, and thus he could pretend none of it was happening.

He reached for his boots. Yes, excellent idea. Out of earshot, out of mind.

He donned the rest of his ensemble with impressive speed and dashed out into the hall, making quick strides toward the stairs.

"Sir Phillip! Sir Phillip!"

Damn. His butler was after him now.

Phillip pretended he didn't hear.

"Sir Phillip!"

"Curse it," he muttered. There was no way he could ignore that bellow unless he was willing to suffer the torture of his servants hovering over him, concerned about his apparent hearing loss.

"Yes," he said, turning around slowly, "Gunning?"

"Sir Phillip," Gunning said, clearing his throat. "We have a caller."

"A caller?" Phillip echoed. "Was that the source of the, ah . . ."

"Noise?" Gunning supplied helpfully.

"Yes."

"No." The butler cleared his throat. "That would have been your children."

"I see," Phillip murmured. "How silly of me to have hoped otherwise."

"I don't believe they broke anything, sir."

"That's a relief and a change."

"Indeed, sir, but there is the caller to consider."

Phillip groaned. Who on earth was visiting at this time of the morning? It wasn't like they were used to receiving callers even during reasonable hours.

Gunning attempted a smile, but one could see that he was out of practice. "We used to have callers, do you recall?"

That was the problem with butlers who'd worked for the family since before one was born. They tended to think highly of sarcasm.

"Who is this caller?"

"I'm not entirely certain, sir."

"You're not certain?" Phillip asked disbelievingly.

"I didn't inquire."

"Isn't that what butlers are meant to do?"

"Inquire, sir?"

"Yes," Phillip ground out, wondering if Gunning was trying to see how red in the face his employer could get without actually collapsing to the floor in an apoplectic fit.

"I thought I'd let you inquire, sir."

"You thought you'd let me inquire." This one came out as a statement, Phillip having realized the futility of asking questions.

"Yes, sir. She's here to see you, after all."

"So are all of our callers, and that has never stopped you from ascertaining their identities before."

"Well, actually, sir—"

"I'm quite certain—" Phillip tried to interrupt.

"We don't have callers, sir," Gunning finished, quite clearly winning the conversational battle.

Phillip opened his mouth to point out that they *did* have callers, there was one downstairs that very moment; but really, what was the point? "Fine," he said, thoroughly irritated. "I'll go downstairs."

Gunning beamed. "Excellent, sir."

Phillip stared at his butler in shock. "Are you unwell, Gunning?"

"No, sir. Why do you ask, sir?"

It didn't seem quite polite to point out that the broad smile made Gunning look a bit like a horse, so Phillip just muttered, "It's nothing," and headed down the stairs.

A caller? Who would be calling? No one had come to visit in nearly a year, since the neighbors had finished making their obligatory condolence calls. He supposed he couldn't really blame them for staying away; the last time one of them had come to visit, Oliver and Amanda had smeared strawberry jam on the chairs.

Lady Winslet had left in a fit of temper quite beyond anything Phillip would have thought healthy for a woman of her years.

Phillip frowned as he reached the bottom of the stairs and turned into the entry hall. It was a she, wasn't it? Hadn't Gunning said his visitor was a she?

Who the devil—

He stopped short; stumbled, even.

Because the woman standing in his entry hall was young, and quite pretty, and when she looked up to meet his gaze, he saw that she had the largest, most achingly beautiful gray eyes he'd ever seen.

He could drown in those eyes.

And Phillip did not, as one might imagine, even *think* the word *drown* lightly.

Chapter 2

... and then, I'm sure you will not be surprised to hear, I talked far too much. I simply couldn't stop talking, but I suppose that is what I do when I am nervous. One can only hope I have less cause for nerves as the rest of my life unfolds.

—from Eloise Bridgerton
to her brother Colin,
upon the occasion of
Eloise's debut into London society

Then she opened her mouth.

"Sir Phillip?" she asked, and before he even had a chance to nod in the affirmative, she said, at quite the speed of lightning, "I'm so terribly sorry to arrive unannounced, but I really had no other option, and to be honest, if I'd sent notice, it probably would have arrived behind me, making the notice really quite moot, as I'm sure you'll agree, and . . ."

Phillip blinked, certain he was supposed to be following what she was saying but no longer able to make out where one word ended and the next began.

"...a long journey, and I'm afraid I didn't sleep, and so I must beg you to forgive my appearance and..."

She was making him dizzy. Would it be rude if he sat down?

"...didn't bring very much, but I had no choice, and..."

This had clearly gone on far too long, with no sign, in truth, that it would ever end. If he allowed her to speak for one moment longer, he was quite certain that he would suffer an inner ear imbalance, or perhaps she would swoon from lack of breath and hit her head on the floor. Either way, one of them would be injured and in debilitating pain.

"Madam," he said, clearing his throat.

If she heard him, she gave no indication, instead saying something about the coach that had apparently conveyed her to his doorstep.

"Madam," he said, a little louder this time.

"...but then I—" She looked up, blinking those devastating gray eyes at him, and for a moment he felt frighteningly off balance. "Yes?" she asked.

Now that he had her attention, he seemed to have forgotten why he'd sought it. "Er," he asked, "who *are* you?"

She stared at him for a good five seconds, her lips parting with surprise, and then she finally answered, "Eloise Bridgerton, of course."

Eloise was fairly certain she was talking too much, and she *knew* she was talking too fast, but she tended to do that when she was nervous, and while she prided herself on the fact that she was rarely nervous, now seemed like a rather deserving time to explore that emotion, and besides, Sir Phillip—if indeed he was the large bear of a man standing before her—was not *at all* what she had expected.

"*You're* Eloise Bridgerton?"

She looked up into his gaping face and felt the first stirrings of annoyance. "Well, of course I am. Who else would I be?"

"I could not possibly imagine."

"You did invite me," she pointed out.

"And you did not respond to my invitation," he returned.

She swallowed. He had a point there. A rather large one, if one wanted to be fair, which she didn't. Not just then, anyway.

"I didn't really have the opportunity," she hedged, and then, when it seemed from his expression that that wasn't enough explanation, she added, "as I mentioned when I spoke earlier."

He stared at her for longer than made her comfortable, his dark eyes inscrutable, and then he said, "I didn't understand a word you said."

She felt her mouth form an oval of . . . surprise? No, annoyance. "Weren't you listening?" she asked.

"I *tried.*"

Eloise pursed her lips. "Very well, then," she said, counting to five in her head—in Latin—before adding, "My apologies. I am sorry to have arrived unannounced. It was dreadfully ill-bred of me."

He was silent for a full three seconds—Eloise counted that as well—before saying, "I accept your apology."

She cleared her throat.

"And of course"—he coughed, glancing around as if in search of someone who might save him from her—"I am delighted that you are here."

It would probably be impolite to point out that he sounded *anything* but delighted, so Eloise just stood there, staring at his right cheekbone as she tried to decide what she *could* say without insulting him.

Eloise considered it a sad state of affairs that she— who generally had something to say for any occasion—couldn't think of a thing.

Luckily, he saved their awkward silence from growing to monumental proportions by asking, "Is this all of your luggage?"

Eloise straightened her shoulders, delighted to move on to a comparatively trivial topic. "Yes. I didn't really—" She broke herself off. Did she really need to tell him that she'd stolen away from home in the middle of the night? It didn't seem to speak well of her, or of her family, for that matter. She wasn't sure why, but she didn't want him to know that she had, for all intents and purposes, run away. She wasn't certain why she thought so, but she had a distinct feeling that if he knew the truth, he'd pack her up and send her back to London posthaste. And while her meeting with Sir Phillip had not thus far proven to be the stuff of romance and bliss she'd imagined it to be, she was not yet prepared to give up.

Especially when that meant running back to her family with her tail between her legs.

"This is all I have," she said firmly.

"Good. I, er . . ." He looked around again, this time a little desperately, which Eloise did not find flattering in the least. "Gunning!" he bellowed.

The butler appeared so quickly that he must have been eavesdropping. "Yes, sir?"

"We . . . ah . . . need to prepare a room for Miss Bridgerton."

"I have already done so," Gunning assured him.

Sir Phillip's cheeks colored slightly. "Good," he grunted. "She will be staying here for . . ." He looked to her in askance.

"A fortnight," she supplied, hoping that was about the right amount of time.

"A fortnight," Sir Phillip reiterated as if the butler wouldn't have heard her reply. "We will do everything in our power to make her comfortable, of course."

"Of course," the butler agreed.

"Good," Sir Phillip said, still looking somewhat uncomfortable with the entire situation. Or if not uncomfortable, precisely, then perhaps weary, which might have been even worse.

Eloise was disappointed. She'd pictured him as a man of easy charm, rather like her brother Colin, who possessed a dashing smile and always knew what to say in any situation, awkward or otherwise.

Sir Phillip, on the other hand, looked as if he'd rather be anywhere else but where he was, which Eloise did not find encouraging, as his present surroundings included her. And what's more, he was supposed to be making at least some effort to make her acquaintance and determine if she would make him an acceptable wife.

And his efforts had better be good ones indeed, because if it was true that first impressions were the most accurate, she rather doubted that she would determine that *he* would make an acceptable husband.

She smiled at him through gritted teeth.

"Would you like to sit down?" he blurted out.

"That would be quite pleasing, thank you."

He looked around with a blank expression on his face, giving Eloise the impression he barely knew his way around his own house. "Here," he mumbled, motioning to a door at the end of the hall, "the drawing room."

Gunning coughed.

Sir Phillip looked at him and scowled.

"Perhaps you intended to order refreshments, sir?" the butler asked solicitously.

"Er, yes, of course," Sir Phillip replied, clearing his throat. "Of course. Er, perhaps . . ."

"A tea tray, perhaps?" Gunning suggested. "With muffins?"

"Excellent," Sir Phillip muttered.

"Or perhaps if Miss Bridgerton is hungry," the butler continued, "I could have a more extensive breakfast prepared."

Sir Phillip swung his gaze over to Eloise.

"Muffins will be lovely," she said, even though she *was* hungry.

Eloise allowed Sir Phillip to take her arm and lead her to the drawing room, where she sat on a sofa covered in striped blue satin. The room was neat and clean, but the furnishings were shabby. The entire house had a vague neglected quality to it, as if the owner had run out of money, or perhaps just didn't care.

Eloise tended to think that it was the latter. She

supposed it was possible that Sir Phillip was short of funds, but the grounds had been magnificent, and she had seen enough of his greenhouse as she was driving in to realize that it was in excellent condition. Given that Sir Phillip was a botanist, that might explain the great care given to the exterior while the interior was left to fade.

Clearly, he needed a wife.

She folded her hands in her lap, then watched as he took a seat across from her, folding his large frame into a chair that had obviously been designed for one much smaller than he.

He looked most uncomfortable and (and Eloise had enough brothers to recognize the signs) rather like he wanted desperately to curse, but Eloise decided it was his own fault for choosing that chair, and so she smiled at him in what she hoped was a polite and encouraging manner, waiting for him to begin the conversation.

He cleared his throat.

She leaned forward.

He cleared his throat again.

She coughed.

He cleared his throat once more.

"Do you need some tea?" she finally asked, unable to bear even the thought of one more *ahem*.

He looked up gratefully, although Eloise wasn't certain whether that was due to her offer of tea or her merciful breaking of the silence. "Yes," he said, "that would be lovely."

Eloise opened her mouth to reply, then remembered she was in *his* house and had no business offering tea. Not to mention that he ought to have remembered that fact as well. "Right," she said. "Well, I'm sure it will be here soon."

"Right," he agreed, shifting in his seat.

"I'm sorry to have come by unannounced," she murmured, even though she'd already said as much. But something *had* to be said; Sir Phillip might be well used to awkward pauses, but Eloise was the sort who liked to fill any silence.

"It's quite all right," he said.

"It's not, actually," she replied. "It was terribly ill-mannered of me to do so, and I apologize."

He looked startled at her frankness. "Thank you," he murmured. "It is no problem, I assure you. I was merely . . ."

"Surprised?" she offered.

"Yes."

She nodded. "Yes, well, anyone would have been. I should have thought of that, and I truly am sorry for the inconvenience."

He opened his mouth, but then closed it, instead glancing out the window. "It's a sunny day," he said.

"Yes, it is," Eloise agreed, thinking that quite obvious.

He shrugged. "I imagine it will still rain by nightfall."

She wasn't quite certain how to respond to that, so she just nodded, surreptitiously studying him while his gaze was still fixed on the window. He was bigger than she'd imagined him, rougher-looking, less urbane. His letters had been so charming and well written; she'd pictured him to be more . . . smooth. More slender, perhaps, certainly not given to fat, but still, less muscled. He looked as if he worked outside like a laborer, especially in those rough trousers and shirt with no cravat. And even though he'd written that his hair was brown, she'd always imagined him as a dark blond, looking rather like a poet (why she always pictured poets with blond hair she did not know). But his hair was exactly as he'd described it—brown, a rather dark shade, actually, bordering on black, with an unruly wave to it. His eyes were brown, much the same shade as his hair, so dark they were utterly unreadable.

She frowned. She hated people she couldn't figure out in a heartbeat.

"Did you travel all night?" he inquired politely.

"I did."

"You must be tired."

She nodded. "I am, quite."

He stood, motioning gallantly to the door. "Would you prefer to rest? I don't wish to keep you here if you'd rather sleep."

Eloise was exhausted, but she was also ferociously hungry. "I'll have just a bite to eat first," she said, "and then I would be grateful to accept your hospitality and rest."

He nodded and started to sit down, trying to fold himself back into the ridiculously small chair, then finally muttering something under his breath, turning to her with a slightly more intelligible, "Excuse me," and moving to another, larger chair.

"I beg your pardon," he said, once he was settled.

Eloise just nodded at him, wondering when she had ever found herself in a more awkward situation.

He cleared his throat. "Er, was your journey a pleasant one?"

"Indeed," she replied, mentally giving him credit

for at least trying to keep up a conversation. One good turn deserved another, so she made her contribution with, "You have a lovely home."

He raised a brow at that, giving her a look that said he didn't believe her false flattery for a second.

"The grounds are magnificent," she added hastily. Who would have thought that he'd actually know his furnishings were faded? Men never noticed such things.

"Thank you," he said. "I am a botanist, as you know, and so I spend a great deal of my time out-of-doors."

"Were you planning to work outside today?"

He answered in the affirmative.

Eloise offered him a tentative smile. "I'm sorry to have disrupted your schedule."

"It is nothing, I assure you."

"But—"

"You really needn't apologize again," he cut in. "For anything."

And then there was that awful silence again, with both of them looking longingly at the door, waiting for Gunning to return with salvation in the form of a tea tray.

Eloise tapped her hands against the cushion of the sofa in a manner that her mother would have deemed horribly ill-bred. She looked over at Sir Phillip and was somewhat gratified to see that he was doing the same. Then he caught her looking and quirked an irritating half-smile as his gaze dropped down to her restless hand.

She stilled herself immediately.

She looked over at him, silently daring—imploring?—him to *say* something. Anything.

He didn't.

This was killing her. She had to break the silence. This was not natural. It was too awful. People were meant to *talk*. This was—

She opened her mouth, driven by a desperation she didn't quite understand. "I—"

But before she could continue on with a sentence she fully intended to make up as she went along, a bloodcurdling scream ripped through the air.

Eloise jumped to her feet. "What was—"

"My children," Sir Phillip said, letting out a haggard sigh.

"You have *children*?"

He noticed that she was standing and rose wearily to his feet. "Of course."

She gaped at him. "You never said you had children."

His eyes narrowed. "Is that a problem?" he asked, quite sharply.

"Of course it isn't!" she said, bristling. "I adore children. I have more nieces and nephews than I can count, and I can assure you that I am their *favorite* aunt. But that does not excuse the fact that you did not mention their existence."

"That is impossible," he said, shaking his head. "You must have overlooked it."

Her chin jerked back so suddenly it was a wonder she didn't snap her neck. "That is not," she said haughtily, "the sort of thing I would overlook."

He shrugged, clearly dismissing her protest.

"You never mentioned them," she said, "and I can prove it."

He crossed his arms, giving her a patently disbelieving look.

She marched to the door. "Where is my valise?"

"Right where you left it, I imagine," he said, watching her with a condescending expression. "Or more likely already up in your room. My servants are not *that* inattentive."

She turned to him with a scowl. "I have every single one of your letters with me, and I can assure you, not one of them contains the words, 'my children.'"

Phillip's lips parted in surprise. "You saved my letters?"

"Of course. Didn't you save mine?"

He blinked. "Uh . . ."

She gasped. "You didn't save them?"

Phillip had never understood women and half the time was quite willing to put aside all current medical thought and declare them a separate species altogether. He fully accepted that he rarely knew what one was supposed to say to them, but this time even he knew he had blundered badly. "I'm sure I have some of them," he tried.

Her jaw clamped into a straight angry line.

"Most of them, I'm sure," he added hastily.

She looked mutinous. Eloise Bridgerton, he was coming to realize, had a formidable will.

"It's not that I would have disposed of them," he said, trying to dig his way out of his bottomless pit. "It is just that I'm not certain precisely where I put them."

He watched with interest as she gained control of her anger, then let out a short breath. Her eyes, however, remained a stormy gray. "Very well," she said. "It hardly signifies, anyway."

Exactly his opinion, Phillip thought, but even he was smart enough not to say so.

Besides, her tone made it quite clear that in her opinion, it did signify. A great deal.

Another scream rent the air, followed by a resounding crash. Phillip winced. It sounded like furniture.

Eloise glanced toward the ceiling, as if expecting plaster to start spinning down at any moment. "Shouldn't you go to them?" she asked.

He should, but by all that was holy, he didn't want to. When the twins were out of control, no one could manage them, which, Phillip supposed, was the definition of "out of control." It was his opinion that it was generally easier to let them run wild until they dropped from exhaustion (which usually didn't take too long) and deal with them then. It probably wasn't the most beneficial course of action, and certainly nothing that any other parent would have recommended, but a man only had so much energy to deal with two eight-year-olds, and he feared he'd run out of his a good six months ago.

"Sir Phillip?" Eloise prodded.

He let out a breath. "You're right, of course." It certainly wouldn't do to appear a disinterested parent in front of Miss Bridgerton, whom he was trying to woo, however clumsily, into the position of mother to the two hellions presently attempting the complete destruction of his home. "If you will excuse me," he said, giving her a nod as he stepped into the hall.

"Oliver!" he bellowed. "Amanda!"

He wasn't sure, but he thought he heard Miss Bridgerton stifle a horrified laugh.

A wave of irritation washed over him, and he glared at her, even though he knew he shouldn't. He supposed she thought she could do a better job with those two hellions.

He strode to the stairs and yelled the twins' names again. On the other hand, maybe he shouldn't be so uncharitable. He rather hoped—no, fervently prayed—that Eloise Bridgerton could do a better job with the twins than he could.

Good God, if she could teach them to mind, he would bloody well kiss the ground she walked upon on a thrice-daily schedule.

Oliver and Amanda rounded the corner in the staircase and descended the rest of the way down to the hall, looking not a bit sheepish.

"What," Phillip demanded, "was that all about?"

"What was what all about?" Oliver replied cheekily.

"The screaming," Phillip ground out.

"That was Amanda," Oliver said.

"It certainly was," she agreed.

Phillip waited for further elucidation, and when it appeared that none was forthcoming, he added, "And *why* was Amanda screaming?"

"It was a frog," she explained.

"A frog."

She nodded. "Indeed. In my bed."

"I see," Phillip said. "Do you have any idea how it got there?"

"I put it there," she replied.

He swung his gaze off of Oliver, to whom he'd addressed his question, and back to Amanda. "You put a frog in your own bed?"

She nodded.

Why why *why*? He cleared his throat. "Why?"

She shrugged. "I wanted to."

Phillip felt his chin thrust forward in disbelief. "You wanted to?"

"Yes."

"Put a frog in your bed?"

"I was trying to grow tadpoles," she explained.

"In your bed?"

"It seemed warm and cozy."

"I helped," Oliver put in.

"Of that I had no doubt," Phillip said in a tight voice. "But why did you scream?"

"I didn't scream," Oliver said indignantly. "Amanda did."

"I was asking Amanda!" Phillip said, just barely resisting the urge to throw his arms up in defeat and retire to his greenhouse.

"You were looking at me, sir," Oliver said. And then, as if his father were too dim to understand what he meant, he added, "When you asked the question."

Phillip took a deep breath before schooling his features into what he hoped was a patient expression and turned back to Amanda. "Why, *Amanda*, did you scream?"

She shrugged. "I forgot I put the frog there."

"I thought she was going to *die*!" Oliver put in, most dramatically.

Phillip decided not to pursue that statement. "I thought," he said, crossing his arms and leveling his sternest gaze at his children, "that we had said no frogs in the house."

"No," Oliver said (with vehement nodding from Amanda), "you said no *toads*."

"No amphibians of any kind," Phillip ground out.

"But what if one of them is dying?" Amanda asked, her pretty blue eyes filling with tears.

"Not even then."

"But—"

"You may tend to it outside."

"What if it's cold and freezing and only needs my care and a warm bed inside the house?"

"Frogs are supposed to be cold and freezing," Phillip shot back. "It's why they are amphibians."

"But what if—"

"*No!*" he bellowed. "No frogs, toads, crickets, grasshoppers, or animals of any kind in the house!"

Amanda started gulping for air. "But but but—"

Phillip let out a long sigh. He never knew what to say to his children, and now his daughter looked as if she might dissolve into a pool of tears. "For the love of—" He caught himself just in time and softened his voice. "What is it, Amanda?"

She gasped, then sobbed, "What about Bessie?"

Phillip felt around unsuccessfully for a wall to sag against. "Naturally," he ground out, "I did not intend to include our beloved spaniel in that statement."

"Well, I wish you'd said so," Amanda sniffed, looking surprisingly—and suspiciously—recovered. "You made me extremely sad."

Phillip gritted his teeth. "I am sorry I made you feel sad."

She nodded at him like a queen.

Phillip groaned. When had the twins gained the upper hand in the conversation? Surely a man of his size and (he'd like to think, anyway) intellect, ought to be able to manage two eight-year-olds.

But no, once again, despite his best intentions, he'd lost all control of the conversation and now he was actually apologizing to *them*.

Nothing made him feel more like a failure.

"Right, then," he said, eager to be done. "Run along. I'm very busy."

They stood there for a moment, just looking up at him with wide, blinking eyes. "All day?" Oliver finally asked.

"All day?" Phillip echoed. What the devil was he talking about?

"Are you going to be busy all day?" Oliver amended.

"Yes," he said sharply, "I am."

"What if we went on a nature walk?" Amanda suggested.

"I can't," he said, even though part of him wanted to. But the twins were so vexing, and they were sure to force him to lose his temper, and nothing terrified him more.

"We could help you in the greenhouse," Oliver said.

Destroy it was more like it. "No," Phillip said. He honestly didn't think he could answer to his temper if they ruined his work.

"But—"

"I can't," he snapped, hating the tone of his voice.

"But—"

"And who is this?" came a voice from behind him.

He turned around. It was Eloise Bridgerton, sticking her nose into what was assuredly not her business, and this after arriving on his doorstep without even so much as a hint of warning.

"I beg your pardon," he said to her, not bothering to hide the irritation in his voice.

She ignored him and faced the twins. "And who might you be?" she asked.

"Who are you?" Oliver demanded.

Amanda's eyes narrowed into slits.

Phillip allowed himself his first true grin of the morning and crossed his arms. Yes, let's see how Miss Bridgerton handled *this*.

"I am Miss Bridgerton," she said.

"You're not our new governess, are you?" Oliver asked, with suspicion bordering on venom.

"Heavens, no," she replied. "What happened to your last governess?"

Phillip coughed. Loudly.

The twins took the hint. "Er, nothing," Oliver said.

Miss Bridgerton didn't look the least bit fooled by the air of innocence the twins were trying to convey, but she wisely did not choose to pursue the subject, and instead just said, "I am your guest."

The twins pondered that for a moment, and then Amanda said, "We don't want any guests."

Followed by Oliver's, "We don't *need* any guests."

"Children!" Phillip interjected, not really wanting to take Miss Bridgerton's side after she'd been so meddlesome, but really having no other choice. He couldn't let his children be so rude.

The twins crossed their arms in unison and gave Miss Bridgerton the cut direct.

"That's it," Phillip boomed. "You will apologize to Miss Bridgerton at once."

They stared at her mutinously.

"Now!" he roared.

"Sorry," they mumbled, but no one could ever have mistaken them for meaning it.

"Back to your room, the both of you," Phillip said sharply.

They marched off like a pair of proud soldiers, noses in the air. It would have been quite an impressive sight, if Amanda hadn't turned around at the bottom of the stairs and stuck out her tongue.

"Amanda!" he bellowed, striding toward her.

She tore up the stairs with the speed of a fox.

Phillip held himself very still for several moments, his hands fisted and shaking at his sides. Just once—*once!*—he would like his children to behave and mind and not answer a question with a question and be polite to guests and not stick out their tongues, and—

Just once, he'd like to feel that he was a good father, that he knew what he was doing.

And not raise his voice. He hated when he raised his voice, hated the flash of terror he thought he saw in their eyes.

Hated the memories it brought back for him.

"Sir Phillip?"

Miss Bridgerton. Damn, he'd almost forgotten she was there. He turned around. "Yes?" he asked, mortified that she'd witnessed his humiliation. Which of course made him irritated with her.

"Your butler brought the tea tray," she said, motioning to the drawing room.

He gave her a curt nod. He needed to get outside. Away from his children, away from the woman who'd seen what a terrible father he was to them. It had started to rain, but he didn't care.

"I hope you enjoy your breakfast," he said. "I will see you after you have rested."

And then he made haste out the door, making his way to his greenhouse, where he could be alone with his nonspeaking, nonmisbehaving, nonmeddlesome plants.

Chapter 3

...you will see why I could not accept his suit. He was too churlish by half and positively possessed of a foul temper. I should like to marry someone gracious and considerate, who treats me like a queen. Or at the very least, a princess. Surely that is not too much to ask.

—from Eloise Bridgerton to her
dear friend Penelope Featherington,
sent by messenger after Eloise
received her first proposal of marriage

By afternoon, Eloise was almost convinced that she had made a terrible mistake.

And in truth, the sole reason she was only *almost* convinced was that the only thing she hated more than making mistakes was the admission thereof. So she was trying to maintain a proverbial stiff upper lip and forcing herself to pretend that this ghastly situation might all work itself out in the end.

She had been left stunned—openmouthed, even—when Sir Phillip had departed with barely more than an "Enjoy your food" and then stalked out the door. She had traveled halfway across England, answering *his* invitation to come and visit, and he left her alone in the drawing room a mere half hour after she arrived?

She hadn't expected him to fall in love at first sight and drop to his knees, professing his undying devotion, but she'd hoped for a little bit more than a curt "Who are you?" and "Enjoy your food."

Or maybe she *had* expected him to fall in love at the first sight of her. She'd built an elaborate dream around her image of this man—an image which she now knew to be untrue. She'd let herself mold him into the perfect man, and it hurt so much to learn that he wasn't just imperfect, he was quite close to abysmal.

And the worst was—she had only herself to blame. Sir Phillip had never misrepresented himself in his letters (although she did think he ought to have mentioned that he was a father, especially before he'd proposed marriage).

Her dreams had been just that—dreams. Wishful illusions, all of her own making. If he wasn't what she'd expected, that was her fault. She'd been expecting something that didn't even exist.

And she should have known better.

What's more, he didn't seem to be a very good father, which was as black a mark as anyone could get in her book.

No, she wasn't being fair. She shouldn't judge him so quickly on that score. The children didn't look ill-treated or malnourished or anything so dire, but Sir

Phillip clearly had no idea how to manage them. He had handled them all wrong this morning, and it was clear from the way they behaved that his relationship with them was distant at best.

Good heavens, they had practically begged him to spend the day with them. Any child who actually received enough attention from his parents would never act in such a way. Eloise and her siblings had spent half their childhood trying to avoid their parents—lack of supervision being, of course, more conducive for mischief.

Her own father had been splendid. She had been only seven when he'd died, but she remembered him well, from the stories he wove at bedtime to the hikes they had taken across the fields of Kent, sometimes with all the Bridgertons in tow, sometimes just with one lucky child, chosen for some special alone time with Father.

It was clear to her that if she hadn't suggested to Sir Phillip that he find out why his children were screaming and knocking over the furniture, he would have left them to their own devices. Or, more to the point, left them to be someone else's problem. And by the end of their conversation, it was apparent that Sir Phillip's main aim in life was to avoid his children.

Which Eloise did not approve of at all.

She pushed herself off of her bed, forcing herself upright even though she was bone-tired. But every time she laid down, something began to quicken in her lungs, and she felt herself gasping in that awful precursor to not just tears, but true, body-shaking sobs. If she didn't get up and do something, she wasn't going to be able to control herself.

And she didn't think she could bear herself if she cried.

She wrenched the window open, even though it was still gray and drizzling outside. There was no wind, so the rain ought not to blow in, and what she really needed right now was a bit of fresh air. A slap of cold on her face might not make her feel better, but it certainly wasn't going to make her feel worse.

From her window she could see Sir Phillip's greenhouse. She assumed that was where he was, since she hadn't heard him here in the house, stomping about and bellowing at his children. The glass was fogged up and the only thing she could see was a blurry curtain of green—his beloved plants, she supposed. What sort of man was he, that he preferred plants to people? Certainly not anyone who appreciated a fine conversation.

She felt her shoulders sag. Eloise had spent half her life in search of a fine conversation.

And if he was such a hermit, why had he bothered to write her back? He had worked just as hard as she had to perpetuate their correspondence. Not to mention his proposal. If he hadn't wanted company, he had no business inviting her here.

She took a few deep breaths of the misty air and then forced herself to stand up straight. She wasn't certain what she was expected to do with herself all day. She'd taken a nap already; exhaustion had quickly won out over misery. But no one had come by to inform her of lunch or of any other plans that might extend to her as a houseguest.

If she stayed here, in this slightly drab and drafty room, she was going to go mad. Or at the very least cry herself into oblivion, which was something she did not tolerate in others, so the thought of doing it herself was horrifying.

There was no reason she couldn't explore the house a bit, was there? And maybe she could find herself some food along the way. She'd eaten all four muffins on the tea tray this morning, all with as much butter and marmalade as she could politely slather on, but she was still famished. At this point she thought she might be willing to commit violence for a ham sandwich.

She changed her clothing, donning a dress of peach muslin that was pretty and feminine without being too frilly. And most importantly, it was easy to get on and off, surely a critical factor when one had run from home without a lady's maid.

A quick glance in the mirror told her that she looked presentable, if no picture of ravishing beauty, and so she stepped out into the hall.

Only to be immediately confronted by the eight-year-old Crane twins, looking very much as if they'd been lying in wait for hours.

"Good afternoon," Eloise said, waiting for them to come to their feet. "How nice of you to greet me."

"We're not here to *greet* you," Amanda blurted out, grunting when Oliver elbowed her in the ribs.

"You're not?" Eloise asked, trying to sound surprised. "Are you here, then, to show me to the dining room? I'm quite hungry, I must say."

"No," Oliver said, crossing his arms.

"Not even that?" Eloise mused. "Let me guess. You're here to take me to your room and show me your toys."

"No," they said, in unison.

"Then it must be to take me on a tour of the house. It's quite large and I might lose my way."

"No."

"No? You wouldn't want me to lose my way, would you?"

"No," Amanda said. "I mean yes!"

Eloise feigned incomprehension. "You want me to lose my way?"

Amanda nodded. Oliver just tightened his arms across his chest and speared her with a sullen stare.

"Hmmm. That's interesting, but it hardly explains your presence right here outside my door, does it? I'm not likely to get lost in the company of you two."

Their lips parted in befuddled surprise.

"You do know your way around the house, don't you?"

"Of course," Oliver grunted, followed by Amanda's, "We're not babies."

"No, I can see that," Eloise said with a thoughtful nod. "Babies wouldn't be allowed to wait by themselves outside my door, after all. They'd be quite busy with nappies and bottles and the like."

They had nothing to add to that.

"Does your father know you're here?"

"He's busy."

"Very busy."

"He's a very busy man."

"Much too busy for *you*."

Eloise watched and listened with interest as the twins shot off their lightning-fast statements, falling all over themselves to demonstrate how busy Sir Phillip was.

"So what you're telling me," Eloise said, "is that your father is busy."

They stared at her, momentarily dumbfounded by her calm retelling of the facts, then nodded.

"But that still doesn't explain your presence," Eloise mused. "Because I don't think your father sent you here in his stead. . . ." She waited until they shook their heads in the negative, then added, "Unless . . . I know!" she said in an excited voice, allowing herself a mental smile over her cleverness. She had nine nephews and nieces. She knew *exactly* how to talk to children. "You're here to tell me you have magical powers and can predict the weather."

"No," they said, but Eloise heard a giggle.

"No? That's a shame, because this constant drizzle is miserable, don't you think?"

"No," Amanda said, quite forcefully. "Father likes the rain, and so do we."

"He likes the rain?" Eloise asked in surprise. "How very odd."

"No, it's not," Oliver replied, his stance defensive. "My father isn't odd. He's perfect. Don't say mean things about him."

"I didn't," Eloise replied, wondering what on earth was going on now. At first she'd merely thought the twins were here to frighten her away. Presumably, they had heard that their father was thinking of marrying her and wanted no part of a stepmother, especially given the stories Eloise had been told by the housemaid of the succession of poor, abused governesses who had come and gone.

But if that were the simple truth, wouldn't they want her to think there was something wrong with

Sir Phillip? If they wanted her gone, wouldn't they be trying to convince her that he would be a terrible candidate for marriage?

"I assure you, I harbor no ill will toward any of you," Eloise said. "In fact, I barely know your father."

"If you make Father sad, I will . . . I will . . ."

Eloise watched the poor little boy's face grow red with frustration as he fought for words and bravado. Carefully, gently, she crouched next to him until her face was on a level with his and said, "Oliver, I promise you, I am not here to make your father sad." He said nothing, so she turned to his twin and asked, "Amanda?"

"You need to go," Amanda blurted out, her arms crossed so tightly that her face was turning red. "We don't want you here."

"Well, I'm not going anywhere for at least a week," Eloise told them, keeping her voice firm. The children needed sympathy, and probably a great deal of love as well, but they also needed a bit of discipline and a clear idea of who was in charge.

And then, out of nowhere, Oliver hurled himself forward and pushed her hard, with both hands against her chest.

Her balance was precarious, crouching as she was on the balls of her feet. Eloise toppled over backward, landing most inelegantly on her bottom and rolling back until she was quite certain the twins had received a nice look at her petticoats.

"Well," she declared, rising to her feet and crossing her arms as she stared sternly down at them. They had both taken several steps back and were staring at her with a mixture of glee and horror, as if they couldn't quite believe that one of them had had the nerve to push her over. "That," Eloise continued, "was inadvisable."

"Are you going to hit us?" Oliver asked. His voice was defiant, but there was a hint of fright there, as if someone *had* hit them before.

"Of course not," Eloise said quickly. "I don't believe in striking children. I don't believe in striking anyone." *Except people who strike children,* she added to herself.

They looked somewhat relieved to hear it.

"I might remind you, however," Eloise continued, "that you struck me first."

"I pushed you," he corrected.

She allowed herself a tiny groan. She ought to have anticipated that one. "If you do not want people striking you, you ought to practice the same philosophy."

"The Golden Rule," Amanda piped up.

"Exactly," Eloise said with a wide smile. She rather doubted she'd changed the course of their lives with one little lesson, but nonetheless it was nice to hope that something she'd said provoked some consideration.

"But doesn't that mean," Amanda said thoughtfully, "that you should go home?"

Eloise felt her small moment of elation crumbling to dust, as she tried to imagine what leap of logic Amanda was about to embark upon to explain why Eloise should be banished to the Amazon.

"We're home," Amanda said, sounding exceedingly supercilious for an eight-year-old. Or maybe she was supercilious as *only* an eight-year-old could be. "So you should go home."

"It doesn't work that way," Eloise said sharply.

"Yes, it does," Amanda replied with a smug little nod. "Do unto others as you would like done to you. *We* haven't gone to your house, so you shouldn't come to ours."

"You're very clever, did you know that?" Eloise asked.

Amanda looked as if she wanted to nod, but she was clearly too suspicious of Eloise's compliment to accept it.

Eloise bent down so that they were face-to-face, all three of them. "But I," she said to them in a very serious—and slightly defiant—voice, "am very clever, too."

They stared at her with wide eyes, their mouths hanging slack as they regarded this person who was clearly so different from any other adult they'd ever met.

"Do we understand each other?" Eloise asked, straightening her spine and smoothing her hands along her skirts in a deceptively casual manner.

They said nothing, so she decided to answer for them. "Good," she said. "Now, then, would you like to show me where the dining room is? I'm famished."

"We have lessons," Oliver said.

"You do?" Eloise asked, arching her brows. "How interesting. Then you must return to them at once. I imagine you've fallen behind after spending so long waiting outside my door."

"How did you know—" Amanda's question was cut short by Oliver's elbow in her ribs.

"I have seven brothers and sisters," Eloise answered, deciding that Amanda's question deserved an answer, even if her brother hadn't allowed her to finish her sentence. "There isn't much about this sort of warfare that I don't already know."

But as the twins scurried down the hall, Eloise was left chewing her lower lip in apprehension. She had a feeling she shouldn't have ended their encounter with such a challenge. She had practically dared Oliver and Amanda to find a way to evict her from the premises.

And while she was quite certain they wouldn't succeed—she was a Bridgerton, after all, and made of sterner stuff than those two even knew existed—she had a feeling that they would throw every fiber of their being into the task.

Eloise shuddered. Eels in the bed, hair dipped in ink, jam on chairs. It had all been done to her at one point or another, and she didn't particularly relish a repeat performance—and certainly not by a pair of children twenty years her junior.

She sighed, wondering what it was she had gotten herself into. She had better find Sir Phillip and get to the task of deciding whether they would suit. Because if she really was leaving in a week or two, never to see any of the Cranes again, she wasn't sure that she wanted to put herself through the trouble of mice and spiders and salt in the sugar bowl.

Her stomach rumbled. Whether it was the thought of salt or sugar that did it, Eloise didn't know. But it was definitely time to find something to eat. And better sooner than later, before the twins had a chance to figure out how to poison her food.

Phillip knew that he'd blundered badly. But deuce it, the bloody woman had given him no warning. If she'd only alerted him of her arrival, he could have prepared himself, thought of a few poetic things to say. Did she really think he'd scribbled all those letters without laboring over every word? He'd never sent out the first draft of any of his missives (although he always wrote it on his best paper, each time hoping that this would be the time he'd get it right on the first try).

Hell, if she'd given him warning, he might have even summoned a romantic gesture or two. Flowers would have been nice, and heaven knew, if there was one thing he was good at, it was flowers.

But instead, she'd simply appeared before him as if conjured from a dream, and he'd mucked everything up.

And it hadn't helped that Miss Eloise Bridgerton was *not* what he had expected.

She was a twenty-eight-year-old spinster, for heaven's sake. She was supposed to be unattractive. Horse-faced, even. Instead she was—

Well, he wasn't exactly certain how one could describe her. Not beautiful, precisely, but still somehow stunning, with thick chestnut hair and eyes of the clearest, crispest gray. She was the sort of woman whose expressions made her beautiful. There was intelligence in her eyes, curiosity in the way she cocked her head to the side. Her features were unique, almost exotic, with her heart-shaped face and wide smile.

Not that he'd seen much of that smile. His less-than-legendary charm had seen to that.

He jammed his hands into a pile of moist soil and scooped some into a small clay pot, leaving it loosely packed for optimal root growth. What the devil was he going to do now? He'd pinned his hopes on his mirage of Miss Eloise Bridgerton, based upon the letters she'd sent to him over the past year. He didn't have time (nor, in truth, the inclination) to court a prospective mother for the twins, so it had seemed perfect (not to mention almost easy) to woo her through letters.

Surely an unmarried woman rapidly approaching the age of thirty would be gratified to receive a proposal of marriage. He hadn't expected her to accept his offer without meeting with him, of course, and he wasn't prepared to formally commit to the idea without making her acquaintance, either. But he *had* expected that she would be someone who was at least a little bit desperate for a husband.

Instead, she'd arrived looking young and pretty and smart and self-confident, and good God, but *why* would a woman like that want to marry someone she didn't even know? Not to mention tie herself to a decidedly rural estate in the farthest corner of Gloucestershire. Phillip might know less than nothing about fashion, but even he could tell that her garments had been well made and most probably of the latest style. She was going to expect trips to London, an active social life, friends.

None of which she was likely to find here at Romney Hall.

It seemed almost useless to even try to make her acquaintance. She wasn't going to stay, and he'd be foolish to get his hopes up.

He groaned, then cursed for good measure. Now he was going to have to court some other woman. Curse it, now he was going to have to *find* some other woman to court, which was going to be nearly as difficult. No one in the district would even look at him. All of the unmarried ladies knew about the twins, and there wasn't a one of them willing to take on the responsibility of his little devils.

He'd pinned all of his hopes on Miss Bridgerton, and now it seemed that he was going to have to give up on her as well.

He set his pot down too hard on a shelf, wincing as the clatter of it rang through the greenhouse.

With a loud sigh, he dunked his muddy hands into a bucket of already dirtied water to wash them off. He'd been rude this morning. He was still rather irritated that she'd come out here and wasted his time—or if she hadn't wasted it yet, she was almost certainly *going* to waste it, since she wasn't likely to turn around and leave this evening.

But that didn't excuse his behavior. It wasn't her fault he couldn't manage his own children, and it certainly wasn't her fault that this failing always put him in a foul mood.

Wiping his hands on a towel he kept by the door, he strode out into the drizzle and made his way to the house. It was probably time for luncheon, and it wouldn't hurt anyone to sit down with her at the table and make polite conversation.

Plus, she was *here*. After all his effort with the letters, it seemed foolish not to at least see if they might get on well enough for marriage. Only an idiot would send her packing—or allow her to leave—without even ascertaining her suitability.

It was unlikely that she would stay, but not, he reckoned, impossible, and he might at least give it a try.

He made his way through the misty drizzle and into the house, wiping his feet on the mat that the housekeeper always left out for him near the side entrance. He was a mess, as he always was after working in the greenhouse, and the servants were used to him in such a state, but he supposed he ought to clean up before finding Miss Bridgerton and inviting her to eat with him. She was from London and would surely object to sitting at table with a man who was less than perfectly groomed.

He cut through the kitchen, nodding genially at a maid washing carrots in a tub of water. The servants' stairs were just outside the other kitchen door and—

"Miss Bridgerton!" he said in surprise. She was sitting at a table in the kitchen, halfway through a very large ham sandwich and looking remarkably at home on her perch on a stool. "What are you doing here?"

"Sir Phillip," she said, nodding at him.

"You don't have to eat in the kitchen," he said, scowling at her for no reason other than that she was not where he'd expected her to be.

That and the fact that he'd actually intended to change his clothes for lunch—something with which he did not ordinarily bother—for her benefit, and here she'd caught him a mess, anyway.

"I know," she replied, cocking her head and blinking those devastating gray eyes at him. "But I was looking for food and company, and this seemed the best place to find both."

Was that an insult? He couldn't be certain, and her eyes looked innocent, so he decided to ignore it and said, "I was just on my way to change into cleaner attire and invite you to share my lunch with me."

"I would be happy to remove myself to the breakfast room and finish my sandwich there, if you wish to join me," Eloise said. "I'm sure Mrs. Smith wouldn't mind making another sandwich for you. This one is delicious." She looked over at the cook. "Mrs. Smith?"

"It's no trouble at all, Miss Bridgerton," the cook said, leaving Phillip nearly gaping at her. It was quite the friendliest tone of voice he had ever heard emerge from her lips.

Eloise edged herself off of her stool and picked up her plate. "Shall we?" she said to Phillip. "I have no objection to your attire."

Before he even realized that he had not agreed to her plan, Phillip found himself in the breakfast room, seated across from her at the small round table he used far more often than the long, lonely one in the formal dining room. A maid had carried Miss Bridgerton's tea service, and after inquiring if he wanted some, Miss Bridgerton herself had expertly prepared him a cup.

It was an unsettling feeling, this. She had maneuvered him quite neatly to serve her purposes, and somehow it didn't quite matter that he'd *intended* to ask her to lunch with him in this very manner. He liked to think he was at least nominally in charge in his own home.

"I met your children earlier," Miss Bridgerton said, lifting her teacup to her lips.

"Yes, I was there," he replied, pleased that she had initiated the conversation. Now he didn't have to.

"No," she corrected, "after that."

He looked up in question.

"They were waiting for me," she explained, "outside my bedchamber door."

An awful feeling began to churn and roll in his stomach. Waiting for her with what? A bag of live frogs? A bag of *dead* frogs? His children had not been kind to their governesses, and he did not imagine they'd be much more charitable to a female guest who was obviously there in the role of prospective stepmother.

He coughed. "I trust you survived the encounter?"

"Oh, yes," she said. "We have reached an understanding of sorts."

"An understanding?" He eyed her warily. "Of sorts?"

She waved away his question as she chewed on her food. "You needn't worry about me."

"Need I worry about my children?"

She looked up at him with an inscrutable smile. "Of course not."

"Very well." He looked down at the sandwich that had been placed in front of him and took a healthy bite. Once he'd swallowed, he looked her straight in the eye and said, "I must apologize for my greeting this morning. I was less than gracious."

She nodded regally. "And I apologize for arriving unheralded. It was quite ill-bred of me."

He nodded back. "You, however, apologized for that this morning, while I did not."

She offered him a smile, a genuine one, and he felt his heart lurch. Good God, when she smiled it transformed her entire face. In all the time he'd been corresponding with her, he'd never dreamed that she would take his breath away.

"Thank you," she murmured, her cheeks flushing

with the barest hint of pink. "That was very gracious of you."

Phillip cleared his throat and shifted uneasily in his seat. What was wrong with him, that he was less comfortable with her smiles than he was with her frowns? "Right," he said, coughing one more time to cover the gruffness in his voice. "Now that we have that out of the way, perhaps we should address your reason for being here."

Eloise set her sandwich down and regarded him with obvious surprise. Clearly, she hadn't expected him to be so direct. "You were interested in marriage," she said.

"Are you?" he countered.

"I'm here," she said simply.

He looked at her assessingly, his eyes searching hers until she squirmed in her seat. "You are not what I expected, Miss Bridgerton."

"Under the circumstances, I would not think it inappropriate for you to use my given name," she said, "and you are not what I expected, either."

He sat back in his seat, looking at her with the vaguest hint of a smile. "And what did you expect?"

"What did *you* expect?" Eloise countered.

He gave her a look that told her he'd noticed she'd avoided his question, then said, quite bluntly, "I didn't expect you to be so pretty."

Eloise felt herself lurch back slightly at the unexpected compliment. She hadn't been looking her best that morning, and even if she had—well, she'd never been considered one of the beauties of the *ton*. Bridgerton women were generally thought to be attractive, vivacious, and personable. She and her sisters were popular, and they'd all received more than one offer of marriage, but men seemed to like them because they *liked* them, not because they were struck dumb by their beauty.

"I . . . ah . . ." She felt herself flushing, which mortified her, which of course caused her cheeks to redden even more. "Thank you."

He nodded graciously.

"I am not certain why my appearance would have come as a surprise to you," she said, thoroughly annoyed with herself for reacting so strongly to his flattery. Heavens, one would think she had never been paid a compliment before. But he was just sitting there, *looking* at her. Looking, and staring, and . . .

She shivered.

And it wasn't the least bit drafty. Could one shiver from feeling too . . . *hot*?

"You yourself wrote that you are a spinster," he said. "There must be some reason you have never married."

"It was not because I received no offers," she felt compelled to inform him.

"Obviously not," he said, tilting his head in her direction as a gesture of compliment. "But I cannot help but be curious as to why a woman like you would feel the need to resort to . . . well . . . *me*."

She looked at him, really looked at him for the first time since she'd arrived. He was quite handsome in a rough, slightly unkempt sort of way. His dark hair looked in dire need of a good trim, and his skin showed signs of a faint tan, which was impressive considering how little sunshine they'd enjoyed lately. He was large and muscular, and sat in his chair with a careless, athletic sort of grace, legs sprawled in a manner that would not have been acceptable in a London drawing room.

And the look on his face told her that he didn't much care that his manners were not de rigeur. It wasn't the same sort of defiant attitude she saw so often among young men of the *ton*. She'd met so many men of that kind—the ones who made such a point of defying convention, and then spoiled the effect by going out of their way to make sure that everyone knew how daring and scandalous they were.

But with Sir Phillip it was different. Eloise would have bet good money that it would simply never have occurred to him to care that he wasn't sitting in a properly formal manner, and it certainly wouldn't have occurred to him to make sure that other people knew he didn't care.

It made Eloise wonder if that was the mark of a truly self-confident person, and if so, why did he need to resort to *her*? Because from what she'd seen of him, curt manners this morning aside, he shouldn't have had too much trouble finding himself a wife.

"I am here," she said, finally remembering that he had asked her a question, "because after refusing *several* offers of marriage"—she knew that a better person would have been more modest and not taken such pains to emphasize the word "several," but she just couldn't help herself—"I find that I still desire a husband. Your letters seemed to indicate that you might be a good candidate. It seemed shortsighted not to meet with you and find out if that was indeed true."

He nodded. "Very practical of you."

"What about you?" she countered. "You were the one who initially brought up the topic of marriage. Why couldn't you simply find yourself a wife among the women here?"

For a moment he did nothing but blink, looking at her as if he couldn't quite believe she hadn't figured it out for herself. Finally, he said, "You've met my children."

Eloise nearly choked on the bite of sandwich she'd just started to chew. "I beg your pardon?"

"My children," he said flatly. "You've met them. Twice, I think. You told me so."

"Yes, but what . . ." She felt her eyes grow wide. "Oh, no, don't tell me they've scared away every prospective wife in the district?"

The look he leveled at her was grim. "Most of the women in the area refuse to even enter the ranks of the prospectives."

She scoffed. "They're not that bad."

"They need a mother," he said baldly.

She raised her brows. "Surely you can find a more romantic way to convince me to be your wife."

Phillip sighed wearily, running a hand through his already ruffled hair. "Miss Bridgerton," he said, then corrected himself with, "Eloise. I'm going to be honest with you, because, to be frank, I have neither the energy nor the patience for fancy romantic words or cleverly constructed stories. I need a wife. My children need a mother. I invited you here to see if you would be willing to assume such a role, and indeed, if you and I would suit."

"Which one?" she whispered.

He clenched his hands, his knuckles brushing the

tablecloth. What was it about women? Did they speak in some sort of *code*? "Which one . . . what?" he asked, impatience coloring his voice.

"Which one do you want," she clarified, her voice still soft. "A wife or a mother?"

"Both," he said. "I should think that was obvious."

"Which one do you want *more*?"

Phillip stared at her for a long while, aware that this was an important question, quite possibly one that could signal the end of his unusual courtship. Finally, he just offered her a helpless shrug and said, "I'm sorry, but I don't know how to separate the two."

She nodded, her eyes serious. "I see," she murmured. "I expect you are right."

Phillip let out a long breath he wasn't even aware he'd been holding. Somehow—God Himself only knew how—he'd answered correctly. Or at the very least, not incorrectly.

Eloise fidgeted slightly in her seat, then motioned to the half-eaten sandwich on his plate. "Shall we continue with our meal?" she suggested. "You've been in your greenhouse all morning. I'm sure you must be quite famished."

Phillip nodded and took a bite of his food, all of a sudden feeling quite pleased with life. He still wasn't certain that Miss Bridgerton was going to consent to become Lady Crane, but if she did . . .

Well, he didn't think he would have any objections.

But wooing her wasn't going to be as easy as he'd anticipated. It was clear to him that he needed her more than the other way around. He'd been counting on her being a desperate spinster, which was clearly not the case, despite her advanced years. Miss Bridgerton, he suspected, had a number of options in her life, of which he was only one.

But still, something must have compelled her to leave her home and travel all the way out to Gloucestershire. If her life in London was so perfect, why, then, had she left?

But as he watched her across the table, watched her face transform with a mere smile, it occurred to him—he didn't much care why she'd left.

He just needed to make sure that she stayed.

Chapter 4

...so sorry to hear that Caroline is colicky and giving you fits. And of course it is too bad that neither Amelia nor Belinda is amenable to her arrival. But you must look upon the bright side, dear Daphne. It would all have been so much more difficult had you birthed twins.

—*from Eloise Bridgerton to her sister the Duchess of Hastings, one month after the birth of Daphne's third child*

Phillip whistled to himself as he walked through the main hall toward the staircase, inordinately pleased with his life. He'd spent the better part of the afternoon in the company of Miss Bridgerton—no, *Eloise*, he reminded himself—and he was now convinced she'd make an excellent wife. She was quite clearly intelligent, and with all those brothers and sisters (not to mention nephews and nieces) she'd told him about, surely she'd know how to manage Oliver and Amanda.

And, he thought with a wolfish smile, she was rather pretty, and more than once this afternoon he'd caught himself looking at her, wondering how she'd feel in his arms, whether she'd respond to his kiss.

His body tightened at the thought. It had been so long since he'd been with a woman. More years than he cared to count.

More years, quite honestly, than any man would care to admit to.

He'd not availed himself of any of the services offered by the barmaids at the local public inn, preferring his women more freshly washed and, in truth, not quite so anonymous.

Or maybe *more* anonymous. None of those barmaids were likely to leave the village during their lifetime, and Phillip enjoyed his time at the public inn too much to ruin it by constantly having to run into women with whom he'd once lain and no longer cared to.

And before Marina's death—well, he'd never even considered being unfaithful to her, despite the fact that they'd not shared a bed since the twins were quite young.

She'd been so melancholy following their birth. Marina had always seemed fragile and overly pensive, but it was only after Oliver and Amanda had arrived that she'd sunk into her own world of sorrow and despair. It had been horrifying for Phillip, watching the life behind her eyes slip away, day by day, until all that was left was an eerie flatness, the barest shadow of the woman who had once existed.

He knew that women couldn't have relations immediately following childbirth, but even once she was physically healed he couldn't have even imagined forcing himself upon her. How was one supposed to lust after a woman who always looked as if she might cry?

When the twins were a bit older, and Phillip had thought—hoped, really—that Marina was getting better, he had visited her in her bedchamber.

Once.

She had not refused him, but nor had she taken part in his lovemaking. She'd just lain there, doing nothing, her head turned to the side, her eyes open, barely blinking.

It was almost as if she hadn't been there at all.

He'd left feeling soiled, morally corrupt, as if he'd somehow violated her, even though she had never uttered the word *no*.

And he had never touched her again.

His needs weren't so great that he needed to slake them upon a woman who lay beneath him like a corpse.

And he never wanted to feel again as he had that final night. Once he'd returned to his own room, he'd promptly emptied the contents of his stomach, shaking and trembling, disgusted with himself. He had behaved like an animal, desperately trying to rouse in her some sort—any sort—of response. When that had proven impossible, he'd grown angry with her, wanted to punish her.

And that had terrified him.

He'd been too rough. He didn't think he'd hurt her, but he hadn't been gentle. And he never wanted to see that side of himself again.

But Marina was gone.

Gone.

And Eloise was different. She wasn't going to cry at the drop of a hat or shut herself in her room, picking at her food and crying into her pillow.

Eloise had spirit. Backbone.

Eloise was *happy*.

And if that wasn't a good criterion for a wife, he didn't know what was.

He paused at the base of the stairs to check his pocket watch. He had told Eloise that supper would be at seven and that he would meet her outside her door to take her down to the dining room. He didn't want to be early and appear too eager.

On the other hand, it wouldn't do to be late. There was little to be gained in making her think he was disinterested.

He snapped his watch shut and rolled his eyes. He was behaving no better than a green boy. This was ridiculous. He was master of his own house and an accomplished scientist. He ought not to be counting minutes just so he could best win a woman's favor.

But even as he thought that, he opened his watch for one more check. Three minutes prior to seven. Excellent. That would give him just enough time to ascend the stairs and meet her outside her door with precisely one minute to spare.

He grinned, enjoying his warm flush of desire at the thought of her in an evening gown. He hoped it was blue. She would look lovely in blue.

His smile deepened. She would look lovely in nothing at all.

* * *

Except when he found her, upstairs in the hall outside her bedchamber, her hair had gone white.

As, it seemed, had the rest of her.

Bloody hell. "Oliver!" he bellowed. "Amanda!"

"Oh, they're long gone," Eloise bit off. She looked
up at him with fuming eyes. Fuming eyes which, he
couldn't help but note, were the only part of her not
covered with a remarkably thick coating of flour.

Well, good for her for closing them in time. He'd
always admired quick reflexes in a woman.

"Miss Bridgerton," he said, his hand moving forward to help her, then retracting as he realized there
was no helping her. "I cannot begin to express—"

"*Don't* apologize for them," she snapped.

"Right," he said. "Of course. But I promise you . . .
I will . . ."

His words trailed off. Truly, the look in her eyes
would have been enough to silence Napoleon himself.

"Sir Phillip," she said . . . slowly, tightly, looking
very much as if she might launch herself at him in a
furious frenzy. "As you can see, I'm not quite ready
for supper."

He took a self-preservational step back. "I gather
the twins paid you a visit," he said.

"Oh, yes," she replied, with no small measure of
sarcasm. "And then scampered away. The little cow-
ards themselves are nowhere to be found."

"Well, they wouldn't be far," he mused, allowing
her the well-deserved insult to his children while he
tried to carry on a conversation as if she didn't look
like some sort of hideous ghostly apparition.

Somehow it seemed the best course of action. Or

at the very least, the one least likely to result in her wrapping her fingers around his throat.

"They'd want to see the results, of course," he said, taking another discreet step back as she coughed, sending up a swirling cloud of flour. "I don't suppose you heard any laughter when the flour came down? Cackling, perhaps?"

She glared at him.

"Right." He winced. "Sorry for that. Stupid joke."

"It was difficult," she said, so tightly he wondered if her jaw might snap, "to hear anything but the sound of the bucket hitting my head."

"Damn," he muttered, following her line of sight until his eyes fell on a large metal bucket lying on its side on the carpet, with a small amount of flour still inside. "Are you hurt?"

She shook her head.

He reached out and took her head in his hands, trying to inspect her skin for bumps or bruises.

"Sir Phillip!" she yelped, attempting to squirm out of his grasp. "I must ask you to—"

"Be still," he ordered, smoothing his thumbs over her temples, feeling for welts. It was an intimate gesture, and one he found oddly satisfying. She seemed just the right height next to him, and had she been clean, he wasn't sure he'd have been able to stop himself from leaning down and dropping a soft kiss on her brow.

"I'm fine," she practically grunted, wrenching herself free. "The flour weighed more than the bucket."

Phillip leaned down and righted the bucket, testing its weight in his hand. It was fairly light and shouldn't have caused too much damage, but still, it wasn't the sort of thing with which one wanted to be struck on the head.

"I shall survive, I assure you," she bit out.

He cleared his throat. "I imagine you will want a bath?"

He *thought* she said, "I imagine I will want those two little wretches on the end of a rope," but the words came out under her breath, and just because that was what he would have said—well, it didn't mean *she* was as uncharitably inclined.

"I'll have one drawn for you," he said quickly.

"Don't bother. The water from my last bath is still in the tub."

He winced. His children's timing couldn't have been more on the spot. "Nonetheless," he said hastily, "I shall see that it is warmed with a few fresh buckets."

He winced again at her glare. Bad choice of words.

"I'll just see to that now," he said.

"Yes," she replied tautly. "Do that."

He strode down the hall to give the order to a maid, except that the minute he turned the corner, he saw that a half dozen servants were already gaping at them, and had in fact set up a betting pool on how long the twins would last before Phillip tanned their hides.

After sending them on their way with instructions to draw a new bath immediately, he returned to Eloise's side. He was already dusted with flour, so he saw no harm in taking her hand. "I'm terribly sorry," he murmured, now trying not to laugh. His immediate reaction had been fury, but now . . . well, she did look rather ridiculous.

She glared at him, clearly sensing his change of mood.

He quickly assumed a sober mien. "Perhaps you should return to your room?" he suggested.

"And sit where?" she snapped.

She had a point. She was likely to ruin anything she touched, or at the very least necessitate a thorough cleaning.

"I'll just keep you company, then," he said, trying to sound jovial.

She gave him a look that was decidedly unamused.

"Right," he said, in an attempt to fill the silence with something other than flour. He glanced up over the door, impressed with the twins' handiwork, despite the unfortunate results. "I wonder how they did it," he mused.

Her mouth fell open. "Does it matter?"

"Well," he said, seeing from her face that this was not the most advisable avenue of conversation, but continuing nonetheless with, "I certainly can't condone their actions, but it was obviously quite cleverly done. I don't see where they attached the bucket, and—"

"They rested it on the top of the door."

"I beg your pardon?"

"I have seven brothers and sisters," she said dismissively. "Do you think I've never seen this prank before? They opened the door—just a crack—and then carefully placed the bucket."

"And you didn't hear them?"

She glared at him.

"Right," he said hastily. "You were in the bath."

"I don't suppose," she said in a haughty voice,

"that you intend to imply that this was my fault for not having heard them."

"Of course not," he said—very quickly. Judging from the murderous look in Miss Bridgerton's eyes, he was fairly certain that his health and welfare were directly dependent upon the speed with which he agreed with her. "Why don't I leave you to your . . ."

Was there really a good way to describe the process of cleaning several pounds of flour off one's person?

"Will I see you at supper?" he asked, deciding that a change of subject was most definitely in order.

She nodded, once, briefly. There wasn't a great deal of warmth in that nod, but Phillip reckoned he should be happy that she wasn't planning to leave the county that night.

"I will instruct the cook to keep supper warm," he said. "And I will see to punishing the twins."

"No," she said, halting him in his tracks. "Leave them to me."

He turned around slowly, a bit unnerved by the tone of her voice. "What, precisely, do you plan to do with them?"

"With them, or *to* them?"

Phillip had never thought the day would come when he'd be frightened by a woman, but as God was his witness, Eloise Bridgerton scared the living wits out of him.

The look in her eyes was positively diabolical.

"Miss Bridgerton," he said, crossing his arms, "I must ask. What do you intend to do to my children?"

"I'm pondering my options."

He considered that. "May I depend upon their still being alive tomorrow morning?"

"Oh, yes," she replied. "Alive, and with every limb intact, I assure you."

Phillip stared at her for several moments, then let his lips spread into a slow, satisfied smile. He had a feeling that Eloise Bridgerton's vengeance—whatever it might be—would be exactly what his children needed. Surely anyone with seven brothers and sisters would know how to wreak havoc in the most cunning, underhanded, and ingenious manner.

"Very well, Miss Bridgerton," he said, almost glad they'd dumped a bucket of flour on her. "They are all yours."

An hour later, just after he and Eloise sat down for supper, the screaming began.

Phillip actually dropped his spoon; Amanda's shrieks had a more terrified tenor than usual.

Eloise didn't even pause as she placed a spoonful of turtle soup between her lips. "She's fine," she murmured, delicately wiping her mouth with her serviette.

The rapid patter of little feet thundered overhead, signaling that Amanda was racing toward the steps.

Phillip half rose in his seat. "Perhaps I should—"

"I put a fish in her bed," Miss Bridgerton said, not quite smiling, but nonetheless looking rather pleased with herself.

"A fish?" he echoed.

"Very well, it was a rather big fish."

The tadpole in his mind quickly grew into a toothy shark, and he found himself choking on air. "Er," he couldn't help but ask, "where did you find a fish?"

"Mrs. Smith," she said, as if his cook handed out large trout every day of the week.

He forced himself to sit back down. He wasn't going to run to save Amanda. He wanted to; he did possess the odd paternal instinct, after all, and she was shrieking as if the fires of hell were licking at her toes.

But his daughter had made her bed; now it was time to lie in the one Miss Bridgerton had stunk up for her. He dipped his spoon in his soup, lifted it a few inches, then paused. "And what did you place in Oliver's bed?"

"Nothing."

He quirked a brow in question.

"It will keep him in suspense," she explained coolly.

Phillip cocked his head toward her in salute. She was good. "They'll retaliate, of course," he felt honor-bound to warn her.

"I'll be ready." She sounded unconcerned. Then she looked up at him, straight in the eye, momentarily startling him with her direct gaze. "I suppose they know that you invited me here for the purpose of asking me to be your wife."

"I never said anything to them."

"No," she murmured, "you wouldn't."

He looked over at her sharply, unable to discern if she meant that as an insult. "I don't feel the need to keep my children apprised of my personal matters."

She shrugged, a delicate little motion that he found infuriating.

"Miss Bridgerton," he said, "I don't need your advice on how to raise my children."

"I didn't say a word on the subject," she returned, "although I might point out that you do appear rather desperate to find them a mother, which would seem to indicate that you *do* want help."

"Until you agree to take on that role," he bit off, "you may keep your opinions to yourself."

She speared him with a frosty stare, then turned her attention back to her soup. After only two spoonfuls, however, she looked back up at him defiantly, and said, "They need discipline."

"Do you think I don't know that?"

"They also need love."

"They get love," he muttered.

"And attention."

"They get that, too."

"From *you*."

Phillip might have been aware that he was far from being a perfect father, but he was damned if he would allow someone else to say so. "And I suppose you have deduced their state of shameful neglect during the *twelve hours* since your arrival."

She snorted her disdain. "It hardly required twelve hours to listen to them this morning, begging you to spend a paltry few minutes in their company."

"They did nothing of the sort," he retorted, but he could feel the tips of his ears growing hot, as they always did when he was lying. He *didn't* spend enough time with them, and he was mortified that she'd managed to figure that out in such a short amount of time.

"They practically begged you not to be busy *all day*," she shot back. "If you spent a bit more time with them—"

"You don't know anything about my children," he hissed. "And you don't know anything about me."

She stood abruptly. "Clearly," she said, heading for the door.

"Wait!" he called, jumping to his feet. Damn. How had this happened? Barely an hour ago he'd been convinced that she would become his wife, and now she was practically on her way back to London.

He let out a frustrated breath. Nothing had the ability to turn his temper like his children, or the discussion thereof. Or, to be more precise, the discussion of his failings as their father.

"I'm sorry," he said, meaning it, too. Or at least meaning it enough not to want her to leave. "Please." He held out his hand. "Don't go."

"I'll not be treated like an imbecile."

"If there is one thing I've learned in the twelve hours since your arrival," he said, purposefully repeating his earlier words, "it's that you're no imbecile."

She regarded him for a few more seconds, then placed her hand in his.

"At the very least," he said, not even caring that he sounded as if he were pleading with her, "you must stay until Amanda arrives."

Her brows rose in question.

"Surely you'll want to savor your victory," he murmured, then added under his breath, "I know I would."

She allowed him to reseat her, but they had only one more minute together before Amanda came shrieking into the room, her nursemaid hot on her heels.

"Father!" Amanda wailed, throwing herself onto his lap.

Phillip embraced her awkwardly. It was some time since he'd done so, and he'd forgotten how it felt. "Whatever can be the problem?" he asked, giving her a pat on the back for good measure.

Amanda pulled her face out of its burrowed position in his neck and pointed one furious, shaking finger at Eloise. "It's her," she said, as if referring to the devil himself.

"Miss Bridgerton?" Phillip asked.

"She put a fish in my bed!"

"And you dumped flour on her head," he said sternly, "so I'd say you're even."

Amanda's little mouth fell open. "But you're my father!"

"Indeed."

"You're supposed to take my side!"

"When you're in the right."

"It was a *fish*," she sobbed.

"So I smell. You'll want a bath, I imagine."

"I don't want a bath!" she wailed. "I want you to punish her!"

Phillip smiled at that. "She's rather big for punishing, wouldn't you agree?"

Amanda stared at him with horrified disbelief, and then finally, her lower lip shaking, she gasped, "You need to tell her to leave. *Right now!*"

Phillip set Amanda down, rather pleased with how the entire encounter was progressing. Maybe it was Miss Bridgerton's calm presence, but he seemed to have more patience than usual. He felt no urge to snap at Amanda, or to avoid the issue altogether by banishing her to her room. "I beg your pardon,

Amanda," he said, "but Miss Bridgerton is my guest, not yours, and she will remain here as long as I wish."

Eloise cleared her throat. Loudly.

"Or," Phillip amended, "as long as she wishes to remain."

Amanda's entire face scrunched in thought.

"Which doesn't mean," he said quickly, "that you may torture her in an attempt to force her away."

"But—"

"No buts."

"But—"

"What did I just say?"

"But she's *mean*!"

"I think she's very clever," Phillip said, "and I wish I'd put a fish in your bed months ago."

Amanda stepped back in horror.

"Go to your room, Amanda."

"But it smells bad."

"You have only yourself to blame."

"But my bed—"

"You'll have to sleep on the floor," he replied.

Face quivering—entire body quivering, truth be told—she dragged herself toward the door. "But . . . but . . ."

"Yes, Amanda?" he asked, in what he thought to be an impressively patient voice.

"But she didn't punish Oliver," the little girl whispered. "That wasn't very fair of her. The flour was his idea."

Phillip raised his brows.

"Well, it wasn't *only* my idea," Amanda insisted. "We thought it up together."

Phillip actually chuckled. "I wouldn't worry

about Oliver if I were you, Amanda. Or rather," he said, giving his chin a thoughtful stroke with his fingers, "I *would* worry. I suspect Miss Bridgerton has plans for him yet."

That seemed to satisfy Amanda, and she mumbled a barely articulate "Good night, Father," before allowing her nursemaid to lead her from the room.

Phillip turned back to his soup, feeling very pleased with himself. He couldn't remember the last time he'd emerged from a run-in with one of the twins in which he'd felt he'd handled everything just right. He took a sip, then, still holding his spoon, looked over at Eloise and said, "Poor Oliver will be quaking in his boots."

She appeared to be trying hard not to grin. "He won't be able to sleep."

Phillip shook his head. "Not a wink, I should think. And you should watch your step. I'd wager he'll set some sort of trap at his door."

"Oh, I have no plans to torture Oliver this evening," she said with a blithe wave of her hand. "That would be far too easy to predict. I prefer the element of surprise."

"Yes," he said with a chuckle. "I can see that you would."

Eloise answered him with a smug expression. "I would almost consider leaving him in perpetual agony, except that it really wouldn't be fair to Amanda."

Phillip shuddered. "I hate fish."

"I know. You wrote me as much."

"I did?"

She nodded. "Odd that Mrs. Smith even had any in the house, but I suppose the servants like it."

They descended into silence, but it was a comfortable, companionable sort of quietude. And as they ate, moving through the courses of the supper as they chatted about nothing in particular, it occurred to Phillip that perhaps marriage wasn't supposed to be so hard.

With Marina he'd always felt like he was tiptoeing around the house, always fearful that she was going to descend into one of her bouts with melancholia, always disappointed when she seemed to withdraw from life, and indeed, almost disappear.

But maybe marriage was supposed to be easier than that. Maybe it was supposed to be like this. Companionable. Comfortable.

He couldn't remember the last time he had spoken with anyone about his children, or the raising thereof. His burdens had always been his alone, even when Marina had been alive. Marina herself had been a burden, and he was still wrestling with the guilt he felt at his relief that she was gone.

But Eloise . . .

He looked across the table at the woman who had so unexpectedly fallen into his life. Her hair glowed almost red in the flickering candlelight, and her eyes, when she caught him staring at her, sparkled with vitality and just a hint of mischief.

She was, he was coming to realize, exactly what he needed. Smart, opinionated, bossy—they weren't the sort of things men usually looked for in a wife, but Phillip so desperately needed someone to come to Romney Hall and fix things. Nothing was quite right, from the house to his children to the slightly hushed pall that had hung over the place when Marina had been alive, and sadly had not lifted even after her death.

Phillip would gladly cede some of his husbandly power to a wife if she would only make everything right again. He'd be more than happy to disappear into his greenhouse and let her be in charge of everything else.

Would Eloise Bridgerton be willing to take on such a role?

Dear God, he hoped so.

Chapter 5

... implore you, Mother, you MUST punish
Daphne. It is NOT FAIR that I am the only one
sent to bed without pudding. And for a week. A
week is far too long. Especially since it was ~~all~~
mostly Daphne's idea.

—from Eloise Bridgerton to her mother,
left upon Violet Bridgerton's night table
during Eloise's tenth year

It was strange, Eloise thought, how much could
change in a single day.

Because now, as Sir Phillip was escorting her
through his home, ostensibly viewing the portrait
gallery but really just prolonging their time together,
she was thinking—

He might make a perfectly fine husband after all.

Not the most poetic way to phrase a concept that
ought to have been full of romance and passion, but
theirs wasn't a typical courtship, and with only two

years remaining until her thirtieth birthday, Eloise couldn't really afford to be fanciful.

But still, there was something . . .

In the candlelight, Sir Phillip was somehow more handsome, perhaps even a little dangerous-looking. The rugged planes of his face seemed to angle and shadow in the flickering light, lending him a more sculptured look, almost like the statues she'd visited at the British Museum. And as he stood next to her, his large hand possessively at her elbow, his entire presence seemed to envelop her.

It was odd, and thrilling, and just a little bit terrifying.

But gratifying, too. She'd done a crazy thing, running off in the middle of the night, hoping to find happiness with a man she'd never met. It was a relief to think that maybe it hadn't all been a complete mistake, that maybe she'd gambled with her future and won.

Nothing would have been worse than slinking back to London, admitting failure and having to explain to her entire family what she'd done.

She didn't want to have to admit that she'd been wrong, to herself or anyone else.

But mostly to herself.

Sir Phillip had proven to be an enjoyable supper companion, even if he wasn't quite so glib or conversational as she was used to.

But he obviously possessed a sense of fair play, which Eloise deemed essential in any spouse. He had accepted—even admired—her fish-in-the-bed technique with Amanda. Many of the men Eloise had met in London would have been horrified that a gently bred lady would even think of resorting to such underhanded tactics.

And maybe, just maybe, this would work. Marriage to Sir Phillip did seem a harebrained scheme when she allowed herself to think about it in a logical manner, but it wasn't as if he were a *complete* stranger—they had been corresponding for over a year, after all.

"My grandfather," Phillip said mildly, gesturing to a large portrait.

"He was quite handsome," Eloise said, even though she could barely see him in the dim light. She motioned to the picture to the right. "Is that your father?"

Phillip nodded once, curtly, the corners of his lips tightening.

"And where are you?" she asked, sensing that he didn't wish to talk about his father.

"Over here, I'm afraid."

Eloise followed his direction to a portrait of Phillip as a young boy of perhaps twelve years, posing with someone who could only have been his brother.

His older brother.

"What happened to him?" she asked, since he had to be dead. If he lived, Phillip could not have inherited his house or baronetcy.

"Waterloo," he answered succinctly.

Impulsively, she placed her hand over his. "I'm sorry."

For a moment she didn't think he was going to say anything, but eventually he let out a quiet, "No one was sorrier than I."

"What was his name?"

"George."

"You must have been quite young," she said, counting back to 1815 and doing the math in her head.

"Twenty-one. My father died two weeks following."

She thought about that. At twenty-one, she was supposed to have been married. All young ladies of her station were expected to have been married by then. One would think that would confer a measure of adulthood, but now twenty-one seemed impossibly young and green, and far too innocent to have inherited a burden one had never thought to receive.

"Marina was his fiancée," he said.

Her breath rushed over her lips, and she turned to him, her hand falling away from his. "I didn't know," she said.

He shrugged. "It doesn't matter. Here, would you like to see her portrait?"

"Yes," Eloise replied, discovering that she did indeed wish to see Marina. They had been cousins, but distant ones, and it had been years since they'd visited with one another. Eloise remembered dark hair and light eyes—blue, maybe—but that was all. She and Marina had been of an age, and so they had been thrust together at family gatherings, but Eloise didn't recall their ever having very much in common. Even when they were barely older than Amanda and Oliver, their differences had been clear. Eloise had been a boisterous child, climbing trees and sliding down banisters, always following her older siblings, begging them to allow her to take part in whatever they were doing.

Marina had been quieter, almost contemplative. Eloise remembered tugging on her hand, trying to get her to come outside and play. But Marina had just wanted to sit with a book.

Eloise had taken note of the pages, however, and she was quite convinced that Marina never moved beyond page thirty-two.

It was a strange thing to remember, she supposed, except that her nine-year-old self had found it so astounding—why would someone choose to stay inside with a book when the sun was shining, and then not even read it? She'd spent the rest of the visit whispering with her sister Francesca, trying to figure out just what it was that Marina was doing with that book.

"Do you remember her?" Phillip asked.

"Just a little," Eloise replied, not sure why she didn't wish to share her memory with him. And anyway, it was the truth. That was the sum of her recollections of Marina—that one week in April over twenty years earlier, whispering with Francesca as Marina stared at a book.

Eloise allowed Phillip to lead her over to Marina's portrait. She had been painted seated, on some sort of ottoman, with her dark red skirts artfully arranged about her. A younger version of Amanda was on her lap, and Oliver stood at her side, in one of those poses young boys were always forced to assume—serious and stern, as if they were miniature adults.

"She was lovely," Eloise said.

Phillip just stared at the image of his dead wife, then, almost as if it required a force of will, turned his head and walked away.

Had he loved her? Did he love her still?

Marina should have been his brother's bride; everything seemed to suggest that Phillip had been given her by default.

But that didn't mean he didn't love her. Maybe he had been secretly in love with her while she had been engaged to his brother. Or maybe he had fallen in love after the wedding.

Eloise stole a look at his profile as he stared sightlessly at a painting on the wall. There had been emotion on his face when he had looked at Marina's portrait. She wasn't sure what he had felt for her, but it was definitely still something. It had only been a year, she reminded herself. A year might make up the official period of mourning, but it wasn't very long to get past the death of a loved one.

Then he turned. His eyes hit hers, and she realized she'd been staring at him, mesmerized by the planes of his face. Her lips parted with surprise, and she wanted to look away, felt as if she ought to blush and stammer at having been caught, but somehow she could not. She just stood there, transfixed, breathless, as a strange heat spread across her skin.

He was ten feet away, at the very least, and it felt as if they were touching.

"Eloise?" he whispered, or at least she thought he did. She saw his lips form the word more than she actually heard his voice.

And then somehow the moment was broken. Maybe it was his whisper, maybe the creak of a windblown tree outside. But Eloise was finally able to move—to think—and she quickly turned back to Marina's portrait, firmly affixing her gaze on her late cousin's serene face. "The children must miss her," Eloise said, needing to say something, anything that would restart the conversation—and restore her composure.

For a moment Phillip said nothing. And then, finally: "Yes, they've missed her for a long time."

It seemed to Eloise a rather odd way to phrase it. "I know how they feel," she said. "I was quite young when my father died."

He looked over at her. "I didn't realize."

She shrugged. "It's not something I talk about a great deal. It was a long time ago."

He crossed back to her side, his steps slow and methodical. "Did it take you very long to get over it?"

"I'm not certain it's something you ever do get over," she said. "Completely, that is. But no, I don't think about him every day, if that's what you want to know."

She turned away from Marina's portrait; she'd been focusing on it for too long and was beginning to feel oddly intrusive. "I think it was more difficult for my older brothers," she said. "Anthony—he is the eldest and was already a young man when it happened—had a particularly difficult time with it. They were very close. And my mother, of course." She looked over at him. "My parents loved each other very much."

"How did she react to his passing?"

"Well, she cried a great deal at first," Eloise said. "I'm sure we weren't meant to know. She always did it in her room at night, after she thought we were all asleep. But she missed him dreadfully, and it couldn't have been easy with seven children."

"I thought there were eight of you."

"Hyacinth was not yet born. I believe my mother was eight months along."

"Good God," she thought she heard him murmur.

Good God was right. Eloise had no idea how her mother had managed.

"It was unexpected," she told him. "He was stung by a bee. A bee. Can you imagine that? He was stung by a bee, and then— Well, I don't need to bore you with the details. Here," she said briskly, "let us leave. It's too dark in here to see the portraits properly, anyway."

It was a lie, of course. It *was* too dark, but Eloise couldn't have cared less about that. Talking about her father's death always made her feel a bit strange, and she just didn't feel like standing there surrounded by paintings of dead people.

"I should like to see your greenhouse," she said.

"Now?"

Put that way, it did seem an odd request. "Tomorrow, then," she said, "when it's light."

His lips curved into a hint of a smile. "We can go now."

"But we won't be able to see anything."

"We won't be able to see everything," he corrected. "But the moon is out, and we'll take a lantern."

She glanced doubtfully out the window. "It's cold."

"You can take a coat." He leaned down with a gleam in his eye. "You're not afraid, are you?"

"Of course not!" she retorted, knowing he was baiting her but falling for it, anyway.

He quirked a brow in a most provoking manner.

"I'll have you know I'm the least cowardly woman you're ever likely to encounter."

"I'm sure you are," he murmured.

"Now you're being patronizing."

He did nothing but chuckle.

"Very well," she said gamely, "lead the way."

"It's so warm!" Eloise exclaimed as Phillip shut the greenhouse door behind her.

"It's actually usually warmer than this," he told her. "The glass allows the sun to warm the air, but except for this morning, it's been quite overcast for the past few days."

Phillip often visited his greenhouse at night, toiling by the light of a lantern when he could not sleep. Or, before he'd been widowed, to keep him busy so that he would not consider entering Marina's bedchamber.

But he had never asked anyone to accompany him in the dark; even during the day, he almost always worked alone. Now he was seeing it all through Eloise's eyes—the magic in the way the pearlescent moonlight threw shadows across the leaves and fronds. During the day, a walk through the greenhouse wasn't so very different from a walk through any wooded area in England, with the exception of the odd rare fern or imported bromeliad.

But now, with the cloak of night playing tricks on the eyes, it was as if they were in some secret, hidden jungle, with magic and surprise lurking around every corner.

"What is this?" Eloise asked, peering down at eight small clay pots, arranged in a line across his workbench.

Phillip walked to her side, absurdly pleased that she seemed truly curious. Most people just feigned interest, or didn't even bother to pretend and made a quick escape. "It's an experiment I've been working on," he said, "with peas."

"The kind we eat?"

"Yes. I'm trying to develop a strain that will grow fatter in the pod."

She peered down at the pots. Nothing was sprouting yet; he'd only planted the seeds a week ago. "How curious," she murmured. "I had no idea one could do that."

"I have no idea if one can," he admitted. "I've been trying for a year."

"With no success? How very frustrating."

"I've had some success," he admitted, "just not as much as I'd like."

"I tried to grow roses one year," she told him. "They all died."

"Roses are more difficult than most people think," he said.

Her lips twisted slightly. "I noticed you have them in abundance."

"I have a gardener."

"A botanist with a gardener?"

He'd heard that question before, many times. "It's no different than a dressmaker with a seamstress."

She considered that for a moment, then moved farther into the greenhouse, stopping to peer at various plants and scold him for not keeping up with her with the lantern.

"You're a bit bossy this evening," he said.

She turned, caught that he was smiling—

half-smiling, at least—and offered him a wicked grin. "I prefer to be called 'managing.'"

"A managing sort of female, eh?"

"I'm surprised you didn't deduce as much from my letters."

"Why do you think I invited you?" he countered.

"You want someone to manage your life?" she asked, tossing the words over her shoulder as she moved flirtatiously away from him.

He wanted someone to manage his children, but now didn't seem like the best time to bring them up. Not when she was looking at him as if . . .

As if she wanted to be kissed.

Phillip had taken two slow, predatory steps in her direction before he even realized what he was doing.

"What is this?" she asked, pointing to something.

"A plant."

"I know it's a plant," she said with a laugh. "If I'd—" But then she looked up, caught the gleam in his eyes, and quieted.

"May I kiss you?" he asked. He would have stopped if she'd said no, he supposed, but he didn't allow her much opportunity, closing the distance between them before she could reply.

"May I?" he repeated, so close that his words were whispered across her lips.

She nodded, the motion tiny but sure, and brushed his mouth against hers, gently, softly, as one was supposed to kiss a woman one thought one might marry.

But then her hands stole around and touched his neck, and God help him, but he wanted more.

Much more.

He deepened the kiss, ignoring her gasp of surprise as he parted her lips with his tongue. But even that wasn't what he wanted. He wanted to feel her, her warmth, her vitality, up and down the length of him, around him, through him, infusing him.

He slid his hands around her, settling one against her upper back, even as another daringly found the lush curve of her bottom. He pressed her against him, hard, not caring that she would feel the evidence of his desire. It had been so long. So damned long, and she was so soft and sweet in his arms.

He wanted her.

He wanted all of her, but even his passion-hazed mind knew that that was impossible this evening, and so he was determined to have the next best thing, which was just the feel of her, the sensation of her in his arms, the heat of her running along the entire length of his body.

And she was responding. Hesitantly, at first, as if she wasn't quite sure what she was doing, but then with greater ardor, making innocently seductive little sounds from the back of her throat.

It drove him wild. *She* drove him wild.

"Eloise, Eloise," he murmured, his voice hoarse and raspy with need. He sank one hand into her hair, tugging at it until her coiffure loosened and one thick chestnut lock slid out to form a seductive curlicue on her breastbone. His lips moved to her neck, tasting her skin, exulting when she arched back and offered him greater access. And then, just when he'd started to sink down, his knees bending as his lips trailed over her collarbone, she wrenched herself away.

"I'm sorry," she blurted out, her hands flying up

to the neckline of her dress even though it wasn't the least bit out of place.

"I'm not," he said baldly.

Her eyes widened at his bluntness. He didn't care. He'd never been particularly fancy with words, and it was probably best that she learned that now, before they did anything permanent.

And then she surprised him.

"It was a figure of speech," she said.

"I beg your pardon?"

"I said I was sorry. I wasn't, really. It was a figure of speech."

She sounded remarkably composed and almost schoolteacherish, for a woman who had just been so soundly kissed.

"People say things like that all the time," she continued, "just to fill the silence."

Phillip was coming to realize that she wasn't the sort of woman who liked silence.

"It's rather like when one—"

He kissed her again.

"Sir Phillip!"

"Sometimes," he said with a satisfied smile, "silence is a good thing."

Her mouth fell open. "Are you saying I talk too much?"

He shrugged, having too much fun teasing her to do anything else.

"I'll have you know that I have been *much* quieter here than I am at home."

"That's difficult to imagine."

"Sir Phillip!"

"Shhh," he said, reaching out and taking her hand, then taking it again, more firmly this time, when she snatched it away. "We need a bit of noise around here."

Eloise woke the following morning as if she were still wrapped in a dream. She hadn't expected him to kiss her.

And she hadn't expected to like it quite so much.

Her stomach let out an angry growl, and she decided to make her way down to the breakfast room. She had no idea if Sir Phillip would be there. Was he an early riser? Or did he like to remain abed until noon? It seemed silly that she didn't know these things about him when she was seriously contemplating marriage.

And if he was there, waiting for her over a plate of coddled eggs, what would she say to him? What did one say to a man after he'd had his tongue in one's ear?

Never mind that it had been a very nice tongue, indeed. It was still quite beyond scandalous.

What if she got there and could barely manage "Good morning?" He'd surely find that amusing, after teasing her about her loquaciousness the night before.

It almost made her laugh. She, who could carry on a conversation about nothing in particular and frequently did, wasn't sure what she was going to say when she next saw Sir Phillip Crane.

Of course, he *had* kissed her. That changed everything.

Crossing the room, she checked to make sure that her door was firmly shut before she opened it. She didn't think that Oliver and Amanda would try the same trick twice, but one never knew. She didn't particularly relish the thought of another flour bath. Or worse. After the fish incident, they were probably thinking more along the lines of something liquid. Something liquid and smelly.

Humming softly to herself, she stepped out into the hall and turned to the right to make her way to the staircase. The day seemed filled with promise; the sun had actually been peeking out through the clouds this morning when she'd looked out the window, and—

"Oh!"

The shriek ripped itself right out of her throat as she plunged forward, her foot caught behind something that had been strung out across the hall. She didn't even have a chance to try to regain her balance; she had been walking quickly, as was her habit, and when she fell, she fell hard.

And without even the time to use her hands to break her fall.

Tears burned her eyes. Her chin—dear God, her chin felt like it was on fire. The side of it, at least. She had just managed to twist her head ever so slightly to the side before she fell.

She moaned something incoherent, the sort of noise one makes when one hurts so badly that one simply cannot keep it all inside. And she kept waiting for the pain to subside, thinking that this would be like a stubbed toe, which throbs mercilessly for a few seconds and then, once the surprise of it is over, slides into nothing more than a dull ache.

But the pain kept burning. On her chin, on the side of her head, on her knee, and on her hip.

She felt beaten.

Slowly, with great effort, she forced herself up

onto her hands and knees, and then into a sitting position. She allowed herself to lean against the wall and lifted her hand to cradle her cheek, taking quick bursts of breath through her nose to try to control the pain.

"Eloise!"

Phillip. She didn't bother to look up, didn't want to move from her curled-up position.

"Eloise, my God," he said, triple-stepping the last few stairs as he rushed to her side. "What happened?"

"I fell." She hadn't meant to whimper, but it came out that way, anyway.

With a tenderness that seemed out of place on a man of his size, he took her hand in his and pulled it from her cheek.

The next words he said were not ones that were often uttered in Eloise's presence.

"You need a piece of meat on that," he said.

She looked up at him with watery eyes. "Am I bruised?"

He nodded grimly. "You may have a blackened eye. It's still too soon to tell."

She tried to smile, tried to put a game face on it, but she just couldn't manage it.

"Does it hurt very badly?" he asked softly.

She nodded, wondering why the sound of his voice made her want to cry even more. It reminded her of when she was small and she'd fallen from a tree. She'd sprained her ankle, quite badly, but somehow she'd managed not to cry until she'd made it back home.

One look from her mother and she'd begun to sob.

Phillip touched her cheek gingerly, his features pulling into a scowl when she winced.

"I'll be fine," she assured him. And she would. In a few days.

"What happened?"

And of course she knew exactly what had happened. Something had been strung across the hall, put in place to make her trip and fall. It didn't require very much intelligence to guess who had done it.

But Eloise didn't want to get the twins in trouble. At least not the sort of trouble they were likely to find themselves in once Sir Phillip got hold of them. She didn't think they'd intended to cause quite so much harm.

But Phillip had already spied the thin length of twine, tightly drawn across the hall and tied around the legs of two tables, both of which had been tugged toward the center of the hall when Eloise had tripped.

Eloise watched as he knelt down, touching the string and twisting it around his fingers. He looked over at her, not with question in his eyes, but rather grim statement of fact.

"I didn't see it," she said, even though that was quite obvious.

Phillip didn't take his eyes off of hers, but his fingers kept twisting the string until it tautened and snapped.

Eloise sucked in her breath. There was something almost terrifying in the moment. Phillip didn't seem aware that he'd broken the string, barely cognizant of his strength.

Or the strength of his anger.

"Sir Phillip," she whispered, but he never heard her.

"Oliver!" he bellowed. "Amanda!"

"I'm sure they didn't mean to injure me," Eloise began, not certain why she was defending them. They'd hurt her, that was true, but she had a feeling her punishment would be considerably less painful than anything coming from their father.

"I don't care what they meant," Phillip snapped. "Look how close you landed to the stairs. What if you'd fallen?"

Eloise eyed the stairs. They were close, but not close enough for her to have taken a tumble. "I don't think . . ."

"They must answer for this," he said, his voice deadly low and shaking with rage.

"I'll be fine," Eloise said. Already the stinging pain was giving way to a duller ache. But it still hurt, enough so that when Sir Phillip lifted her into his arms, she let out a little cry.

And his fury grew.

"I'm putting you in bed," he said, his voice rough and curt.

Eloise offered no disagreement.

A maid appeared on the landing, gasping when she saw the darkening bruise on Eloise's face.

"Get me something for this," Sir Phillip ordered. "A piece of meat. Anything."

The maid nodded and ran off as Phillip carried Eloise into her room. "Are you hurt anywhere else?" he asked.

"My hip," Eloise admitted as he settled her on top of her covers. "And my elbow."

He nodded grimly. "Do you think you've broken anything?"

"No!" she said quickly. "No, I—"

"I'll need to check, anyway," he said, brushing aside her protests as he lightly examined her arm.

"Sir Phillip, I—"

"My children just nearly killed you," he said, without a trace of humor in his eyes. "I should think you could dispense with the *sir*."

Eloise swallowed as she watched him cross the room to the door, his strides long and powerful. "Get me the twins immediately," he said, presumably to some servant hovering outside in the hall. Eloise couldn't imagine that the children hadn't heard his earlier bellow, but she also couldn't blame them for attempting to delay judgment day at the hands of their father.

"Phillip," she said, trying to coax him back into the room with the sound of her voice, "leave them to me. I was the injured party, and—"

"They are my children," he said, his voice harsh, "and I will punish them. God knows it's long past due."

Eloise stared at him with growing horror. He was nearly shaking with rage, and while she could have happily swatted the children on their bottoms herself, she didn't think he ought to be meting out punishment in his state.

"They hurt you," Phillip said in a low voice. "That is not acceptable."

"I'll be fine," she assured him again. "In a few days I won't even—"

"That is not the point," he said sharply. "If I

had . . ." He stopped, tried again with, "If I hadn't . . ." He stopped, beyond words, and leaned against the wall, his head hanging back as his eyes searched the ceiling—for what, she didn't know. Answers, she supposed. As if one could find answers with the simple upward sweep of the eyes.

He turned, looked at her, his eyes grim, and Eloise saw something on his face she hadn't expected to see there.

And that was when she realized it—all that rage in his voice, in the shaking of his body—it wasn't directed at the children. Not really, and certainly not entirely.

The look on his face, the bleakness in his eyes—it was self-loathing.

He didn't blame his children.

He blamed himself.

Chapter 6

... should not have let him kiss you. Who knows
what liberties he will attempt to take the next time
you meet? But what's done is done, I suppose, so all
there is left is to ask: Was it lovely?

—*from Eloise Bridgerton to her sister Francesca,*
slid under the door of her bedroom
the night Francesca met the Earl of Kilmartin,
whom she would marry two months later

When the children entered the room, half dragged
and half pushed by their nursemaid, Phillip forced
himself to remain rigidly in his position against the
wall, afraid that if he went to them he'd beat them
both within an inch of their lives.

And even more afraid that when he was through,
he wouldn't regret his actions.

So instead he just crossed his arms and stared, letting them squirm under the heat of his fury, while he
tried to figure out what the hell he meant to say.

Finally, Oliver spoke up, his voice trembling as he said, "Father?"

Phillip said the only thing that came to mind, the only thing that seemed to matter. "Do you see Miss Bridgerton?"

The twins nodded, but they didn't quite look at her. At least not at her face, which was beginning to purple around the eye.

"Do you notice anything amiss about her?"

They said nothing, forcing a silence until a maid appeared in the doorway with a "Sir?"

Phillip acknowledged her arrival with a nod, then strode to take hold of the piece of meat she'd brought for Eloise's eye.

"Hungry?" he snapped at his children. When they didn't reply, he said, "Good. Because sadly, none of us will be eating this, will we?"

He crossed the room to the bed, then sat down gently at Eloise's side. "Here," he said, still too angry for his voice to be anything but gruff. Brushing aside her efforts to help, he set the meat against her eye, then arranged a piece of cloth over it so that she would not have to dirty her fingers while keeping it in place.

Then, when he was done, he walked over to where the twins were cowering, and stood in front of them, arms crossed. And waited.

"Look at me," he ordered, when neither removed their gaze from the floor.

When they did, he saw terror in their eyes, and it sickened him, but he didn't know how else he was supposed to act.

"We didn't mean to hurt her," Amanda whispered.

"Oh, you didn't?" he bit off, turning on them both

with palpable fury. His voice was icy, but his face clearly showed his anger, and even Eloise shrank back in her bed.

"You didn't think she might possibly be hurt when she tripped over the string?" Phillip continued, his sarcasm lending him a controlled air that was even more frightening. "Or perhaps you realized correctly that the string itself wasn't likely to cause injury, but it didn't occur to you that she might be hurt when she actually fell."

They said nothing.

He looked at Eloise, who had lifted the meat from her face and was gingerly touching her cheekbone. The bruise under her eye seemed to be worsening by the minute.

The twins had to learn that they couldn't continue like this. They needed to learn that they had to treat people with more respect. They needed to learn . . .

Phillip swore under his breath. They needed to learn *some*thing.

He jerked his head toward the door. "You will come with me." He walked into the hall, turned back at them, and snapped, "Now."

And as he led them from the room, he prayed that he could control himself.

Eloise tried not to listen, but she couldn't seem to stop herself from straining her ears. She didn't know where Phillip was taking the children—it could be the next room, it could be the nursery, it could be outside. But one thing was certain. They were going to be punished.

And while she thought they *should* be punished— what they had done was inexcusable and they were certainly old enough to have realized that—she still found herself oddly worried for them. They had looked terrified when Phillip had led them away, and there was that niggling memory from the day before, when Oliver had blurted out the question, "Are you going to hit us?"

He had recoiled when he'd said it, as if he were expecting to be hit.

Surely Sir Phillip didn't . . . No, that was impossible, Eloise thought. It was one thing to give children a spanking at a time like this, but surely he didn't strike his children habitually.

She couldn't have made such a misjudgment about a person. She had let the man kiss her the night before, kissed him in return, even. Surely she would have felt that something was wrong, sensed an inner cruelty if Phillip were the sort who beat his children.

Finally, after what seemed like an eternity, Oliver and Amanda filed in, looking somber and red-eyed, followed by a grim-faced Sir Phillip, whose job at the rear was clearly to keep the children walking at a pace that exceeded that of a snail.

The children shuffled over to her bedside, and Eloise turned her head so that she could see them. She couldn't see out of her left eye with the meat covering it, and of course that was the side the children had chosen.

"We're sorry, Miss Bridgerton," they mumbled.

"Louder," came their father's sharply worded directive.

"We're sorry."

Eloise gave them a nod.

"It won't happen again," Amanda added.

"That's certainly a relief to hear," Eloise said.

Phillip cleared his throat.

"Father says we must make it up to you," Oliver said.

"Er . . ." Eloise wasn't exactly certain how they meant to do that.

"Do you like sweets?" Amanda blurted out.

Eloise looked at her, blinking her good eye in confusion. "Sweets?"

Amanda's chin shook up and down.

"Well, yes, I suppose I do. Doesn't everyone?"

"I have a box of lemon drops. I've saved them for months. You can have them."

Eloise swallowed against the lump in her throat as she watched Amanda's tortured expression. There was something wrong with these children. Or if not with them, then for them. Something wasn't right in their lives. With all of her nieces and nephews, Eloise had seen enough happy children to know this. "That will be all right, Amanda," she said, her heart wrenching. "You may keep your lemon drops."

"But we have to give you something," Amanda said, casting a fearful glance at her father.

Eloise was about to tell her that that wasn't necessary, but then, as she watched Amanda's face, she realized that it was. In part, of course, because Sir Phillip had obviously insisted upon it, and Eloise wasn't about to undermine his authority by saying otherwise. But also because the twins needed to understand the concept of making amends. "Very well," Eloise said. "You may give me an afternoon."

"An afternoon?"

"Yes. Once I'm feeling better, you and your brother may give me an afternoon. There is much here at Romney Hall with which I'm unfamiliar, and I imagine you two know every last corner of the house and grounds. You may take me on a tour. Provided, of course," she added, because she did value her health and well-being, "that you promise there will be no pranks."

"None," Amanda said quickly, her chin bobbing in an earnest nod. "I promise."

"Oliver," Phillip growled, when his son did not speak quickly enough.

"There will be no pranks that afternoon," Oliver muttered.

Phillip strode across the room and grabbed his son by the collar.

"Ever!" Oliver said in a strangled voice. "I promise! We shall leave Miss Bridgerton completely alone."

"Not completely, I hope," Eloise said, glancing up at Phillip and hoping he correctly interpreted that to mean, *You may now put down the child.* "After all, you do owe me an afternoon."

Amanda offered her a tentative smile, but Oliver's scowl remained firmly in place.

"You may leave now," Phillip said, and the children fled through the open doorway.

The two adults remained in silence for a full minute after they left, both staring at the door with hollow, weary expressions. Eloise felt drained, and wary, almost as if she'd been dropped into a situation she didn't quite understand.

A burst of nervous laughter almost escaped her lips. What was she thinking? Of *course* she had been dropped into a situation she didn't understand, and she was lying to herself if she thought she knew what to do.

Phillip walked over to the bed, but when he got there, he stood rather stiffly. "How are you?" he asked Eloise.

"If I don't remove this meat soon," she said quite frankly, "I think I might be sick."

He picked up the platter the meat had arrived upon and held it out. Eloise put the steak down, grimacing at the wet, slopping sound it made. "I believe I would like to wash my face," she said. "The smell is rather overwhelming."

He nodded. "First let me look at your eye."

"Do you have very much experience with this sort of thing?" she asked, glancing at the ceiling when he asked her to look up.

"A bit." He pressed gently against the ridge of her cheekbone with his thumb. "Look right."

She did. "A bit?"

"I boxed at university."

"Were you good?"

He turned her head to the side. "Look left. Good enough."

"What does *that* mean?"

"Close your eye."

"What does that *mean*?" she persisted.

"You're not closing your eye."

She did, shutting them both, because whenever she winked only one eye she ended up squeezing it far too tightly. "What does it mean?"

She couldn't see him, but she could feel him pause. "Has anyone ever told you you can be a bit stubborn?"

"All the time. It's my only flaw."

She heard his smile in the tenor of his breath. "The only one, eh?"

"The only one worth commenting upon."

She opened her eyes. "You didn't answer my question."

"I've quite forgotten what it was."

She opened her mouth to repeat it, then realized he was teasing her, so she scowled instead.

"Close your eye again," he said. "I'm not yet finished." When she obeyed his command, he added, "*Good enough* meant I never had to fight if I didn't want to."

"But you weren't the champion," she surmised.

"You can open your eye now."

She did, then blinked when she realized how close he still was.

He stepped back. "I wasn't the champion."

"Why not?"

He shrugged. "I didn't care about it enough."

"How does it look?" she asked.

"Your eye?"

She nodded.

"I don't think there is anything to be done to stop the bruising."

"I didn't think I hit my eye," she said, letting out a frustrated sigh. "When I fell. I thought I hit my cheek."

"You don't have to hit your eye to bruise there. I can see from your face that you landed right here"—he touched her cheekbone, right where she'd hit, but he was so gentle that she felt no pain—"and that's close enough for the bleeding to spread to the eye area."

She groaned. "I'm going to look a fright for weeks."

"It might not take weeks."

"I have brothers," she said, giving him a look that

said she knew what she was talking about. "I've seen blackened eyes. Benedict had one that didn't completely fade away for two months."

"What happened to him?" Phillip asked.

"My other brother," she said wryly.

"Say no more," he said. "I had a brother of my own."

"Beastly creatures," she muttered, "the lot of them." But there was love in her voice as she said it.

"Yours probably won't take that long," he said, helping her to stand so that she could make her way to the washbasin.

"But it might."

Phillip nodded, then, once she was splashing the smell of the meat off her skin, said, "We need to get you a chaperone."

She froze. "I'd quite forgotten."

He let several seconds go by before replying, "I hadn't."

She picked up a towel and patted herself dry. "I'm sorry. It's my fault, of course. You had written that you would arrange for a chaperone. In my haste to leave London, I quite forgot that you would need time to make the arrangements."

Phillip watched her closely, wondering if she realized that she had slipped and said more than she'd probably meant to. It was difficult to imagine a woman such as Eloise—open, bright, and extremely talkative—as having secrets, but she had been quite close-lipped about her reasons for coming to Gloucestershire.

She'd said that she was looking for a husband, but he suspected that her reasons had as much to do with what she'd left behind in London as they did with what she hoped to find here in the country.

And then she'd said—*in my haste*.

Why had she left in a hurry? What had happened there?

"I have already contacted my great-aunt," he said, helping her back into her bed even though she quite clearly wanted to do it herself. "I sent her a letter the morning you arrived. But I doubt she could be here any earlier than Thursday. She only lives in Dorset, but she's not the sort to leave her home at the drop of a hat. She will want time to pack, I'm sure, and do all those things"—he waved his hand about in a slightly dismissive manner—"that women need to do."

Eloise nodded, her expression serious. "It's only four days. And you've a great many servants. It's not as if we're alone together at some remote hunting box."

"Nonetheless, your reputation could be seriously compromised should people learn of your visit."

She let out a long exhale, then lifted her shoulders in a fatalistic gesture. "Well, there isn't much I can do about it now." She motioned to her eye. "If I returned, my current appearance would cause more comment than the fact that I left in the first place."

He nodded slowly, signaling his agreement even as his mind flew off in other directions. Was there a reason she was so unconcerned for her reputation? He'd not spent much time in society, but it was his experience that unmarried ladies, regardless of their age, were always concerned for their reputations.

Was it possible that Eloise's reputation had been ruined before she'd arrived on his doorstep?

And more to the point, did he care?

He frowned, unable to answer the latter question just yet. He knew what he wanted—no, make that what he *needed*—in a wife, and it had little to do with purity and chastity and all those other ideals that proper young ladies were meant to embody.

He needed someone who could step in and make his life easy and uncomplicated. Someone who would run his house and mother his children. He was quite frankly pleased to have found in Eloise a woman for whom he felt a great deal of desire as well, but even if she'd been ugly as a crone—well, he'd have been happy to marry a crone as long as she was practical, efficient, and good with his children.

But if all that were true, why did he feel rather annoyed by the possibility that Eloise had had a lover?

No, not annoyed, precisely. He couldn't quite put his finger on the correct word for his feelings. Irritated, he supposed, the way one was irritated by a pebble in one's shoe or a mild sunburn.

It was that feeling that something wasn't quite right. Not dreadfully, catastrophically wrong, but just not . . . *right*.

He watched her settle herself against the pillows. "Do you want me to leave you to your rest?" he asked.

She sighed. "I suppose, although I'm not tired. Bruised, perhaps, but not tired. It's barely eight in the morning."

He glanced at a clock on a shelf. "Nine."

"Eight, nine," she said, shrugging off the difference. "Whichever, it's still morning." She looked longingly out the window. "And it's finally not raining."

"Would you prefer to sit in the garden?" he inquired.

"I'd prefer to *walk* in the garden," she replied pertly, "but my hip does ache a bit. I suppose I should try to rest for a day."

"More than a day," he said gruffly.

"You're most probably right, but I can assure you I won't be able to manage it."

He smiled. She wasn't the sort of woman who would ever choose to spend her days sitting quietly in a drawing room, working on her embroidery or sewing, or whatever it was women were supposed to do with needles and thread.

He looked over at her as she fidgeted. She wasn't the sort of woman who would ever choose to sit still, period.

"Would you like to take a book with you?" he asked.

Her eyes clouded with disappointment. He knew that she'd expected him to accompany her to the garden, and heaven knew, part of him wanted to, but somehow he felt he had to get away, almost as a measure of self-preservation. He still felt off balance, desperately ill-at-ease from having had to spank the children.

It seemed that every fortnight they did something that required punishment, and he didn't know what else to do. But he drew no pleasure from the act. He hated it, absolutely hated it, felt almost as if he might retch every time, and yet what was he supposed to do when they misbehaved that badly? The little things he tried to brush aside, but when they glued their governess's hair to her bedsheets while she slept, how was he supposed to brush aside *that*? Or what about the time they had broken an entire shelf of terra-cotta pots in his greenhouse? They had claimed it was an accident, but Phillip knew better. And the look in their eyes as they protested their innocence told him that even they hadn't thought he'd actually believe them.

And so he disciplined them in the only way he knew how, although thus far he'd been able to avoid using anything other than his hand. When, that is, he did anything at all. Half the time—more than half, really—he was so overcome by memories of his own father's brand of discipline that he just stumbled away, shaking and sweating, horrified by the way his hand itched to swat them on their behinds.

He worried that he was too lenient. He probably was, since the children didn't seem to be getting any better. He told himself he needed to be more stern, and once he'd even strode out to the stables and grabbed the whip . . .

He shuddered at the memory. It was after the glue incident, and they'd had to cut away Miss Lockhart's hair just to free her, and he'd been so angry—so unbelievably, overpoweringly angry. His vision had gone red, and all he'd wanted to do was punish them, and make them behave, and teach them how to be good people, and he'd snatched the whip . . .

But it had burned in his hands, and he'd dropped it in horror, afraid of what he would become if he actually used it.

The children had gone unpunished for an entire day. Phillip had fled to his greenhouse, shaking with disgust, hating himself for what he'd almost done.

And for what he was unable to do.

Make his children better people.

He didn't know how to be a father to them. That much was clear. He didn't know how, and maybe he simply wasn't suited to the task. Maybe some men were born knowing what to say and how to act, and some of them simply couldn't do a good job of it no matter how hard they tried.

Maybe one needed a good father oneself to know how to be the same.

Which had left him doomed from birth.

And now here he was, trying to make up for his deficiencies with Eloise Bridgerton. Perhaps he could finally stop feeling so guilty about being such a bad father if he could only provide them with a good mother.

But nothing was ever as simple as one wanted it to be, and Eloise, in the single day she'd been in residence, had managed to turn his life upside down. He'd never expected to want her, at least not with the intensity he felt every time he stole a glance at her. And when he'd seen her on the floor—why was it that his first thought had been terror?

Terror for her well-being, and, if he was honest, terror that the twins might have convinced her to leave.

When poor Miss Lockhart had been glued to the bed, Phillip's first emotion had been rage at his children. With Eloise, he'd spared only the merest of thoughts for them until he'd assured himself that she was not seriously injured.

He hadn't wanted to care about her, hadn't wanted anything other than a good mother for his children. And now he didn't know what to do about it.

And so even though a morning in the garden with Miss Bridgerton sounded like heaven, somehow he couldn't quite allow himself the pleasure.

He needed some time alone. He needed to think. Or rather, to *not* think, since the thinking just left him angry and confused. He needed to bury his hands in some dirt and prune some plants, and shut himself away until his mind was no longer screaming with all of his problems.

He needed to escape.

And if he was a coward, so be it.

Chapter 7

...have never been so bored in all of my life. Colin, you must come home. It is interminably boring without you, and I don't think I can bear such boredom another moment. Please do return, for I have clearly begun to repeat myself, and nothing could be more of a bore.

—from Eloise Bridgerton to her brother Colin,
during her fifth season as a debutante,
sent (but never received)
while Colin was traveling in Denmark

Eloise spent the entire day in the garden, lounging on an exceedingly comfortable chaise that she was quite convinced had been imported from Italy, since it was her experience that neither the English nor the French had any clue as to how to fashion comfortable furniture.

Not that she normally spent a great deal of time pondering the construction of chairs and sofas, but stuck outside by herself in the Romney Hall garden, it wasn't as if she had anything else to ponder.

No, not a thing. Not a single thing to think about other than the comfortable chaise beneath her, and maybe the fact that Sir Phillip was an ill-mannered beast for leaving her alone for the entire day after his two little monsters—whose existence, she added into her thoughts with a mental flourish, he had never seen fit to reveal in his correspondence—had given her a blackened eye.

It was a perfect day, with a blue sky and a light breeze, and Eloise didn't have a single thing in the world to think about.

She had never been so bored in her life.

It wasn't in her nature to sit still and watch the clouds float by. She would much rather be out *doing* something—taking a walk, inspecting a hedgerow, anything other than just sitting like a lump on the chaise, staring aimlessly at the horizon.

Or if she *had* to sit here, at least she could have done so in the company of another person. She supposed the clouds might have been more interesting if she weren't quite so alone, if someone were here to whom she might say, *Goodness, but that one looks rather like a rabbit, don't you think?*

But no, she'd been left quite on her own. Sir Phillip was off in his greenhouse—she could see it from here, even see him moving about from time to time—and while she really wanted to get up and join him, if for no other reason than the fact that his plants had to be more interesting than the blasted clouds, she wasn't about to give him the satisfaction of seeking him out.

Not after he'd rejected her so abruptly this afternoon. Good heavens, the man had practically fled from her company. It had been the oddest thing. She'd thought they were dealing with each other rather well, and then he'd grown quite abrupt, making up some sort of excuse about how he needed to work and fleeing the room as if she were plagued.

Odious man.

She picked up the book she'd selected from the library and held it resolutely in front of her face. She was going to read the blasted thing this time if it killed her.

Of course, that was what she'd told herself the last four times she'd picked it up. She never managed to get past a single sentence—a paragraph if she was really disciplined—before her mind wandered and the text on the page grew unfocused and, it went without saying, unread.

Served her right, she supposed, for being so irritated with Sir Phillip that she hadn't paid any attention in the library and she'd snatched up the first book she'd seen.

The Botany of Ferns? What had she been thinking?

Even worse, if he saw her with it, he'd surely think she'd chosen it because she wanted to learn more about his interests.

Eloise blinked with surprise when she realized that she had reached the end of her page. She didn't recall a single sentence, and in fact wondered if perhaps her eyes had only slid along the words without actually reading the letters.

This was ridiculous. She thrust the book aside and stood up, taking a few steps to test out the tenderness of her hip. Allowing herself a satisfied smile when she realized that the pain wasn't bad at all, and in fact couldn't even be called anything beyond mild discomfort, she walked all the way to the riotous mass of rosebushes off to the north, leaning forward to sniff the buds. They were still tightly closed—it was early in the season, after all—but maybe they'd have a scent, and—

"*What the devil are you doing?*"

Eloise just managed to avoid falling into the rosebush as she turned around. "Sir Phillip," she said, as if that weren't completely obvious.

He looked irate. "You're supposed to be sitting down."

"I was sitting down."

"You were supposed to *stay* sitting down."

She decided the truth would make an excellent explanation. "I was bored."

He glanced over at the chaise in the distance. "Didn't you get a book from the library?"

She shrugged. "I finished it."

He quirked a brow in patent disbelief.

She returned his expression with an arch look of her own.

"Well, you need to sit down," he said gruffly.

"I'm perfectly fine." She patted her hip gently. "It hardly hurts at all now."

He stared at her for some time, his expression irritable, as if he wanted to say something but didn't know what. He must have left the greenhouse in a hurry, because he was quite filthy, with dirt along his arms, under every fingernail, and streaked quite liberally on his shirt. He looked a fright, at least by the standards Eloise had grown used to in London, but there was something almost appealing about him, something rather primitive and elemental as he stood there scowling at her.

"I can't work if I have to worry about you," he grumbled.

"Then don't work," she replied, thinking the solution quite obvious.

"I'm in the middle of something," he muttered, sounding, in Eloise's opinion, at least, rather like a sullen child.

"Then I'll accompany you," she said, brushing past him on the way to the greenhouse. Really, how did he expect them to decide if they would suit if they didn't spend any time together?

He reached out to grab her, then remembered that his hand was covered with dirt. "Miss Bridgerton," he said sharply, "you can't—"

"Couldn't you use the help?" she interrupted.

"No," he said, and in such a tone that she really couldn't continue the argument along those lines.

"Sir Phillip," she ground out, completely losing patience with him, "may I ask you a question?"

Visibly startled by her sudden turn of conversation, he just nodded—once, curtly, the way men liked to do when they were annoyed and wanted to pretend they were in charge.

"Are you the same man you were last night?"

He looked at her as if she were a lunatic. "I beg your pardon."

"The man I spent the evening with last night," she said, just barely resisting the urge to cross her arms as she spoke, "the one with whom I shared a meal and then toured the house and greenhouse, actually *spoke* to me, and in fact, seemed to enjoy my company, astonishing as it might seem."

He did nothing but stare at her for several seconds, then muttered, "I enjoy your company."

"Then why," she asked, "have I been sitting alone in the garden for three hours?"

"It hasn't been three hours."

"It doesn't matter how long—"

"It's been forty-five *minutes*," he said.

"Be that as it may—"

"Be that as it *is*."

"Well," she declared, mostly because she suspected he might have been correct, which put her in something of an awkward position, and *well*, seemed all she could say without embarrassing herself further.

"Miss Bridgerton," he said, his clipped voice a reminder that just the night before he'd been calling her Eloise.

And kissing her. "As you might have guessed," he continued sharply, "this morning's episode with my children has left me in a foul mood. I thought merely to spare you my company, such as it is."

"I see," she said, rather impressed with the supercilious edge to her voice.

"Good."

Except that she was quite certain she *did* see. That he was lying, to be precise. Oh, his children had put him in a foul mood, that much was true, but there was something else at work as well.

"I will leave you to your work, then," she said, motioning to the greenhouse with a gesture that was meant to seem as if she were waving him away.

He eyed her suspiciously. "And what do you plan to do?"

"I suppose I shall write some letters and then go for a walk," she replied.

"You will *not* go for a walk," he growled.

Almost, Eloise thought, as if he actually *cared* about her.

"Sir Phillip," she replied, "I assure you that I am perfectly fine. I'm quite certain I look a great deal worse than I feel."

"You had better look worse than you feel," he muttered.

Eloise scowled at him. It was a blackened eye, after all, and thus only a temporary blight on her appearance, but truly, he didn't need to *remind* her that she looked a fright.

"I shall remain out of your way," she told him, "which is all that really matters, correct?"

A vein began to twitch in his temple. Eloise took great pleasure in that.

"Go," she said. And when he didn't, she turned and began to walk through a gate to another segment of the garden.

"Stop this instant," Sir Phillip ordered, closing the distance between them with a single step. "You may *not* go for a walk."

Eloise wanted to ask him if he intended to tie her down, but she held her tongue, fearing that he might actually approve of the suggestion.

"Sir Phillip," she said, "I fail to see how— Oh!"

Grumbling something about foolish women (and using another adjective which Eloise considered considerably less complimentary), Sir Phillip scooped her into his arms and strode over to the chaise, where he dumped her quite unceremoniously back onto the cushion.

"Stay there," he ordered.

She sputtered, trying to find her voice after his unbelievable display of arrogance. "You can't—"

"Good God, woman, you could try the patience of a saint."

She glared at him.

"What," he asked with weary impatience, "would it take to keep you from moving from this spot?"

"I can't think of a thing," she answered, quite honestly.

"Fine," he said, his chin jutting out in a furiously stubborn manner. "Hike the entire countryside. Swim to France."

"From Gloucestershire?" she asked, her lips twitching.

"If anyone could figure out a way to do it," he said, "it would be you. Good day, Miss Bridgerton."

And then he stalked off, leaving Eloise exactly where she'd been ten minutes earlier. Sitting on the chaise, so surprised by his sudden departure that she quite forgot that she'd meant to get up and leave.

If Phillip hadn't already been convinced that he had made an ass of himself earlier that day, Eloise's short missive informing him that she intended to take supper in her room that evening made it quite clear.

Considering she'd spent the afternoon complaining that she had no company, her decision to pass the evening by herself was a pointed insult, indeed.

He ate alone, in silence, as he had for so many

months. Years, really, since Marina had rarely left her room to dine when she'd been alive. One would have thought he'd have grown used to it, but now he was restless and uncomfortable, ever aware of the servants, who all knew that Miss Bridgerton had rejected his company.

He grumbled to himself as he chewed his beefsteak. He knew that one was supposed to ignore the servants and go about daily life as if they didn't exist, or if they did, as if they were an entirely different species altogether. And while he had to admit he didn't have much interest in their lives outside of Romney Hall, the fact remained that they had interest in his, and he rather detested being the subject of gossip.

Which he surely would be tonight, as they gathered for supper in the alcove off the kitchen.

He took a vicious bite of his roll. He hoped they had to eat that damned fish from Amanda's bed.

He made his way through the salad and the poultry and the pudding, even though the soup and the meat had proven quite enough. But there was always the chance that Eloise would change her mind and join him for supper. It didn't seem likely, given her stubborn streak, but if she decided to bend her will, he wanted to be present when it happened.

When it became apparent that this was nothing but wishful thinking on his part, he considered going up to her, but even out here in the country, that was quite inappropriate, and besides, he doubted she wanted to see him.

Well, that wasn't quite true. He rather thought that she *did* want to see him, but she wanted him humbled and apologetic. And even if he didn't utter a single word resembling either *I'm* or *sorry*, his very appearance would be tantamount to eating crow.

Which wouldn't be the worst thing in the world, considering that he'd already decided he'd be willing to wrap himself around her feet and beg her piteously to marry him if she would only consent to stay and mother his children. This, even though he had botched it up completely this afternoon—and morning, really, if one were to be honest about it.

But wanting to woo a woman didn't mean one actually knew how to go about it.

His brother had been the one born with all the charm and flair, always knowing what to say and how to act. George would never have even noticed that the servants were eyeing him as if they were going to gossip about him ten minutes later, and in truth, the point was moot, because all that the servants had ever had to say was along the lines of, "That Master George is such a rascal." All said with a smile and a blush, of course.

Phillip, on the other hand, had been quieter, more thoughtful, and certainly less suited to the role of father and lord of the manor. He'd always planned to leave Romney Hall and never look back, at least while his father was still alive. George was to marry Marina and have a half dozen perfect children, and Phillip would be the gruff and slightly eccentric uncle who lived over in Cambridge, spending all his time in his greenhouse, conducting experiments that no one else understood or in truth even cared about.

That was how it was supposed to be, but it had all changed on a battlefield in Belgium.

England had won the war, but that had been little comfort to Phillip when his father had dragged him back to Gloucestershire, determined to mold him into a proper heir.

Determined to change him into George, who had always been his favorite.

And then his father had died. Right there, right in front of Phillip, his heart gave out in a screaming rage, surely exaggerated by the fact that his son was now too large to be hauled over his knee and beaten with a paddle.

And Phillip became Sir Phillip, with all the rights and responsibilities of a baronet.

Rights and responsibilities he had never, ever wanted.

He loved his children, loved them more than life itself, so he supposed he was glad for the way it had all turned out, but he still felt as if he were failing. Romney Hall was doing well—Phillip had introduced several new agricultural techniques he'd learned at university, and the fields were turning a profit for the first time since . . . well, Phillip didn't know since when. They certainly hadn't earned any money while his father had been alive.

But the fields were only fields. His children were human beings, flesh and blood, and every day he grew more convinced that he was failing them. Every day seemed to bring worse trouble (which terrified him; he couldn't imagine what could possibly be worse than Miss Lockhart's glued hair or Eloise's blackened eye) and he had no idea what to do. Whenever he tried to talk to them, he seemed to say the wrong thing. Or do the wrong thing. Or not do anything, all because he was so scared that he'd lose his temper.

Except for that one time. Supper last night with

Eloise and Amanda. For the first time in recent memory, he'd handled his daughter *exactly* right. Something about Eloise's presence had calmed him, lent him a clarity of thought he usually lacked when it came to his children. He was able to see the humor in the situation, where he usually saw nothing but his own frustration.

Which was all the more reason he needed to make sure Eloise stayed and married him. And all the more reason he wasn't going to go to her tonight and try to make amends.

He didn't mind eating crow. Hell, he would have eaten an entire flock if that was what it took.

He just didn't want to muck up the situation any worse than it already was.

Eloise rose quite early the following morning, which wasn't surprising, since she'd crawled into bed at only half eight the night before. She'd regretted her self-imposed exile almost the moment after she'd sent the note down to Sir Phillip informing him of her decision to take supper in her room.

She'd been thoroughly annoyed with him earlier in the day, and she'd allowed her irritation to rule her thinking. The truth was, she hated eating by herself, hated sitting alone at a table with nothing to do but stare at her food and guess how many bites it might take to finish one's potatoes. Even Sir Phillip in his most obstinate and uncommunicative of moods would have been better than nothing.

Besides, she still wasn't convinced that they wouldn't suit, and dining apart wasn't going to offer her any further insight into his personality and temperament.

He could be a bear—and a grumpy one, at that—but when he smiled . . . Eloise suddenly understood what all those young ladies were talking about when they'd waxed rhapsodic over her brother Colin's smile (which Eloise found rather ordinary; it was *Colin*, after all.)

But when Sir Phillip smiled, he was transformed. His dark eyes assumed a devilish twinkle, full of humor and mischief, as if he knew something she didn't. But that wasn't what sent her heart fluttering. Eloise was a Bridgerton, after all. She'd seen plenty of devilish twinkles and prided herself on being quite immune to them.

When Sir Phillip looked at her and smiled, there was an air of shyness to it, as if he weren't quite used to smiling at women. And she was left with the feeling that he was a man who, if all the pieces of their puzzle fell together in just the right way, might someday come to treasure her. Even if he never loved her, he would value her and not take her for granted.

And it was for that reason that Eloise was not yet prepared to pack her bags and leave, despite his rather gruff behavior of the previous day.

Stomach growling, she made her way down to the breakfast room, only to be informed that Sir Phillip had already come and gone. Eloise tried not to be discouraged. It didn't mean he was trying to avoid her; it was entirely possible, after all, that he had assumed she was not an early riser and had elected not to wait for her.

But when she peeked into his greenhouse and found it empty, she declared herself stymied and went looking for other company.

Oliver and Amanda owed her an afternoon,

didn't they? Eloise marched resolutely up the stairs. There was no reason they couldn't make it a morning, instead.

"You want to go swimming?"

Oliver was looking at her as if she were mad.

"I do," Eloise replied with a nod. "Don't you?"

"No," he said.

"I do," Amanda piped up, sticking her tongue out at her brother when he shot her a ferocious glare. "I love to swim, and so does Oliver. He's just too cross with you to admit it."

"I don't think they should go," replied their nursemaid, a rather stern-looking woman of indeterminate years.

"Nonsense," Eloise said breezily, disliking the woman immediately. She looked the sort to tug on ears and rap hands. "It is unseasonably warm and a bit of exercise will be quite healthful."

"Nevertheless—" the nursemaid said, her testy voice demonstrating her irritation at having her authority challenged.

"I shall give them lessons while we go about it," Eloise continued, using the tone of voice her mother used when it was clear she would brook no argument. "They are currently without a governess, aren't they?"

"Indeed," the nurse said, "the two little monsters glued—"

"Whatever the reason for her departure," Eloise interrupted, quite certain she didn't want to know what they had done to their last governess, "I'm sure it has been a monstrous burden upon you to assume both roles these last few weeks."

"Months," the nursemaid bit off.

"Even worse," Eloise agreed. "One would think you deserve a free morning, wouldn't one?"

"Well, I wouldn't mind a brief trip into town. . . ."

"Then it's settled." Eloise glanced down at the children and allowed herself a small moment of self-congratulation. They were staring at her in awe. "Off you go," she said to the nurse, bustling her out the door. "Enjoy your morning."

She shut the door behind the still-bewildered nurse and turned to face the children.

"You are very clever," Amanda said breathlessly.

Even Oliver couldn't help but nod his agreement.

"I hate Nurse Edwards," Amanda said.

"Of course you don't," Eloise said, but her heart wasn't into the statement; she hadn't much liked Nurse Edwards, either.

"Yes, we do," Oliver said. "She's horrid."

Amanda nodded. "I wish we could have Nurse Millsby back, but she had to leave to care for her mother. She's sick," she explained.

"Her mother," Oliver said, "not Nurse Millsby."

"How long has Nurse Edwards been here?" Eloise asked.

"Five months," Amanda said glumly. "Five very long months."

"Well, I'm sure she's not as bad as all that," Eloise said, intending to say more, but closing her mouth when Oliver interrupted with—

"Oh, she is."

Eloise wasn't about to disparage another adult, especially one who was meant to have some authority over them, so instead she decided to sidestep the issue by saying, "It doesn't matter this morning, does it, because you have me instead."

Amanda reached out shyly and took her hand. "I like you," she said.

"I like you, too," Eloise replied, surprised by the tears forming in the corners of her eyes.

Oliver said nothing. Eloise wasn't insulted. It took some people longer to warm up to a person than others. Besides, these children had a right to be wary. Their mother had left them, after all. Granted, it was through death, but they were young; all they would know was that they had loved her and she was gone.

Eloise remembered well the months following the death of her father. She had clung to her mother at every opportunity, telling herself that if she just kept her nearby (or even better, holding her hand), then her mother couldn't leave, either.

Was it any wonder that these children resented their new nursemaid? They had probably been cared for by Nurse Millsby since birth. Losing her so soon after Marina's death must have been doubly difficult.

"I'm sorry we blackened your eye," Amanda said.

Eloise squeezed her hand. "It looks much worse than it actually is."

"It looks dreadful," Oliver admitted, his little face beginning to show signs of remorse.

"Yes, it does," Eloise agreed, "but it's starting to grow on me. I think I look rather like a soldier who's been to battle—and won!"

"You don't look like you've won," Oliver said, one corner of his mouth twisting in a dubious expression.

"Nonsense. Of course I do. Anyone who actually comes home from battle wins."

"Does that mean Uncle George lost?" Amanda asked.

"You father's brother?"

Amanda nodded. "He died before we were born."

Eloise wondered if they knew that their mother was originally to have married him. Probably not. "Your uncle was a hero," she said with quiet respect.

"But not Father," Oliver said.

"Your father couldn't go to war because he had too many responsibilities here," Eloise explained. "But this is a very serious conversation for such a fine morning, don't you think? We should be out swimming and having a grand time."

The twins quickly caught her enthusiasm, and in no time they were changed into their bathing costumes and headed across the fields to the lake.

"We must practice our arithmetic!" Eloise called out as they skipped ahead.

And much to her surprise, they actually did. Who would have known that sixes and eights could be so much fun?

Chapter 8

... how fortunate you are to be at school. We girls
have been presented with a new governess, and she
is misery personified. She drones on about sums
from dawn until dusk. Poor Hyacinth now breaks
into tears every time she hears the word "seven."
(Although I must confess that I don't understand
why one through six do not elicit similar reac-
tions.) I don't know what we shall do. Dip her hair
in ink, I suppose. (Miss Haversham's, that is, not
Hyacinth's, although I would never rule out the
latter.)

—*from Eloise Bridgerton to her brother Gregory,*
during his first term as a student at Eton

When Phillip returned from the rose garden, he was
surprised to find his home quiet and empty. It was a
rare day when the air wasn't exploding with the
sound of some overturned table or shriek of outrage.

The children, he thought, pausing to savor the silence. Clearly, they had been vacated from the premises. Nurse Edwards must have taken them out for a walk.

And, he supposed, Eloise would still be abed, although in truth it was already nearly ten, and she did not seem the sort to laze the day away under her covers.

Phillip stared down at the roses in his hand. He'd spent an hour choosing exactly the right ones; Romney Hall boasted three rose gardens, and he'd had to go to the far one to find the early-blooming varieties. He'd then painstakingly picked them, careful to snip at the exact right spot so as to encourage further blooming, and then meticulously sliced away each thorn.

Flowers he could do. Green plants he could do even better, but somehow he didn't think Eloise would find much romance in a fistful of ivy.

He wandered over to the breakfast room, expecting to see food laid out, awaiting Eloise's arrival, but the sideboard was tidy and spotless, signaling that the morning meal had come to an end. Phillip frowned and stood in the middle of the room for a moment, trying to figure out what he ought to do next. Eloise had obviously already arisen and eaten breakfast, but deuced if he knew where she was.

Just then a maid came through, holding a feather duster and a rag. She bobbed a quick curtsy when she saw him.

"I'll need a vase for these," he said, holding up the flowers. He'd hoped to hand them to Eloise directly, but he didn't feel like clutching them all morning while he hunted her down.

The maid nodded and started to leave, but he

stopped her with, "Oh, and do you happen to know where Miss Bridgerton might have gone off to? I noticed that breakfast has been cleared."

"Out, Sir Phillip," the maid said. "With the children."

Phillip blinked in surprise. "She went out with Oliver and Amanda? Willingly?"

The maid nodded.

"That's interesting." He sighed, trying not to envision the scene. "I hope they don't kill her."

The maid looked alarmed. "Sir Phillip?"

"It was a joke . . . ah . . . Mary?" He didn't mean to finish his sentence on a questioning note, but the truth was, he wasn't quite certain of her name.

She nodded in such a way that he couldn't be sure whether he'd gotten it right or she was just being polite.

"Do you happen to know where they went?" he asked.

"Down to the lake, I believe. To go swimming."

Phillip's skin went cold. "Swimming?" he asked, his voice sounding disembodied and hollow to his ears.

"Yes. The children were wearing their bathing costumes."

Swimming. Dear God.

For a year now, he'd avoided the lake, always taken the long route around, just to spare himself the sight of it. And he had forbidden the children from ever visiting the site.

Or had he?

He'd told Nurse Millsby not to allow them near the water, but had he remembered to do the same with Nurse Edwards?

He took off at a run, leaving the floor littered with roses.

"Last one in is a hermit crab!" Oliver shrieked, tearing into the water at top speed, only to laugh when it reached his waist and he was forced to slow down.

"I'm not a hermit crab. *You're* a hermit crab!" Amanda yelled back as she splashed around in the shallower depths.

"You're a *rotten* hermit crab!"

"Well, you're a *dead* hermit crab!"

Eloise laughed as she waded through the water a few yards away from Amanda. She hadn't brought a bathing costume—indeed, who would have thought she might need one?—so she had tied her skirt and petticoat up, baring her legs to just above her knees. It was an awful lot of leg to be showing, but that hardly mattered in the company of two eight-year-olds.

Besides, they were having far too much fun tormenting each other to give her legs even a passing glance.

The twins had warmed up to her during their walk down to the lake, laughing and chattering the entire way, and Eloise wondered if all they truly needed was a bit of attention. They'd lost their mother, their relationship with their father was distant at best, and then their beloved nurse had left them. Thank heavens they had each other.

And maybe, perhaps, her.

Eloise bit her lip, not sure whether she ought even to be allowing her thoughts to veer in that direction.

She hadn't yet decided whether she wanted to marry Sir Phillip, and much as these two children seemed to need her—and they did need her, she just knew they did—she couldn't make her decision based on Oliver and Amanda.

She wasn't going to be marrying *them*.

"Don't go any deeper!" she called out, mindful that Oliver had been inching away.

He pulled the sort of face boys do when they think they are being mollycoddled, but she noticed that he took two large steps back toward the shore.

"You should come in further, Miss Bridgerton," Amanda said, sitting down on the lake bottom and then squealing, "Oh! It's cold!"

"Why did you sit down, then?" Oliver said. "You knew how cold it was."

"Yes, but my feet were used to it," she replied, hugging her arms to her body. "It didn't feel so cold anymore."

"Don't worry," he told her with a supercilious grin, "your bottom will get used to it soon, too."

"Oliver," Eloise said sternly, but she was fairly certain she'd ruined the effect by smiling.

"He's right!" Amanda exclaimed, turning to Eloise with an expression of surprise. "I can't feel my bottom at all anymore."

"I'm not so sure that's a good thing," Eloise said.

"You should swim," Oliver prodded. "Or at least go as far as Amanda. You've barely got your feet wet."

"I don't have a bathing costume," Eloise said, even though she'd explained this to them at least six times already.

"I think you don't know how to swim," he said.

"I assure you I know very well how to swim," she returned, "*and* that you're not likely to provoke a demonstration while I'm wearing my third-best morning dress."

Amanda looked over at her and blinked a few times. "I should like to see your first- and second-best. That's a very pretty frock."

"Why, thank you, Amanda," Eloise said, wondering who picked out the young girl's clothing. The crotchety Nurse Edwards, probably. There was nothing wrong with what Amanda was wearing, but Eloise would wager that no one had ever thought to offer her the fun of choosing her own garments. She smiled at Amanda and said, "If you would like to go shopping sometime, I would be happy to take you."

"Oh, I should adore that," Amanda said breathlessly. "Above all else. Thank you!"

"Girls," Oliver said disdainfully.

"You'll be glad for us someday," Eloise remarked.

"Eh?"

She just shook her head with a smile. It would be some time before he thought girls were good for anything other than tying their plaits together.

Oliver just shrugged and went back to hitting the surface of the water with the heel of his hand at just the right angle so as to splash the maximum amount of water on his sister.

"Stop it!" Amanda hollered.

He cackled and splashed some more.

"Oliver!" Amanda stood up and advanced menacingly toward him. Then, when walking proved too slow, she dove in and began to swim. He shrieked with laughter and swam away, coming up for air only long enough to taunt her.

"I'll get you yet!" Amanda growled, stopping for a moment to tread water.

"Don't go too far out!" Eloise called, but it really wasn't very important. It was clear that both children were excellent swimmers. If they were like Eloise and her siblings, they'd probably been swimming since age four. The Bridgerton children had spent countless summer hours splashing around in the pond near their home in Kent, although, in truth, the swimming had been curtailed after the death of their father. When Edmund Bridgerton had been alive, the family had spent most of their time in the country, but once he was gone, they had found themselves in town more often than not. Eloise had never known if it was because her mother preferred town or simply that their home in the country held too many memories.

Eloise adored London and had certainly enjoyed her time there, but now that she was here in Gloucestershire, splashing in a pond with two boisterous young children, she realized how much she'd missed the country way of living.

Not that she was prepared to give up London and all the friends and amusements it offered, but still, she was beginning to think she didn't need to spend *quite* so much time in the capital.

Amanda finally caught up with her brother and launched herself on top of him, causing them both to go under. Eloise watched carefully; she could see a hand or foot break the surface every few seconds until they both came up for air, laughing and gasping and vowing to beat each other in what was clearly extremely important warfare.

"Be careful!" Eloise called out, mostly because she felt she should. It was strange to find herself in the position of authoritative adult; with her nieces and nephews she got to be the fun and permissive aunt. "Oliver! Do *not* pull your sister's hair!"

He stopped but then immediately moved to the collar of her bathing costume, which could not have been comfortable for Amanda, and indeed, she began to sputter and cough.

"Oliver!" Eloise yelled. "Stop that at once!"

He did, which surprised and pleased her, but Amanda used the momentary reprieve to jump on top of him, sending him under while she sat on his back.

"Amanda!" Eloise yelled.

Amanda pretended not to hear.

Oh, blast, now she was going to have to wade out there to put an end to it herself, and she was going to be completely soaked in the process. "Amanda, stop that this instant!" she called out, making one last attempt to save her dress and her dignity.

Amanda did, and Oliver came up gasping, "Amanda Crane, I'm going to—"

"No, you're not," Eloise said sternly. "Neither one of you is going to kill, maim, attack, or even hug the other for at least thirty minutes."

They were clearly appalled that Eloise had even mentioned the possibility of a hug.

"Well?" Eloise demanded.

They were completely silent, then Amanda asked, "Then what *will* we do?"

Good question. Most of Eloise's own memories of swimming involved the same sort of war games. "Maybe we'll dry off and rest for a spell," she said.

They both looked horrified by the suggestion.

"We certainly ought to work on lessons," Eloise added. "Perhaps a bit more arithmetic. I did promise Nurse Edwards that we would do something constructive with our time."

That suggestion went over about as well as the first.

"Very well," Eloise said. "What do you suggest we do?"

"I don't know," came Oliver's muttered reply, punctuated by Amanda's shoulder shrug.

"Well, there is certainly no point in standing here doing nothing," Eloise said, planting her hands on her hips. "Aside from the fact that it's exceedingly boring, we're likely to fr—"

"Get out of the lake!"

Eloise whirled around, so surprised by the furious roar that she slipped and fell in the water. Drat and blast, there went her dry intentions and her dress. "Sir Phillip," she gasped, thankful that she'd broken her fall with her hands and had not landed on her bottom. Still, the front of her dress was completely soaked.

"Get out of the water," Phillip growled, striding into the lake with astonishing force and speed.

"Sir Phillip," Eloise said, her voice cracking with surprise as she staggered to her feet, "what—"

But he had already grabbed both of his children, his arms wrapped around each of their rib cages, and was hauling them to shore. Eloise watched with fascinated horror as he set them none-too-gently down on the grass.

"I told you never, ever to go near the lake," he yelled, shaking each by a shoulder. "You know you're supposed to stay away. You—"

He stopped, clearly shaken by something, and by the need to catch his breath.

"But that was last year," Oliver whimpered.

"Did you hear me rescind the order?"

"No, but I thought—"

"You thought wrong," Phillip snapped. "Now get back to the house. Both of you."

The two children recognized the deadly serious intent in their father's eyes and quickly fled up the hill. Phillip did nothing as they left, just watched them run, and then, as soon as they were out of earshot, he turned to Eloise with an expression that caused her to take a step back and said, "What the hell did you think you were doing?"

For a moment she could say nothing; his question seemed too ludicrous for a reply. "Having a spot of fun," she finally said, probably with a bit more insolence than she ought.

"I do not want my children near the lake," he bit off. "I have made those wishes clear—"

"Not to me."

"Well, you should have—"

"How was I meant to know that you wanted them to stay away from the water?" she asked, interrupting him before he could accuse her of irresponsibility or whatever it was he was going to say. "I told their nurse where we intended to go, *and* what we intended to do, and she gave no indication that it was forbidden."

She could see from his face that he knew he had no valid argument, and it was making him all the more furious. Men. The day they learned to admit to a mistake was the day they became women.

"It's a hot day," she continued, her voice clipping along in the way it always did when she was determined not to lose an argument.

Which, for Eloise, generally meant any argument.

"I was trying to mend the breach," she added, "since I don't particularly relish the thought of another blackened eye."

She said it to make it him feel guilty, and it must have worked, since his cheeks turned ruddy and he muttered something that might have been an assurance under his breath.

Eloise paused for a few seconds to see if he would say more, or, even better, say something with a tone that approached intelligible speech, but when he did nothing but glare at her, she continued with, "I thought that doing something *fun* might go a long way. Heaven knows," she muttered, "the children could use a spot of fun."

"What are you saying?" he asked, his voice angry and low.

"Nothing," she said quickly. "Just that I didn't see any harm in going swimming."

"You put them in danger."

"Danger?" she sputtered. "From swimming?"

Phillip said nothing, just glared at her.

"Oh, for heaven's sake," she said dismissively. "It would only have been dangerous if I couldn't swim."

"I don't care if *you* can swim," he bit off. "I only care that my children can't."

She blinked. Several times. "Yes, they can," she said. "In fact, they're both quite proficient. I'd assumed you'd taught them."

"What are you talking about?"

Her head tilted slightly, perhaps out of concern, perhaps out of curiosity. "Didn't you know they could swim?"

For a moment, Phillip felt as if he couldn't breathe. His lungs tightened and his skin prickled, and his body seemed to freeze into a hard, cold statue.

It was awful.

He was awful.

Somehow this moment seemed to crystallize all of his failings. It wasn't that his children could swim, it was that he hadn't *known* they could swim. How could a father not know such a thing about his own children?

A father ought to know if his children could ride a horse. He ought to know if they could read and count to one hundred.

And for the love of God, he ought to know if they could swim.

"I—" he said, his voice giving out after a single word. "I—"

She took a step forward, whispering, "Are you all right?"

He nodded, or at least he thought he nodded. Her voice was ringing in his head—*Yes they can yes they can they can they can*—and it didn't even matter what she was saying. It had been the tone. Surprise, and maybe even a hint of disdain.

And he hadn't *known.*

His children were growing and changing and he

didn't know them. He saw them, he recognized them, but he didn't know who they were.

He felt himself take a gasp of air. He didn't know what their favorite colors were.

Pink? Blue? Green?

Did it matter, or did it only matter that he didn't know?

He was, in his own way, every bit as awful a father as his own had been. Thomas Crane may have beaten his children to within an inch of their lives, but at least he knew what they were up to. Phillip ignored and avoided and pretended—anything to keep his distance and avoid losing his temper. Anything to stop him from becoming his father all over again.

Except maybe distance wasn't always such a good thing.

"Phillip?" Eloise whispered, laying a hand on his arm. "Is something the matter?"

He stared at her, but he still felt blinded, and his eyes couldn't seem to focus.

"I think you should go home," she said, slowly and carefully. "You don't look well."

"I'm—" He meant to say *I'm fine*, but the words didn't quite come out. Because he wasn't fine, and he wasn't good, and these days he wasn't even sure what he was.

Eloise chewed on her lower lip, then hugged her arms to her chest and glanced up at the sky as a shadow passed over her.

Phillip followed her gaze, watched as a cloud slid over the sun, dropping the temperature of the air at least ten degrees. He looked at Eloise, his breath catching in his throat as she shivered.

Phillip felt colder than he ever had in his life. "You need to get inside," he said, grabbing her arm and attempting to haul her up the hill.

"Phillip!" she yelped, stumbling along behind him. "I'm fine. Just a little chilled."

He touched her skin. "You're not just a little chilled, you're bloody well freezing." He yanked off his coat. "Put this on."

Eloise didn't argue, but she did say, "Truly, I'm fine. There is no need to *run*."

The last word came out halfway strangled as he yanked her forward, nearly off her feet. "Phillip, *stop*," she yelped. "Please, just let me walk."

He halted so quickly that she stumbled, whirling around and hissing, "I will not be responsible for your freezing yourself into a lung fever."

"But it's May."

"I don't care if it's bloody July. You will not remain in those wet clothes."

"Of course not," Eloise replied, trying to sound reasonable, since it was quite clear that argument was simply going to make him dig his heels in even further. "But there is no reason I cannot *walk*. It's only ten minutes back to the house. I'm not going to die."

She hadn't thought that blood could literally drain from a person's face, but she had no idea how else to describe the sudden blanching of his skin.

"Phillip?" she asked, growing alarmed. "What is wrong?"

For a moment she didn't think he was going to answer, and then, almost as if he weren't aware that he was making a noise, he whispered, "I don't know."

She touched his arm and gazed up at his face. He looked confused, almost dazed, as if he'd been dropped into a theatrical play and didn't know his lines. His eyes were open, and they were on her, but she didn't think he saw anything, just a memory of something that must have been very awful indeed.

Her heart broke for him. She knew bad memories, knew how they could squeeze a heart and haunt one's dreams until one was afraid to blow out the candle.

Eloise had, at the age of seven, watched her father die, shrieked and sobbed as he'd gasped for air and collapsed to the ground, then beaten against his chest when he could no longer speak, begging him to wake up and *say* something.

It was obvious now that he'd already been dead by that point, but somehow that made the memory even worse.

But Eloise had managed to put that behind her. She didn't know how—it was probably all due to her mother, who had come to her side every night and held her hand and told her it was all right to talk about her father. And it was all right to miss him.

Eloise still remembered, but it no longer haunted her, and she hadn't had a nightmare in over a decade.

But Phillip . . . his was a different story. Whatever had happened to him in the past, it was still very much with him.

And unlike Eloise, he was facing it alone.

"Phillip," she said, touching his cheek. He didn't move, and if she hadn't felt his breath on her fingers, she would have sworn he was a statue. She said his name again, stepping even closer.

She wanted to erase that shattered look from his eyes; she wanted to heal him.

She wanted to make him the person she knew he was, deep down in his heart.

She whispered his name one last time, offering him compassion and understanding and the promise of help, all in one single word. She hoped he heard; she hoped he listened.

And then, slowly, his hand covered hers. His skin was warm and rough, and he pressed her hand against his cheek, as if he were trying to sear her touch into his memory. Then he moved her hand to his mouth and kissed her palm, intensely, almost reverently, before sliding it down to his chest.

Across his beating heart.

"Phillip?" she whispered, question in her voice even though she knew what he intended to do.

His free hand found the small of her back, and he pulled her to him, slowly but surely, with a firmness she could not deny. And then he touched her chin and tilted her face to his, stopping only to whisper her name before capturing her mouth in a kiss that was blinding in its intensity. He was hungry, needy, and he kissed her as if he would die without her, as if she were his very food, his air, his body and soul.

It was the type of kiss a woman could never forget, the sort Eloise had never even dreamed possible.

He pulled her even closer, until the entire length of her body was pressed up against his. One of his hands traveled down her back to her bottom, cupping her, pulling her against him until she gasped at the intimacy of it.

"I need you," he groaned, the words sounding as if they were ripped from his throat. His lips slid off her mouth to her cheek, then down her neck, teasing and tickling as they went.

She was melting. *He* was melting her, until she didn't know who she was or what she was doing.

All she wanted was him. More of him. All of him. Except . . .

Except not like this. Not when he was using her like some sort of succor to heal his wounds.

"Phillip," she said, somehow finding the strength to pull back. "We can't. Not like this."

For a moment she didn't think he would let her go, but then, abruptly, he did. "I'm sorry," he said, breathing hard. He looked dazed, and she didn't know if that was from the kiss or simply from the tumultuous events of the morning.

"Don't apologize," she said, instinctively smoothing her skirts, only to find them wet and unsmoothable. But she ran her hands along them anyway, feeling nervous and uncomfortable in her own body. If she didn't move, didn't force herself into some sort of meaningless motion, she was afraid she would launch herself back into his arms.

"You should go back to the house," he said, his voice still low and hoarse.

She felt her eyes widen with surprise. "Aren't you coming as well?"

He shook his head and said in an oddly flat voice, "You won't freeze. It's May, after all."

"Well, yes, but . . ." She let her words trail off, since she didn't really know what to say. She supposed she'd been hoping he'd interrupt her.

She turned to walk up the hill, then stopped when she heard his voice, quiet and intent behind her.

"I need to think," he said.

"About what?" She shouldn't have asked, shouldn't have intruded, but she'd never been able to mind her own business.

"I don't know." He shrugged helplessly. "Everything, I suppose."

Eloise nodded and continued back to the house.

But the bleak look in his eyes haunted her all day.

Chapter 9

. . . we all miss Father, especially this time of year. But think how lucky you were to have had eighteen years with him. I remember so little, and I do wish he could have known me, and all that I've grown up to be.

—*from Eloise Bridgerton to her*
brother Viscount Bridgerton,
upon the occasion of the tenth
anniversary of their father's death

Eloise was purposefully late for supper that evening. Not by much—it was not in her nature to be tardy, especially since it was a trait she didn't care to tolerate in others. But after the events of that afternoon, she had no idea if Sir Phillip was even going to show up for supper, and she couldn't bear the thought of waiting in the drawing room, trying not to twiddle her thumbs as she wondered if she was to dine alone.

At precisely ten minutes past seven, she reckoned

she could assume that if he wasn't waiting for her, he wasn't joining her, and she could then proceed to the dining room on her own and act as if she'd planned to eat by herself all the while.

But much to her surprise and, if she was honest, her great relief as well, Phillip was standing by the window when she entered the drawing room, elegantly dressed in evening kit that was, if not the very latest in style, obviously well made and tailored to perfection. Eloise noticed that his attire was strictly black and white, and she wondered if he was still in partial mourning for Marina, or if perhaps that was simply his preference. Her brothers rarely wore the peacock colors that were so popular among a certain set of the *ton*, and Sir Phillip didn't seem the type, either.

Eloise stood in the doorway for a moment, staring at his profile, wondering if he'd even seen her. And then he turned, murmured her name, and crossed the room.

"I hope you will accept my apologies for this afternoon," he said, and although his voice was reserved, she could see the entreaty in his eyes, sense that her forgiveness was very much desired.

"No apology is necessary," she said quickly, and it was the truth, she supposed. How could she know if he should apologize when she didn't even understand what had transpired?

"It is," he said haltingly. "I overreacted. I—"

She said nothing, just watched his face as he cleared his throat.

He opened his mouth, but it was several seconds before he said, "Marina nearly drowned in that lake."

Eloise gasped, not realizing that her hand had

flown up to cover her mouth until she felt her fingers on her lips.

"She wasn't a strong swimmer," he explained.

"I'm so sorry," she whispered. "Were you—" How to ask it without appearing morbidly curious? There was no way to avoid it, and she couldn't help herself; she had to know. "Were you there?"

He nodded grimly. "I pulled her out."

"How lucky for her," Eloise murmured. "She must have been terrified."

Phillip said nothing. He didn't even nod.

She thought about her father, thought about how helpless she had felt when he'd collapsed to the ground in front of her. Even as a child, she'd been the sort who needed to *do* things. She'd never been one of life's observers; she'd always wanted to take action, to fix things, to fix people, even. And the one time it had all truly mattered, she'd been impotent.

"I'm glad you were able to save her," she murmured. "It would have been horrible for you if you hadn't."

He looked at her oddly, and she realized how strange her words had been, so she added, "It's . . . very difficult . . . when someone dies, and you can only watch, and you can't do anything to stop it." And then, because the moment seemed to call for it, and she felt oddly connected to this man standing so quiet and stiff in front of her, she said softly, and perhaps a bit mournfully as well, "I know."

He looked up at her, the question clearly in his eyes.

"My father," she said simply.

It wasn't something she shared with many people; in fact, her good friend Penelope was probably the only person outside her immediate family who knew that Eloise had been the sole witness to her father's strange and untimely death.

"I'm sorry," he murmured.

"Yes," she said wistfully. "So am I."

And then he said the oddest thing. "I didn't know my children could swim."

It was so unexpected, such a complete non sequitur, that it was all she could do to blink and say, "I beg your pardon?"

He held out his arm to lead her to the dining room. "I didn't know they could swim," he repeated, his voice bleak. "I don't even know who taught them."

"Does it matter?" Eloise asked softly.

"It does," he said bitterly, "because *I* should have done so."

It was difficult to look at his face. She couldn't recall ever seeing a man so pained, and yet in an odd way it warmed her heart. Anyone who cared so much for his children—even if he didn't quite know how to act around them—well, he had to be a good man. Eloise knew that she tended to see the world in blacks and whites, that she sometimes leapt to judgment because she didn't stop to analyze the gradations of gray, but of this she was certain.

Sir Phillip Crane was a good man. He might not be perfect, but he was good, and his heart was true.

"Well," she said briskly, since that was her manner, and she preferred to deal with problems by charging ahead and fixing them rather than stopping to lament, "there's nothing to be done about it now. They can't very well unlearn what they already know."

He stopped, looked at her. "You're right, of course." And then, more softly, "But no matter who did the teaching, I should have known they were able."

Eloise agreed with him, but he was so obviously distressed, a scolding seemed inappropriate, not to mention unfeeling. "You still have time, you know," she said softly.

"What," he said, his mocking tone turned upon himself, "to teach them the backstroke so that they might expand their repertoire?"

"Well, yes," she said, her tone slightly sharp, since she'd never had much patience for self-pity, "but also to learn other things about them. They're charming children."

He looked at her dubiously.

She cleared her throat. "They do misbehave on occasion—"

One of his brows shot up.

"Very well, they misbehave quite often, but truly, all they want is a little attention from you."

"They told you this?"

"Of course not," she said, smiling at his naïveté. "They're only eight. They're not going to say it in so many words. But it's quite clear to me."

They reached the dining room, so Eloise took the seat held out for her by a footman. Phillip sat across from her, put his hand on his wineglass, then drew it back. His lips moved, but very slightly, as if he had something to say but wasn't quite certain how to phrase it. Finally, after Eloise had taken a sip of her own wine, he asked, "Did they enjoy it? Swimming, I mean."

She smiled. "Very much. You should take them."

He closed his eyes and held them that way, not for very long, but still, more than a blink. "I don't think I'd be able," he said.

She nodded. She knew the power of memories. "Perhaps somewhere else," she suggested. "Surely there must be another lake nearby. Or even a mere pond."

He waited for her to pick up her spoon, then dipped his own in his soup. "That's a fine idea. I think . . ." He stopped, cleared his throat. "I think I could do that. I shall ponder where we might go."

There was something so heartbreaking about his expression—the uncertainty, the vulnerability. The awareness that even though he wasn't sure he was doing the right thing, he was going to try to do it anyway. Eloise felt her heart lurch, skip a beat, even, and she wanted to reach across the table and touch his hand. But of course she couldn't. Even if the table weren't a foot longer than the length of her arm, she couldn't. So in the end, she just smiled and hoped that her manner was reassuring.

Phillip ate a bit of his soup, then dabbed at his mouth with his napkin and said, "I hope that you will join us."

"Of course," Eloise said, delighted. "I would be desolate if I weren't invited."

"I'm quite certain you overstate," he said with a wry twist to his lips, "but nonetheless, we would be honored, and to be quite honest, I would be relieved to have you there." At her curious expression, he added, "The outing is certain to be a successful one with your presence."

"I'm sure you—"

He stopped her midsentence. "We will all enjoy ourselves much better with your accompaniment," he said quite emphatically, and Eloise decided to stop arguing and graciously accept the compliment.

He was, in all likelihood, correct. He and his children were so unused to spending time together that they would probably benefit from having Eloise along to smooth the way.

Eloise found she didn't mind the idea one bit. "Perhaps tomorrow," she suggested, "if the fine weather holds out."

"I think it will," Phillip said conversationally. "The air didn't feel changeable."

Eloise glanced at him as she sipped her soup, a chicken broth with bits of vegetables that needed a touch more salt. "Do you predict the weather, then?" she asked, quite certain her skepticism showed on her face. She had a cousin who was convinced he could predict the weather, and every time she listened to him, she ended up soaked to the skin or freezing her toes off.

"Not at all," he replied, "but one can—" He stopped, craned his neck a bit. "What was that?"

"What was what?" Eloise answered, but as the words left her lips, she heard what Phillip must have heard. Argumentative voices, growing louder by the second. Heavy footfall.

A forceful stream of invective was followed by a yelp of terror that could only have come from the butler . . .

And then Eloise *knew*.

"Oh, dear God," she said, her grip on her spoon growing slack until the soup dribbled off, splashing back into her bowl.

"What the devil?" Phillip asked, standing up, obviously preparing to defend his home against invasion.

Except that he had no idea what sort of invaders

he was about to face. What sort of annoying, meddlesome, and diabolical invaders he was going to have to meet in, oh, approximately ten seconds.

But Eloise did. And she knew that *annoying, meddlesome*, and *diabolical* meant nothing compared to *furious, unreasonable*, and *downright large* when it came to Phillip's imminent safety.

"Eloise?" Phillip asked, his brows shooting up when they both heard someone bellow her name.

She felt the blood drain from her body. Positively felt it, *knew* it had happened, even though she couldn't see it pooling about her feet. There was no way she could survive a moment such as this, no way she could make it through without killing someone, preferably someone to whom she was quite closely related.

She stood, her fingers gripping the table. The footsteps (which, to be honest, sounded rather like a rabid horde) grew closer.

"Someone you know?" Phillip asked, quite mildly for someone who was about to face his demise.

She nodded, and somehow managed to eke out the words: "My brothers."

It occurred to Phillip (as he was pinned up against the wall with two sets of hands around his throat) that Eloise might have given him a bit more warning.

He didn't need *days*, although that would have been nice, if still insufficient against the collective strength of four very large, very angry, and, from the looks of them, rather closely related men.

Brothers. He should have considered that. It was probably best to avoid courting a woman with brothers.

Four of them, to be precise.

Four. It was a wonder he wasn't dead already.

"Anthony!" Eloise shrieked. "Stop!"

Anthony, or at least Phillip presumed he was Anthony—they hadn't exactly bothered to go through the necessary introductions—tightened his grip on Phillip's neck.

"Benedict," Eloise pleaded, turning her attention to the largest of the lot. "Be reasonable."

The other one—well, the other one squeezing his throat; there were two others, but they were just standing around glowering—loosened his grip slightly to turn around and look at Eloise.

Which was a huge mistake, since, in their haste to rip every limb from his body, none of them had yet looked at her long enough to see that she sported a nasty blackened eye.

Which of course they would think *he* was responsible for.

Benedict let out an unholy growl and jammed Phillip against the wall so tightly that his feet came off the ground.

Wonderful, Phillip thought. *Now I really am going to die.* The first squeeze was merely uncomfortable, but this . . .

"Stop!" Eloise yelled, hurling herself onto Benedict's back and yanking his hair. Benedict howled as his head jerked backward, but unfortunately Anthony's strangulatory grip held firm, even as Benedict was forced to let go to fight off Eloise.

Who was, Phillip noted as well as he could, given his lack of oxygen, fighting like a fury crossed with a banshee, crossed with Medusa herself. Her right hand was still pulling out Benedict's hair, even as her left arm wrapped around his throat, with her forearm lodged quite neatly up under his chin.

"Good Christ," Benedict cursed, whirling around as he tried to dislodge his sister. "Someone get her off of me!"

Not surprisingly, none of the other Bridgertons rushed to his aid. In fact, the one back against the wall looked rather amused by the whole thing.

Phillip's vision began to curl and turn black at the edges, but he couldn't help but admire Eloise's fortitude. It was a rare woman who knew how to fight to win.

Anthony's face suddenly appeared very close to his. "Did . . . you . . . hit her?" he growled.

As if he could speak, Phillip thought woozily.

"No!" Eloise cried out, momentarily taking her attention off tearing Benedict's hair out. "Of course he didn't hit me."

Anthony looked over at her with a sharp expression as she resumed pummeling Benedict. "There's no *of course* about it."

"It was an accident," she insisted. "He had nothing to do with it." And then, when none of her brothers made any indication that they believed her, she added, "Oh, for heaven's sake. Do you really think that *I* would defend someone who'd struck me?"

That seemed to do the trick, and Anthony abruptly let go of Phillip, who promptly sagged to the floor, gasping for breath.

Four of them. Had she told him she had four brothers? Surely not. He would never have considered marriage to a woman with four brothers. Only a fool would shackle himself to such a family.

"What did you do to him?" Eloise demanded, jumping off Benedict and hurrying to Phillip's side.

"What did he do to *you*?" one of the other brothers demanded. The one who, Phillip realized, had punched him in the chin right before the others had decided to strangle him instead.

She shot him a scathing look. "What are *you* doing here?"

"Protecting my sister's honor," he shot back.

"As if I need protection from you. You're not even twenty!"

Ah, thought Phillip, he must be the one whose name began with G. George? No, that wasn't right. Gavin? No . . .

"I'm twenty-three," the young one bit off, with all the irritability of a younger sibling.

"And I'm twenty-eight," she snapped. "I didn't need your help when you were in nappies, and I don't need it now."

Gregory. That's right. Gregory. She'd said as much in one of her letters. Ah, damn. If he knew that, then he must have known about the flock of brothers. He really had no one to blame but himself.

"He wanted to come along," said the one in the corner, the only one who hadn't yet tried to kill Phillip. Phillip decided he liked this one best, especially when he wrapped his hand around Gregory's forearm to prevent the younger man from launching himself at Eloise.

Which, Phillip thought, feeling rather ironically-minded there on the floor, was nothing more than she deserved. Nappies, indeed.

"Well, you should have stopped him," Eloise said, oblivious to Phillip's mental defection. "Do you have any idea how mortifying this is?"

Her brothers stared at her, quite rightly, in Phillip's opinion, as if she'd gone mad.

"You lost the right," Anthony bit off, "to feel mortified, embarrassed, chagrined, or in fact any emotion other than blindingly stupid when you ran off without a word."

Eloise looked a bit mollified but still muttered, "It's not as if I would listen to anything he has to say."

"As opposed to us," the one who had to be Colin murmured, "with whom you are the soul of meekness and obeisance."

"Oh, for the love of God," Eloise said under her breath, sounding rather fetchingly unladylike to Phillip's stinging ears.

Stinging? Had someone boxed his ears? It was difficult to recall. Four-to-one odds against did tend to muddle one's memory.

"You," snapped the one Phillip was almost certain was Anthony, with a finger jabbed in Phillip's direction, "don't go anywhere."

As if that were even worth contemplating.

"And you," Anthony said to Eloise, his voice even deadlier, although Phillip wouldn't have thought it possible, "what the hell did you think you were doing?"

Eloise tried to sidestep the question with one of her own. "What are you doing here?"

And succeeded, because her brother actually answered her. "Saving you from ruin," he yelled. "For the love of God, Eloise, do you have any idea how worried we've been?"

"And here I'd thought you hadn't even noticed my departure," she tried to joke.

"Eloise," he said, "Mother is beside herself."

That sobered her in an instant. "Oh, no," she whispered. "I didn't think."

"No, you didn't," Anthony replied, his stern tone exactly what one would expect from a man who'd been the head of his family for twenty years. "I ought to take a whip to you."

Phillip started to intervene, because, really, he couldn't countenance a whipping, but then Anthony added, "Or at the very least, a muzzle," and Phillip decided that brother knew sister very well, indeed.

"Where do you think you're going?" demanded Benedict, and Phillip realized that he must have started to stand before plopping back to his rather impotent position on the floor.

Phillip looked to Eloise. "Perhaps introductions are in order?"

"Oh," Eloise said, gulping. "Yes, of course. These are my brothers."

"I'd gathered," he said, his voice as dry as dust.

She shot him an apologetic look, which, Phillip thought, was really the least she could do after nearly getting him tortured and killed, then turned to her brothers and motioned to each in turn, saying, "Anthony, Benedict, Colin, Gregory. These three," she added, motioning to A, B, and C, "are my elders. This one"—she waved dismissively at Gregory—"is an infant."

Gregory looked near ready to throttle her, which suited Phillip just fine, since it deflected the murderous intentions off of *him*.

And then Eloise finally turned back to Phillip and

said to her brothers, "Sir Phillip Crane, but I expect you know that already."

"You left a letter in your desk," said Colin.

Eloise closed her eyes in agony. Phillip thought he saw her lips form the words, *Stupid, stupid, stupid.*

Colin smiled grimly. "You ought to be more careful in the future, should you decide to run off again."

"I'll remember that," Eloise shot back, but she was losing her fire.

"Would now be a good time to stand?" Phillip inquired, directing his question to no one in particular.

"*No.*"

It was difficult to discern which Bridgerton brother spoke the loudest.

Phillip remained on the floor. He didn't tend to think himself a coward, and he was, if he did say so himself, quite proficient with his fists, but hell, there were *four* of them.

Boxer he might be. Suicidal fool he was not.

"How did you get that eye?" Colin asked quietly.

Eloise paused before answering, "It was an accident."

He considered her words for a moment. "Would you care to expand upon that?"

Eloise swallowed uncomfortably and glanced down at Phillip, which he really wished she wouldn't do. It only made *them* (as he was coming to think of the quartet) even more convinced that he was the one responsible for her injury.

A misapprehension that could only lead to his death and dismemberment. They didn't seem the sorts to allow anyone to lay a hand on their sisters, much less blacken an eye.

"Just tell them the truth, Eloise," Phillip said wearily.

"It was his children," she said, wincing on the words. But Phillip didn't worry. As close as they'd come to strangling him, they didn't seem the sort to harm innocent children. And certainly Eloise would not have said anything if she'd thought it might place Oliver and Amanda in peril.

"He has children?" Anthony asked, eyeing him with a slightly less derogatory expression.

Anthony, Phillip decided, must be a father as well.

"Two," Eloise replied. "Twins, actually. A boy and a girl. They're eight."

"My felicitations," Anthony murmured.

"Thank you," Phillip answered, feeling rather old and weary in that moment. "Sympathies are probably more to the point."

Anthony looked at him curiously, almost—but not quite—smiling.

"They weren't especially keen on my presence here," Eloise said.

"Smart children," Anthony said.

She shot him a decidedly unamused look. "They set a trip wire," she said. "Rather like the one Colin"—she turned to spear him with a hostile glare—"set for me in 1804."

Colin's lips twisted into a disbelieving expression. "You remember the *date*?"

"She remembers everything," Benedict commented.

Eloise turned to glare at *him*.

Aching throat notwithstanding, Phillip was actually beginning to enjoy the interaction.

Eloise turned back to Anthony, regal as a queen. "I fell," she said simply.

"On your eye?"

"On my hip, actually, but I didn't have time to break my fall, and I hit my cheek. I imagine the bruising spread to the eye area."

Anthony looked down at Phillip with a ferocious expression. "Is she telling the truth?"

Phillip nodded. "On my brother's grave. The children will own up to it as well, should you feel the need to interrogate them."

"Of course not," Anthony said gruffly. "I would never—" He cleared his throat, then ordered, "Stand up." But he tempered his tone by offering Phillip his hand.

Phillip took it, having already decided that Eloise's brother would make a far finer ally than enemy. He eyed the four male Bridgertons warily, though, and his stance was defensive. He stood no chance if all four decided to charge at him at once, and he wasn't convinced that that was not still a likely possibility.

At the end of the day, he was going to find himself either dead or married, and he wasn't quite prepared to let the Bridgerton brothers take the matter to a vote.

And then, after Anthony silenced his four younger siblings with nothing more than a stare, he turned to Phillip and said, "Perhaps you should tell me what happened."

Out of the corner of his eye, Phillip saw Eloise open her mouth to interrupt, then close it again, sitting down on a chair with an expression that, if it wasn't meek, was at least meeker than anything he'd ever expected to see gracing her face.

Phillip decided that he needed to learn how to glare like Anthony Bridgerton. He'd have his children in line in no time.

"I don't think Eloise will be interrupting us now," Anthony said mildly. "Please, go on."

Phillip glanced over at Eloise. She looked about ready to explode. But still, she held her tongue, which seemed a remarkable feat indeed, for one such as her.

Phillip briefly recounted the events that had led to Eloise's arrival at Romney Hall. He told Anthony about the letters, beginning with Eloise's letter of condolence, and how they had begun a friendly correspondence, pausing in his story only when Colin shook his head and murmured, "I always wondered what she was writing up in her room."

When Phillip looked at him quizzically, he held up his hands and added, "Her fingers. They were always ink-stained, and I never knew why."

Phillip finished his tale, concluding with, "So, as you see, I was looking for a wife. From the tone of her letters, she seemed intelligent and reasonable. My children, as you will come to realize should you remain long enough to meet them, can be rather, er"—he searched for the least unflattering adjective— "rambunctious," he said, satisfied with his word choice. "I'd been hoping she would be a calming influence on them."

"Eloise?" Benedict snorted, and Phillip could see from their expressions that the other three brothers agreed with his assessment.

And while Phillip might smile at Benedict's comment about Eloise remembering everything, and even *agree* with Anthony about the muzzle, it was becoming apparent that the Bridgerton males did not hold their sister in the regard she deserved. "Your sister," he said, his voice coming off sharp, "has been a marvelous influence upon my children. You would do well not to disparage her in my presence."

He'd probably just issued his own death warrant. There were four of them, after all, and it wasn't in his best interest to be insulting. But even if they had charged halfway across the country to protect Eloise's virtue, there was no way he was going to stand here and listen to them snort and snuff and make a mockery of her.

Not Eloise. Not in front of him.

But to his great surprise, not a one of them had a retort, and in fact Anthony, who was still clearly the one in charge, held him with a level stare, assessing him as if he were peeling the layers back until he could see what lay hidden in his core.

"We have a great deal to talk about, you and I," Anthony said quietly.

Phillip nodded. "I expect you will need to speak with your sister as well."

Eloise shot him a grateful look. He wasn't surprised. He couldn't imagine she would take well to being left out of any decisions pertaining to her life. Hell, she wasn't the sort to take well to being left out of anything.

"Yes," Anthony said, "I do. In fact, I think we shall conduct our interview first, if you don't mind."

As if Phillip was stupid enough to argue with one Bridgerton while three more were glaring at him.

"Please use my study," he offered. "Eloise can show you the way."

It was the wrong thing to say. None of the brothers cared to be reminded that Eloise had been in residence long enough to know her way around.

Anthony and Eloise left the room without another word, leaving Phillip alone with the remaining Bridgerton brothers.

"Mind if I sit?" Phillip asked, since he suspected he was going to be stuck here in the dining room for some time.

"Go right ahead," Colin said expansively. Benedict and Gregory just continued to glare. Colin, Phillip noted, didn't look particularly eager to strike up a friendship, either. He might have been marginally more amiable than his brothers, but his eyes showed a sharp shrewdness that Phillip rather thought he ought not underestimate.

"Please," Phillip said, motioning to the food still on the table, "eat."

Benedict and Gregory scowled at him as if he'd offered poison, but Colin sat across from him and plucked a crusty roll off a plate.

"They're quite good," Phillip said, even though he'd not had the opportunity to partake that evening.

"Good," Colin muttered, taking a bite. "I'm famished."

"How can you think of food?" Gregory said angrily.

"I always think of food," Colin replied, his eyes searching the table until he located the butter. "What else is there?"

"Your wife," Benedict drawled.

"Ah, yes, my wife," Colin said with a nod. He turned to Phillip, leveled a hard stare at him, and said, "Just so that you are aware, I would have rather spent the night with my wife."

Phillip couldn't think of a reply that might not hint at insult to the absent Mrs. Bridgerton, so he just nodded and buttered a roll of his own.

Colin took a huge bite, then spoke with his mouth full, the etiquette breach a clear insult to his host. "We've only been married a few weeks."

Phillip raised one of his brows in question.

"Still newlyweds."

Phillip nodded, since some sort of response seemed to be required.

Colin leaned forward. "I *really* did not want to leave my wife."

"I see," Phillip murmured, since truly, what else could he have said?

"Do you understand what he's saying?" Gregory demanded.

Colin turned and sent a chilling look at his brother, who was clearly too young to have mastered the fine art of nuance and circumspect speech. Phillip waited until Colin had turned back to the table, offered him a plate of asparagus (which he took), then said, "I gather you miss your wife."

There was a beat of silence, and then Colin said, after sending one last disdainful glance at his brother, "Indeed."

Phillip looked over at Benedict, since he was the only one uninvolved in the latest spat.

Big mistake. Benedict was flexing his hands, still looking as if he regretted not strangling him when he had his chance.

Phillip then turned his gaze to Gregory, whose arms were crossed angrily over his chest. His entire body practically quivered with fury, perhaps aimed at Phillip, perhaps at his family, who'd been treating him like a green boy all evening. Phillip's glance was not met with favor. Gregory's chin jutted angrily out, his teeth clenched, and—

And Phillip had had enough of that. He looked back to Colin.

Colin was still working on his food, having somehow managed to charm the servants into bringing him a bowl of soup. He'd set down his spoon, though, and was presently examining his other hand, idly flexing each finger in turn, murmuring a word as each pointed out toward Phillip.

"Miss. My. Wife."

"Bloody hell," Phillip finally burst out. "If you're going to break my legs, would you just go ahead and do it now?"

Chapter 10

. . . you will never know how unfortunate you are, dearest Penelope, to have sisters only. Brothers are ever so much more fun.

*—from Eloise Bridgerton
to Penelope Featherington,
following a midnight ride in Hyde Park
with her three older brothers*

"Here are your choices," Anthony said, sitting behind Phillip's desk as if he owned the place. "You can marry him in one week, or you can marry him in two."

Eloise's mouth fell open into a horrified oval. "Anthony!"

"Did you expect me to suggest an alternative?" he asked mildly. "I suppose we might stretch it to three, given a sufficiently compelling reason."

She hated when he spoke like that, as if he were reasonable and wise, and she were nothing more than a recalcitrant child. It was far better when he ranted and raved. Then, at least, she could pretend he was mad in the head and she was a poor, beleaguered innocent.

"I don't see why you would object," he continued. "Didn't you come here with the intention to marry him?"

"No! I came here with the intention to *find out* if he was suitable for marriage."

"And is he?"

"I don't know," she said. "It's only been two days."

"And yet," Anthony said, idly examining his fingernails in the dim candlelight, "that's still more than enough time to ruin your reputation."

"Does anyone know I was gone?" she quickly asked. "Outside the family, that is."

"Not yet," he admitted, "but someone will find out. Someone always finds out."

"There was supposed to be a chaperone," Eloise said sullenly.

"Was there?" he asked, his voice perfectly conversational, as if he were asking if there was supposed to have been lamb for dinner, or maybe a hunting expedition arranged for his entertainment.

"She's coming soon."

"Hmmm. Too bad for her I arrived first."

"Too bad for everyone," Eloise muttered.

"What was that?" he asked, but again he used that awful voice, the one that made it clear he'd heard every word.

"Anthony," Eloise said, and his name came out like a plea, even though she had no idea what it was she was pleading for.

He turned to her, his dark eyes blazing, the force of his stare so violent that it was only then that she realized she ought to have been grateful he'd been pretending to examine his fingernails.

She took a step back. Anyone would have when faced with Anthony Bridgerton in such a fury.

But when he spoke, his voice was even and controlled. "You've made yourself a rather messy little bed here," he said, his cadence slow and precise. "I'm afraid you're going to have to lie in it."

"You would have me marry a man I don't know?" she whispered.

"Is that even the truth?" Anthony responded. "Because you seemed to know him very well indeed in the dining room. You certainly leapt to his defense at every conceivable opportunity."

Anthony was talking her into a corner, and it was driving her mad. "It's not enough for marriage," she insisted. "At least not yet."

But Anthony wasn't the sort to let up. "If not now, then when? One week? Two?"

"Stop!" she burst out, wanting to throw her hands over her ears. "I can't think."

"You *don't* think," he corrected. "If you'd taken one moment to think, to use that tiny portion of your brain reserved for common sense, you would never have run off."

She crossed her arms, looking away. She had no argument, and it was killing her.

"What are you going to do, Eloise?" Anthony asked.

"I don't know," she muttered, hating how stupid she sounded.

"Well," he said, still continuing in that awful, reasonable voice, "that puts us in a bit of a bind, doesn't it?"

"Can't you just say it?" she asked, her fists clenching against her rib cage. "Do you have to end everything with a question?"

He smiled humorlessly. "And here I thought you'd appreciate my soliciting your opinion."

"You're being condescending and you know it."

He leaned forward, thunder in his eyes. "Do you have any idea how much effort it requires to keep my temper in check?"

Eloise thought it best not to hazard a guess.

"You ran off in the middle of the night," he said, rising to his feet, "without a word, without even a note—"

"I left a note!" she burst out.

He looked at her with patent disbelief.

"I did!" she insisted. "I left it on the side table in the front hall. Right next to the Chinese vase."

"And this mysterious note said . . ."

"It said not to worry, that I was fine and would contact you all within a month."

"Ah," Anthony said mockingly. "*That* would have set my mind at ease."

"I don't know why you didn't get it," Eloise muttered. "It probably got mixed up with a pile of invitations."

"For all we knew," Anthony continued, taking a step toward her, "you'd been kidnapped."

Eloise paled. She'd never even considered that her family might think such a thing. It had never occurred to her that her note might go astray.

"Do you know what Mother did?" Anthony asked, his voice deathly serious. "*After* nearly collapsing with worry?"

Eloise shook her head, dreading the answer.

"She went to the bank," Anthony continued. "Do you know why?"

"Could you just tell me?" Eloise asked wearily. She hated the questions.

"She went there," he said, walking toward her in a terrifying manner, "to make sure that all her funds were in the proper order so that she could withdraw them *should she need to ransom you!*"

Eloise shrank back at the fury in her older brother's voice. *I left a note,* she wanted to say again, but she knew it would come out the wrong way. She'd been wrong, and she'd been foolish, and she didn't want to compound her stupidity by trying to excuse it.

"Penelope was the one who finally figured out what you'd done," Anthony said. "We asked her to search your room, since she's probably spent more time there than any of the rest of us."

Eloise nodded. Penelope had been her closest friend—still was, in fact, even though she'd married Colin. They'd spent countless hours up in her room, talking about anything and everything. Phillip's letters were the only secret Eloise had ever kept from her.

"Where did she find the letter?" Eloise asked. Not that it mattered, but she couldn't help her curiosity.

"It had fallen behind your desk." Anthony crossed his arms. "Along with a pressed flower."

Somehow that seemed fitting. "He's a botanist," she whispered.

"I beg your pardon?"

"A botanist," she said, more loudly this time. "Sir Phillip. He took a first at Cambridge. He would have been an academic if his brother hadn't died at Waterloo."

Anthony nodded, digesting that fact, and the fact that she knew it. "If you tell me that he's a cruel man, that he will beat you, that he will insult you and demean you, I will not force your hand. But before you speak, I want you to consider my words. You are a Bridgerton. I don't care who you marry or what your name becomes when you stand up before a priest and say your vows. You will always be a Bridgerton, and we behave with honor and honesty, not because it is expected of us, but because *that is what we are.*"

Eloise nodded, swallowing as she fought the tears that were stinging in her eyes.

"So I will ask you right now," he said. "Is there any reason you cannot marry Sir Phillip Crane?"

"No," she whispered. She didn't even hesitate. She wasn't ready for this, wasn't yet ready for the marriage, but she wouldn't sully the truth by hesitating on her answer.

"I thought not."

She stood still, almost deflated, not certain what to do or say next. She turned, aware that Anthony had to know she was crying, but not wanting him to see her tears, nonetheless. "I'll marry him," she said, choking on the words. "It's just that I—I'd wanted—"

He held silent for a moment, respecting her distress, but then, when she did not continue, he asked, "What did you want, Eloise?"

"I'd hoped for a love match," she said, so softly she barely heard herself.

"I see," he said, his hearing superb as always. "You should have thought of that before you ran off, shouldn't you?"

She hated him in that moment. "You have a love match. You should understand."

"*I*," he said, the tone of his voice indicating that he did not appreciate her trying to make the conversation about him, "married my wife after we were caught in a compromising position by the biggest bloody gossip in England."

Eloise let out a long breath, feeling stupid. It had been so many years since Anthony had married. She'd forgotten the circumstances.

"I didn't love my wife when I married her," he continued, "or," he added, his voice growing a bit softer, more gruff and nostalgic, "if I did, I did not yet realize it."

Eloise nodded. "You were very lucky," she said, wishing she knew if she could be that lucky with Phillip.

And then Anthony surprised her, because he didn't scold, and he didn't reprimand. All he said was, "I know."

"I felt lost," she whispered. "When Penelope and Colin married . . ." She sank into a chair, letting her head drop into her hands. "I'm a terrible person. I must be a terrible person, horrible and shallow, because when they married, all I could think about was myself."

Anthony sighed, and he crouched beside her. "You're not a terrible person, Eloise. You know that."

She looked up at him, wondering when it was that

this man, her brother, had become so wise. If he'd yelled one more word, spent one more minute speaking to her in that mocking voice, she would have broke. She would have broke, or she would have hardened, but either way, something between them would have been ruined.

But here he was, Anthony of all people, who was arrogant and proud and every inch the arch noble-man he'd been born to be, kneeling at her side, plac-ing his hand on hers, and speaking with a kindness that nearly broke her heart.

"I was happy for them," she said. "I *am* happy for them."

"I know you are."

"I should have felt nothing but joy."

"If you had, you wouldn't be human."

"Penelope became my *sister*," she said. "I should have been happy."

"Didn't you say that you were?"

She nodded. "I am. I am. I know that I am. I'm not just saying it."

He smiled benignly and waited for her to con-tinue.

"It's just that I suddenly felt so lonely, and so *old*." She looked up at him, wondering if he could possibly understand. "I never thought I would be left behind."

He chuckled. "Eloise Bridgerton, I don't think anyone would *ever* make the mistake of leaving you behind."

She felt her lips curve into a wobbly smile, mar-veling that her brother of all people could actually say the *exact* right thing. "I suppose I never really thought I'd always be a spinster," she said. "Or, if I was, then at least that Penelope would always be one, too. It wasn't very kind of me, and I don't even think I really thought about it much, but—"

"But that's just how it was," he said, doing her the kindness of finishing the sentiment. "I don't think even Penelope ever thought she'd marry. And to be honest, I doubt Colin did, either. Love can rather creep up on a person, you know."

She nodded, wondering if it could creep up on her. Probably not. She was the sort of person who would need it whacked over the head.

"I'm glad they're married," Eloise said.

"I know you are. I am, too."

"Sir Phillip," she said, motioning toward the door, even though he was actually down the hall and around two corners in the dining room. "We had been corresponding for over a year. And then he mentioned marriage. And he did it in such a sensible manner. He didn't propose, he just inquired if I might like to visit, to see if we would suit. I told myself he was mad, that I couldn't even consider such an offer. Who would marry someone she didn't know?" She let out a shaky little laugh. "And then Colin and Penelope announced their engagement. It was as if my entire world flipped sideways. And that was when I started thinking about it. Every time I looked at my desk, at the drawer where I kept his letters, it was as if they were burning a hole right through the wood."

Anthony said nothing, just squeezed her hand, as if he understood.

"I had to do something," she said. "I couldn't just sit and wait for life to happen to me any longer."

A chuckle burst from her brother's throat. "Eloise,"

he said, "that is the last thing I would ever worry about on your behalf."

"Anth—"

"No, let me finish," he said. "You're one of the special ones, Eloise. Life never *happens* to you. Trust me on this. I've watched you grow up, had to be your father at times when I wanted only to be your brother."

Her lips parted as something squeezed around her heart. He was right. He *had* been a father to her. It was a role neither of them had wanted for him, but he had done it for years, without complaint.

And this time she squeezed his hand, not because she loved him, but because it was only now that she realized how very much she did.

"*You* happen to life, Eloise," Anthony said. "You've always made your own decisions, always been in control. It might not always feel that way, but it's true."

She closed her eyes for a moment, shaking her head as she said, "Well, I was trying to make my own decisions when I came here. It seemed a good plan."

"And maybe," Anthony said quietly, "you'll find that it was indeed a good plan. Sir Phillip seems an honorable sort."

Eloise couldn't hide her peevish expression. "You were able to deduce this while you had your hands wrapped around his throat?"

He shot her a superior look. "You'd be surprised what men can deduce about one another while fighting."

"You call that fighting? It was four against one!"

He shrugged. "I never said it was *fair* fighting."

"You're incorrigible."

"An interesting adjective considering *your* recent activities."

Eloise felt herself flush.

"Very well," Anthony said, his brisk tone signaling a change of topic. "Here is what we are going to do."

And Eloise knew that whatever he said, it was what she'd be doing. His voice was that resolute.

"You will pack your bags immediately," Anthony said, "and we will all travel to My Cottage and remain there for a week."

Eloise nodded. My Cottage was the rather odd name of Benedict's home, situated not too far from Romney Hall in Wiltshire. He lived there with his wife Sophie and their three sons. It wasn't a particularly large home, but it was comfortable, and there was certainly enough room for a few extra Bridgertons.

"Your Sir Phillip may come visit each day," Anthony continued, and Eloise understood his words perfectly to mean, *Your Sir Phillip will come visit each day.*

She nodded again.

"If, at the end of the week, I determine that he is good enough to marry my sister, you will do so. Immediately."

"You're certain you can judge the measure of a man's character in one week?"

"It rarely takes longer," Anthony stated. "And if I'm unsure, we'll merely wait another sennight."

"Sir Phillip might not care to marry me," Eloise felt compelled to point out.

Anthony leveled a hard stare at her face. "He hasn't that option."

Eloise gulped.

One of Anthony's brows rose into an arrogant arch. "Do we understand each other?"

She nodded. His plan seemed reasonable—more reasonable, in fact, than most older brothers would have allowed—and if something went horribly wrong, if she decided that she couldn't possibly marry Sir Phillip Crane, well then, she had a week to figure out how to get out of it. A lot could happen in a week.

Just look at the last one.

"Shall we return to the dining room?" Anthony queried. "I imagine you're hungry, and if we tarry much longer, Colin is sure to have eaten our host out of house and home."

Eloise nodded. "Either that, or they've all killed him by now."

Anthony paused to consider that. "It would save me the expense of a wedding."

"Anthony!"

"It's a joke, Eloise," he said, giving his head a weary shake. "Come along, now. Let's make sure your Sir Phillip still resides among the ranks of the living."

"And then," Benedict was saying as Anthony and Eloise reentered the dining room, "the tavern wench arrived and she had the *biggest*—"

"Benedict!" Eloise exclaimed.

Benedict looked over at his sister with a supremely guilty expression, yanked back his hands, which were demonstrating the size of what was clearly an impossibly endowed female, and muttered, "Sorry."

"You're married," Eloise scolded.

"But not blind," Colin said with a grin.

"You're married, too!" she accused.

"But not blind," he said again.

"Eloise," Gregory said with what was quite possibly the most annoying use of condescension she'd ever had cause to hear, "there are some things that are impossible not to see. Especially," he added, "when you're a man."

"It's true," admitted Anthony. "I saw it myself."

Eloise gasped as she looked from brother to brother, looking for some sane spot in this cesspool of madness. Her eyes fell on Phillip, who, by the looks of him, not to mention his slightly inebriated state, had formed a lifelong bond with her brothers during the short time she'd been closeted away with Anthony.

"Sir Phillip?" she asked, waiting for him to say something acceptable.

But he just offered her a loopy grin. "I know who they're talking about," he said. "Been to that inn any number of times. Lucy's quite famous in these parts."

"Even I've heard of her," Benedict said, with a knowing nod. "I'm only an hour away on horseback. Less, if you push hard."

Gregory leaned toward Phillip, his blue eyes gleaming with interest as he asked, "So, did you? Ever?"

"Gregory!" Eloise practically yelled. This was really too much. Her brothers should never have been talking about such things in front of her, but even more, the last thing she wanted to know was whether Sir Phillip had tupped a tavern wench with bosoms the size of soup tureens.

But Phillip just shook his head. "She's married," he said. "As was I."

Anthony turned to Eloise and whispered in her ear, "He'll do."

"I'm glad you have such high standards for your beloved sister," she muttered.

"I told you," Anthony remarked, "I've seen Lucy. This is a man with restraint."

She planted her hands on her hips and looked her older brother squarely in the eye. "Were *you* tempted?"

"Of course not! Kate would slit my throat."

"I'm not talking about what Kate would do to you if you strayed, although I'm of the opinion that she would not start at your throat—"

Anthony winced. He knew it was true.

"—I want to know if you were tempted."

"No," he admitted, shaking his head. "But don't tell anyone. I used to be considered something of a rake, after all. Wouldn't want people to think I was completely tamed."

"You're appalling."

He grinned. "And yet, my wife still loves me to distraction, which is all that really matters, isn't it?"

Eloise supposed he was right. She sighed. "What are we going to do about them?" She motioned to the quartet of men sitting around the dining room table, which was littered with empty dishes. Phillip, Benedict, and Gregory were sitting back and relaxing, looking quite sated. Colin was still eating.

Anthony shrugged. "I don't know what you want to do, but I'm going to join them."

Eloise just stood in the doorway, watching as he sat down and poured himself a glass of wine. The conversation had thankfully moved on from Lucy and her tremendous bosoms, and now they were talking about boxing. Or at least that's what she assumed they were talking about. Phillip was demonstrating some sort of hand maneuver to Gregory.

Then he punched him in the face.

"So sorry," Phillip said, patting Gregory on the back. But Eloise noticed that the right corner of his mouth was curving ever so slightly into a smile. "Won't hurt for long, I'm sure. *My* chin's feeling better already."

Gregory grunted something that was clearly meant to mean that it didn't hurt, but he rubbed his chin nonetheless.

"Sir Phillip?" Eloise said loudly. "Might I have a word?"

"Of course," he said, standing up immediately, although in all truth, *all* of the men should have been standing, since she'd never vacated her position in the doorway.

Phillip walked to her side. "Is something amiss?"

"I was worried they were going to kill you," she hissed.

"Oh." He smiled, that lopsided, three-glasses-of-wine sort of smile. "They didn't."

"I see that," she ground out. "What happened?"

He looked back over at the table. Anthony was eating the meager scraps that Colin had left behind (almost certainly only because he hadn't realized they were there), and Benedict was tipping back in his chair, trying to balance it on two legs. Gregory was humming to himself, his eyes closed as he smiled beatifically, presumably thinking of Lucy, or, more likely, certain large and squishy parts of Lucy.

Phillip turned back to her and shrugged.

"When," Eloise said with exaggerated patience, "did you all become the best of friends?"

"Oh," he said, nodding. "Funny thing, actually. I asked them to break my legs."

Eloise just stared at him. As long as she lived, she'd never understand men. She had four brothers, and quite frankly should have understood them better than most women, and maybe it had taken all of her twenty-eight years to come to this realization, but men were, quite simply, freaks.

Phillip shrugged again. "It seemed to break the ice."

"Clearly."

She stared at him, and he stared at her, and all the while she could see Anthony staring at them both, and then suddenly Phillip seemed to sober.

"We'll have to marry," he said.

"I know."

"They really will break my legs if I don't."

"That's not all they would do," she grumbled, "but even so, a lady might like to think she's been chosen for a reason other than osteopathic health."

He blinked at her in surprise.

"I'm not stupid," she muttered. "I've studied Latin."

"Right," he said slowly, in that way men do when they are trying to cover up the fact that they're not sure what to say.

"Or at least," she tried desperately, searching for something that might be even loosely interpreted as a compliment, "if not a reason *other*, then perhaps a reason *in addition*."

"Right," he said, nodding, but still not saying anything more.

Her eyes narrowed. "How much wine have you drunk?"

"Only three." He stopped, considered that. "Maybe four."

"Glasses or bottles?"

He didn't seem to know the answer to that.

Eloise looked over at the table. There were four bottles of wine littered among the remains of supper. Three were empty.

"I wasn't gone that long," she said.

He shrugged. "It was either drink with them or let them break my legs. It seemed a fairly straightforward decision."

"Anthony!" she called out. She'd had enough of Phillip. She'd had enough of them all, of everything, of men, of marriage, of broken legs and empty wine bottles. But most of all, she'd had enough of herself, of feeling so out of control, so helpless against the tides of her life.

"I want to go," she said.

Anthony nodded and grunted, still chewing the solitary piece of chicken that Colin had missed.

"*Now*, Anthony."

And he must have heard the crack in her voice, the hollow note that choked on the syllables, because he stood immediately and said, "Of course."

Eloise had never been so glad to see the inside of a carriage in all her life.

Chapter 11

...cannot abide a man who drinks to excess. Which is why I'm sure you will understand why I could not accept Lord Wescott's offer.

—from Eloise Bridgerton to her brother Benedict, upon refusing her second proposal of marriage

"No!" gushed Sophie Bridgerton, Benedict's petite and almost ethereal-looking wife. "They didn't!"

"They did," Eloise said grimly, as she sat back in her lawn chair and sipped a cup of lemonade. "And then they all got drunk!"

"Fiends," Sophie muttered, leading Eloise to realize that what she'd really been sick of the night before was that horribly chummish and collegial manner of men. Clearly, all she'd needed was one sensible female with whom she might disparage the lot of them.

Sophie scowled. "Don't tell me they were talking about that poor Lucy woman again."

Eloise gasped. "You know about her?"

"Everyone knows about her. Heaven knows, one can't *miss* her if you pass in the street."

Eloise stopped, thought, tried to imagine. She couldn't.

"Truth be told," Sophie said, whispering under her breath even though there wasn't a soul nearby who might hear, "I feel sorry for the woman. All that unwanted attention, and, well, it can't be good for her back."

Eloise tried to stifle her laugh, but a little snort made it through.

"Posy once even asked her about it!"

Eloise's mouth fell open. Posy was Sophie's step-sister, who had lived for several years with the Bridgertons before marrying the rather jolly vicar who lived just five miles from Benedict and Sophie. She was also, quite honestly, the friendliest person of Eloise's acquaintance, and if anyone was going to befriend a married serving wench with large bosoms, it would have been her.

"She's in Hugh's parish," Sophie explained, refer-ring to Posy's husband. "So of course they would have met."

"What did she say?" Eloise asked.

"Posy?"

"No. Lucy."

"Oh. I don't know." Sophie pulled a face. "Posy wouldn't tell me. Can you believe that? I don't think Posy has kept a secret from me in all her life. She said she couldn't betray the confidence of a parishioner."

Eloise thought that rather noble of Posy.

"It doesn't concern me, of course," Sophie said,

with all the confidence of a woman who knows she is loved. "Benedict would never stray."

"Of course not," Eloise said quickly. Benedict and Sophie's love story was legendary in their family. It had been one of the reasons Eloise had refused so many proposals of marriage. She'd wanted that kind of love and passion and drama. She'd wanted more than, "I have three homes, sixteen horses, and forty-two hounds," which is what one of her suitors had informed her when he asked for her hand.

"But," Sophie continued, "I don't think it's so much to ask that he manage to keep his mouth closed when she walks by."

Eloise was about to offer her firm and vehement agreement when she saw Sir Phillip walking across the lawn in her direction.

"Is that him?" Sophie asked, smiling.

Eloise nodded.

"He's very handsome."

"Yes, I suppose," Eloise said slowly.

"You suppose?" Sophie snorted with impatience. "Don't play coy with me, Eloise Bridgerton. I was once your lady's maid, and I know you better than anyone ought."

Eloise forbore to point out that Sophie had been her lady's maid for all of two weeks before she and Benedict had come to their senses and decided to marry. "Very well," she allowed, "he's quite handsome, if you like the rough, rural sort."

"Which you do," Sophie said pertly.

To her complete mortification, Eloise felt herself blush. "Perhaps," she muttered.

"And," Sophie said approvingly, "he brought flowers."

"He's a botanist," Eloise said.

"That doesn't make the gesture any less sweet."

"No, just easier."

"Eloise," Sophie said disapprovingly, "stop this right now."

"Stop what?"

"Trying to cut the poor man down before he even has a chance."

"That's not what I was doing at all," Eloise protested, but she knew she was lying the moment the words left her lips. She hated that her family was trying to run her life, no matter how well intentioned they were, and it had left her feeling sullen and uncooperative.

"Well, I think the flowers are very sweet," Sophie declared firmly. "I don't care if he had eight thousand different varieties available to him. He still thought to bring them."

Eloise nodded, hating herself. She wanted to feel better, wanted to be all smiles and cheer and optimism, but she just couldn't manage it.

"Benedict didn't give me all the details," Sophie continued, ignoring Eloise's distress. "You know how men are. They never tell you what you want to know."

"What do you want to know?"

Sophie looked over at Sir Phillip, gauging how long she'd have before he reached their side. "Well, for one thing, is it true you'd not met him before you ran off?"

"Not face-to-face, no," Eloise admitted. It all sounded so stupid when she recounted the tale. Who would have thought that she, a Bridgerton, would run away to a man she'd never met?

"Well," Sophie said, her voice matter-of-fact, "if it all works out in the end, what a romantic tale it will be."

Eloise swallowed uncomfortably. It was still too soon to know if it would "all work out in the end." She rather suspected—no, in truth she was quite certain—that she'd find herself married to Sir Phillip, but who knew what sort of marriage it would be? She didn't love him, not yet, anyway, and he didn't love her, and she'd thought that would be all right, but now that she was here in Wiltshire, trying not to notice how Benedict looked at Sophie, she was wondering if she'd made a terrible mistake.

And did she really want to wed a man who was looking primarily for a mother for his children?

If one didn't have love, was it better, then, to be alone?

Unfortunately, the only way to answer these questions was to marry Sir Phillip and see how it went. And if it didn't go well . . .

She'd be stuck.

The easiest way out of marriage was death, and frankly, that wasn't something Eloise cared to contemplate.

"Miss Bridgerton."

Phillip was standing in front of her, holding out a bouquet of white orchids. "I brought these for you."

She smiled at him, heartened by the slightly nervous, giddy feeling that arose within her at his appearance. "Thank you," she murmured, taking them and smelling the blooms. "They're lovely."

"Wherever did you find orchids?" Sophie asked. "They're exquisite."

"I grew them," he answered. "I keep a greenhouse."

"Yes, of course," Sophie said. "Eloise mentioned that you are a botanist. I do like to garden myself, although I must say that most of the time I haven't the least idea what I'm doing. Our caretakers here consider me the bane of their existence, I'm sure."

Eloise cleared her throat, aware that she had not yet made introductions. "Sir Phillip," she said, motioning to her sister-in-law, "this is Benedict's wife Sophie."

He bowed over her hand, murmuring, "Mrs. Bridgerton."

"I'm very pleased to meet you," Sophie said in her most friendly manner. "And please, do use my Christian name. I'm told you already do so with Eloise, and furthermore, it sounds as if you are practically a member of the family already."

Eloise flushed.

"Oh!" Sophie exclaimed, instantly embarrassed. "I did not mean that in relation to you, Eloise. I would never assume— Oh, dear. What I meant to say was that I meant it because the men . . ." Her cheeks turned a deep red as she looked down at her hands. "Well," she mumbled, "I'd heard there was a great deal of wine."

Phillip cleared his throat. "A detail I'd prefer not to remember."

"The fact that you remember at all is remarkable," Eloise said sweetly.

He looked over at her, his expression clearly indicating that he had not been taken in by her sugary tone. "You're too kind."

"Does your head ache?" she asked.

He winced. "Like the devil."

She should have been concerned. She should have been kind, especially since he'd gone to the trouble of bringing her rare orchids. But she couldn't help feeling it was no more than he deserved, so she said (quietly, but still said it), "Good."

"Eloise!" Sophie said disapprovingly.

"How is Benedict feeling?" Eloise asked her sweetly.

Sophie sighed. "He's been a bear all morning, and Gregory hasn't even risen from bed."

"I seemed to have fared well by comparison, then," Phillip said.

"Except for Colin," Eloise told him. "He never feels the aftereffects of alcohol. And of course Anthony drank little last night."

"Lucky man."

"Would you care for something to drink, Sir Phillip?" Sophie asked, adjusting her bonnet so that it better shaded her eyes. "Of the benign, nonintoxicating variety, of course, given the circumstances. I would be happy to have someone bring you a glass of lemonade."

"That would be most appreciated. Thank you." He watched as she rose and walked up the slight incline to the house, then sat in her place across from Eloise.

"It is good to see you this morning," he said, clearing his throat. He was never the most talkative of men, and he was clearly making no exceptions this morning, despite the rather extraordinary circumstances that had led to this moment.

"And you," she murmured.

He shifted in his seat. It was too small for him;

most chairs were. "I must apologize for my behavior last night," he said stiffly.

She looked over at him, staring into his dark eyes for just a moment before her gaze slid down to a patch of grass beside him. He seemed sincere; he probably was. She didn't know him well—certainly not well enough to marry, although it seemed that point was now moot—but he didn't seem the sort to make false apologies. Still, she wasn't quite ready to fall all over him with gratitude, so when she answered, she did so in a sparing fashion. "I have brothers," she said. "I am used to it."

"Perhaps, but I am not. I assure you I do not make a habit of overimbibing."

She nodded, accepting his apology.

"I have been thinking," he said.

"As have I."

He cleared his throat, then tugged at his cravat, as if it had suddenly grown too tight. "We will, of course, have to marry."

It was nothing more than she knew, but there was something awful in the way he said it. Maybe it was the lack of emotion in his voice, as if she were a problem he had to solve. Or maybe it was the way he said it so matter-of-factly, as if she had no choice (which, in truth, she did not, but she didn't care to be reminded of that).

Whatever it was, it made her feel strange, and itchy, as if she needed to jump out of her skin.

She had spent her adult life making her own choices, had considered herself the luckiest of females because her family had allowed her to do so. Maybe that was why it now felt so unbearable to be forced onto a path before she was ready.

Or maybe it was unbearable because she was the one who had set this entire farce into motion. She was furious with herself, and it was making her snippy with everyone.

"I'll do my best to make you happy," he said gruffly. "And the children need a mother."

She smiled weakly. She'd wanted her marriage to be about more than just children.

"I'm sure you'll be a great help," he said.

"A great help," she echoed, hating the way it sounded.

"Wouldn't you agree?"

She nodded, mostly because she was afraid that if she opened her mouth, she might scream.

"Good," he said. "Then it's all settled."

It's all settled. For the rest of her life, that would be her grand proposal of marriage. *It's all settled.* And the worst part of it was—she had no right to complain. She was the one who'd run off without giving Phillip enough time to arrange for a chaperone. She was the one who'd been so eager to make her own destiny. She was the one who'd acted without thinking, and now all she had to show for it was—

It's all settled.

She swallowed. "Wonderful."

He looked at her, blinking in confusion. "Aren't you happy?"

"Of course," she said hollowly.

"You don't sound happy."

"I'm happy," she snapped.

Phillip muttered something under his breath.

"What did you say?" she asked.

"Nothing."

"You said something."

He gave her an impatient look. "If I'd meant for you to hear it, I would have said it out loud."

She sucked in her breath. "Then you shouldn't have said it at all."

"Some things," Phillip muttered, "are impossible to keep inside."

"What did you *say*?" she demanded.

Phillip raked his hand through his hair. "Eloise—"

"Did you insult me?"

"Do you really want to know?"

"Since it appears we are to be wed," she bit off, "yes."

"I don't recall my exact words," Phillip shot back, "but I believe I may have uttered the words *women* and *lack of sense* in the same breath."

He shouldn't have said it. He *knew* he shouldn't have said it; it would have been rude under any circumstances, and it was especially wrong right now. But she had pushed and pushed and pushed and wouldn't back down. It was like she'd sliced a needle under his skin, and then decided to jab just for the fun of it.

And besides, why was she in such a terrible mood, anyway? All he'd done was state the facts. They *would* have to marry, and frankly, she should have been glad that if she'd been compromised, at least it had been with a man who was willing to do the right thing and wed her.

He didn't expect gratitude. Hell, this was as much his fault as it was hers; he was the one who'd issued the initial invitation, after all. But was it too much to expect a smile and a pleasant mood?

"I'm glad we had this conversation," Eloise said quite suddenly. "This has been good."

He looked up, instantly suspicious. "I beg your pardon."

"Very beneficial," she said. "One should always understand one's spouse before one marries, and—"

He groaned. This was not going to end well.

"And," she added sharply, glaring at his groan, "it is certainly provident that I now know how you feel about my gender."

He was the sort who usually walked away from conflict, but really, this was too much. "If I recall correctly," he shot back, "I never did tell you exactly what I thought of women."

"I inferred it," she retorted. "The phrase 'lack of sense' pointed me in the correct direction."

"Did it?" he drawled. "Well, I'm thinking differently now."

Her eyes narrowed. "What do you mean?"

"I mean that I've changed my mind. I've decided I don't have difficulties with women in general, after all. It's *you* I find insufferable."

She drew back, clearly affronted.

"Has no one called you insufferable before?" He found that difficult to believe.

"No one who wasn't related to me," she grumbled.

"You must live in a very polite society." He squirmed in his seat again; really, did no one make chairs for large men anymore? "Either that," he muttered, "or you've simply terrified everyone into bending to your every whim."

She flushed, and he couldn't tell if it was because she was embarrassed by his spot-on assessment of her personality or just because she was angry beyond words.

Probably both.

"I'm sorry," she muttered.

He turned to her in surprise. "I beg your pardon?" He couldn't have heard correctly.

"I said I'm sorry," she repeated, making it clear that she was not going to say the words a third time, so he'd better be listening well.

"Oh," he said, too stunned to say much of anything else. "Thank you."

"You're welcome." Her tone was less than gracious, but she seemed to be trying hard, nonetheless.

For a moment he said nothing. Then he had to ask. "What for?"

She looked up, obviously irritated that that hadn't been the end of it. "Did you have to ask?" she grumbled.

"Well, yes."

"I am sorry," she ground out, "because I am in a horrid mood and have been behaving badly. And if you ask *how* I have been behaving badly, I swear I will get up and walk away and you will never see me again, because I assure you, this apology is difficult enough without my having to explain it further."

Phillip decided he couldn't possibly hope for more. "Thank you," he said softly. He held his tongue for a minute, quite possibly the longest minute of his life, then he decided he might as well just go ahead and say it.

"If it makes you feel any better," he told her, "I had decided we would suit before your brothers arrived. I was already planning to ask you to be my wife. Properly, with a ring and whatever else it is I'm supposed to do. I don't know. It's been a long while since I've proposed marriage to anyone, and last time wasn't under normal circumstances in any case."

She looked up at him, surprise in her eyes . . . and perhaps a little bit of gratitude as well.

"I'm sorry that your brothers came along and made it all happen faster than you are ready for," he added, "but I'm not sorry that it's happening."

"You're not?" she whispered. "Really?"

"I'll give you as long as you need," he said, "within reason, of course. But I cannot—" He glanced up the hill; Anthony and Colin were ambling down toward them, followed by a footman carrying a tray of food. "I cannot speak for your brothers. I daresay they won't care to wait as long you might prefer. And quite frankly, if you were my sister, I'd have marched you to a church last night."

She looked up the hill at her brothers; they were still at least a half a minute away. She opened her mouth, then closed it in obvious thought. Finally, after several seconds, during which he could practically see the wheels of her mind churning and turning, she blurted out, "Why did you decide we would suit?"

"I beg your pardon?" It was a stalling tactic, of course. He hadn't expected such a direct question.

Although heaven knew why not. This was Eloise, after all.

"Why did you decide we would suit?" she repeated, her voice pointed and undeniable.

But of course that would be how she would ask it. There was nothing subtle or deniable about Eloise Bridgerton. She would never skirt around an issue when she could just walk right in and stick her nose directly into the heart of the matter.

"I . . . ah . . ." He coughed, cleared his throat.

"You don't know," she stated, sounding disappointed.

"Of course I know," he protested. No man liked to be told he didn't know his own mind.

"No, you don't. If you did, you wouldn't be sitting there choking on air."

"Good God, woman, do you have a charitable bone in your body? A man needs time to formulate an answer."

"Ah," came Colin Bridgerton's ever-genial voice. "Here's the happy couple."

Phillip had never been so glad to see another human being in all his life. "Good morning," he said to the two Bridgerton men, inordinately pleased to have escaped Eloise's interrogation.

"Hungry?" Colin inquired as he sat in the chair next to Phillip. "I took the liberty of having the kitchen prepare breakfast alfresco."

Phillip looked over at the footman and wondered if he ought to offer to help. The poor man looked nearly ready to collapse under the weight of the food.

"How are you this morning?" Anthony asked as he sat down on the cushioned bench next to Eloise.

"Fine," she replied.

"Hungry?"

"No."

"Cheerful?"

"Not for you."

Anthony turned to Phillip. "She's usually more conversational."

Phillip wondered if Eloise would hit him. It wouldn't be more than he deserved.

The tray of food came down on the table with a loud clatter, followed by the footman's abject apology for being so clumsy, followed by Anthony's assurance that it was no trouble at all, that Hercules himself could not carry enough food to suit Colin.

The two Bridgerton brothers served themselves, then Anthony turned to Eloise and Phillip and said, "The two of you certainly seem well suited this morning."

Eloise looked at him with open hostility. "When did you reach that conclusion?"

"It only took a moment," he said with a shrug. He looked at Phillip. "It was the bickering, actually. All the best couples do it."

"I'm glad to hear it," Phillip murmured.

"My wife and I often have similar conversations before she comes around to my way of thinking," Anthony said affably.

Eloise shot him a peevish expression.

"Of course, my wife might offer a different interpretation," he added with a shrug. "I *allow* her to think that I'm coming 'round to her way of thinking." He turned back to Phillip and smiled. "It's easier that way."

Phillip stole a glance at Eloise. She appeared to be working very hard to hold her tongue.

"When did you arrive?" Anthony asked him.

"Just a few minutes ago," he replied.

"Yes," Eloise said. "He proposed marriage, I'm sure you'll be happy to hear."

Phillip coughed with surprise at her sudden announcement. "I beg your pardon?"

Eloise turned to Anthony. "He said, 'We'll have to marry.'"

"Well, he's right," Anthony replied, settling a level stare directly on her face. "You do have to marry. And my compliments to him for not beating around the bush about it. I'd think you of all people would appreciate direct conversation."

"Scone, anyone?" Colin asked. "No? More for me, then."

Anthony turned to Phillip and said, "She's just a bit irritated because she hates being ordered about. She'll be fine in a few days."

"I'm fine right now," Eloise ground out.

"Yes," Anthony murmured, "you look fine."

"Don't you have somewhere to *be*?" Eloise asked. Through her teeth.

"An interesting question," her brother replied. "One might say that I ought to *be* in London, with my wife and children. In fact, if I did have somewhere else to *be*, I imagine that would be it. But strangely enough, I seem to be here. In Wiltshire. Where, when I woke in my comfortable bed *in London* three days ago, I would never have guessed I would be." He smiled blandly. "Any other questions?"

She was quiet at that.

Anthony handed an envelope to Eloise. "This arrived for you."

She looked down, and Phillip could see that she instantly recognized the handwriting.

"It's from Mother," Anthony said, even though it was clear she already knew that.

"Do you want to read it?" Phillip asked.

She shook her head. "Not now."

Which meant, he realized, not in front of her brothers.

And then suddenly he knew what he had to do.

"Lord Bridgerton," he said to Anthony, standing up, "might I request a moment alone with your sister?"

"You just had a moment alone with her," Colin said between bites of bacon.

Phillip ignored him. "My lord?"

"Of course," Anthony said, "if she's agreeable."

Phillip grabbed Eloise's hand and yanked her to her feet. "She's agreeable," he said.

"Mmmm," Colin remarked. "She looks very agreeable."

Phillip decided then and there that *all* the Bridgertons ought to be fitted with muzzles. "Come with me," he said to Eloise, before she had a chance to argue.

Which of course she would, since she was Eloise, and she would never smile politely and follow when an argument was a possibility.

"Where are we going?" she gasped, once he had pulled her away from her family and was striding across the lawn, unmindful of how she had to run to keep up.

"I don't know."

"You don't *know*?"

He stopped so quickly that she crashed into him. It was rather nice, actually. He could feel every last bit of her, from her breasts to her thighs, although she recovered all too quickly and stepped away before he could savor the moment.

"I've never been here before," he said, explaining it to her as if she were a small child. "I'd have to be a bloody clairvoyant to know where I'm going."

"Oh," she said. "Well then, lead the way."

He pulled her back to the house, making his way to a side door. "Where does this go?" he asked.

"Inside," she replied.

He gave her a sarcastic look.

"Through Sophie's writing room to the hall," Eloise expounded.

"Is Sophie in her writing room?"

"I doubt it. Didn't she go to fetch you lemonade?"

"Good." He pulled the door open, muttering a quick thanks that it was unlocked, and poked his head inside. The room was empty, but the door to the hall was open, so he strode across and pulled it shut. When he turned back around, Eloise was still standing in the open doorway to the outside, watching him with a blend of curiosity and amusement.

"Shut the door," he ordered.

Her brows rose. "I beg your pardon?"

"Shut it." It wasn't a tone of voice he used often, but after a year of floating along, of feeling lost amid the currents of his life, he was finally taking control.

And he knew exactly what he wanted.

"Shut the door, Eloise," he said in a low voice, moving slowly across the room toward her.

Her eyes widened. "Phillip?" she whispered. "I—"

"Don't talk," he said. "Just shut the door."

But she was frozen in place, staring at him as if she didn't know him. Which, in truth, she didn't. Hell, he wasn't so sure he knew himself any longer.

"Phillip, you—"

He reached behind her and shut the door for her, turning the lock with a loud and ominous click.

"What are you doing?" she asked.

"You were worried," he said, "that we might not suit."

Her lips parted.

He stepped forward. "I think it's time I showed you that we do."

Chapter 12

...and how did you know that you and Simon were well-suited for marriage? For I vow I have not met a man about which I might say the same, and this after three long seasons on the Marriage Mart.

—*from Eloise Bridgerton to her sister the Duchess of Hastings, upon refusing her third proposal of marriage*

Eloise had time to breathe—barely—before his mouth came down on hers. And it was a good thing she did, because it didn't feel as if he had any plans to release her until, oh, the next millennium.

But then, abruptly, he drew back, his large hands cradling her face. And he looked at her.

Just looked at her.

"What?" she asked, uncomfortable with his scrutiny. She knew she was considered to be attractive, but she was no legendary beauty, and he was examining her as if he wanted to catalogue her every feature.

"I wanted to see you," he whispered. He touched her cheek, then smoothed his thumb down the line of her jaw. "You're always in motion. I don't get to just *see* you."

Her legs turned wobbly, and her lips parted, but she couldn't seem to make them work, couldn't seem to do anything other than stare up into his dark eyes.

"You're so beautiful," he murmured. "Do you know what I thought when I saw you the first time?"

She shook her head, desperate for his words.

"I thought I could drown in your eyes. I thought"— he moved in closer, his words now as much breath as sound—"I could drown in *you*."

She felt herself swaying toward him.

He touched her lips, tickling the tender skin with his forefinger. The motion sent ripples of pleasure throughout her, right down to the center of her being, to places forbidden even to her.

And she realized that she had never really understood the power of desire until that very moment. Never really understood what it was at all.

"Kiss me," she whispered.

He smiled. "You always order me about."

"Kiss me."

"Are you sure?" he murmured, his mouth curved into a teasing smile. "Because once I do, I might not be able to—"

She grabbed the back of his head and yanked him down.

He chuckled against her lips, his arms tightening around her with uncompromising strength. She opened her mouth, welcoming his invasion, moaning with pleasure as his tongue swept in, exploring her warmth. He nibbled and licked, slowly stirring a fire within her, all the while pressing her closer and closer against him until his heat poured through her clothing, wrapping her in a haze of desire.

His hands stole around her back, then down to her derriere, squeezing and kneading, then tilting her up until—

She gasped. She was twenty-eight years old, old enough to have heard indiscreet whispers. She knew what his hardness meant. She'd just never expected it to feel quite so hot, so insistent.

She jerked back, the motion more instinct than anything else, but he wouldn't let her go, pulled her closer and groaned, rubbing her against him. "I want to be inside you," he groaned in her ear.

Her legs completely gave out.

It didn't matter, of course; he just held her even tighter, then sank her onto the sofa, coming down atop her until the full length of him pressed her into the soft, cream-colored cushions. He was heavy, but his weight was thrilling, and she could do nothing but loll her head back as his lips left hers to travel down the column of her throat.

"Phillip," she moaned, and then again, as if his name were the only word left to her.

"Yes," he grunted, "yes." His words seemed torn from his throat, and she had no idea what he was talking about, only that whatever he was saying yes to, she wanted it, too. She wanted everything. Anything he wanted, anything possible.

She wanted everything that was possible and everything impossible, too. There was no more reason, only sensation. Only need and desire and this overwhelming sense of *now*.

This wasn't about yesterday and it wasn't about tomorrow. This was now, and she wanted it all.

She felt his hand on her ankle, rough and callused as it moved up her leg until it reached the edge of her stocking. He didn't pause, did nothing to implicitly ask her permission, but she gave it anyway, urging her legs apart until he settled more firmly between them, giving him more room to caress, more space to tickle her skin.

He moved up and up and up, pausing every now and then to squeeze, and she thought she might die from the waiting. She was on fire, burning for him, feeling strange and wet and so completely unlike herself she thought she might dissolve into a pool of nothingness.

Or evaporate completely. Or maybe even explode.

And then, just when she was quite convinced that nothing could be stranger, nothing could wind her even tighter than she was, he touched her.

Touched her.

Touched her where no one had ever touched her, where she didn't dare touch herself. Touched her so intimately, so tenderly that she had to bite her lip to keep from screaming his name.

And as his finger slid inside, she knew that in that moment she no longer belonged to herself.

She was his.

Sometime later, much later, she'd be herself again, back in control, with all her powers and faculties, but for now she was his. In this moment, for this second, she lived for him, for all he could make her feel, for every last whisper of pleasure, each moan of desire.

"Oh, Phillip," she gasped, his name a plea, a promise, a question. It was whatever she needed to say to make sure he didn't stop. She had no idea where this was all heading, whether she'd even be the same person when it was done, but it had to go *some*where. She couldn't possibly continue in this state forever. She was wound so tight, so tense that she'd surely shatter.

She was near the end. She had to be.

She needed something. She needed release, and she knew that only he could give it to her.

She arched to him, pressed up with a power she would never have imagined she possessed, actually lifting them both off the sofa with her need. Her hands found his shoulders, biting into his muscles, then moved down to the small of his back in an effort to pull him even closer against her.

"Eloise," he groaned, sliding his other hand up her skirt until it found her backside. "Do you have any idea—"

And then she had no idea what he did—he probably didn't know, either—but her entire body went impossibly tense. She couldn't speak, couldn't even breathe as her mouth opened into a silent scream of surprise and delight and a hundred other things all rolled into one. And then, just when she thought she couldn't possibly survive even a second longer, she shuddered and collapsed beneath him, panting with exhaustion, so limp and spent she couldn't have moved even her littlest finger.

"Oh, my God," she finally said, the blasphemy the

only words coursing through her mind. "Oh, my God."

His hands tightened on her backside.

"Oh, my God."

His hand moved, came up to stroke her hair. He was gentle, achingly gentle, even though his body was rigid and tense.

Eloise just lay there, wondering if she'd ever be able to move again, breathing against him as she felt his breath on her temple. Eventually he shifted and moved, mumbling something about being too heavy for her, and then there was nothing but air, and when she looked to the side, he was kneeling next to the sofa, smoothing her skirts back down.

It seemed a rather tender and gentlemanly gesture, given her recent wantonness.

She looked into his face, knowing she must have the silliest smile on hers. "Oh, Phillip," she sighed.

"Is there a washroom?" he asked hoarsely.

She blinked, noticing for the first time that he looked rather strained. "A washroom?" she echoed.

He nodded stiffly.

She pointed to the door leading to the hall. "Out and to the right," she said. It was hard to believe he needed to relieve himself right after such a thrilling encounter, but who was she to attempt to understand the workings of the male body?

He walked to the door, put his hand on the knob, then turned around. "Do you believe me now?" he asked, one of his brows rising into an impossibly arrogant arch.

Her lips parted in confusion. "About what?"

He smiled. Slowly. And all he said was, "We'll suit."

*   *   *

Phillip had no idea how long it would take Eloise to regain her composure and restore her appearance. She'd looked quite delectably disheveled when he'd left her on the sofa in Sophie Bridgerton's little office. He never could understand the intricacies of a woman's toilette, and was quite certain he never would, but he was fairly sure she was going to need to redress her hair at the very least.

As for him, he required less than a minute in the washroom to find his release; he was wound that tight from his encounter with Eloise.

Dear God, she was magnificent.

It had been so long since he'd been with a woman. He'd known that when he finally found one he wanted to bed that his body would react strongly. He'd had more years than he'd cared to count with only his hand to satisfy his needs; a female body seemed like pure bliss.

And heaven knew he had imagined one often enough.

But this had been different, not at all what he'd pictured in his mind. He'd been mad for her. For *her*. For the sounds that escaped her throat, for the scent of her skin, for the way his body seemed to fit perfectly in the crook of hers. Even though he'd had to finish off himself, he'd still felt more, and more intensely, than he'd ever thought possible.

He'd thought almost any female body would do, but it was now quite clear to him that there was a reason he'd never availed himself of the services of the whores and barmaids who'd expressed their willingness. There was a reason he'd never found himself a discreet widow.

He'd needed more.

He'd needed Eloise.

He wanted to sink himself into her and never come out.

He wanted to own her, to possess her, and then to lay back and let her torture him until he screamed.

He'd had fantasies before. Hell, every man did. But now his fantasy had a face, and he feared he was going to find himself walking around with a constant erection if he didn't learn how to control his thoughts.

He needed a wedding. Fast.

He groaned, giving his hands a quick wash in the basin. She didn't know she'd left him in such a state. She didn't even realize. She'd just looked at him with that blissful smile, too caught in her own passion to notice that he was ready to explode.

He pushed open the door, his feet moving quickly along the marble floor as he made his way back to the lawn. He'd have plenty of time to explode soon enough. And when he did, she'd be right there along with him.

The thought brought a smile to his lips, and very nearly sent him back into the washroom.

"Ah, there he is," Benedict Bridgerton said as Phillip walked toward him across the lawn. Phillip saw the gun in his hand and stopped in his tracks, wondering if he ought to be worried. Benedict couldn't possibly know what had just happened in his wife's office, could he?

Phillip swallowed, thinking hard. No, there was no way. And besides, Benedict was smiling.

Of course, he could be the sort who would enjoy

picking off the spoiler of his sister's innocence . . .

"Er, good morning," Phillip said, glancing at everyone else in an attempt to gauge the situation.

Benedict nodded his greeting, then said, "Do you
shoot?"

"Of course," Phillip replied.

"Good." He jerked his head toward a target. "Join
us."

Phillip noted with relief that the target seemed to
be firmly in place, indicating that *he* would not have
to play that role. "I didn't bring a pistol," he said.

"Of course not," Benedict replied. "Why would
you? We're all friends here." His brows rose. "Aren't
we?"

"One would hope."

Benedict's lips curved, but it wasn't the sort of
smile that inspired confidence in one's well-being.
"Don't worry about the pistol," he said. "We'll provide one."

Phillip nodded. If this was to be how he was to
prove his manhood to Eloise's brothers, so be it. He
could shoot as well as the best of them. It had been
one of those manly pursuits his father had been so
insistent he learn. He'd spent countless hours outside Romney Hall, his arm outstretched until his
muscles burned, holding his breath as he aimed for
whatever it was his father was out to destroy. Every
shot was accompanied by a fervent prayer that his
aim would be true.

If he hit the target, his father wouldn't hit him. It
was as simple—and desperate—as that.

He walked over to a table with several pistols on
it, murmuring his hellos to Anthony, Colin, and Greg-

ory. Sophie was sitting about ten or so yards away, her nose in a book.

"Let's get on with this," Anthony said, "before Eloise returns." He looked over at Phillip. "Where *is* Eloise?"

"She went off to read the letter from your mother," Phillip lied.

"I see. Well, that won't take long," Anthony said with a frown. "We'd better hurry, then."

"Maybe she'll want to reply," Colin said, picking up a gun and examining it. "That'll buy us a few extra minutes. You know Eloise. She's always writing someone a letter."

"Indeed," Anthony replied. "Got us into this mess, didn't it?"

Phillip just looked at him with an inscrutable smile. He was far too pleased with himself this morning to rise to any bait Anthony Bridgerton cared to offer.

Gregory chose a gun. "Even if she replies, she'll be back soon. She's fiendishly fast."

"At writing?" Phillip queried.

"At everything," Gregory said grimly. "Let's shoot."

"Why are you all so eager to get started without Eloise?" Phillip asked.

"Er, no reason," Benedict said, at precisely the same moment Anthony mumbled, "Who said anything about that?"

They all had, of course, but Phillip didn't remind them of it.

"Age before beauty, old chap," Colin said, slapping Anthony on the back.

"You're too kind," Anthony murmured, stepping

up to a chalk line someone had drawn in the grass. He lifted his arm, took aim, and fired.

"Well done," Phillip said, once the footman had brought forth the bull's-eye. Anthony had not hit dead center, but he was only an inch off.

"Thank you." He set his pistol down. "How old are you?"

Phillip blinked at the unexpected question, then replied, "Thirty."

Anthony jerked his head toward Colin. "You're after Colin, then. We always do these things by age. It's the only way to keep track."

"By all means," Phillip said, watching as Benedict and Colin took their turns. They were both good shots, neither dead center, but certainly close enough to kill a man, had that been their goal.

Which, thankfully, it didn't seem to be, at least not that morning.

Phillip selected a pistol, tested its weight in his hand, then stepped up to the chalk line. It had only been recently that he'd stopped thinking of his father every time he took aim at a target. It had taken years, but he'd finally allowed himself to realize that he actually liked shooting, that it didn't have to be a chore. And then suddenly his father's voice, so often at the back of his mind, always yelling, always criticizing, was gone.

He lifted his arm, his muscles rock steady, and fired.

He squinted toward the target. It looked good. The footman brought it forward. One-half inch, at most, off the center. Closer than anyone else thus far.

The target went back, and Gregory took his turn, proving himself to be Phillip's equal.

"We do five rounds," Anthony told Phillip. "Best out, and if there's a tie, the leaders face off."

"I see," Phillip said. "Any particular reason?"

"No," Anthony said, picking up his gun. "Just that we've always done it this way."

Colin looked at Phillip with deadly serious eyes. "We take our games seriously."

"I'm gathering."

"Do you fence?"

"Not well," Phillip said.

One corner of Colin's mouth turned up. "Excellent."

"Be quiet," Anthony barked, looking testily over at them. "I'm trying to aim."

"Such need for silence will not serve you well at a time of crisis," Colin remarked.

"Shut up," Anthony bit off.

"If we were attacked," Colin continued, one of his hands moving expressively as he wove his tale, "it would be quite noisy, and frankly, I find it disturbing to think—"

"Colin!" Anthony bellowed.

"Don't mind me," Colin said.

"I'm going to kill him," Anthony announced. "Does anyone mind if I kill him?"

No one did, although Sophie did look up and mention something about blood and messes and not wanting to have to clean up.

"It's an excellent fertilizer," Phillip said helpfully, since, after all, that was his area of expertise.

"Ah." Sophie nodded and turned back to her book. "Kill him, then."

"How's that book, darling?" Benedict called out to her.

"It's quite good, actually."

"Will you all *shut up*?" Anthony ground out. Then, his cheeks coloring slightly, he turned to his sister-in-law and mumbled, "Not you, of course, Sophie."

"Glad to be exempted," she said cheerfully.

"Do try not to threaten my wife," Benedict said mildly.

Anthony turned to his brother and skewered him with a glare. "The lot of you should be drawn and quartered," he grunted.

"Except for Sophie," Colin reminded him.

Anthony turned to him with a deadly expression. "You do realize this gun is loaded, don't you?"

"Lucky for me fratricide is considered quite beyond the pale."

Anthony clamped his mouth shut and turned back toward the target. "Round two," he called out, taking aim.

"*Waaaaaaait!*"

All four Bridgerton men sagged and turned around, groaning as they saw Eloise careening down the hill.

"Are you shooting?" she demanded, stumbling to a halt.

No one answered. No one really needed to. It was quite obvious.

"Without me?"

"We're not shooting," Gregory said. "Just standing about with guns."

"Near a target," Colin added helpfully.

"You're shooting."

"Of course we're shooting," Anthony snapped. He flicked his head off to the right. "Sophie is by herself. You should keep her company."

Eloise planted her hands on her hips. "Sophie is reading a book."

"A good one, too," Sophie put in, returning her attention to the pages.

"You should read a book, too, Eloise," Benedict suggested. "They're very improving."

"I don't need any improving," she shot back. "Give me a gun."

"I'm not giving you a gun," Benedict retorted. "We don't have enough to go around."

"We can share," Eloise ground out. "Have you ever tried sharing? It's very improving."

Benedict scowled at her in a manner that wasn't particularly fitting for a man of his years.

"I think," Colin said, "that what Benedict was trying to say is that he's as improved as he's ever going to be."

"For certain," Sophie said, not even raising her eyes from her book.

"Here," Phillip said magnanimously, handing his gun to Eloise, "have mine." The four Bridgerton men groaned, but he decided he rather enjoyed annoying them.

"Thank you," Eloise said graciously. "From Anthony's bark of 'Round two' I deduce that you've each taken one shot?"

"Indeed," Phillip replied. He looked over at her brothers, all of whom wore dejected expressions. "What's wrong?"

Anthony just shook his head.

Phillip looked to Benedict.

"She's a freak of nature," Benedict muttered.

Phillip looked back at Eloise with renewed interest. She didn't look particularly freakish to him.

"I'm dropping out," Gregory muttered. "I haven't eaten breakfast yet."

"You'll have to ring for more," Colin told him. "I already finished it all."

Gregory let out an annoyed sigh. "It's a wonder I haven't starved," he grumbled, "younger brother that I am."

Colin shrugged. "You've got to be quick if you want to eat."

Anthony looked at the two of them with disgust. "Did the two of you grow up in an orphanage?" he asked.

Phillip bit his lip to contain his smile.

"Are we going to shoot?" Eloise demanded.

"*You* certainly are," Gregory said, slumping against a tree. "I'm leaving to eat."

He stayed, though, watching his sister with a bored expression as she lifted her arm and, without even appearing to aim, fired.

Phillip blinked in surprise as the footman brought forth the target.

Dead center.

"Where did you learn to do that?" he asked, trying not to gape.

She shrugged. "I couldn't tell you. I've always been able to do it."

"Freak of nature," Colin muttered. "Clearly."

"I think it's splendid," Phillip said.

Eloise looked at him with glowing eyes. "Do you really?"

"Of course. Should I ever need to defend my home, I shall know who to send out to the front line."

She beamed. "Where's the next target?"

Gregory threw his arms up in disgust. "I forfeit. I'm getting something to eat."

"Get something for me, too," Colin called out.

"Of course," Gregory muttered.

Eloise turned to Anthony. "Is it your turn now?"

He took the gun from her hands and set it on the table to be reloaded. "As if it matters."

"We have to do all five rounds," she said officiously. "You were the one who made the rules."

"I know," he said glumly. He lifted his arm and fired off a shot, but his heart clearly was not into it, and he was off by five inches.

"You're not even trying!" Eloise accused.

Anthony just turned to Benedict and said, "I hate shooting with her."

"Your turn," Eloise said to Benedict.

He took his turn, as did Colin, both men putting in a bit more effort than Anthony had, but still coming up off the mark.

Phillip stepped up to the chalk line, pausing only to listen as Eloise said, "Don't you decide to give up."

"I wouldn't dream of it," he murmured.

"Good. It's no fun to play with *bad sports*." She directed the last two words quite vehemently toward her brothers.

"That's the point," Benedict said.

"They do this every time," Eloise said to Phillip. "They shoot badly until I decide the match isn't worth it, and *then* they all have fun."

"Be quiet," Phillip told her, lips twitching. "I'm aiming."

"Oh." She shut her mouth with alacrity, watching with interest as he focused on the target.

Phillip took his shot, allowing himself a slow, satisfied smile as the target was brought forward.

"Perfect!" Eloise exclaimed, clapping her hands together. "Oh, Phillip, that was wonderful!"

Anthony muttered something under his breath that he probably ought not to have said in his sister's presence, then added, directing his words to Phillip, "You are going to marry her, aren't you? Because frankly, if you get her off of our hands and allow her to shoot with you so that she doesn't pester us, I'll gladly double her dowry."

Phillip was quite certain at that point that he'd wed her for nothing, but he just grinned and said, "It's a deal."

Chapter 13

...and as I'm sure you can imagine, they were all possessed of a most foul temper. Is it my fault I am so superior? I think not. No more, I suppose, than it is their fault they were born men and thus without the barest hint of common sense or innate good manners.

—from Eloise Bridgerton
to Penelope Featherington,
*after trouncing six men (three not
related to her) in a shooting match*

The following day Eloise traveled to Romney Hall for lunch, along with Anthony, Benedict, and Sophie. Colin and Gregory had declared that the rest of the family had the situation well enough in hand and decided to return to London, Colin back to his new wife, and Gregory back to whatever it was the young unmarried men of the *ton* did to fill their daily lives.

Eloise was happy to see them go; she loved her brothers, but truly, the four of them at once was more than any woman ought to be expected to bear.

She was feeling optimistic as she stepped down from the carriage; the previous day had gone far better than she could ever have hoped. Even if Phillip hadn't taken her into Sophie's office to prove to her that they "would suit" (Eloise could now think of those words only as if they were in quotations), the day would have been a success. Phillip had more than held his own against the collective force of the Bridgerton brothers, which had left her feeling quite pleased and more than a little proud.

Funny how it hadn't occurred to her until then that she could never marry a man who couldn't square off with each and any of her brothers and emerge unscathed.

And in Phillip's case, he'd taken on all four at once. Most impressive.

Eloise still had reservations about the marriage, of course. How could she not? She and Phillip had developed a sense of mutual respect and hopefully even affection, but they were not in love, and Eloise had no way of knowing if they ever would be.

Still, she was convinced that she was doing the right thing by marrying him. She had little choice in the matter, of course; it was either marry Phillip or face complete ruin and a life alone. But even so, she thought he would make a fine husband. He was honest and honorable, and if he was at times too quiet, at least he seemed to have a sense of humor, which Eloise felt was essential for any prospective spouse.

And when he kissed her . . .

Well, it was quite obvious that he knew exactly how to turn her knees to butter.

And the rest of her as well.

Eloise was, of course, a pragmatic. She always had been, and she knew that passion was not enough to sustain a marriage.

But, she thought with a wicked smile, surely it couldn't hurt.

Phillip checked the clock on the mantel for about the fifteenth time in as many minutes. The Bridgertons were due to arrive at half noon, and it was already thirty-five past the hour. Not that five minutes was anything to worry about when one had to travel over country roads, but still, it was deuced hard to keep Oliver and Amanda neat and tidy and, above all, well behaved as they waited with him in the drawing room.

"I hate this jacket," Oliver said, tugging on his little coat.

"It's too small," Amanda told him.

"I *know*," he replied, with clear disdain. "If it weren't too small, I wouldn't have complained."

Phillip rather thought he'd have found something else to complain about, but there seemed little reason to express this opinion.

"And anyway," Oliver continued, "your dress is too small, too. I can see your ankles."

"You're supposed to be able to see my ankles," Amanda said, frowning down at her lower legs.

"Not so much of them."

She looked down again, this time with an expression of alarm.

"You're only eight years old," Phillip said in a

weary voice. "The dress is perfectly suitable." Or at least he hoped it was, little that he knew of such things.

Eloise, he thought, her name echoing through his head like the answer to his prayers. Eloise would know these things. She would know if a child's dress was too short and when a girl should start wearing her hair up and even whether a boy should attend Eton or Harrow.

Eloise would know all these things.

Thank God.

"I think they're late," Oliver announced.

"They're not late," Phillip said automatically.

"I think they *are* late," Oliver said. "I can read the clock now, you know."

Phillip didn't know, which depressed him. It was rather like the swimming thing. Too much like it, really.

Eloise, he reminded himself. Whatever his failings as a father, he was making up for all of that by marrying the perfect mother for them. He was, for the first time since their birth, doing the exact right thing for his children, and the sense of relief was almost overwhelming.

Eloise. She couldn't get here soon enough.

Hell, he couldn't marry her soon enough. How did one procure a special license, anyway? It hadn't been the sort of thing he'd ever thought he'd need to know, but the last thing he wanted to do was wait several weeks to have banns read.

Weren't weddings meant to be held on Saturday mornings? Could they manage it by this Saturday? It was only two days away, but if they could get that special license . . .

Phillip caught Oliver by the collar as he tried to race out the door. "No," he said firmly. "You will wait here for Miss Bridgerton. And you will do so quietly, without incident, and with a smile on your face."

Oliver made at least some attempt to settle down at the mention of Eloise's name, but his "smile" (performed obediently at his father's order) was a ghastly stretch of the lips that left Phillip feeling like he'd just had an audience with an anemic gorgon.

"That wasn't a smile," Amanda immediately said.

"It was, too."

"No. Your lips didn't even curve up. . . ."

Phillip sighed as he attempted to block his ears from the inside out. He'd talk to Anthony Bridgerton about the special license this afternoon. It seemed like the sort of thing the viscount would know about.

Saturday couldn't come soon enough. He could turn the twins over to Eloise during the day, and . . .

He smiled to himself. She could turn herself over to *him* at night.

"Why are you smiling?" Amanda demanded.

"I'm not smiling," Phillip said, feeling himself begin to—dear *God*—blush.

"You *are* smiling," she accused. "And now your cheeks are turning pink."

"Don't be silly," he muttered.

"I'm not silly," she insisted. "Oliver, look at Father. Don't his cheeks look pink?"

"One more word about my cheeks," Phillip threatened, "and I'm going to . . ."

Hell, he'd been about to say *horsewhip,* but they all knew he would never do that.

". . . do something," he finished, in a lame attempt at a threat.

Amazingly, it worked, and they held still and silent for a moment. Then Amanda swung her legs from her perch on the sofa and knocked over a footstool.

Phillip looked at the clock.

"Oops," she said, jumping down and then bending over to right it. "Oliver!" she howled.

Phillip tore his eyes away from the minute hand, which was, inexplicably, not even to the eight. Amanda was sprawled on the floor, glaring at her brother.

"He pushed me," Amanda said.

"Did not."

"Did too."

"Did—"

"Oliver," Phillip cut in. "*Some*one pushed her, and I'm fairly certain it was not I."

Oliver chewed on his lower lip, having forgotten to consider the fact that his culpability would be quite obvious. "Maybe she fell over on her own," he suggested.

Phillip just stared at him, hoping that the ferocious expression would be enough to nip *that* idea in the bud.

"Very well," Oliver admitted. "I pushed her. I'm sorry."

Phillip blinked with surprise. Maybe he was getting better at fatherhood. He couldn't recall the last time he'd heard an unsolicited apology.

"You can push me back," Oliver said to Amanda.

"Oh, no," Phillip said quickly. Bad idea. Very, very bad idea.

"All right," Amanda said brightly.

"No, Amanda," Phillip said, jumping to his feet. "Do not—"

But she'd already pressed both of her little hands to her brother's chest and heaved.

Oliver went tumbling back with a loud burst of laughter. "Now I get to push *you!*" he yelled with glee.

"You will *not* push your sister!" Phillip roared, jumping over an ottoman.

"She pushed me!" Oliver hollered.

"Because you asked her to, you miserable little wretch." Phillip swung his hand out to grab Oliver's sleeve before he slithered away, but the sneaky little bugger was slippery as an eel.

"Push me!" Amanda squealed. "Push me!"

"Do not push her!" Phillip yelled. Visions of his drawing room floated ominously in his brain, the image strewn with broken furniture and overturned lamps.

Good God, and with the Bridgertons due at any moment.

He reached Oliver just as Oliver reached Amanda, and the three of them went tumbling down, taking two cushions off the sofa with them. Phillip thanked the Lord for small favors. At least the cushions were not breakable.

Crash.

"What the devil?"

"I think it was the clock," Oliver gulped.

How on earth they'd managed to topple the clock off the mantel, Phillip would never know. "The two of you are hereby banished to your rooms until you're sixty-eight," he hissed.

"Oliver did it," Amanda said quickly.

"I don't give a—care who did it," Phillip bit off. "You *know* that Miss Bridgerton is expected at any—"

"Ahem."

Phillip turned slowly to the doorway, horrified—but not surprised—to see Anthony Bridgerton standing there, Benedict, Sophie, and Eloise right behind him.

"My lord," Phillip said, his voice too curt. Really, he should have been more gracious—it wasn't the viscount's fault that his children were just one transgression short of being complete monsters—but Phillip just couldn't manage good cheer at the moment.

"Perhaps we're interrupting?" Anthony said mildly.

"Not at all," Phillip replied. "As you can see, we're merely . . . ah . . . rearranging the furniture."

"And doing an excellent job of it," Sophie said brightly.

Phillip shot her a grateful smile. She seemed like the type of woman who always went out of her way to make others feel more comfortable, and at the moment he could have kissed her for it.

He rose, stopping to right the overturned ottoman as he did so, then grabbed both of his children by the arms and hauled them to their feet. Oliver's little cravat was now completely undone, and Amanda's hair clip hung limply near her ear. "May I present my children," he said, with all the dignity he could muster, "Oliver and Amanda Crane."

Oliver and Amanda mumbled their greetings, both looking rather uncomfortable at being paraded before so many adults. Either that, or maybe they were actually shamefaced for their abominable behavior, unlikely as that seemed.

"Very well," Phillip said, once the twins had done their duty. "You can run along now."

They looked at him with woeful expressions.

"What now?"

"Can we stay?" Amanda asked in a small voice.

"No," Phillip answered. He'd invited the Bridgertons over for lunch and a tour of his greenhouse, and he needed the children to disappear back to the nursery if either endeavor was to be successful.

"Please?" Amanda pleaded.

Phillip studiously avoided looking at his guests, aware that they were all witnessing his supreme lack of command over his children. "Nurse Edwards is waiting for you in the hall," he said.

"We don't like Nurse Edwards," Oliver said. Amanda nodded beside him.

"Of course you like Nurse Edwards," Phillip said impatiently. "She's been your nurse for months."

"But we don't *like* her."

Phillip looked over at the Bridgertons. "Excuse me," he said in a clipped voice. "I apologize for the interruption."

"It's no bother," Sophie said quickly, her face taking on a maternal air as she assessed the situation.

Phillip guided the twins to the far corner of the room, then crossed his arms and stared down at them. "Children," he said sternly, "I have asked Miss Bridgerton to be my wife."

Their eyes lit up.

"Good," he grunted. "I see that you agree with me that this is a superior idea."

"Will she—"

"Don't interrupt me," Phillip interrupted, too impatient by now to deal with any of their questions. "I want you to listen to me. I still need to gain approval from her family, and for that I need to entertain them and offer them lunch, and all this without children underfoot." It was almost the truth, at least. The twins didn't need to know that Anthony had practically ordered the wedding and that approval was no longer an issue.

But Amanda's lower lip started wobbling, and even Oliver looked upset. "What now?" Phillip asked wearily.

"Are you ashamed of us?" Amanda asked.

Phillip sighed, feeling utterly sick of himself. Dear God, how had it come to this? "I'm not—"

"May I be of assistance?"

He looked over at Eloise as if she were his savior. He watched in silence as she knelt down near his children, telling them something in a voice so soft that he couldn't understand the words, only the gentle quality of the tone.

The twins said something which was obviously in protest, but Eloise cut them off, gesticulating with her hands as she spoke. Then, to his complete and utter amazement, the twins said their farewells and walked out into the hall. They didn't look especially happy to go, but they did it all the same.

"Thank God I'm marrying you," Phillip said under his breath.

"Indeed," she murmured, brushing past him with a secretive smile as she walked back to her family.

Phillip followed her and immediately apologized to Anthony, Benedict, and Sophie for his children's behavior. "They have been difficult to manage since their mother passed," he explained, trying to put it in the most excusable terms possible.

"There is nothing more difficult than the death of a parent," Anthony said quietly. "Please, do not feel any need to apologize on their behalf."

Phillip nodded his thanks, grateful for the older man's understanding. "Come," he said to the group, "let's go on to lunch."

But as he led them to the dining room, Oliver's and Amanda's faces loomed large in his mind. Their eyes had been sad as they'd walked away.

He'd seen his children obstinate, insufferable, even in full-fledged tantrums, but he'd not seen them sad since their mother had died.

It was very troubling.

After lunch and a tour through the greenhouse, the quintet broke into two groups. Benedict had brought along an artist's pad, so he and Sophie remained near the house, chattering contentedly as he sketched the exterior. Anthony, Eloise, and Phillip decided to take a walk around the grounds, but Anthony very discreetly allowed Eloise and Phillip to tarry a good many yards behind, affording the affianced couple the opportunity to speak with some privacy.

"What did you say to the children?" Phillip immediately asked.

"I don't know," Eloise said quite honestly. "I just tried to act like my mother." She shrugged. "It seemed to work."

He thought about that. "It must be nice to have parents one can emulate."

She looked at him curiously. "Didn't you?"

He shook his head. "No."

She hoped he would say more, gave him time, even, but he did not speak. Finally, she decided to press the matter and asked, "Was it your mother or your father?"

"What do you mean?"

"Which of your parents was so difficult?"

He looked at her for a long moment, his dark eyes inscrutable as his brows ever-so-slightly came together. Then he said, "My mother died at my birth."

She nodded. "I see."

"I doubt you do," he said in a tight, hollow voice, "but I appreciate your trying."

They walked along, keeping their pace slow, not wanting to come within earshot of Anthony, even though neither broke the silence for several minutes. Finally, as they turned along the path toward the back side of the house, Eloise uttered the question she'd been dying to ask all day—

"Why did you take me into Sophie's study yesterday?"

He spluttered and stumbled. "I should think that would be obvious," he mumbled, his cheeks turning pink.

"Well, yes," Eloise said, blushing as she realized exactly what it was she had asked. "But surely you didn't think *that* was going to happen."

"A man can always hope," he muttered.

"You don't mean that!"

"Of course I do. But," he added, looking rather like he couldn't believe he was having this conversation, "as it happens, no, it never crossed my mind that matters would get quite so out of hand." He gave her a sly, sideways sort of look. "I'm not sorry, however, that they did."

She felt her cheeks turn hot. "You still haven't answered my question."

"I haven't?"

"No." She knew she was being persistent to the point of unseemliness, but as matters went, this seemed an important one to press. "Why did you take me in there?"

He stared at her for a full ten seconds, presumably to ascertain if she was daft, then shot a quick look at Anthony to make sure he was out of earshot before answering, "Well, if you must know, yes, I did intend to kiss you. You were yapping on about the marriage and asking me all sorts of ridiculous questions." He planted his hands on his hips and shrugged. "It seemed a good way to prove once and for all that we are well suited."

She decided to let his description of her as a yapping female pass. "But passion is surely not enough to sustain a marriage," she persisted.

"It's certainly a good start," he muttered. "May we talk of something else?"

"No. What I'm trying to say—"

He snorted and rolled his eyes. "You are always trying to say something."

"It's what makes me charming," she said peevishly.

He looked at her with exaggerated patience. "Eloise. We are well suited and will enjoy a perfectly pleasant and amiable marriage. I don't know what else to say or do to prove it."

"But you don't love me," she said, her voice soft.

That seemed to knock the wind out of him, and he just stopped and stared at her for the longest moment. "Why do you say things like that?" he asked.

She shrugged helplessly. "Because it's important."

For a moment he did nothing but stare. "Hasn't it ever occurred to you that every thought and feeling doesn't need to be given voice?"

"*Yes*," she said, a lifetime of regrets wrapped into that single syllable. "All the time." She looked away, discomforted by the odd, hollow sensation rumbling in her throat. "I can't seem to help myself, though."

He shook his head, obviously perplexed, which didn't surprise her. Half the time she perplexed herself. *Why* had she forced the issue? Why couldn't she ever be subtle, coy? Her mother had once told her that she could catch more flies with honey than a sledgehammer, but Eloise never could learn to keep her thoughts to herself.

She had practically asked Sir Phillip if he loved her, and his silence was as much of an answer as *no* would have been. Her heart twisted. She hadn't really thought he would contradict her, but her disappointment was proof that some tiny part of her had been hoping that he'd drop to his knees and cry out that he did love her, that he cherished her, and was in fact quite certain that he would die without her.

Which was all nothing but rot, and she didn't know why she'd even wished for it, when she didn't love him, either.

But she could. She had this feeling that if she gave it enough time, she could love this man. And maybe she'd just wanted him to say the same.

"Did you love Marina?" she asked, the words

crossing her lips before she'd even had a chance to ponder the wisdom of asking. She winced. There she went again, asking questions that were far too personal.

It was a wonder he hadn't thrown up his arms and run screaming in the opposite direction already.

He didn't answer for the longest moment. They just stood there, watching one another, trying to ignore Anthony, who was studiously examining a tree some thirty yards away. Finally, in a low voice, Phillip said, "No."

Eloise didn't feel elated; she didn't feel sorrow. She didn't feel anything at all at his pronouncement, which surprised her. But she did let out a long breath, one she hadn't realized she'd been holding. And she did feel rather glad that she now knew.

She hated the not knowing. About anything.

And so she really shouldn't have been surprised when she whispered, "Why did you marry her?"

A rather blank expression washed over his eyes, and finally he just shrugged and said, "I don't know. It seemed like the right thing to do."

She nodded. It all made so much sense. It was exactly the sort of thing he would do. Phillip was always doing the right thing, the honorable thing, apologizing for his transgressions, shouldering everyone's burdens . . .

Honoring his brother's promises.

And then she had one more question. "Did you . . ." she whispered, almost losing her nerve. "Did you feel passion for her?" She knew she shouldn't ask, but after that afternoon, she had to know. The answer didn't matter—or at least she told herself it didn't.

But she had to know.

"No." He turned away, began to walk, his long stride forcing her to jump to attention and follow. But then, just when she'd gathered enough speed to catch up, he stopped, causing her to stumble and put her hands out against his arm just to keep her balance.

"I have a question for you," he said, his voice abrupt.

"Of course," she murmured, surprised by his sudden change of demeanor. Still, it was only fair. She'd practically interrogated the poor man.

"Why did you leave London?" he asked.

She blinked in surprise. She hadn't been expecting something with such an easy answer. "To meet you, of course."

"Balderdash."

Her mouth fell open at his palpable disdain.

"That's why you came," he said, "not why you left."

It hadn't occurred to her until that very minute that there was a difference, but he was right. He'd had nothing to do with why she'd left London. He'd just provided an easy means of escape, a way to leave without feeling she was running away.

He'd given her something to run to, which was so much easier to justify than running *from*.

"Did you have a lover?" he asked, his voice low.

"No!" she answered, loud enough so that Anthony actually turned around, forcing her to smile and wave at him, assuring him that all was well. "Just a bee," she called out.

Anthony's eyes widened, and he started to stride in their direction.

"It's gone now!" Eloise called quickly, shooing him away. "Nothing about it!" She turned to Phillip and explained, "He's rather morbidly afraid of bees." She grimaced. "I forgot. I should have said it was a mouse."

Phillip looked over at Anthony, curiosity on his face. Eloise wasn't surprised; it was difficult to imagine that a man such as her brother was afraid of bees, but it did make sense, seeing as how their father had died after being stung by one.

"You didn't answer my question."

Damn. She'd thought she'd got him off the subject. "How could you even ask it?" she asked.

Phillip shrugged. "How could I not? You ran away from home, not bothering to tell your family where you were going—"

"I left a note," she interrupted.

"Yes, of course, the note."

Her mouth fell open. "Don't you believe me?"

He nodded. "I do, actually. You're much too organized and officious to leave without making sure all of your loose ends were tied up."

"It's not my fault it got shuffled into Mother's invitations," she muttered.

"The note is not the issue," he stated, crossing his arms.

Crossing his arms? She clenched her teeth together. It made her feel a child, and there was nothing she could do or say about it, because she had a feeling that whatever he was about to say concerning her recent behavior, he was right.

Much as it pained her to admit it.

"The fact of the matter," he continued, "is that you fled London like a criminal in the middle of the night. It simply occurred to me that something might have happened to . . . ah . . . stain your reputation." At her peevish expression, he added, "It's not an unreasonable conclusion to reach."

He was right, of course. Not about her reputation—that was still as pure and clean as snow. But it did look odd, and frankly, it was a wonder he hadn't inquired after it already.

"If you had a lover," he said quietly, "it won't change my intentions."

"It's not that at all," she said quickly, mostly just to make him stop talking about it. "It was . . ." Her voice trailed off, and she sighed. "It was . . ."

And then she told him everything. All about the marriage proposals she'd received, and the ones Penelope hadn't, and the plans they'd jokingly made to grow old and spinsterish together. And she told him how guilty she'd felt when Penelope and Colin had married, and she couldn't stop thinking about herself and how alone she was.

She told him all that and more. She told him what was in her mind and what was in her heart, and she told him things she'd never told another soul. And it occurred to her that for a woman who opened her mouth every other second, there was an awful lot inside of her that she'd never shared.

And then, when she was done (and, in truth, she didn't even realize she'd finished; she just kind of ran out of energy and dwindled off into silence), he reached out and took her hand.

"It's all right," he said.

And it was, she realized. It actually was.

Chapter 14

...I grant that Mr. Wilson's face does have a certain amphibious quality, but I do wish you would learn to be a bit more circumspect in your speech. While I would never consider him an acceptable candidate for marriage, he is certainly not a toad, and it ill-behooved me to have my younger sister call him thus, and in his presence.

—from Eloise Bridgerton to her sister Hyacinth, upon refusing her fourth offer of marriage

Four days later, they were married. Phillip had no idea how Anthony Bridgerton had managed it, but he'd procured a special license, allowing them to be wed without banns and on a Monday, which, Eloise assured him, was no worse than Tuesday or Wednesday, just that it wasn't Saturday, as was proper.

Eloise's entire family, minus her widowed sister in Scotland, who hadn't had time to make the journey, had trooped out to the country for the wedding. Normally, the ceremony would have taken place in Kent, at the Bridgerton family seat, or at the very least in London, where the family attended church regularly at St. George's in Hanover Square, but such arrangements were not possible on such a hastened schedule, and this wasn't an ordinary sort of wedding in any case. Benedict and Sophie had offered their home for the reception, but Eloise had felt that the twins would be more comfortable at Romney Hall, so they'd held the ceremony at the parish church down the lane, followed by a small, intimate reception on the lawn outside Phillip's greenhouse.

Later in the day, just as the sun was beginning to dip in the sky, Eloise found herself in her new bedchamber with her mother, who was busying herself by pretending to tuck away items in Eloise's hastily gathered trousseau. It all, of course, had been taken care of by Eloise's lady's maid (brought up from London with the family) earlier that morning, but Eloise didn't comment upon her mother's idle busywork. It seemed like Violet Bridgerton simply needed something to do while she talked.

Eloise, of all people, understood that need perfectly.

"I should complain that I'm being denied my proper moment of glory as the mother of the bride," Violet said to her daughter as she folded her lacy veil and placed it gently on top of a bureau, "but in truth I'm just happy to see you a bride."

Eloise smiled gently at her mother. "You'd quite despaired of it, hadn't you?"

"Quite." But then she cocked her head to the side

and added, "Actually, no. I always thought you might surprise us in the end. You frequently do."

Eloise thought of all those years since her debut, all those rejected marriage proposals. All those weddings they'd attended, with Violet watching another of her friends marrying off another of their daughters to another fabulously eligible gentleman.

Another gentleman, of course, who could now no longer marry Eloise, Lady Bridgerton's famously on-the-shelf spinster daughter.

"I'm sorry if I've disappointed you," Eloise whispered.

Violet gazed at her with a wise expression. "My children never disappoint me," she said softly. "They merely . . . astonish me. I believe I like it that way."

Eloise found herself lurching forward to hug her mother. She felt awkward doing so; she didn't know why, since hers was a family that had never discouraged such displays of affection in the privacy of their own home. Maybe it was because she was so perilously close to tears; maybe it was because she sensed her mother was the same. But she felt an awkward girl again, all gangly arms and legs and bony elbows and a mouth that always opened when it should be closed.

And she wanted her mother.

"There, there," Violet said, sounding very much as she had years ago, when fussing over a skinned knee or bruised feelings. "Now," she said, her face turning pink. "Now, then."

"Mother?" Eloise murmured. She looked very strange indeed, as if she'd eaten bad fish.

"I dread this," Violet muttered.

"Mother?" Surely she couldn't have heard correctly.

Violet took a deep, fortifying breath. "We have to have a little talk." She leaned back, looked her daughter in the eye, then added, *"Do* we have to have a little talk?"

Eloise wasn't certain whether her mother was asking her if she knew of the details *of* intimacy or if she actually knew them . . . intimately. "Uhhh . . . I haven't . . . ah . . . If you mean . . . That is to say, I'm still . . ."

"Excellent," Violet said with a heartfelt sigh. "But do you—that is to say, are you aware . . . ?"

"Yes," Eloise said quickly, eager to spare both of them undue embarrassment. "I don't believe I need anything explained."

"Excellent," Violet said again, her sigh even more heartfelt. "I must say, I do detest this part of motherhood. I can't even recall what I said to Daphne, just that I spent the entire time blushing and stammering, and honestly, I have no idea if she left the encounter any better informed than when she arrived." The corners of her mouth turned down. "Probably not, I'm afraid."

"She seems to have adapted to married life quite well," Eloise murmured.

"Yes, she has. Hasn't she?" Violet said brightly. "Four little children and a husband who dotes upon her. One certainly can't hope for more."

"What did you say to Francesca?" Eloise asked.

"I beg your pardon?"

"Francesca," Eloise repeated, referring to her younger sister who had married six years earlier—and was tragically widowed two years after that.

"What did you say to her when she married? You mentioned Daphne, but not Francesca."

Violet's blue eyes clouded, as they always did when she thought of her third daughter, widowed so young. "You know Francesca. I expect she could have told me a thing or two."

Eloise gasped.

"I don't mean it *that* way, of course," Violet hastened to add. "Francesca was as innocent as . . . well, as innocent as you are, I imagine."

Eloise felt her cheeks grow hot and thanked her maker for the cloudy day, which left the room somewhat darkened. That and the fact that her mother was busy inspecting a torn hem on her dress. She was *technically* untouched, of course, and she'd certainly pass inspection if examined by a physician, but she didn't feel quite so innocent any longer.

"But you know Francesca," Violet continued, shrugging and looking back up when she realized that there was nothing she could do about the hem. "She's so sly and knowing. I expect she bribed some poor housemaid into explaining it all to her years earlier."

Eloise nodded. She didn't want to tell her mother that she and Francesca had in fact pooled their pin money to bribe the housemaid. It had been worth every penny, however. Annie Mavel's explanation had been detailed and, Francesca had later informed her, absolutely correct.

Violet smiled wistfully, then reached up and touched her daughter's cheekbone, right near the corner of her eye. The skin was still slightly discolored, but the purple had faded through blue and green to a rather sickly (but certainly less unsightly) shade of yellow. "Are you certain you'll be happy?" she asked.

Eloise smiled ruefully. "It's a little late to wonder, don't you think?"

"It might be too late to do anything about it, but it's never too late to wonder."

"I think I'll be happy," Eloise said. *I hope so*, she added, but just in her mind.

"He seems a nice man."

"He's a very nice man."

"Honorable."

"He is that."

Violet nodded. "I think you'll be happy. It might take time until you realize it, and you might doubt yourself at first, but you'll be happy. Just remember—" She stopped, chewing on her lip.

"What, Mother?"

"Just remember," she said slowly, as if she were choosing each word with great care, "that it takes time. That's all."

What takes time? Eloise wanted to scream.

But her mother had already stood up and was briskly smoothing her skirts. "I expect I shall have to usher the family out, or they will never leave." She fiddled with a bow on her dress as she turned slightly away. One of her hands reached up to her face, and Eloise tried not to notice that she was brushing aside a tear.

"You're very impatient," Violet said, facing the door. "You always have been."

"I know," Eloise said, wondering if this was a scolding, and if so, *why* was her mother choosing to do it now?

"I always loved that about you," Violet said. "I always loved everything about you, of course, but for some reason I always found your impatience especially charming. It was never because you wanted *more*, it was because you wanted everything."

Eloise wasn't so sure that sounded like such a good trait.

"You wanted everything for everyone, and you wanted to know it all and learn it all, and . . ."

For a moment Eloise thought her mother might be done, but then Violet turned around and added, "You've never been satisfied with second-best, and that's good, Eloise. I'm glad you never married any of those men who proposed in London. None of them would have made you happy. Content, maybe, but not happy."

Eloise felt her eyes widen with surprise.

"But don't let your impatience become all that you are," Violet said softly. "Because it isn't, you know. There's a great deal more to you, but I think sometimes you forget that." She smiled, the gentle, wise smile of a mother saying goodbye to her daughter. "Give it time, Eloise. Be gentle. Don't push too hard."

Eloise opened her mouth but found herself entirely incapable of speech.

"Be patient," Violet said. "Don't push."

"I . . ." Eloise had meant to say *I won't*, but her words fell away, and all she could do was stare at her mother's face, only now realizing what it truly meant that she was married. She'd been thinking so much about Phillip that she hadn't thought of her family.

She was leaving them. She would always have them in all the ways that mattered, but still, she was leaving.

And she hadn't realized until that very moment how often she sat down with her mother and just talked. Or how very precious those moments were. Violet always seemed to know just what her children needed, which was remarkable, really, since there were eight of them—eight very different souls, each with unique hopes and dreams.

Even Violet's letter—the one she'd written and asked Anthony to give to her at Romney Hall—it was exactly right, precisely what Eloise had needed to hear. Violet could have scolded, she could have hurled accusations; she would have been perfectly within her rights to do either—or more.

But all she'd written was, "I hope you are well. Please remember that you are my daughter and you will always be my daughter. I love you."

Eloise had bawled. Thank goodness she'd forgotten to read it until late in the night, when she was able to do so in the privacy of her room at Benedict's house.

Violet Bridgerton had never wanted for anything, but her true wealth lay in her wisdom and her love, and it occurred to Eloise, as she watched Violet turn back to the door, that she was more than just her mother—she was everything that Eloise aspired to be.

And Eloise couldn't believe it had taken her this long to realize it.

"I imagine you and Sir Phillip will want some privacy," Violet said, placing her hand on the doorknob.

Eloise nodded even though her mother couldn't see the gesture. "I shall miss you all."

"Of course you will," Violet said, her brisk tone obviously her way of recovering her composure.

"And we shall miss you. But you won't be far. And you'll live so close to Benedict and Sophie. And Posy, too. I expect I shall be coming out this way more often for visits now that I have two more grandchildren to spoil."

Eloise brushed away tears of her own. Her family had accepted Phillip's children instantly and unconditionally. She had expected no less, but still, it warmed her heart more than she would ever have imagined. Already the twins were playing raucously with the Bridgerton grandchildren, and Violet had insisted that they call her Grandmama. They had agreed with alacrity, especially after Violet had produced an entire bag of peppermint drops that she claimed must have fallen into her valise back in London.

Eloise had already said her goodbyes to her family, so when her mother departed, she felt well and truly Lady Crane. Miss Bridgerton would have returned to London with the rest of the family, but Lady Crane, wife of a Gloucestershire landowner and baronet, remained here at Romney Hall. She felt strange and different and chided herself for it. One would think, at twenty-eight, that marriage would not seem such a momentous step. After all, she wasn't a green girl, and hadn't been for some time.

Still, she told herself, she had every right to feel that her life had changed forever. She was married, for heaven's sake, and the mistress of her own home. Not to mention mother to two children. None of her siblings had had to take on the responsibilities of parenthood so suddenly.

But she was up to the task. She had to be. She squared her shoulders, looking determinedly at her reflection in the mirror as she brushed her hair. She was a Bridgerton, even if it was no longer her legal surname, and she was up to anything. And as she wasn't the sort to tolerate an unhappy life, then she would simply have to make certain that hers was anything but.

A knock sounded at the door, and when Eloise turned around, Phillip had entered the room. He closed the door behind him but remained where he was, presumably to offer her a bit of time to collect herself.

"Wouldn't you like your maid for that?" he asked, nodding toward her hairbrush.

"I told her to take a free evening," Eloise said. She shrugged. "It seemed odd to have her here, almost an intrusion, I think."

He cleared his throat as he tugged at his cravat, a motion that had become endearingly familiar. He was never quite at home in formal attire, she realized, always tugging or shifting and quite obviously wishing he was in his more comfortable work clothes.

How strange to have a husband with an actual vocation. Eloise had never thought to marry a man like that. Not that Phillip was in trade, but still, his work in the greenhouse was certainly something more than what most of the idle young men of her acquaintance had to fill their lives.

She liked it, she realized. She liked that he had a purpose and a calling, liked that his mind was sharp and engaged in intellectual inquiry rather than horses and gambling.

She liked *him*.

It was a relief, that. What a bind she would have been in if she didn't.

"Would you like a few more minutes?" he asked.

She shook her head. She was ready.

A rush of air blew past his lips. Eloise thought she might have heard the words "Thank God," and then she was in his arms, and he was kissing her, and whatever else she'd been thinking, it was gone.

Phillip supposed that he should have devoted a bit more of his mental energy to his wedding, but the truth was, he couldn't keep his mind on the events of the day, not when the events of the night loomed tantalizingly close. Every time he looked at Eloise, every time he even sniffed her scent, which seemed to be everywhere, standing out among all the delicate perfumes of the Bridgerton women, he felt a telltale tightening in his body, a shiver of anticipation as he recalled what it felt like to have her in his arms.

Soon, he told himself, forcing his body to relax, then thanking God that he was actually successful in the endeavor. *Soon.*

And then soon became now, and they were alone, and he couldn't quite believe how lovely she was with her long, chestnut hair cascading in soft waves down her back. He had never seen it down, he realized, never imagined the length of it when it had been tucked away in a tidy little bun at the nape of her neck.

"I always wondered why women kept their hair up," he murmured, once he'd finished with his seventh kiss.

"It's expected, of course," Eloise said, looking puzzled at the comment.

"That's not why," he said. He touched her hair, ran his fingers through it, then lifted it to his face and breathed in the scent. "It's for the protection of other men."

Her eyes flew to his with surprise and confusion. "Surely you mean the protection *from*."

He shook his head slowly. "I'd have to kill anyone who saw you thus."

"Phillip." Her tone was meant to be scolding, he was quite sure of that, but she was blushing and looking rather absurdly pleased by his statement.

"No one who saw this could resist you," he said, winding a length of her silky hair around his fingers. "I'm quite sure of it."

"Many men have found me quite resistible," she said, offering him a self-deprecating smile as she looked up at him. "Quite a lot, actually."

"They're fools," he said simply. "And besides, it only proves my point, does it not? This"—he held one long thick lock up between their faces, then tickled it against his lips, breathing in its heady scent— "has been hidden away in a bun for years."

"Since I was sixteen," she said.

He tugged her toward him, gently but inexorably. "I'm glad. You'd never have been mine if you'd tugged out your hairpins. Someone else would have snatched you up years ago."

"It's just hair," she whispered, her voice a little trembly.

"You're right," he agreed. "You must be, because on anyone else, I don't think it would be nearly so intoxicating. It must be you," he whispered, letting the strands drop from his fingers. "Only you."

He cradled her face in his hands, tilting it slightly to the side so that he might more easily kiss her. He knew what her lips tasted like, had kissed them, in fact, just minutes earlier. But even with that, he was startled by her sweetness, by the warmth of her breath and her mouth, and the way his body turned to fire from one simple kiss.

Except that it would never be just a simple kiss. Not with her.

His fingers found the fastenings of her gown, small fabric-covered buttons marching down her back. "Turn around," he ordered, breaking the kiss. He wasn't so experienced at seduction that he could slip them from their loops without the advantage of sight.

Besides, he rather enjoyed this—this slow disrobing, each button revealing another half inch of creamy skin.

She was his, he realized, sliding one finger down her spine before attending to the third-to-last button. His for eternity. It was hard to imagine how he had been so lucky, but he resolved not to wonder at his good fortune, just to enjoy it.

Another button. This one revealed a square of flesh near the base of her spine.

He touched her. She shivered.

His fingers went to the last button. He didn't really need to attend to it; her dress was more than loose enough to slip from her shoulders. But somehow he needed to do this right, to disrobe her properly, to savor the moment.

Besides, this last one revealed the curve of her buttocks.

He wanted to kiss her. He wanted to kiss her right there. Right at the top of her cleft while she stood facing the other way, shivering not from cold but from excitement.

He leaned toward her, pressed his lips to the back of her neck as both of his hands found her shoulders. There were some things that were too wicked for an innocent like Eloise.

But she was his. His wife. And she was fire and passion and energy all wrapped into one. She wasn't Marina, he reminded himself, delicate and breakable, unable to express emotion other than sorrow.

She wasn't Marina. It seemed necessary to remind himself of this, not just now, but continually, throughout the day, each time he looked at her. She wasn't Marina, and he didn't need to hold his breath around her, afraid of his own words, afraid of his facial expressions, afraid of anything that might cause her to sink into herself, into her own despair.

This was Eloise. *Eloise.* Strong, magnificent Eloise.

Unable to stop himself, he sank to his knees, holding Eloise's hips firmly between his hands when she let out a soft murmur of surprise and tried to turn around.

And he kissed her. Right there, at the base of her spine, in the spot that had tempted him so, he kissed her. And then—he didn't know why; his experience with women had been limited, but his imagination was clearly making up for that lack—he ran his tongue along that central line, down her spine to the beginning of her cleft, tasting the sweet saltiness of her skin, stopping—but not removing his lips—when she moaned, putting her hands out against the wall to support herself when she could no longer stand.

"Phillip," she gasped.

He rose and turned her around, leaning down until they were nearly nose to nose. "It was there," he said helplessly, as if that would explain everything. And in truth, that was all the explanation there was. It was there, that tantalizing little patch of skin, pink and peachy and waiting for a kiss.

She was there, and he had to have her.

He kissed her mouth again as he let her gown slide from her body. She'd been married in blue, a pale version of the color that made her eyes look deeper and more tempestuous than ever, rather like a cloudy sky just before a rainstorm.

It was a heavenly dress—he'd heard her sister Daphne say that to her earlier that day. But it was even more heavenly to rid her of it.

She wasn't wearing a chemise, and he knew that she was bared to him, heard her suck in her breath as the tips of her breasts grazed the fine linen of his shirt. But instead of looking, he ran his hand along the side of her breast, his knuckles lightly nuzzling the side of the swell. Then, as he continued to kiss her, his hand curved around until he was cupping her, feeling the exquisite weight of her in his fingers.

"Phillip," she moaned, the word sinking into his mouth like a benediction.

He moved his hand again until he covered her, her pert nipple sliding between his fingers. And as he squeezed—gently, reverently—he could, after all, hardly believe this had all come to pass.

And then he couldn't wait any longer. He had to see her, to see every bit of her and watch her face as he did so. He pulled back, breaking their kiss with a whispered promise that he'd be back.

He sucked in his breath as he gazed down at her. It was not yet dark, and the last vestiges of sunlight still filtered in through the windows, bathing her skin in a red-gold glow. Her breasts were larger than he'd imagined, full and round and plump, and it was all he could do not to sweep her into bed that very moment. He could feast forever on those breasts, love them and worship them until . . .

Dear God, who was he trying to fool? Until his own need grew too intense, and he had to have her, to plunge into her, devour her.

With shaking fingers, he went to work on his own buttons, watching her watching him as he tore the shirt from his body. And then he forgot, and he turned . . .

And she gasped.

He froze.

"What happened?" she whispered.

He didn't know why he was so surprised by the moment, by the fact that he would have to explain. She was his wife, and she was going to see him naked every day for the rest of his life, and if anyone was going to know the nature of his scars, it would be her.

He was able to avoid them, as they were quite out of his sight on his back, but Eloise would not be so lucky.

"I was whipped," he said, not turning around. He should probably spare her the sight, but she was going to have to get used to it sometime.

"Who did this to you?" Her voice was low and angry, and her outrage warmed his heart.

"My father." Phillip well remembered the day. He had been twelve, home from school, and his father had forced him to accompany him on a hunt. Phillip was a good horseman, but not good enough for the jump his father had taken ahead of him. He'd tried it, though, knowing he'd be branded a coward if he did not make the attempt.

He'd fallen, of course. Been thrown, really. Miraculously, he'd walked away without injury, but his father had been livid. Thomas Crane possessed a very narrow vision of English manhood, and it did not include tumbles off horseback. His sons would ride and shoot and fence and box and excel and excel and excel.

And God help them if they did not.

George had made the jump, of course. George was always a hair better at all things sporting. And George was also two years his elder, two years bigger, two years stronger. He'd tried to intercede, to save Phillip from punishment, but then Thomas had just whipped him as well, berating him for meddling. Phillip needed to learn how to be a man, and Thomas would not tolerate anyone interfering, even George.

Phillip wasn't sure what had been different about the punishment that day; usually his father used a belt, which, over a shirt, left no marks. But they'd already been out by the stables, and the whip was handy, and his father had been so damned angry, even angrier than normal.

When the whip sliced through Phillip's shirt, Thomas didn't stop.

It was the only time his father's beatings had left visible scars.

And Phillip was stuck with the reminder for the rest of his life.

He glanced over at Eloise, who was watching him with an oddly intense look in her eyes. "I'm sorry," he said, even though he wasn't. There was nothing to be sorry for, save for having forced her into the horror of his childhood.

"I'm not sorry," she growled, her eyes narrow and fierce.

His eyes widened with surprise.

"I'm furious."

And then he couldn't help it. He laughed. He threw his head back and laughed. She was absolutely perfect, naked and angry, ready to march down to hell itself to drag his father out for a tongue-lashing.

She looked slightly alarmed at his oddly timed laughter, but then she smiled, too, as if recognizing the importance of the moment.

He took her hand and, desperate for her to touch him, brought it to his heart, pressing it flat until her fingers spread out, sinking into the soft, springy hair on his chest.

"So strong," she whispered, her hand sliding gently along his skin. "I had no idea it was such difficult work, toiling away in the greenhouse."

He felt like a boy of sixteen, so pleased was he by her compliment. And the memory of his father quietly slipped away. "I do work outside, too," he said gruffly, unable to simply say thank you.

"With the laborers?" she murmured.

He looked at her with amusement. "Eloise Bridgerton—"

"Crane," she corrected.

A burst of pleasure shot through him at her words. "Crane," he repeated. "Don't tell me you've been harboring secret fantasies about the farm laborers."

"Of course not," she said, "although . . ."

There was no way he was going to let those words trail off into oblivion. "Although?" he prompted.

She looked a little sheepish. "Well, they do look terribly . . . *elemental* . . . out there in the sun, toiling away."

He smiled. Slowly, like a man about to feast upon his dream come true. "Oh, Eloise," he said, bringing his lips to her neck and moving down, down, down. "You have no idea of elemental. No idea at all."

And then he did what he'd been dreaming of for days—well, one of the things he'd been dreaming of—and he took her nipple into his mouth, running his tongue around the edge before closing around to suck.

"Phillip!" she nearly shrieked, sinking into him.

He swept her into his arms and carried her to the bed, already turned down and waiting for the newlyweds. He laid her atop the sheets, stopping to enjoy the sight of her before attending to her stockings, which were all that was left on her body. Her hands went instinctively to cover her sex, and he allowed her her modesty, knowing that his turn would come soon.

He looped his fingers under the edge of one stocking, caressing her through the whisper-fine silk before sliding it down her leg. She moaned as he passed her knee, and he couldn't help looking up and asking, "Ticklish?"

She nodded. "And more."

And more. He loved that. He loved that she felt more, that she wanted more.

The other stocking was disposed of more quickly, and then he stood beside her, his fingers moving to the fastenings on his trousers. He paused for a moment and looked at her, waiting for her to tell him with her eyes that she was ready.

And then, with a speed and agility he'd never dreamed he possessed, he'd stripped himself of his remaining garments and laid down beside her. She stiffened for a moment, then relaxed as he stroked her, his lips making shushing sounds as they moved to her temple, and then to her lips.

"There is nothing to be afraid of," he murmured.

"I'm not afraid," she said.

He drew back, looked her in the face. "You're not?"

"Nervous, but not afraid."

He shook his head in wonder. "You are magnificent."

"I keep telling everyone that," she said with a nonchalant shrug, "but you seem to be the only one to believe me."

He chuckled at that, shaking his head in wonder, barely able to believe that here he was, on his wedding night, and he was laughing. Twice now, she had made him laugh, and he was beginning to realize that this was a gift. An amazing, priceless gift, one that he was truly blessed to receive.

Intercourse had always been about need, about his body and his lust and whatever it was that made him a man. It had never been about this joy, this wonder at discovering another person.

He took her face in his hands and kissed her again, this time with all the feeling and emotion coursing through him. He kissed her mouth, then he kissed her cheek, then her neck. And he moved down, exploring her body, from her shoulders to her belly to the side of her hip.

He skipped only one place, one place he would have very much liked to explore, but he decided that would come later, when she was ready.

When *he* was ready. Marina had never let him kiss her there—no, that wasn't fair; in truth, he'd never even asked. It had just seemed so wrong as she lay beneath him, still and silent, as if she were performing a duty. There had been women before his marriage, but they'd been of the experienced sort, and he'd never wanted to be quite so intimate with them.

Later, he promised himself as he stopped, briefly, to nuzzle her curls.

Soon. Definitely soon.

He wrapped his large hands around her calves, then slid them up, nudging her legs apart so that he could settle between them. He was hard, *really* hard, afraid he was going to embarrass himself, and so he took deep breaths as he touched her opening, trying to calm his blood so that he would be able to make this last long enough for her to enjoy herself.

"Oh, Eloise," he said, although in truth it was more of a grunt. He wanted her more than anything, more than life itself, and he had no idea how he was going to last.

"Phillip?" she asked, her voice sounding vaguely alarmed.

He pulled back so that he could see her face.

"You're very big," she whispered.

He smiled. "Don't you know that's *exactly* what a man wishes to hear?"

"I'm sure," she said, nibbling on her lower lip. "It does seem the sort of thing you'd brag about while you're racing horses and playing cards and being competitive for no particular reason."

He wasn't sure whether he was shaking with laughter or dismay. "Eloise," he managed to say, "I assure you—"

"How much is it going to hurt?" she blurted out.

"I don't know," he said honestly. "I've never been in your position. A little, I imagine. I hope not too much."

She nodded, seeming to appreciate his candor. "I keep . . ." Her words trailed off.

"Tell me," he urged.

For several seconds she did nothing but blink, then she said, "I keep getting swept away, like the other day, but then I see you, or I feel you, and I can't *imagine* how this will work, and I worry I'll be torn apart, and I lose it. The magic," she explained. "I lose the magic."

And then he decided—to hell with it. Why should he wait? Why should *she* wait? He leaned down, kissed her quickly on the mouth. "Wait right here," he said. "Don't go anywhere."

Before she could ask questions—and she was Eloise, so of course she had questions—he slithered down, and spread her legs wide, the way he'd lain awake imagining at night, and kissed her.

She screamed.

"Good," he murmured, his words disappearing

into the very heart of her. His hands held her firm; he had no choice, she was squirming and bucking like a wild woman. He licked and kissed, and he tasted every inch, every tantalizing crevice. He was voracious, and he devoured her, thinking that this had to be quite simply the *best* thing he'd ever done in his entire life, and dear *God*, he was thankful he was a married man now and could do it as often as he liked.

He'd heard other men talk about it, of course, but never ever had he dreamed it would be this good. He was a hairbreadth away from losing himself completely, and she hadn't even touched him. Not that he would have wanted her to at that moment— the way she was gripping the sheets, her knuckles white and straining, hell, she would have ripped him in two.

He should have let her finish, should have kissed her until she exploded into his mouth, but at that point his own needs took over, and he simply had no choice. This was his wedding night, and when he spilled himself, it was going to be into her, not the sheets, and dear God, but if he didn't feel her squeezing around him soon, he was quite certain he was going to burst into flame.

And so he lifted himself, ignoring her cry of distress as he removed his lips, and he moved up, settling his member against her one more time, then using his fingers to part her even more as he pushed forward.

She was wet—very, very wet, a mix of her and him, and it was nothing like he'd ever felt before. He slid right in, her passage somehow easy and tight at the same time.

She gasped his name, and he gasped hers, and then, unable to keep his pace slow, he plunged forward, breaking through her last barrier until he was embedded to the hilt. And maybe he should have stopped, maybe he should have asked if she was all right, if she felt any pain, but he just couldn't. It had been so damned long, and he needed her so damned much, and once his body began to move there wasn't a thing he could do to stop it.

He was fast and he was rough, but she must have liked it because she was fast and rough beneath him, her hips grinding against his with needy force as her fingers bit into his back.

And when she moaned, it wasn't his name. It was, "More!"

He slid his fingers beneath her, grabbing on to her buttocks, squeezing hard as he tilted her up to allow him even easier entry, and the change of position must have done something to change the way he was rubbing her, or maybe she had just reached her limit, because she arched beneath him, going so stiff she shook, and then a cry was ripped from her throat as he felt her muscles convulse around him.

He could take no more. With one final shout he plunged forward, shuddering and shaking as he emptied himself, claiming her finally and indelibly as his own.

Chapter 15

... I cannot believe that you will not tell me more. As your elder sister (by a full year, I should not have to remind you) I am owed a certain measure of respect, and while I appreciate your informing me that Annie Mavel's account of married love was correct, I should have liked a few details beyond that brief account. Surely you are not so wrapped in your own bliss that you cannot spare a few words (adjectives, in particular, would be helpful) for your beloved sister.

—from Eloise Bridgerton to her
sister the Countess of Kilmartin,
two weeks after Francesca's wedding

One week later, Eloise was sitting in the small parlor that had recently been converted into an office for her, chewing on the end of her pencil as she attempted to go over the household accounts. She was supposed to be counting funds, and bags of flour, and the servants' wages, and the like, but in truth all she could count was the number of times she and Phillip had made love.

Thirteen, she thought. No, fourteen. Well, fifteen, actually, if she counted that time when he hadn't actually gone inside of her, but they'd both . . .

She blushed, even though there wasn't a soul in the room besides her, and it wasn't as if anyone would have known what she was thinking, anyway.

But good God, had she really *done* that? Kissed him *there*?

She hadn't even known such a thing was possible. Annie Mavel certainly hadn't described anything like that when she'd delivered her little lesson to Eloise and Francesca all those years ago.

Eloise scrunched her face as she thought back. She wondered if Annie Mavel had even known such things were possible. It was difficult to imagine Annie doing it, but then, it was difficult to imagine *anyone* doing it, most especially herself.

It was amazing, she thought, utterly amazing and beyond wonderful to have a husband who was so mad for her. They didn't see one another too terribly often during the day—he had his work, after all, and she had hers, of a sort—but at night, after he'd given her five minutes for her toilette (it had started at twenty, but it seemed to be getting progressively shorter, and she could even hear his footsteps pacing outside the door during the scant minutes he now allowed her) . . .

At night, he pounced upon her like a man possessed. A starving man, really. His energy seemed endless, and he was always trying new things, positioning her in new ways, teasing and tormenting until she was screaming and begging, never sure whether it was for him to stop or keep going.

He'd said that he hadn't felt passion for Marina, but Eloise found that hard to believe. He was a man of *hearty* appetites (it was a silly word, but she could not think of any other way to describe it), and the things he did with his hands . . .

And his mouth . . .

And his teeth . . .

And his tongue . . .

She blushed again. The things he did—well, a woman would have to be half dead not to respond.

She looked back down at the columns in her ledger. The numbers hadn't miraculously added themselves up while she daydreamed, and every time Eloise tried to concentrate they began swimming around before her eyes. She glanced out the window; she couldn't see Phillip's greenhouse from her position, but she knew it was just around the corner, and that he was in it, toiling away, snipping leaves and planting seeds and whatever else it was that he did there all day.

All day.

She frowned. It was actually a very apt phrase. Phillip did spend the entire day in the greenhouse, often even having his midday meal brought in on a tray. She knew it wasn't terribly abnormal for man and wife to lead separate lives during the day (and, for many couples, at night as well), but they had only been married one week.

And in truth, she was in many ways still learning who her new husband was. The marriage had come about so precipitously; she really knew very little about him. Oh, she knew he was honest and honorable and would treat her well, and now she knew that he possessed a carnal side that she would never have dreamed lurked beneath his reserved exterior.

But aside from what she had learned about his father, she didn't know his experiences, his opinions, what had happened in his life to make him the man he now was. She tried, sometimes, to draw him out in conversation, and she sometimes succeeded, but more often than not, her attempts melted away.

Because he never seemed to want to talk when he could kiss. And that, inevitably, led to his nudging her into the bedroom, where words were forgotten.

And on the few occasions when she did manage to engage him in conversation, it proved to be nothing more than an exercise in frustration. She would ask his opinion on anything relating to the household, for example, and he would just shrug and tell her that she should handle it how she saw fit. Sometimes she wondered if he'd married her just to gain a housekeeper.

And, of course, a warm body in his bed.

But there could be more. Eloise knew there could be more to a marriage, knew there could be more *in* a marriage. She couldn't recall much of her parents' union, but she'd seen her siblings with their spouses, and she thought she and Phillip might find the same bliss if they would only spend a little time together outside the bedroom.

She stood abruptly and walked to the door. She should talk to him. There was no reason she couldn't go to the greenhouse and talk to him. Maybe he'd even appreciate it if she asked about his work.

She wasn't going to interrogate him, exactly, but surely there could be no harm in a question or two, peppered into the conversation. And if he even hinted that she was bothering him or making it difficult to work, she'd leave immediately.

But then she heard her mother's voice echoing in her head.

Don't push, Eloise. Don't push.

It took willpower she'd never thought she possessed, since it went against her every last natural inclination, but she stopped, turned around, and sat back down.

She'd never known her mother to be wrong about anything truly important, and if Violet had seen fit to give advice on her wedding night, Eloise rather suspected she ought to pay it careful attention.

This, she thought with a grumpy frown, must have been what her mother had meant when she'd said to give it time.

She jammed her hands under her bottom, as if to keep them from reaching forward and leading her back toward the door. She glanced out the window, then had to avert her gaze because even though she couldn't see the greenhouse, she knew it was right there, just around the corner.

This was not, she thought through clenched teeth, her natural state. She'd never been the sort who could sit still and smile while she did so. She was meant to be moving, doing, exploring, questioning. And if she were to be honest—bothering, pestering, and stating her opinions to anyone who would listen as well.

She frowned, sighing. Put that way, she didn't sound a terribly attractive person.

She tried to remember her mother's wedding-night speech. Surely there was something positive in there as well. Her mother loved her, after all. She must have said *some*thing good. Hadn't there been something about her being charming?

She sighed. If she recalled correctly, her mother had said she found her impatience charming, which wasn't really the same as finding someone's *good* temperament charming.

How awful this was. She was eight and twenty, for heaven's sake. She'd sailed through her entire life feeling perfectly happy with who she was and how she conducted herself.

Well, almost perfectly happy. She knew she talked too much and was perhaps a little too direct at times, and very well, not everybody liked her, but most people did, and she'd long since decided that that was fine with her.

So why now? Why was she suddenly so unsure of herself, so fearful of doing or saying the wrong thing?

She stood. She couldn't stand this—the indecision, the lack of action. She'd heed her mother's advice and give Phillip a bit of privacy, but by God, she couldn't sit here doing nothing one moment longer.

She looked down at the incomplete ledgers. Oh, dear. If she'd been doing what she was *supposed* to be doing, she wouldn't have been doing nothing, would she?

With a little huff of irritation, she slammed the ledgers shut. It didn't really matter if she could be adding her sums, because she knew herself well enough to know that she *wouldn't* be adding them, even if she sat here, so she might as well go off and do something else.

The children. That was it. She'd become a wife a

week ago, but she'd also become a mother. And if anyone needed interfering in their lives, it was Oliver and Amanda.

Buoyed by her newfound sense of purpose, she strode out the door, feeling once again like her old self. She needed to oversee their lessons, make sure they were learning properly. Oliver was going to need to prepare himself for Eton, where he really ought to enroll in the fall term.

And then there was their clothing. They'd quite outgrown everything in their wardrobes, and Amanda deserved something prettier, and . . .

She sighed with contentment as she hurried up the stairs. Already she was ticking off her projects on her fingers, mentally planning for the dressmaker and the tailor, not to mention devising the wording for the advertisement she intended to place to secure the services of a few more tutors, because they desperately needed to learn French and the pianoforte, and, of course, sums—and were they too young for long division?

Feeling rather jaunty, she pushed open the door to the nursery, and then . . .

She stopped short, trying to figure out what was going on.

Oliver's eyes were red, as if he'd been crying, and Amanda was sniffling, wiping her nose with the back of her hand. Both were taking those hiccuppy gasps of breath that one does when one is upset.

"Is something wrong?" Eloise asked, looking first at the children and then at their nurse.

The twins said nothing, but they looked at her with wide, imploring eyes.

"Nurse Edwards?" Eloise asked.

The nurse's lips were twisted into an unpleasant frown. "They are merely sulking because they were punished."

Eloise nodded slowly. It wasn't the least bit surprising that Oliver and Amanda might do something requiring punishment, but nonetheless, there was something wrong about what she was seeing. Maybe it was the broken look in their eyes, as if they'd tried defiance and had given up on it.

Not that she wanted to encourage defiance, especially not against their nurse, who needed to maintain her position of authority in the schoolroom, but nor did she ever want to see this expression in their eyes—so totally humbled, so meek and sorrowful.

"Why were they punished?" Eloise asked.

"Disrespectful speech," came their nurse's immediate reply.

"I see." Eloise sighed. The twins probably had deserved punishment; they did often speak with disrespect and it was something she herself had scolded them about on several occasions. "And what punishment was meted out?"

"They were rapped on the knuckles," Nurse Edwards said, her back ramrod stiff.

Eloise forced herself to unclench her jaw. She didn't like corporal punishment, but at the same time, rapped knuckles were a staple in all the best schools. She was quite certain all of her brothers had had their knuckles rapped on numerous occasions at Eton; she couldn't imagine they had made it through all those years without a number of disciplinary transgressions.

Still, she didn't like the look in the children's eyes, so she took Nurse Edwards aside and said softly, "I understand their need for discipline, but if you must do this again, I must ask that you do it more softly."

"If I do it softly," the nurse said quite sharply, "they won't learn their lesson."

"I will be the judge of their learned lessons," Eloise said, bristling at the nurse's tone. "And I am no longer asking. I am telling you, they are children, and you must be more gentle."

Nurse Edwards's lips pursed, but she nodded. Once, sharply, to show that she would do as asked, but that she disagreed—and disapproved of Eloise's interference.

Eloise turned back to the children and said in a loud voice, "I am quite certain they have learned their lesson for today. Perhaps they might take a short break with me."

"We are practicing our penmanship," Nurse Edwards said. "We can't afford to take any time off. Especially not if I am meant to act as both nurse and governess."

"I assure you that I plan to address that problem with all possible haste," Eloise said. "And as for today, I will be happy to practice penmanship with the children. You may be assured that they will not fall behind."

"I do not think—"

Eloise speared her with a glare. She was not a Bridgerton for nothing, and by God, she knew how to deal with recalcitrant servants. "You need only to inform me of your lesson plans."

The nurse looked exceedingly grumpy, but she informed Eloise that today they were practicing *M*, *N*, and *O*. "*Both* uppercase and lowercase," she added sharply.

"I see," Eloise said, giving her voice a supercilious lilt. "I am fairly certain that I am qualified in that particular area of scholarly pursuit."

Nurse Edwards's face turned red at the sarcasm. "Will that be all?" she bit off.

Eloise nodded. "Indeed. You are dismissed. Do enjoy your free time—surely you don't get enough of it, serving double duty as you do, as both nurse and governess—and please return to see to their lunch."

Head held high, Nurse Edwards left the room.

"Well then," Eloise announced, turning her attention to the two children, who were still sitting at their little table, gazing up at her as if she were a minor deity, come down to earth for the sole purpose of saving children from evil witches. "Shall we—"

But she couldn't finish her question, because Amanda had launched herself at her, throwing her arms around her midsection with enough force to knock her back against the wall. And Oliver soon followed.

"There, there," Eloise said, patting their hair in confusion. "Whatever could be wrong?"

"Nothing," came Amanda's muffled reply.

Oliver pulled back and stood straight like the little man people were always telling him to be. Then he ruined the effect by wiping his nose with the back of his hand.

Eloise handed him a handkerchief.

He used it, nodded his thanks, and said, "We like you better than Nurse Edwards."

Eloise couldn't imagine liking anyone worse than Nurse Edwards, and she privately vowed to look into finding a replacement as soon as possible. But she wasn't going to say anything to the children about this; they would almost certainly relate the information to the nurse, who would either give her notice immediately, leaving them all in a terrible bind, or take her frustration and ire out on the children, which wouldn't do at all.

"Let's sit down," she said, steering them toward the table. "I don't know about the rest of you, but *I* don't want to have to face her if we haven't practiced our *Ms, Ns*, and *Os*."

And she thought to herself—*I really must speak with Phillip about this.*

She looked down at Oliver's hands. They didn't look abused, but one of the knuckles looked a little bit red. It might have been her imagination, but still . . .

She needed to talk to Phillip. As soon as she was able.

Phillip hummed to himself as he carefully transplanted a seedling, well aware that prior to his marriage, he had always labored in complete and utter silence.

He had never felt like whistling before, he realized, never once wanted to sing softly to himself or hum. But now . . . well, now it seemed as if music were simply in the air, all around him. He felt more relaxed, too, and the constant knots of tension in his shoulders had started to dissolve.

Marrying Eloise was, quite simply, the best thing he could have done. Hell, he'd even go so far as to say it was the best thing he'd *ever* done.

He was, for the first time in recent memory, happy.

It seemed such a simple thing now, to be happy.

And he wasn't even sure that he'd realized he wasn't happy before. He had certainly laughed on occasion, and enjoyed himself from time to time—it wasn't, as it had been for Marina, that he'd been completely and constantly unhappy.

But he hadn't been *happy*. Not in the way he was now, waking up each day with the feeling that the world was indeed a wonderful place and that it would still be a wonderful place when he went to bed that night and still yet again when he got up the following morning.

He couldn't remember the last time he'd felt like that. Probably not since his university days, when he'd had his first taste of the thrill of intellectual discovery—and he was far enough away from his father that he didn't have to worry about the constant threat of the rod.

It was difficult to count the ways that Eloise had improved his life. There was, of course, their time in the bedroom, which was quite beyond anything he might have imagined. If he'd even dreamed that sexual intercourse could be so splendid, there was no way he would have remained celibate for so long. No way he could have, quite frankly, if his current appetite was any indication.

But he simply hadn't known. Lovemaking certainly hadn't been like that with Marina. Or with any of the women he'd fumbled with as a university lad, before his marriage.

But if he were honest with himself—and that was a difficult task, considering how completely besotted his body was with Eloise's—the intercourse wasn't the main reason for his current sense of contentment.

It was this feeling—this knowledge, really—that

he had finally, and truly, for the first time since he'd become a father, done the absolute right thing for the twins.

He'd never be a perfect father. He knew that, and even if he hated it, he accepted it. But he had finally done the next best thing, and gotten them the perfect mother.

It was as if a thousand pounds of guilt had been lifted from his shoulders.

No wonder his muscles finally felt unknotted and relaxed.

He could go into his greenhouse in the morning and *not worry*. He couldn't remember the last time he'd done that, simply gone in and worked without cringing every time he heard a loud noise or shriek. Or been able to concentrate on his work without his mind wandering into guilt, unable to focus on anything other than his lacks as a father.

But now he walked in and forgot all his cares. Hell, he had no cares.

It was splendid. Magical.

A relief.

And if sometimes his wife looked at him as if she wanted him to say something different or do something different—well, he chalked that up to the simple fact that he was a man and she was a woman, and his sort would never understand her sort, and truly, he ought just to be grateful that Eloise almost always said exactly what she meant, which was a very good thing, since he wasn't constantly left guessing what was expected of him.

What was that thing his brother had always said— Beware a woman asking questions. You will never answer correctly.

Phillip smiled to himself, enjoying the memory. Put that way, there was no reason to worry if occasionally their conversations dwindled off into nothingness. Most of the time they dwindled right into bed, which was perfectly fine by him.

He looked down at the bulge forming in his breeches. Damn. He was going to have to stop thinking about his wife in the middle of the day. Or at the very least, find a way to get discreetly back to the house in his condition and find her quickly.

But then, almost as if she'd known he was standing there thinking how perfect she was, and she wanted to prove it one more time, she opened the door to the greenhouse and poked her head in.

Phillip looked around and wondered why he'd built the structure entirely of glass. He might need to install some sort of privacy screen if she was going to come visiting on a regular basis.

"Am I intruding?"

He thought about that. She was, actually; he was quite in the middle of something, but he realized he didn't mind. Which was odd and rather pleasing at the same time. He'd always been irritated by interruptions before. Even when it was someone whose company he enjoyed, after a few minutes he found himself wishing they would just leave so that he could get back to whatever project he'd had to put aside for their benefit. "Not at all," he said, "if you are not offended by my appearance."

She looked at him, taking in the dirt and mud, including the smudge he was rather certain he sported on his left cheek, and she shook her head. "It's no problem at all."

"What is troubling you?"

"It's the children's nurse," she said without pre-amble. "I don't like her."

That was not what he expected. He set down his spade. "You don't? What's wrong with her?"

"I don't know exactly. I just don't like her."

"Well, that's hardly a reason to terminate her employment."

Eloise's lips thinned slightly, a sure sign, he was coming to realize, that she was irritated. She said, "She rapped the children across the knuckles."

He sighed. He didn't like the thought of someone striking his children, but then again, it was just a knuckle rap. Nothing that didn't occur in every schoolroom across the country. And, he thought resignedly, his children were not exactly models of good behavior. And so, wanting to groan, he asked, "Did they deserve it?"

"I don't know," Eloise admitted. "I wasn't there. She said they spoke to her disrespectfully."

Phillip felt his shoulders sag a bit. "Unfortunately," he said, "I do not find that difficult to believe."

"No, of course not," Eloise said. "I'm sure they were little beasts. But still, something didn't seem right."

He leaned back against his workbench, tugging her hand until she tumbled against him. "Then look into it."

Her lips parted with surprise. "Don't *you* want to look into it?"

He shrugged. "I'm not the one with concerns. I've never had cause to doubt Nurse Edwards before, but if you feel uncomfortable, by all means, you should investigate. Besides, you're better at this sort of thing than I am."

"But"—she squirmed slightly as he pulled her against him and nuzzled her neck—"you're their father."

"And you're their mother," he said, his words coming out thick and hot against her skin. She was intoxicating, and he was aching with desire, and if he could only get her to stop talking, he could probably maneuver her to the bedroom, where they could have considerably more fun. "I trust your judgment," he said, thinking that would placate her—and besides, it was the truth. "It's why I married you."

Clearly, his answer surprised her. "It's why you . . . *what*?"

"Well, this, too," he murmured, trying to figure out just how much he could fondle her with so many clothes between them.

"Phillip, stop!" she cried out, wrenching herself away.

What the devil? "Eloise," he asked—cautiously, since it was his experience, limited though it was, that one should always tread carefully with a woman in a temper—"what is wrong?"

"What is *wrong*?" she demanded, her eyes flashing dangerously. "How can you even ask that?"

"Well," he said slowly, and with just a touch of sarcasm, "it might be because I don't know what is wrong."

"Phillip, this is not the time."

"To ask you what is wrong?"

"No!" she nearly shrieked.

Phillip took a step back. Self-preservation, he thought wryly. Surely that had to be what the male side of marital spats was all about. Self-preservation and nothing else.

She began waving her arms in a bizarre fashion. "To do this."

He looked around. She was waving at the workbench, at the pea plants, at the sky above, winking in through the panes of glass. "Eloise," he said, his voice deliberately even, "I am not an unintelligent man, but I have no idea what you're talking about."

Her mouth fell open, and he knew he was in trouble. "You don't *know*?" she asked.

He probably should have heeded his own warnings about self-preservation, but some little devil— some annoyed male devil, he was sure—forced him to say, "I don't read minds, Eloise."

"It is not the time," she finally ground out, "to be intimate."

"Well, of course not," he agreed. "We haven't a bit of privacy. But"—he smiled just thinking about it— "we could always go back to the house. I know it's the middle of the day, but—"

"That is not what I meant at all!"

"Very well," he said, crossing his arms. "I give up. What do you mean, Eloise? Because I assure you, I haven't a clue."

"Men," she muttered.

"I'll take *that* as a compliment."

Her glare could have frozen the Thames. It quite froze off his desire, which irritated him no end, since he'd been looking forward to getting rid of it in another fashion altogether.

"It wasn't meant as such," she said.

He leaned back against the workbench, his casual posture meant to irritate her. "Eloise," he said calmly, "try to afford a small measure of respect for my intelligence."

"It is difficult," she shot back, "when you display so little."

That was *it*. "I don't even know why we are arguing!" he exploded. "One minute you were willing in my arms, and the next you're shrieking like a banshee."

She shook her head. "I was never willing in your arms."

It was as if the bottom dropped out of his world.

She must have seen the shock on his face, because she quickly added, "Today. I meant just today. Just now, actually."

His body sagged with relief, even as the rest of him seethed with anger.

"I was trying to talk with you," she explained.

"You're always trying to talk with me," he pointed out. "That's all you ever do. Talk talk talk."

She drew back. "If you didn't like it," she said in a snippy voice, "you shouldn't have married me."

"It wasn't as if I had a choice in the matter," he bit off. "Your brothers were ready to castrate me. And just so you don't paint me completely black, I don't *mind* your talking. Just not, for the love of God, all of the time."

She looked like she was trying to say something utterly clever and cutting, but all she could do was gape like a fish and make sounds like, "Unh! Unh!"

"Every now and then," he said, feeling quite superior, "you might consider shutting your mouth and using it for some other purpose."

"You," she fumed, "are insufferable."

He raised his brows, knowing it would irritate her.

"I'm sorry you find my propensity for speech so offensive," she ground out, "but I was trying to talk to you about something important, and you tried to kiss me."

He shrugged. "I always try to kiss you. You're my wife. What the hell else am I supposed to do?"

"But sometimes it's not the right time," she said. "Phillip, if we want to have a good marriage—"

"We do have a good marriage," he interrupted, his voice defensive and bitter.

"Yes, of course," she said quickly, "but it can't always be about . . . you know."

"No," he said, deliberately obtuse. "I don't know."

Eloise ground her teeth together. "Phillip, don't be like this."

He said nothing, just tightened his already crossed arms and stared at her face.

She closed her eyes, and her chin bobbed slightly forward as her lips moved. And he realized that she was talking. She wasn't making a sound, but she was still talking.

Dear God, the woman never stopped. Even now she was talking to herself.

"What are you doing?" he finally asked.

She didn't open her eyes as she said, "Trying to convince myself it's all right to ignore my mother's advice."

He shook his head. He would never understand women.

"Phillip," she finally said, just when he'd decided that he was going to leave and let her talk to herself in private. "I very much enjoy what we do in bed—"

"That's nice to hear," he bit off, still too irritated to be gracious.

She ignored his lack of civility. "But it can't be just about that."

"It?"

"Our marriage." She blushed, clearly uncomfortable with such frank speech. "It can't be just about making love."

"It can certainly be a great deal about it," he muttered.

"Phillip, why won't you discuss this with me? We have a problem, and we need to talk about it."

And then something within him simply snapped. He was convinced that his was the perfect marriage, and she was *complaining*? He'd been so sure he'd gotten it right this time. "We've been married one week, Eloise," he ground out. "One week. What do you expect of me?"

"I don't know. I—"

"I'm just a man."

"And I'm just a woman," she said softly.

For some reason, her quiet words only irritated him more. He leaned forward, deliberately using his size to intimidate her. "Do you know how long it had been since I'd lain with a woman?" he hissed. "Do you have any idea?"

Her eyes grew impossibly wide, and she shook her head.

"Eight years," he bit off. "Eight long years with nothing but my own hand for comfort. So the next time I seem to be enjoying myself while I'm driving into you, please do excuse my immaturity and my *maleness*—" He spoke the word as she might, with sarcasm and anger. "I'm simply having a ripping good time after a long dry spell."

And then, unable to bear her for one moment longer—

No, that wasn't true. He was unable to bear himself.

Either way, he left.

Chapter 16

...you do have the right of it, dearest Kate. Men are so easy to manage. I cannot imagine ever losing an argument with one. Of course, had I accepted Lord Lacye's proposal, I should not have had even the opportunity. He rarely speaks, which I do find most odd.

—from Eloise Bridgerton to her
sister-in-law Viscountess Bridgerton,
upon refusing her fifth offer of marriage

Eloise remained in the greenhouse for nearly an hour, unable to do anything but stare off into space, wondering—

What had happened?

One minute they were talking—very well, they were arguing, but in a relatively reasonable and civilized manner—and the next he was out of his head, his face pinched with fury.

And then he'd left. Left. He actually *walked away*

from her in the middle of an argument and left her standing there in his greenhouse, her mouth hanging open and her pride more than pricked.

He'd walked away. That was what really bothered her. How could someone walk away in the middle of an argument?

Granted, she'd been the one to instigate the discussion—oh, very well, argument—but still, nothing had transpired that warranted such a storming off on his part.

And the worst of it was, she didn't know what to do.

All her life, she'd known what to do. She hadn't always turned out to be *right*, but at least she'd felt sure of herself when she had made her decisions. And as she sat there on Phillip's workbench, feeling utterly confused and inept, she realized that for her, at least, it was a great deal better to act and be wrong than it was to feel helpless and impotent.

And as if all that weren't enough, she couldn't get her mother's voice out of her head. *Don't push, Eloise. Don't push.*

And all she could think was— She *hadn't* pushed. Good heavens, what had she done but come to him with a concern about his children? Was it so very wrong to actually want to *speak* rather than race off to the bedroom? She supposed it might be wrong, if the couple in question never spent any intimate time together, but they had . . . they were . . .

It had just been that morning!

No one could say that they had any problems in the bedroom. No one.

She sighed and slumped. She'd never felt so alone in all her life. Funny, that. Who'd have thought she'd have to go and get married—join her life for *eternity* with another person—in order to feel alone?

She wanted her mother.

No, she didn't want her mother. She definitely didn't want her mother. Her mother would be kind and understanding and everything a mother should be, but a talk with her mother would just leave her feeling like a small child, not like the adult she was supposed to be.

She wanted her sisters. Not Hyacinth, who was barely one and twenty and knew nothing of men, but one of her married sisters. She wanted Daphne, who always knew what to say, or Francesca, who never said what one wanted to hear but always managed to eke out a smile nonetheless.

But they were too far away, in London and Scotland respectively, and Eloise was *not* going to run off. She'd made her bed when she'd married, and she was quite contentedly lying in it every night with Phillip. It was just the days that were a bit off.

She wasn't going to play the coward and leave, even if only for a few days.

But Sophie was near, just an hour away. And if they weren't sisters by birth—well, they were sisters of the heart.

Eloise looked out the door. It was too cloudy to see the sun, but she was fairly sure it wasn't much past noon. Even with the travel time, she could spend most of the day with Sophie and be back by supper.

Her pride didn't want anyone to know she was miserable, but her heart wanted a shoulder to cry on.

Her heart won out.

* * *

Phillip spent the next several hours stomping across his fields, viciously yanking weeds from the ground.

Which kept him fairly busy, since he wasn't in a cultivated area, which meant that pretty much every bit of growth could be classified as a weed, if one was so inclined.

And he *was* so inclined. He was more than inclined. If he had his way, he'd yank every damned plant from the earth.

And he, a botanist.

But he didn't want to plant things right now, didn't want to watch anything bloom or grow. He wanted to kick and maim and destroy. He was angry and frustrated and cross with himself and cross with Eloise and he was quite prepared to be upset with anyone who happened across his path.

But after an afternoon of this, of kicking and stomping, and yanking the heads off wildflowers and tearing blades of grass down the middle, he sat on a rock and let his head hang in his hands.

Hell.

What a muck.

What a bloody muck, and the really ironic bit of it was—he'd thought they were happy.

He'd thought his marriage perfect, and all this time—oh, very well, it had only been a week, but it had been a week of, in his opinion, perfection. And she'd been miserable.

Or if not miserable, then not happy.

Or maybe a little bit happy, but certainly not caught up in blissful rapture, as he had been.

And now he had to go and *do* something about it, which was the last thing he wanted to do. Talking with Eloise, actually asking questions and trying to deduce what was wrong, not to mention figuring out what to do to fix it—it was just the sort of thing he always bungled.

But he didn't have much of a choice, did he? He'd married Eloise in part—well, more than in part; almost in whole, in truth—because he'd wanted her to take charge, to take over all the annoying little tasks in his life, to free him up for the things that really mattered. The fact that he was growing to care for her had been an unexpected bonus.

He suspected, however, that one's marriage didn't count as an annoying little task, and he couldn't just leave it to Eloise. And as painful as a heart-to-heart discussion was, he was going to have to bite the bullet and give it a go.

He was quite certain he'd botch it up but good, but at least he could say he'd tried.

He groaned. She was probably going to ask him about his *feelings*. Was there no woman alive who understood that men did not talk about feelings? Hell, half of them didn't even have feelings.

Or maybe he could take the easy way out and simply apologize. He wasn't certain what he'd be apologizing for, but it would appease her and make her happy, and that was all that mattered.

He didn't want Eloise to be unhappy. He didn't want her to regret her marriage, even for one moment. He wanted his marriage back to the way he'd thought it was—easy and comfortable by day, fiery and passionate by night.

He trudged up the hill back to Romney Hall, rehearsing what he'd say in his mind and scowling over how asinine it all sounded.

But his efforts were moot, anyway, because when he arrived at the house and found Gunning, all the butler had to say was, "She's not here."

"What do you mean, she's not here?" Phillip demanded.

"She's not here, sir. She went to her brother's house."

Phillip's stomach clenched. "Which brother?"

"I believe the one who lives close by."

"You believe?"

"I'm rather certain," Gunning corrected.

"Did she say when she planned to return?"

"No, sir."

Phillip swore viciously under his breath. Surely Eloise hadn't *left* him. She wasn't the sort to bail out on a sinking ship, at least not without making sure every last passenger had left safely before her.

"She did not bring a bag, sir," Gunning said.

Oh, now, *that* made him feel good. His butler felt the need to reassure him that he'd not been abandoned by his wife. "That will be all, Gunning," Phillip said through gritted teeth.

"Very good, sir," Gunning said. He inclined his head, as he always did when he excused himself, and left the room.

Phillip stood in the hall for several minutes, stock-still, his hands fisted angrily at his sides. What the devil was he supposed to do now? He wasn't about to go running after Eloise. If she so desperately wanted to be out of his company, then by God that's what he would give her.

He started to walk to his office, where he could stew and fume in private, but then, when he was just a few steps away from the door, he stopped, glancing at the large grandfather clock at the end of the hall. It was a bit past three, just about the time the twins usually took their afternoon snack. Before they'd married, Eloise had accused him of not taking enough interest in their welfare.

He planted his hands on his hips, his foot pivoting slightly, as if unsure which way to turn. He might as well go up to the nursery and spend a few unexpected minutes with his children. It wasn't as if he had anything better to do with his time, stuck here waiting for his errant wife to return. And when she did get back—well, she wouldn't have anything to complain about, not after he'd twisted himself into one of those tiny chairs and eaten milk and biscuits with the twins.

With a decisive turn, he headed up the stairs to the nursery, located on the top floor of Romney Hall, tucked neatly away under the eaves. It was the same set of rooms in which he'd grown up, with the same furniture and toys, and presumably the same crack in the ceiling over the small beds, the one that looked like a duck.

Phillip frowned as he stepped off the final stair onto the third-floor hallway. He probably ought to see if that crack was still there, and if it was, inquire what his children thought it looked like. George, his brother, had always sworn it resembled a pig, but Phillip had never understood how he'd mistaken the bill for a snout.

Phillip shook his head. Good heavens, how anyone could mistake a duck for a pig, he'd never know. Even the—

He stopped short, just two doors down from the nursery. He'd heard something, and he wasn't quite certain what it was, except that he didn't like it. It was . . .

He listened again.

It was a whimper.

His first inclination was to storm forward and burst through the nursery door, but he held himself back when he realized that the door was ajar by two inches, and so he crept forward instead, peeking through the crack as unobtrusively as he could.

It required only half a second to realize what was happening.

Oliver was curled up in a ball on the floor, shaking with silent sobs, and Amanda was standing in front of a wall, bracing herself with her tiny little hands, whimpering as her nurse beat her across the back with a large, heavy book.

Phillip slammed through the door with a force that nearly took it off its hinges. "What the hell do you think you're doing?" he nearly roared.

Nurse Edwards turned around in surprise, but before she could open her mouth to speak, Phillip snatched the book away and hurled it behind him against the wall.

"Sir Phillip!" Nurse Edwards cried out in shock.

"How dare you strike these children," he said, his voice shaking with fury. "And with a book."

"I was told—"

"And you did it where no one would see." He felt himself growing hot, agitated, itching to lash out. "How many children have you beaten, making sure to leave the bruises where no one would see?"

"They spoke disrespectfully," Nurse Edwards said stiffly. "They had to be punished."

Phillip stepped forward, close enough so that the nurse was forced to retreat. "I want you out of my house," he said.

"You told me to discipline the children as I see fit," Nurse Edwards protested.

"Is this how you see fit?" he hissed, using every ounce of his restraint to hold his arms at his sides. He wanted to swing them wildly, to lash out, to grab a book and beat this woman just as she had done to his children.

But he held on to his temper. He had no idea how, but he did it.

"You beat them with a book?" he continued furiously. He looked over at his children; they were cowering in a corner, presumably as scared of their father in such a mood as they were of their nurse. It sickened him that they were seeing him this way, so close to a total loss of control, but there was nothing more he could do to rein himself in.

"There was no switch," Nurse Edwards said haughtily.

Wrong thing to say. Phillip felt his skin grow even hotter, fought against the red haze that had begun to cloud his vision. There *had* been a switch in the nursery; the hook it had hung upon was still there, right by the window.

Phillip had burned it the day of his father's funeral, had stood in front of the fire and watched it turn to ash. He hadn't been satisfied with just tossing it in; he'd needed to see it destroyed, completely and forever.

And he thought of that switch, thought of the hundreds of times it had been used upon him, thought of the pain, of the indignity, of all the effort he had used, trying to keep himself from crying out.

His father had hated crybabies. Tears only resulted in another round with the switch. Or with the belt. Or the riding crop. Or, when there was nothing else available, his father's hand.

But never, Phillip thought with a strange sort of detachment, a book. Probably his father had never thought of it.

"Get out," Phillip said, his voice barely audible. And then, when Nurse Edwards did not immediately respond, he roared it. "Get out! Get out of this house!"

"Sir Phillip," she protested, scooting away from him, out of reach of his long, strong arms.

"Get out! Get out! Get out!"

He didn't know where it was all coming from anymore. From somewhere deep inside, never tamed, but held down by sheer force of will.

"I need to gather my things!" she cried out.

"You have one half hour," Phillip said, his voice low but still quavering with the exertion of his outburst. "Thirty minutes. If you have not departed by then, I will throw you out myself."

Nurse Edwards hesitated at the door, started to walk through, then turned around. "You are ruining those children," she hissed.

"They are mine to ruin."

"Have it your way, then. They are nothing but little monsters, anyway, ill-tempered, misbehaved—"

Had she no care for her own safety? Phillip's control was dangling by one very thin thread, and he was this close to grabbing the damned woman by the arm and hurling her out the door himself.

"Get out," he growled, for what he prayed was the last time. He couldn't hold on much longer. He stepped forward, punctuating his words with movement, and finally—*finally*—she ran from the room.

For a moment Phillip simply held still, trying to calm himself, to calm his breathing and wait for his rushing blood to settle down. His back was to the twins, and he dreaded turning around. He was dying inside, ravaged by guilt that he'd hired that woman, that monster, to care for his children. And he'd been too busy trying avoid them to see that they were suffering.

Suffering in the same way he had.

Slowly, he turned around, terrified of what he'd see in their eyes.

But when he raised his gaze off the floor and looked into their faces, they hurled into motion, launching themselves at him with almost enough force to knock him over.

"Oh, Daddy!" Amanda cried out, using an endearment she hadn't uttered for ages. He'd been "Father" for years now, and he'd forgotten how sweet the other sounded.

And Oliver—he was hugging him, too, his small, thin arms wrapped tightly around Phillip's waist, his face buried against his shirt so that his father would not see him cry.

But Phillip could feel it. The tears soaked through his shirt, and every sniffle rumbled against his belly.

His arms went around his children, tightly, protectively. "Shhhh," he crooned. "It's all right. I'm here now." They were words he'd never said, words he'd never imagined saying; he'd never thought that his presence might be the one to make everything all right. "I'm sorry," he choked out. "I'm so sorry."

They had told him they didn't like their nurse; he hadn't listened.

"It's not your fault, Father," Amanda said.

It was, but there seemed little point in belaboring the fact. Not now, not when the time was ripe for a fresh start.

"We'll find you a new nurse," he assured them.

"Someone like Nurse Millsby?" Oliver asked, sniffling as his tears finally subsided.

Phillip nodded. "Someone just like her."

Oliver looked at him with great sincerity. "Can Miss—Mother help to choose?"

"Of course," Phillip replied, tousling his hair. "I expect she'll want a say. She is a woman of a great many opinions, after all."

The children giggled.

Phillip allowed himself a smile. "I see you two know her well."

"She does like to talk," Oliver said hesitantly.

"But she is terribly clever!" Amanda put in.

"Indeed she is," Phillip murmured.

"I rather like her," Oliver said.

"As do I," his sister added.

"I'm glad to hear that," Phillip told them. "Because I do believe she is here to stay."

And so am I, he added silently. He'd spent years avoiding his children, fearing that he'd make a mistake, terrified that he'd lose his temper. He'd thought he was doing the best thing for them, keeping them at arm's length, but he'd been wrong. So very wrong.

"I love you," he said to them, hoarsely, with great emotion. "You know that, don't you?"

They nodded, their eyes bright.

"I will always love you," he whispered, crouching down until they were all of a level. He drew them close, savoring their warmth. "I will always love you."

Chapter 17

...regardless, Daphne, I do not think you should
have run off.

*—from Eloise Bridgerton to her
sister the Duchess of Hastings,
during Daphne's brief separation
from her husband,
mere weeks into their marriage*

The ride to Benedict's was rutted and bumpy, and
by the time Eloise stepped down at her brother's
front steps, her mood had gone from bad to foul. To
make matters worse, when the butler opened the
door he looked at her as if she were a madwoman.

"Graves?" Eloise finally asked, when it became
clear that he was beyond speech.

"Are they expecting you?" he asked, still gaping.

"Well, no," Eloise said, looking quite pointedly
beyond him into the house, since that, after all, was
where she wanted to be.

It had started to drizzle, and she was not dressed for the rain.

"But I hardly think . . ." she began.

Graves stepped aside, belatedly remembering himself and allowing her entrance. "It's Master Charles," he said, referring to Benedict and Sophie's eldest son, just five and a half years old. "He's quite ill. He—"

Eloise felt something awful and acidic rise in her throat. "What is wrong?" she asked, not even bothering to temper her urgency. "Is he . . ." Good heavens, how did one ask if a young child was dying?

"I'll get Mrs. Bridgerton," Graves said, swallowing convulsively. He turned and scurried up the stairs.

"Wait!" Eloise called out, wanting to ask him more, but he was already gone.

She slumped into a chair, feeling sick with worry, and then, as if that weren't enough, rather disgusted with herself for having been even the least bit dissatisfied with her own lot in life. Her troubles with Phillip, which in truth weren't even troubles at all but nothing more than small irritants—well, they seemed very small and insignificant next to *this*.

"Eloise!"

It was Benedict, not Sophie, who came down the stairs. He looked haggard, his eyes red-rimmed, his skin pale and pasty. Eloise knew better than to ask him how long it had been since he'd slept; the question would be beyond annoying, and besides, the answer was right there on his face—he hadn't closed his eyes for days.

"What are you doing here?" he asked.

"I came for a visit," she said. "Just to say hello. I had no idea. What is wrong? How is Charles? I saw him just last week. He looked fine. He— What is wrong?"

Benedict required several seconds to muster the energy to speak. "He has a fever. I don't know why. On Saturday, he woke up fine, but by luncheon he was—" He sagged against the wall, closing his eyes in agony. "He was burning up," he whispered. "I don't know what to do."

"What did the doctor say?" Eloise asked.

"Nothing," Benedict said in a hollow voice. "Nothing of use, anyway."

"May I see him?"

Benedict nodded, his eyes still closed.

"You need to rest," Eloise said.

"I can't," he said.

"You must. You're no good to anyone like this, and I'd wager Sophie is no better."

"I made her sleep an hour ago," he said. "She looked like death."

"Well, you don't look any better," Eloise told him, keeping her tone purposefully brisk and businesslike. Sometimes that was what people needed at times like this—to be ordered about, told what to do. Compassion would only make her brother cry, and neither of them wanted to be witness to that.

"You must go to bed," Eloise ordered. "*Now*. I'll care for Charles. Even if you sleep only an hour, you'll feel so much better."

He didn't reply; he'd fallen asleep standing up.

Eloise quickly took charge. She directed Graves to put Benedict to bed, and she took over the sickroom, trying not to gasp when she first stepped in and saw her small nephew.

He looked tiny and frail in the large bed; Benedict and Sophie had had him moved to their bedchamber, where there was more room for people to tend to him. His skin was flushed, but his eyes, when he opened them, were glassy and unfocused, and when he wasn't lying unnaturally still, he was thrashing about, mumbling incoherently about ponies and treehouses and marzipan candy.

It made Eloise wonder what she would mumble incoherently about, were she ever to be gripped by a fever.

She mopped his brow, and she turned him and helped the maids change his sheets, and she didn't notice as the sun slipped below the horizon. She just thanked the heavens that Charles did not worsen under her care, because according to the servants, Benedict and Sophie had been at his side for two days straight, and Eloise did not want to have to wake either of them up with bad news.

She sat in the chair by the bed, and she read to him from his favorite book of children's tales, and she told him stories of when his father was young. And she doubted that he heard a word, but it all made her feel better, because she couldn't just sit there and do nothing.

And it wasn't until eight in the evening, when Sophie finally rose from her stupor and asked after Phillip, that it occurred to her that she ought to send a note, that he might be growing worried.

So she scrawled something short and hasty and resumed her vigil. Phillip would understand.

* * *

By eight in the evening, Phillip realized that one of two things had happened to his wife. She had either perished in a carriage accident, or she had left him.

Neither prospect was terribly appealing.

He didn't *think* she would have left him; she seemed mostly happy in their marriage, despite their quarrel that afternoon. And besides, she hadn't taken any of her belongings with her, although that didn't mean much; most of her belongings had yet to arrive from her home in London. It wasn't as if she'd be leaving much behind here at Romney Hall.

Just a husband and two children.

Good God, and he'd just said to them this afternoon— *I do believe she's here to stay.*

No, he thought savagely, Eloise would not leave him. She would never do such a thing. She didn't have a cowardly bone in her body, and she would never slink off and abandon their marriage. If she was displeased in some way, she'd tell him so, right to his face and without mincing words.

Which, he realized, yanking on his coat as he practically hurled himself out the front door, meant that she was dead in some ditch on the Wiltshire road. It had been raining steadily all evening, and the roads between his house and Benedict's were not well tended to begin with.

Hell, it would almost be better if she'd left him.

But as he rode up the drive to My Cottage, Benedict Bridgerton's absurdly named house, soaking wet and in a terrible temper, it was starting to look more like Eloise had decided to abandon her marriage.

Because she hadn't been lying in a ditch by the side of the road, and there hadn't been any sign of any sort of carriage accident, and furthermore, she hadn't been holed up at either of the two inns along the way.

And as there was only one route between his home and Benedict's, it wasn't as if she were in some other inn on some other road, and this entire farce could be chalked up to nothing more than a big misunderstanding.

"Temper," he said under his breath as he stomped up the front steps. "Temper."

Because he had never been so close to losing his.

Maybe there was a logical explanation. Maybe she hadn't wanted to drive home in the rain. It wasn't *that* bad, but it was more than a drizzle, and he supposed she might not have cared to travel.

He lifted up the knocker on the door and slammed it down. Hard.

Maybe the carriage had broken a wheel.

He banged the knocker again.

No, that couldn't explain it. Benedict could easily have sent her home in his carriage.

Maybe . . .

Maybe . . .

His mind searched fruitlessly for some other reason why she would be here with her brother and not at home with her husband. He couldn't think of one.

The curse that hissed out of his mouth was one he had not uttered in years.

He reached up for the knocker again, this time prepared to yank the damned thing off the door and hurl it through the window, but just then the door opened, and Phillip found himself staring at Graves, whom he had met less than a fortnight earlier, during his farce of a courtship.

"My wife?" Phillip practically growled.

"Sir Phillip!" the butler gasped.

Phillip didn't move, even though the rain was streaming down his face. Damned house didn't have a portico. Whoever heard of such a thing, in England, of all places?

"My wife," he bit off again.

"She's here," Graves assured him. "Come in."

Phillip stepped in. "I want my wife," he said again. "Now."

"Let me get your coat," Graves said.

"I don't give a damn about my coat," Phillip snapped. "I want my wife."

Graves froze, his hands still poised to take Phillip's coat. "Did you not receive Lady Crane's note?"

"No, I did not receive a note."

"I thought you'd arrived rather quickly," Graves murmured. "You must have crossed with the messenger. You'd better come in."

"I am in," Phillip reminded him testily.

Graves let out a long breath, almost a sigh, which was remarkable for a butler bred not to show even a hint of emotion. "I think you will be here for some time," he said softly. "Take off your coat. Get dry. You will want to be comfortable."

Phillip's anger suddenly slid into bone-deep terror. Had something happened to Eloise? Good God, if anything— "What is going on?" he whispered.

He'd just found his children. He wasn't ready to lose his wife.

The butler just turned to the stairs with sad eyes. "Come with me," he said softly.

Phillip followed, each step filling him with dread.

Eloise had, of course, attended church nearly every Sunday of her life. It was what was expected of her, and it was what good, honest people did, but in truth she'd never been a particularly God-fearing or religious sort. Her mind tended to wander during the sermons, and she sang along with the hymns not out of any great sense of spiritual uplifting but rather because she very much liked the music, and church was the only acceptable place for a tin ear like herself to raise her voice in song.

But now, tonight, as she looked down upon her small nephew, she prayed.

Charles hadn't worsened, but he hadn't improved, and the doctor, who had come and gone for the second time that day, had pronounced it "in God's hands."

Eloise hated that phrase, hated how doctors resorted to it when faced with illness beyond their skills, but if the physician was correct, and it was indeed in God's hands, then by the heavens above, that was to whom she would appeal.

When she wasn't placing a cooling cloth on Charles's forehead or spooning lukewarm broth down his throat, that was. But there was only so much to be done, and most of her time in the sickroom was spent rather helplessly in vigil.

And so she just sat there, her hands folded tightly in her lap, whispering, "Please. *Please.*"

And then, as if the wrong prayer had been answered, she heard a noise in the doorway, and somehow it was Phillip, even though she'd only sent the messenger an hour earlier. He was soaked from the rain, his hair plastered inelegantly against his forehead, but he was the dearest sight she'd ever seen, and before she had a clue what she was doing, she'd run across the room and thrown herself into his arms.

"Oh, Phillip," she sobbed, finally allowing herself to cry. She'd been so strong all day, forcing herself to be the rock that her brother and sister-in-law needed. But now Phillip was here, and as his arms came around her, he felt so solid and good, and for once she could allow someone else to be strong for her.

"I thought it was you," Phillip whispered.

"What?" she asked, confused.

"The butler—he didn't explain until we were up the stairs. I thought it was—" He shook his head. "Never mind."

Eloise said nothing, just looked up at him, a tiny, sad smile on her face.

"How is he?" he asked.

She shook her head. "Not good."

He looked over at Benedict and Sophie, who had risen to greet him. They looked rather "not good" as well.

"How long has he been this way?" Phillip asked.

"Two days," Benedict replied.

"Two and a half," Sophie corrected. "Since Saturday morning."

"You need to get dry," Eloise said, pulling away from him. "And now I do, too." She looked ruefully down at her dress, now soaked through the front from Phillip's wet clothing. "You'll end up in no better a state than Charles."

"I'm fine," Phillip said, brushing past her as he came to the little boy's bedside. He touched his forehead, then shook his head and glanced back at his parents. "I can't tell," he said. "I'm too cold from the rain."

"He's feverish," Benedict confirmed grimly.

"What have you done for him?" Phillip asked.

"Do you know something of medicine?" Sophie asked, her eyes filling with desperate hope.

"The doctor bled him," Benedict answered. "It didn't seem to help."

"We've been giving him broth," Sophie said, "and cooling him when he grows too hot."

"And warming him when he grows too cold," Eloise finished miserably.

"Nothing seems to work," Sophie whispered. And then, in front of everyone, she simply crumpled. Collapsed against the side of the bed and sobbed.

"Sophie," Benedict choked out. He dropped to his knees beside her and held her as she wept, and Phillip and Eloise both looked away as they realized that he was crying, too.

"Willow bark tea," Phillip said to Eloise. "Has he had any?"

"I don't think so. Why?"

"It's something I learned at Cambridge. It used to be given for pain, before laudanum became so popular. One of my professors insisted that it also helped to reduce fever."

"Did you give the tea to Marina?" Eloise asked.

Phillip looked at her in surprise, then remembered that she still thought Marina had died of lung fever, which, he supposed, was mostly true. "I tried," he answered, "but I couldn't get much down her throat. And besides, she was much sicker than Charles." He swallowed, remembering. "In many ways."

Eloise looked up into his face for a long moment, then turned briskly to Benedict and Sophie, who were quiet now, but still kneeling on the floor together, lost in their private moment.

Eloise, however, being Eloise, had little reverence for private moments at such a time, and so grabbed her brother's shoulder and turned him around. "Do you have any willow bark tea?" she asked him.

Benedict just looked at her, blinking, and then finally said, "I don't know."

"Mrs. Crabtree might," Sophie said, referring to one half of the old couple who had cared for My Cottage before Benedict had married, when it had been nothing more than an occasional place for him to lay his head. "She always has things like that. But she and Mr. Crabtree went to visit their daughter. They won't be home for several days."

"Can you get into their house?" Phillip asked. "I will recognize it if she has it. It won't be a tea. Just the bark, which we'll soak in hot water. It might help to bring down the fever."

"Willow bark?" Sophie asked doubtfully. "You mean to cure my son with the bark of a *tree*?"

"It certainly can't hurt him now," Benedict said gruffly, striding toward the door. "Come along, Crane. We have a key to their cottage. I will take you there myself." But as he reached the doorway, he turned to Phillip and asked, "Do you know what you are about?"

Phillip answered the only way he knew how. "I don't know. I hope so."

Benedict stared him in the face, and Phillip knew that the older man was taking his measure. It was one thing for Benedict to allow him to marry his sister. It was quite another to let him force strange potions down his son's throat.

But Phillip understood. He had children, too.

"Very well," Benedict said. "Let's go."

And as Phillip hurried out of the house, all he could do was pray that Benedict Bridgerton's trust in him had not been misplaced.

In the end it was difficult to say whether it was the willow bark or Eloise's whispered prayers or just dumb luck, but by the following morning Charles's fever had broken, and although the boy was still weak and listless, he was indubitably on the mend. By noontime, it was clear that Eloise and Phillip were no longer needed and in fact were getting in the way, and so they climbed into their carriage and headed home, both eager to collapse into their large, sturdy bed and, for once, do nothing but sleep.

The first ten minutes of the ride home were spent in silence. Eloise, astonishingly, found herself too tired to speak. But even in her exhaustion, she was too restless, too tightly wound from the stress and worry of the previous night to sleep. And so she contented herself with staring out the window at the dampened countryside. It had stopped raining right about the time Charles's fever broke, suggesting a divine intervention that might have pointed to Eloise's prayers as the young boy's savior, but as Eloise stole a glance at her husband, sitting beside her in the carriage with his eyes closed (although not, she was quite certain, asleep), she knew it was the willow bark.

She didn't know how she knew, and she was quite cognizant of the fact that she could never prove it, but her nephew's life had been saved by a cup of tea.

And to think how unlikely it was that Phillip had even been at her brother's house that evening. It had been quite a singular chain of events. If she hadn't gone in to see the twins, if she hadn't gone to tell Phillip that she didn't like their nurse, if they hadn't quarreled . . .

Put that way, little Charles Bridgerton was quite the luckiest little boy in Britain.

"Thank you," she said, not realizing that she'd intended to speak until the words left her lips.

"For what?" Phillip murmured sleepily, without opening his eyes.

"Charles," she said simply.

Phillip did open his eyes at that, and he turned to her. "It might not have been my doing. We'll never know if it was the willow bark."

"*I* know," she said firmly.

His lips curved into the barest of smiles. "You always do."

And she thought to herself— Was this what she'd been waiting for her entire life? Not the passion, not the gasps of pleasure she felt when he joined her in bed, but *this*.

This sense of comfort, of easy companionship, of sitting next to someone in a carriage and knowing with every fiber of your being that it was where you belonged.

She placed her hand on his. "It was so awful," she

said, surprised that she had tears in her eyes. "I don't think I have ever been so scared in my life. I can't imagine what it must have been like for Benedict and Sophie."

"Nor I," Phillip said softly.

"If it had been one of our children . . ." she said, and she realized it was the first time she'd said that. *Our* children.

Phillip was silent for a long time. When he spoke, he was looking out the window. "The entire time I was watching Charles," he said, his voice suspiciously hoarse, "all I kept thinking was, thank God it's not Oliver or Amanda." And then he turned back to her, his face pinched with guilt. "But it shouldn't be anyone's child."

Eloise squeezed his hand. "I don't think there is anything wrong with such feelings. You're not a saint, you know. You're just a father. A very good one, I think."

He looked at her with an odd expression, and then he shook his head. "No," he said gravely, "I'm not. But I hope to be."

She cocked her head. "Phillip?"

"You were right," he said, his mouth tightening into a grim line. "About their nurse. I didn't want anything to be wrong, and so I paid no attention, but you were right. She was beating them."

"*What?*"

"With a book," he continued, his voice almost dispassionate, as if he'd already used up all of his emotions. "I walked in and she was beating Amanda with a book. She had already finished with Oliver."

"Oh, no," Eloise said, as tears—of sorrow *and* anger—filled her eyes. "I never dreamed. I didn't like her, of course. And she'd rapped them on the knuckles, but . . . *I've* been rapped on the knuckles. Everyone has been rapped on the knuckles." She slumped in her seat, guilt weighing her shoulders down. "I should have realized. I should have seen."

Phillip snorted. "You've barely been in residence a fortnight. I've been living with that bloody woman for months. If I didn't see, why should you have done?"

Eloise had nothing to say to this, nothing at least that would not make her already guilt-ridden husband feel worse. "I assume you dismissed her," she finally said.

He nodded. "I told the children you would help to find a replacement."

"Of course," she said quickly.

"And I—" He stopped, cleared his throat, and looked out the window before continuing. "I—"

"What is it, Phillip?" she asked softly.

He didn't turn back to her when he said, "I'm going to be a better father. I've pushed them away for too long. I was so afraid of becoming my father, of being like him, that I—"

"Phillip," Eloise murmured, laying her hand on his, "you're not like your father. You could never be."

"No," he said, his voice hollow, "but I thought I could. I got a whip once. I went to the stables and I grabbed the whip." His head fell into his hands. "I was so angry. So bloody angry."

"But you didn't use it," she whispered, knowing that her words were true. They had to be.

He shook his head. "But I wanted to."

"But you didn't," she said again, keeping her voice as firm as she was able.

"I was so angry," he said again, and she wasn't even sure he'd heard her, so lost was he in his own memory. But then he turned to her, and his eyes pierced hers. "Do you understand what it is to be terrified by your own anger?"

She shook her head.

"I'm not a small man, Eloise," he said. "I could hurt someone."

"So could I," she replied. And then, at his dry look, she added, "Well, maybe not you, but I'm certainly big enough to hurt a child."

"You would never do that," he grunted, turning away.

"Neither would *you*," she repeated.

He was silent.

And then, suddenly, she understood. "Phillip," she said softly, "you said you were angry, but . . . with *whom* were you angry?"

He looked at her uncomprehendingly. "They glued their governess's hair to the sheets, Eloise."

"I know," she said, with a dismissive wave of her hand. "I'm quite certain I would have wanted to throttle them both, had I been present. But that's not what I asked." She waited for him to make some sort of response. When he did not, she added, "Were you angry with them because of the glue, or were you angry with yourself, because you didn't know how to make them mind?"

He didn't say anything but they both knew the answer.

Eloise reached out and touched his hand. "You're nothing like your father, Phillip," she repeated. "Nothing."

"I know that now," Phillip said softly. "You have

no idea how badly I wanted to tear that bloody Nurse Edwards from limb to limb."

"I can imagine," Eloise said, snorting as she settled back in her seat.

Phillip felt his lips twitch. He had no idea why, but there was something almost funny in his wife's tone, something comforting, even. Somehow they had found humor in a situation where there ought not to be any. And it felt good.

"She deserved nothing less," Eloise added with a shrug. And then she turned and looked at him. "But you didn't touch her, did you?"

He shook his head. "No. And if I managed to keep my temper with her, then I'm damn well not ever going to lose it with my children."

"Of course not," Eloise said, as if it had never been an issue. She patted his hand, then glanced out the window, clearly unconcerned.

Such faith in him, Phillip realized. Such faith in his inner goodness, in the quality of his soul, when he'd been wracked by doubt for so many years.

And then he felt he had to be honest, had to come clean, and before he knew what he was about, he blurted out, "I thought you'd left me."

"Last night?" She turned to him in shock. "Whyever would you think that?"

He shrugged self-deprecatingly. "Oh, I don't know. It might be because you left for your brother's house and never came back."

She hmmphed at that. "It's clear now why I was detained, and besides, I would never leave you. You should know that."

He quirked a brow. "Should I?"

"Of course you should," she said, looking rather

cross with him. "I made a vow in that church, and I assure you I do not take such things lightly. Besides, I made a commitment to Oliver and Amanda to be their mother, and I would never turn my back on that."

Phillip regarded her steadily, then murmured, "No. No, you wouldn't. Silly of me not to have thought of that."

She sat back and crossed her arms. "Well, you should have done. You know me better than that." And then, when he did not say anything more, she added, "Those poor children. They have already lost one mother through no fault of their own. I'm certainly not going to run off and make them go through all that again."

She turned to him with a supremely irritated expression. "I cannot believe you even thought that of me."

Phillip was beginning to wonder the same thing himself. He'd only known Eloise—Dear God, could it possibly have been only two weeks? It felt, in many ways, like a lifetime. Because he did feel he knew her, inside and out. She'd always have her secrets, of course, as all people did, and he was quite certain he'd never *understand* her, since he couldn't imagine ever understanding anyone female.

But he knew her. He was quite certain he knew her. And he should have known better than to have worried that she'd abandoned their marriage.

It must have been panic, pure and simple. And, he supposed, because it was better to think she'd left him than to imagine her dead in a ditch by the side of the road. With the former he could at least storm her brother's house and drag her home.

If she'd died . . .

He was unprepared for the pain he felt in his gut at the mere thought.

When had she come to mean so much to him? And what was he going to do to keep her happy?

Because he needed her happy. Not just, as he'd been telling himself, because a happy Eloise meant that his life would continue to run smoothly. He needed her happy because the mere thought of her unhappy was like a knife in his heart.

The irony was well aimed, indeed. He'd told himself, over and over, that he'd married her to be a mother to his children, but just now, when she'd declared that she would never leave their marriage, that her commitment to the twins was too strong—

He'd felt jealous.

He'd actually felt jealous of his own children. He'd wanted her to mention the word *wife*, and all he'd heard was mother.

He wanted her to want him. Him. Not just because she'd made a vow in a church, but because she was quite convinced she could not live without him. Maybe even because she loved him.

Loved him.

Dear God, when had this happened? When had he come to want so much from marriage? He'd married her to mother his children; they both knew that.

And then there was the passion. He was a man, for God's sake, and he'd not lain with a woman for eight years. How could he not be drunk on the feel of Eloise's skin next to his, on the sound of her whimpers and moans when she exploded around him?

On the pure force of his own pleasure every time he entered her?

He'd found everything he'd ever wanted in a marriage. Eloise ran his life to perfection by day and warmed his bed with the skill of a courtesan by night. She fulfilled his every desire so well that he hadn't noticed that she'd done something more.

She'd found his heart. She'd touched it, changed it. Changed him.

He loved her. He hadn't been looking for love, hadn't even given a thought to it, but there it was, and it was the most precious thing imaginable.

He was at the dawn of a new day, the first page of a new chapter of his life. It was thrilling. And terrifying. Because he did not want to fail. Not now, not when he'd finally found everything he needed. Eloise. His children. Himself.

It had been years since he'd felt comfortable in his own skin, since he'd trusted his instincts. Since he'd looked in the mirror without avoiding his own gaze.

He glanced out the window. The carriage was slowing down, pulling up alongside Romney Hall. Everything looked gray—the skies, the stone of the house, the windows, which reflected the clouds. Even the grass seemed a little less green without the sun to brighten its hue.

It suited his contemplative mood perfectly.

A footman appeared to help Eloise down, and once Phillip had hopped down beside her, she turned to him and said, "I'm exhausted, and you look the same. Shall we go take a nap?"

He was just about to agree, since he was exhausted, but then, just before the words could leave his lips, he shook his head and said, "You go along without me."

She opened her mouth to question him, but he silenced her with a gentle squeeze on her shoulder. "I'll be up shortly," he said. "But right now, I think I want to hug my children."

Chapter 18

...I do not tell you often enough, dear Mother, how very grateful I am that I am yours. It is a rare parent who would offer a child such latitude and understanding. It is an even rarer one who calls a daughter friend. I do love you, dear Mama.

—*from Eloise Bridgerton to her mother, upon refusing her sixth offer of marriage*

When Eloise awoke from her nap, she was surprised to see that the sheets on the other side of the bed were neat and unrumpled. Phillip had been just as tired as she had been, probably more so, since he had ridden all the way to Benedict's house the night before, in the wind and rain, no less.

After she'd tidied herself, she set about to locate him, but he was nowhere to be found. She told herself not to worry, that they'd had a difficult few days, that he probably just needed some time to himself, to think.

Just because she tended not to prefer solitude didn't mean everyone else agreed with her.

She laughed humorlessly to herself. That was a lesson she'd been trying—unsuccessfully—to learn her entire life.

And so she forced herself to stop looking for him. She was married now, and suddenly she understood what it was her mother had been trying so hard to tell her on her wedding night. Marriage was about compromise, and she and Phillip were very different people. They might be perfect for one another, but that didn't mean they were the same. And if she wanted him to change some of his ways for her, well then, she was going to have to do the same for him.

She didn't see him for the rest of the day, not when she took tea in the afternoon, not when she bade the twins good night, and not at supper, which she was forced to take by herself, feeling very small and very alone at the large mahogany table. She dined in silence, ever aware of the watchful eyes of the footmen, both of whom smiled at her sympathetically as they brought forth her food.

Eloise smiled back, because she did believe in being polite in all things, but inside she was sighing with resignation. It was a sad state of affairs when the footmen (*men*, for goodness' sakes, who were normally oblivious to another's distress) felt sorry for you.

But then again, here she was, only one week into her marriage and dining alone. Who wouldn't have pitied her?

Besides, the last the servants knew, Sir Phillip had raged out the door to fetch his wife, who had presumably fled to her brother's house after a horrible row.

Put that way, Eloise thought with a sigh, it wasn't quite so surprising that Phillip might have thought she'd left him.

She ate sparingly, not wanting to prolong the meal any longer than was necessary, and when she finished her obligatory two bites of pudding, she rose, fully intending to take herself off to bed, where, she presumed, she would pass her time as she had all day—alone.

But as she stepped into the hall, she found herself restless, not quite ready to retire. And so she began to walk, somewhat aimlessly, through the house. It was a chilly night for late May, and she was glad she'd brought a shawl. Eloise had spent time in many grand country homes, where all the fireplaces were lit at night, leaving the house in a blaze of light and warmth, but Romney Hall, while snug and comfortable, held no such delusions of self-importance, and so most of the rooms were kept closed off for the night, with the fireplaces only lit when needed.

And blast it, it was *cold*.

She pulled her shawl closer around her shoulders as she walked along, rather enjoying finding her way with only the dim moonlight to guide her. But then, as she approached the portrait gallery, she saw the unmistakable light of a lantern.

Someone was there, and she knew, even before she'd taken another step forward, that it was Phillip.

She approached quietly, glad that she'd worn her soft-soled slippers, and peered through the doorway.

The sight she saw nearly broke her heart.

Phillip was standing there, stock-still, in front of Marina's portrait. He moved not at all, save for the occasional blink of his eyes. He just stood there, looking at her, looking at his dead wife, and the expression on his face was so bleak and sorrowful that Eloise almost gasped.

Had he lied to her when he'd said that he hadn't loved Marina? When he'd said he hadn't felt passion?

And did it matter? Marina was dead. It wasn't as if she was a true competitor for Phillip's affections. And even if she was, did it matter? Because he didn't love Eloise, either, and she didn't—

Or maybe, she realized, in one of those flashes that knock the very breath from one's lungs, she did.

It was hard to imagine when it had happened, or even how it had happened, but this feeling she had for him, this affection and respect, had grown into something deeper.

And oh, how she wanted him to feel the same way.

He needed her. Of that she was quite sure. He needed her maybe even more than she needed him, but that wasn't it. She loved being needed, being wanted, being indispensable, even, but there was more to her feelings.

She loved the way he smiled, slightly lopsided, a little boyish, and with a little lilt of surprise, as if he couldn't quite believe in his own happiness.

She loved the way he looked at her, as if she were the most beautiful woman in the world, when she knew, quite patently, that she was not.

She loved the way he actually listened to what she had to say, and the way he didn't allow her to cow him. She even loved the way he told her she talked too much, because he almost always did it with a smile, and because, of course, it was true.

And she loved the way he still listened to her, even after he told her she talked too much.

She loved the way he loved his children.

She loved his honor, his honesty, and his sly sense of humor.

And she loved the way she fit into his life, and the way he fit into hers.

It was comfortable. It was right.

And this, she finally realized, was where she belonged.

But he was standing there, staring at a portrait of his dead wife, and from the way he was so still and unmoving . . . well, God only knew how long he'd been doing that. And if he still loved her . . .

She choked back a wave of guilt. Who was she to feel anything but sorrow on behalf of Marina? She had died so young, so unexpectedly. And she'd lost what Eloise considered every mother's God-given right—to watch her children grow up.

To feel jealous of a woman like that was unconscionable.

And yet . . .

And yet Eloise must not be as good a person as she ought, because she couldn't watch this scene, couldn't watch Phillip staring at the portrait of his first wife without envy squeezing around her heart. She'd just realized she loved this man, and would, to the very last of her days. *She* needed him, not a dead woman.

No, she thought fiercely. He didn't still love Marina. Maybe he'd never loved Marina. He'd said the morning before that he hadn't been with a woman for eight years.

Eight *years*?

It sank in, finally.

Good God.

She'd spent the past two days in such a flurry of emotion that she hadn't really stopped and thought—really thought—about what he'd said.

Eight years.

It was not what she would have expected. Not from a man such as Phillip, who clearly enjoyed— no, clearly *needed*—the physical aspects of married love.

Marina had only been dead for fifteen months. If Phillip had gone without a woman for eight years, that meant they hadn't shared a bedroom since the twins had been conceived.

No . . .

Eloise did some mental arithmetic. No, it would have been after the twins had been born. A little bit after.

Of course, Phillip could have been off in his dates, or perhaps exaggerating, but somehow Eloise didn't think so. She rather thought he knew exactly when he and Marina had last slept together, and she feared, especially now that she had pinpointed the date of it, that it had been a terrible occasion indeed.

But he had not betrayed her. He had remained faithful to a woman from whose bed he'd been banned. Eloise wasn't surprised, given his innate sense of honor and dignity, but she didn't think she would have thought less of him if he had sought comfort elsewhere.

And the fact that he hadn't—

It made her love him all the more.

But if his time with Marina had been so difficult and disturbing, why had he come here tonight? Why was he staring at her portrait, standing there as if he couldn't move from the spot? Gazing upon her as if he were pleading with her, begging her for something.

Begging the favor of a dead woman.

Eloise couldn't stand it any longer. She stepped forward and cleared her throat.

Phillip surprised her by turning instantly; she'd thought that he was so completely lost in his own world that he would not hear her. He didn't say anything, not even her name, but then . . .

He held out his hand.

She walked forward and took it, not knowing what else to do, not even knowing—as strange as it seemed—what to say. So she just stood beside him and stared up at Marina's portrait.

"Did you love her?" she asked, even though she'd asked him before.

"No," he said, and she realized that a small part of her must have still been very worried, because the rush of relief she felt at his denial was surprising in its force.

"Do you miss her?"

His voice was softer, but it was sure. "No."

"Did you hate her?" she whispered.

He shook his head, and he sounded very sad when he said, "No."

She didn't know what else to ask, wasn't sure what she *should* ask, so she just waited, hoping he would speak.

And after a very long while, he did.

"She was sad," he said. "She was always sad."

Eloise looked up at him, but he did not return the glance. His eyes were on Marina's portrait, as if he had to look at her while he spoke about her. As if maybe he owed her that.

"She was always somber," he continued, "always a bit too serene, if that makes any sense, but it was worse after the twins were born. I don't know what happened. The midwife said it was normal for women to cry after childbirth but that I shouldn't worry, that it would clear away in a few weeks."

"But it didn't," Eloise said softly.

He shook his head, then harshly brushed one dark lock of hair aside when it fell onto his brow. "It just got worse. I don't know how to explain it. It was almost as if . . ." He shrugged helplessly as he searched for words, and when he continued, he was whispering. "It was almost as if she'd disappeared. . . . She rarely left her bed. . . . I never saw her smile. . . . She cried a lot. A great deal."

The sentences came forth, not in a rush, but one at a time, as if each piece of information were being brought forth from his memory in slow succession. Eloise didn't say anything, didn't feel it her place to interrupt him or to try to inject her feelings on a matter she knew nothing about.

And then, finally, he turned away from Marina to Eloise, and looked her squarely in the eye.

"I tried everything to make her happy. Everything in my power. Everything I knew. But it wasn't enough."

Eloise opened her mouth, made a small sound, the beginnings of a murmur meant to assure him that he'd done his best, but he cut her off.

"Do you understand, Eloise?" he asked, his voice growing louder, more urgent. "It wasn't enough."

"It wasn't your fault," she said softly, because even though she hadn't known Marina as an adult, she knew Phillip, and she knew that had to be the truth.

"Eventually I just gave up," he said, his voice flat. "I stopped trying to help her at all. I was so sick and tired of beating my head against a wall where she was concerned. And all I tried to do was protect the children, and keep them away when she was in a really bad spell. Because they loved her so much." He looked at her pleadingly, maybe for understanding, maybe for something else Eloise didn't understand. "She was their mother."

"I know," she said softly.

"She was their mother, and she didn't . . . she couldn't . . ."

"But *you* were there," Eloise said fervently. "You were there."

He laughed harshly. "Yes, and a fat lot of good that did them. It's one thing to be born with one dreadful parent, but to have two? I would never have wished that on my children, and yet . . . here we are."

"You are not a bad father," Eloise said, unable to keep the scolding tone out of her voice.

He just shrugged and turned back to the portrait, clearly unable to consider her words.

"Do you know how much it hurt?" he whispered. "Do you have any idea?"

She shook her head, even though he'd turned away.

"To try so hard, so damned hard, and never succeed? Hell—" He laughed, a short, bitter sound, full of self-loathing. "Hell," he said again, "I didn't even like her and it hurt so much."

"You didn't like her?" Eloise asked, her surprise pitching her words into a different register.

His lips quirked ironically. "Can you like someone you don't even know?" He turned back to her. "I didn't know her, Eloise. I was married to her for eight years, and I never knew her."

"Maybe she didn't let you know her."

"Maybe I should have tried harder."

"Maybe," Eloise said, infusing her voice with all the surety and conviction she could, "there was nothing more you could have done. Some people are born melancholy, Phillip. I don't know why, and I doubt anyone knows why, but that's just the way they are."

He looked at her sardonically, his dark eyes clearly dismissing her opinion, and so she leapt back in with, "Don't forget, I knew her, too. As a child, long before you even knew she existed."

Phillip's expression changed then, and his gaze grew so intense upon her face that she nearly squirmed under the pressure of it.

"I never heard her laugh," Eloise said softly. "Not even once. I've been trying to remember her better since I met you, trying to recall why my memories of her always seemed so strange and odd, and I think that's it. She never laughed. Whoever heard of a child who doesn't laugh?"

Phillip was silent for a few moments, then he said, "I don't think I ever heard her laugh, either. Sometimes she would smile, usually when the children came to see her, but she never laughed."

Eloise nodded. And then she said, "I'm not Marina, Phillip."

"I know," he said. "Believe me, I know. It's why I married you, you know."

It wasn't quite what she wanted to hear, but she stifled her disappointment and allowed him to continue.

The creases in his forehead deepened, and he rubbed them hard. He looked so burdened, so tired of his responsibilities. "I just wanted someone who wasn't going to be sad," he said. "Someone who would be present for the children, someone who wouldn't—"

He cut himself off, turned away.

"Someone who wouldn't what?" she asked urgently, sensing that this was important.

For the longest time she thought he wasn't going to answer, but then, just when she'd quite given up on him, he said, "She died of influenza. You know that, don't you?"

"Yes," she said, since his back was to her and he wouldn't see her nod.

"She died of influenza," he repeated. "That's what we told everyone—"

Eloise suddenly felt very sick, because she knew, absolutely *knew* what he was going to say.

"Well, it was the truth," he said bitterly, surprising her with his words. She'd been so sure he was going to say that they'd been lying all the while.

"It's the truth," he said again. "But it wasn't all of the truth. She did die of influenza, but we never told anyone why she fell ill."

"The lake," Eloise whispered, her words coming

forth unbidden. She hadn't even realized she'd been thinking them until she spoke.

He nodded grimly. "She didn't fall in by accident."

Her hand flew to cover her mouth. No wonder he'd been so upset that she'd taken the children there. She felt awful. Of course she didn't know, couldn't have known, but still . . .

"I got her just in time," he said. "Just in time to save her from drowning, that is. Not in time to save her from lung fever three days later." He choked back bitter laughter. "Not even my famed willow bark tea could do the job for *her*."

"I'm so sorry," Eloise whispered, and she was, even though Marina's death had, in so many ways, made her own happiness possible.

"You don't understand," he said, not looking at her. "You couldn't possibly."

"I have never known someone who took their own life," she said cautiously, not certain if these were the words one was meant to say in such a situation.

"That's not what I mean," he said, almost snapped, really. "You don't know what it's like to feel trapped, stuck, hopeless. To try so hard and never, *ever*"—he turned to her then, and his eyes were flashing fire—"break through. I tried. Every day I tried. I tried for me and I tried for Marina, and most of all for Oliver and Amanda. I did everything I knew how, everything everyone told me to do, and nothing, not one thing made it work. I tried, and she cried, and then I tried again and again and again, and all she ever did was dig herself deeper into her damned bed and pull up the covers over her head. She lived in darkness with her curtains drawn and the lights dimmed and then she picked the one god-damned sunny day to go and kill herself."

Eloise's eyes widened.

"A sunny day," he said. "We'd had a bloody month of overcast skies, and then finally the sun came out, and she had to kill herself." He laughed, but the sound was short and bitter. "After everything she'd done, she had to go and ruin sunny days for me."

"Phillip," Eloise said, placing her hand on his arm. But he just shook her off. "And if that weren't enough, she couldn't even kill herself properly. Well, no," he said harshly, "I suppose that was *my* fault. She would have been quite good and dead if I hadn't come along and forced her to torture us all for three more days, wondering if she might live or die." He crossed his arms and snorted in disgust. "But of course she died. I don't know why we even held out hope. She didn't fight it at all, didn't use even an ounce of energy to fight the illness. She just laid there and let it claim her, and I kept waiting for her to smile, as if she were finally happy because now she'd succeeded in the one thing she wanted to do."

"Oh, my God," Eloise whispered, sickened by the image. "Did she?"

He shook his head. "No. She didn't have even the energy for that. She just died with the same expression on her face she always had. Empty."

"I'm so sorry," Eloise said, even though she knew her words could never be enough. "No one should have to go through something like that."

He stared at her for the longest time, his eyes searching hers, looking for something, searching for an answer that she wasn't sure she had. Then he turned abruptly away and walked to the window, staring out at the inky night sky. "I tried so hard," he said, his voice quiet with resignation and regret, "and still, every day I wished I were married to someone else." His head tipped forward, until his forehead was leaning against the glass. "Anyone else."

He was silent for a very long time. Too long, in Eloise's estimation, and so she stepped forward, murmuring his name, just to hear his response. Just to know that he was all right.

"Yesterday," he said, his voice abrupt, "you said we have a problem—"

"No," she cut in, as quickly as she was able. "I didn't mean—"

"You said we have a problem," he repeated, his voice so low and forceful she didn't think he'd hear another interruption even if she tried. "But until you live through what I lived through," he continued, "until you've been trapped in a hopeless marriage, to a hopeless spouse, until you've gone to bed alone for years wishing for nothing more than the touch of another human being . . ."

He turned around, stepped toward her, his eyes alight with a fire that humbled her. "Until you've lived through all that," he said, "don't you *ever* complain about what we have. Because to me . . . to me . . ." He choked on the words, but he barely paused before he continued. "This—us—is heaven. And I can't bear to hear you say otherwise."

"Oh, Phillip," she said, and then she did the only thing she knew to do. She closed the distance between them and threw her arms around him and held on for all she was worth. "I'm so sorry," she murmured, her tears soaking into his shirt. "I'm so sorry."

"I don't want to fail again," he choked out, burying his face in the crook of her neck. "I can't—I couldn't—"

"You won't," she vowed. "*We* won't."

"You've got to be happy," he said, his words sounding as if they'd been ripped from his throat. "You have to be. Please say—"

"I *am*," she assured him. "I am. I promise you."

He pulled back and took her face in his hands, forcing her to look deeply into his eyes. He seemed to be searching for something in her expression, desperately seeking confirmation, or maybe absolution, or maybe just a simple promise.

"I *am* happy," she whispered, covering his hands with her own. "More than I ever dreamed possible. And I am proud to be your wife."

His face seemed to tighten, and his lower lip began to quiver. Eloise caught her breath. She'd never seen a man cry, never really even thought it possible, but then a tear rolled slowly down his cheek, settling into the dimple at the corner of his mouth until she reached out and brushed it away.

"I love you," he said, choking on the words. "I don't even care if you don't feel the same way. I love you and . . . and . . ."

"Oh, Phillip," she whispered, reaching up and touching the tears on his face. "I love you, too."

His lips moved as if trying to form words, and then he gave up on speech, and he reached out for her, crushing her to him with a strength and intensity that humbled her. He buried his face in her neck, murmuring her name over and over again, and then his words became kisses, and he moved along her skin until he found her mouth.

How long they stood there, kissing as if the world were to end that very night, Eloise would never know. Then he swept her into his arms and carried her out of the portrait gallery and up the stairs, and before she knew it, she was on her bed, and he was on top of her.

And his lips had never left hers.

"I need you," he said hoarsely, pulling her dress from her body with shaking fingers. "I need you like I need breath. I need you like food, like water."

She tried to say she needed him, too, but she couldn't, not when his mouth had closed around her nipple, not when he was sucking in such a way that made her feel it down in her belly, a warm, slow heat that curled and grew, taking her hostage until she could do nothing but reach for this man, her husband, and give herself to him with everything that she had.

He lifted himself away from her, just long enough to yank off his own clothing, and then he rejoined her, this time lying beside her. He pulled her to him until they were belly to belly, and then he stroked her hair, softly, gently, and his other hand splayed at the small of her back.

"I love you," he whispered. "I want nothing more than to grab you and—" He swallowed. "You have no idea how much I want you right now."

Her lips curved. "I think I have some idea."

That made him smile. "My body is dying. It's like nothing I've ever felt, and yet . . ." He leaned in closer and brushed his lips across hers. "I had to stop. I had to tell you."

She couldn't speak, could barely breathe. And she felt the tears coming, burning in her eyes until they spilled out, flowing over his hands.

"Don't cry," he whispered.

"I can't help it," she said, her voice shaking. "I love you so much. I didn't think—I'd always hoped, but I guess I never really thought—"

"I never thought, either," he said, and they both knew what they were thinking—

I never thought it would happen to me.

"I'm so lucky," he said, and his hands moved, sliding down her rib cage, over her belly, and then around to her backside. "I think I've waited my entire life for you."

"I know I've been waiting for you," Eloise said.

He squeezed and pulled her against him, nearly burning her with his touch. "I'm not going to be able to go slowly," he said, his voice shaking. "I think I used up my entire allotment of willpower just now."

"Don't go slowly," she said, sliding onto her back and pulling him atop her. She spread her legs, opening until he settled between them, his sex coming to rest right at the opening of her womanhood. Her hands found his hair and sank in, pulling his head down until his mouth was right at hers. "I don't want it slow," she said.

And then, in a single fluid motion, so fast that it took her breath away, he was inside her, embedded to the hilt, knocking against her womb with enough force to jolt a surprised little "Oh!" from her lips.

He smiled wickedly. "You said you wanted it fast."

She responded by curling her legs around his, locking him to her. She tilted her hips, which pulled him in even deeper, and smiled back. "You're not doing anything," she said to him.

And then he did.

All words were lost as they moved. They weren't graceful, and they didn't move as one. Their bodies weren't in tune, and the sounds they made were not musical or lovely.

They just moved, with need and fire and total abandon, reaching for each other, reaching for the summit. The wait was not long. Eloise tried to make it last, tried to hold out, but there was no way. With every stroke, Phillip unleashed a fire within her that could not be denied. And then finally, when she couldn't contain herself one moment longer, Eloise cried out and arched beneath him, lifting them both from the bed with the force of her fulfillment. Her body quivered and shook, and she gasped for breath, and all she could do was clutch his back, her fingers surely leaving bruises on his skin as she clung to him.

And then, before she could even fall back down to earth, Phillip cried out, and he slammed forward over and over again, emptying himself within her until he collapsed, the full weight of him pinning her into the mattress.

But she didn't mind. She loved the feel of him atop her, loved the heaviness, loved the smell and the taste of the sweat on his skin.

She loved *him*.

It was that simple.

She loved him, and he loved her, and if there was anything more, anything else important in her world, it just didn't matter. Not right there, not right then.

"I love you," he whispered, finally rolling off of her and allowing her lungs to fill with air.

I love you.

It was all she needed.

Chapter 19

... days are filled with endless amusements. I shop and attend luncheons and pay calls (and have calls paid upon me). In the evenings I usually attend a ball or musicale, or perhaps a smaller party. Sometimes I remain at home with my own company and read a book. Truly, it is a full and lively existence; I have no cause for complaint. What more, I often ask, could a lady want?

—from Eloise Bridgerton to Sir Phillip Crane,
six months into their unusual correspondence

For the rest of her days, Eloise would remember the following week as one of the most magical of her life. There were no stupendous events, no bursts of fine weather, no birthdays, no extravagant gifts or unexpected visitors.

But still, even though it all seemed, on the outside at least, very ordinary . . .

Everything changed.

It wasn't the sort of thing that hit one like a thunderbolt, or even, Eloise thought with a wry smile, like a slammed door or high C at the opera. It was a slow, creeping kind of change, the sort of thing that begins without one realizing it, and ends before one even knows it has begun.

It started a few mornings after she'd come across Phillip in the portrait gallery. When she woke, he was sitting fully dressed at the foot of the bed, staring at her with an indulgent smile on his face.

"What are you doing there?" Eloise asked, tucking the sheets under her arms as she scooted into a sitting position.

"Watching you."

Her lips parted with surprise, and then she couldn't help but smile. "It can't be very interesting."

"To the contrary. I can't think of anything that could keep my attention for so long."

She blushed, mumbling something about his being silly, but in truth, his words made her want to yank him right back into bed. She had a feeling he wouldn't resist—he never did—but she put a hold on her desire, since he had, after all, got himself completely dressed, and she rather thought he'd done so for a reason.

"I brought you a muffin," he said, holding out a plate.

Eloise thanked him and took his proffered dish. While she was munching away (and wishing he'd thought to bring something to drink as well), he said, "I thought we might go on an outing today."

"You and I?"

"Actually," he said, "I thought the four of us might go."

Eloise froze, her teeth lodged in the muffin, and looked at him. This was, she realized, the first time he'd suggested such a thing. The first time, to her knowledge, at least, that he'd reached out to his children rather than setting them aside, hoping that someone else would see to them.

"I think that's a fine idea," she said softly.

"Good," he said, rising to his feet. "I'll leave you to your morning routine and inform that poor housemaid you bullied into acting as their nurse that we will be taking them for the day."

"I'm sure she'll be relieved," Eloise said. Mary hadn't really wanted to take the position as nurse-maid, even on a temporary basis. None of the servants had; they all knew the twins too well. And poor long-haired Mary vividly recalled having to burn the bedsheets after they'd been unable to remove the last governess's glued-on hair.

But there was nothing else to be done, and Eloise had extracted a promise from both children that they would treat Mary with the respect due to, say, the queen, and so far they had been living up to their word. Eloise even had her fingers crossed that Mary might relent and agree to the position on a permanent basis. It did pay better than cleaning, after all.

Eloise looked over at the door and was surprised to see Phillip standing quite still, frowning. "What is wrong?" she asked.

He blinked, then looked in her direction, his brows still pulled down in thought. "I'm not sure what to do."

"I believe the doorknob will turn in either direction," she teased.

He shot her a look, then said, "There are no fairs or events occurring in the village. What should we do with them?"

"Anything," Eloise said, smiling at him with all the love in her heart. "Or nothing at all. It doesn't matter, really. All they want is you, Phillip. All they want is you."

Two hours later Phillip and Oliver were standing outside the Larkin's Fine Tailor and Dressmaker in the village of Tetbury, waiting somewhat impatiently while Eloise and Amanda completed their purchases inside.

"Did we have to go *shopping*?" Oliver groaned, as if he'd been asked to wear pigtails and a frock.

Phillip shrugged. "It is what your mother wished to do."

"Next time, it's the men's turn to pick," Oliver grumbled. "If I'd known having a mother would mean *this* . . ."

Phillip had to force himself not to laugh. "Men must make sacrifices for the women we love," he said in serious tones, patting his son on the shoulder. "It's the way of the world, I'm afraid."

Oliver let out a long-suffering sigh, as if he'd been making such sacrifices on a daily basis.

Phillip looked through the window. Eloise and Amanda showed no signs of wrapping up their business. "But as pertains to the issue of shopping, and who gets to decide upon the next joint activity," he said, "I agree wholeheartedly."

Just then, Eloise poked her head outside. "Oliver?" she asked. "Would you care to come in?"

"No," Oliver replied, shaking his head emphatically.

Eloise pursed her lips. "Allow me to rephrase," she said. "Oliver, I would like you to come in."

Oliver looked up to his father, his eyes pleading.

"I'm afraid you must do as she says," Phillip said.

"So many sacrifices," Oliver grumbled, shaking his head as he hauled himself up the steps.

Phillip coughed to cover a laugh.

"Are you coming, too?" Oliver asked.

Hell, no, Phillip almost said, but managed to catch himself in time to change it to, "I need to remain outside to watch the carriage."

Oliver's eyes narrowed. "Why does the carriage need watching?"

"Er, strain on the wheels," Phillip mumbled. "All our packages, you know."

He was unable to hear what Eloise said under her breath, but the tone was not complimentary.

"Run along, Oliver," he said, patting his son on the back. "Your mother needs you."

"And you, too," Eloise said sweetly, just to torture him, he was sure. "You need new shirts."

Phillip groaned. "Can't we have the tailor come out to the house?"

"Don't you want to choose the fabric?"

He shook his head and said, quite grandly, "I trust you implicitly."

"I think he needs to watch the carriage," Oliver said, still hovering in the threshold.

"He's going to need to watch his back," Eloise muttered, "if he doesn't—"

"Oh, very well," Phillip said. "I'll come in. But only for a moment." He found himself standing in the women's half of the shop, a frilly, feminine place if ever there was one, and shuddered. "Anything more, and I'm likely to perish of claustrophobia."

"A big, strong man like you?" Eloise said in a mild voice. "Nonsense." And then she looked up at him and motioned to him with her chin to come close.

"Yes?" he asked, wondering what this was all about.

"Amanda," she whispered, nodding toward a door at the back of the room. "When she comes out, make a fuss."

He looked about the store doubtfully. He might as well have been in China, so out of place did he feel. "I'm not very good at fussing."

"Learn," she ordered, then turned her attention to Oliver with a: "Now it's your turn, Master Crane. Mrs. Larkin—"

Oliver's groan would have done a dying man justice. "I want Mr. Larkin," he protested. "Like Father."

"You would like to see the tailor?" Eloise asked.

Oliver nodded vigorously.

"Really?"

He nodded again, although without quite as much conviction.

"Even though," Eloise continued, with enough inflection to put her on the Drury Lane stage, "not an hour ago you vowed that wild horses could not drag you inside a storefront unless there were guns or toy soldiers in the window?"

Oliver's mouth went slack, but he nodded. Barely.

"You're good," Phillip murmured in her ear as he watched Oliver drag himself through the doorway that separated Mr. Larkin's half of the store from Mrs. Larkin's.

"It's all a matter of showing them how much worse the alternative is," Eloise said. "Getting fitted by Mr. Larkin is tedious, but *Mrs. Larkin*—now, that would be wretched."

An indignant howl rent the air, and Oliver came running back in—straight to Eloise, which left Phillip feeling a little bereft. He wanted his children to run to him, he realized.

"He stuck me with a pin!" Oliver declared.

"Were you squirming?" Eloise asked, without even batting an eyelash.

"No!"

"Not even a little bit?"

"Only the tiniest bit."

"Right, then," Eloise said. "Don't move next time. I assure you that Mr. Larkin is very good at his job. If you don't move, you won't get jabbed. It's as simple as that."

Oliver digested that, then turned to Phillip with a pleading look in his eyes. It was rather nice to be perceived as an ally, but Phillip wasn't going to contradict Eloise and undermine her authority. Especially not when he agreed with her wholeheartedly.

But then Oliver surprised him. He didn't beg to be set free from Mr. Larkin's clutches, and he didn't say something horrid about Eloise, which, Phillip was sure, he would have done just a few weeks earlier, about any adult who thwarted his wishes.

Oliver just looked up at him and asked, "Will you come with me, Father? Please."

Phillip opened his mouth to reply, but then, inexplicably, had to stop. His eyes began to sting with unshed tears, and he realized that he was, quite simply, overcome.

It wasn't just the moment, the fact that his son wanted his company for a male rite of passage. Oliver had begged his company before.

But this was the first time that Phillip felt truly able to say yes, confident that if he went, he would do the right thing and say the right words.

And even if he didn't, it wouldn't matter. He wasn't his father, would never be—*could* never be like him. He couldn't afford to be a coward, to keep pushing his children toward other people, all because he was worried he'd make a mistake.

He *would* make mistakes. It was inevitable. But they wouldn't be huge ones, and with Eloise at his side, he was quite confident he could do anything.

Even manage the twins.

He placed his hand on Oliver's shoulder. "I would be delighted to accompany you, son." He cleared his throat, which had gone hoarse on the final word. Then he bent down and whispered, "The last thing we want is women over on the men's side."

Oliver nodded his vigorous agreement.

Phillip straightened, preparing to follow his son back to Mr. Larkin's side of the establishment. Then he heard Eloise, clearing her throat behind him. He turned, and she was gesturing with her head toward the back of the room.

Amanda.

Looking very grown up in her new lavender frock, showing just a hint of the woman she would one day become.

For the second time in as many minutes, Phillip's eyes began to burn.

This was what he'd been missing. In his fear, in his self-doubt, he'd been missing this.

They'd been growing up without him.

Phillip patted his son on the shoulder to signal that he'd be right back, and then crossed the room to his daughter's side. Without a word, he picked up her hand and kissed it. "You, Miss Amanda Crane," he said, his heart in his eyes, his voice, his smile, "are the most beautiful girl I have ever seen."

Her eyes grew wide and her lips formed a tiny little *O* of sheer delight. "What about Miss—Mother?" she whispered frantically.

Phillip looked over at his wife, who appeared close to tears herself, and then turned back to Amanda, leaning over to whisper in her ear, "Let's make a deal, you and I. You can think your mother is the most beautiful woman alive. But I get to think it's you."

And later that night, after he'd tucked them into bed, kissed each on the forehead, and headed for the door, he heard his daughter whisper, "Father?"

He turned. "Amanda?"

"This was the best day ever, Father," she whispered.

"Ever," Oliver agreed.

Phillip nodded. "For me as well," he said softly. "For me as well."

* * *

It started with a note.

Later that night, as Eloise finished her supper and her plate was cleared away, she realized that there had been a piece of paper tucked underneath, folded twice until it formed a small rectangle.

Her husband had excused himself, claiming that he needed to find a book that contained a poem they had been discussing over pudding, and so, with no one watching her, not even the footman, who was busy transporting the dishes to the kitchen, Eloise unfolded the paper.

I have never been good with words,

it said, in Phillip's unmistakable handwriting. And then, smaller, in the corner:

Proceed to your office.

Intrigued, she stood and exited the dining room. A minute later she entered her office.

And there, in the middle of her desk, was another piece of paper.

But it all started with a letter, did it not?

Followed by instructions to take herself to the sitting room. She did, this time having to concentrate quite hard on keeping her half walk, half skip from turning into a full-fledged run.

A small piece of paper, again folded twice, sat on a red cushion positioned at the very center of the sofa.

And so if it started with words, it ought to continue with them, too.

This time she was directed to the front hall.

But there are no words to thank you for all you have given me, so I will use the only ones at my disposal, and I will tell you the only way I know how.

And at the bottom corner of the note, she was directed to her bedroom.

Eloise headed up the stairs slowly, her heart beating with anticipation. This was her final destination, she was sure of it. Phillip would be waiting for her, waiting to take her hand, to lead her into their future together.

It had, she realized, all started with a note. Something so innocent, so innocuous, and it had grown into this, a love so full and rich she could barely contain it.

She reached the upstairs hall and on quiet feet made her way to the bedroom door. It was slightly ajar, just an inch or so, and with shaking hand she pushed it open, all the way—

And she gasped.

For there, on the bed, were flowers. Hundreds and hundred of blooms, some clearly out of season, picked from Phillip's special collection in his greenhouse. And written in blossoms of red, against the backdrop of white and pink petals:

I LOVE YOU.

"Words aren't enough," Phillip said softly, stepping out of the shadows behind her.

She turned to him, barely cognizant of the tears trickling down her cheeks. "When did you do this?"

He smiled. "Surely you'll allow me a few secrets."

"I—I—"

He took her hand, pulled her close. "Speechless?" he murmured. "You? I must be better at this than I thought."

"I love you," she said, choking on the words. "I love you so much."

His arms came around her, and as she laid her cheek against his chest, his chin came down to rest gently on her head. "Today," he said softly, "the twins told me it was the best day ever. And I realized they were right."

Eloise nodded, beyond words.

"But then," he continued, "I realized they were wrong."

She looked up at him, question in her eyes.

"I couldn't choose a day," he confessed. "Any day with you, Eloise. Any day with you."

He touched her chin, brought his lips to hers. "Any week," he murmured, "any month, any hour."

He kissed her then, softly, but with all the love in his soul. "Any moment," he whispered, "as long as I'm with you."

Epilogue

There is so much I hope to teach you, little one. I hope that I may do so by example, but I feel the need to put the words to paper as well. It is a quirk of mine, one which I expect you will recognize and find amusing by the time you read this letter.

Be strong.

Be diligent.

Be conscientious. There is never anything to be gained by taking the easy road. (Unless, of course, the road is an easy one to begin with. Roads sometimes are. If that should be the case, do not forge a new, more difficult one. Only martyrs go out looking for trouble.)

Love your siblings. You have two already, and God willing, there will be more. Love them well, for they are your blood, and when you are unsure, or times are difficult, they will be the ones to stand by your side.

Laugh. Laugh out loud, and laugh often. And when circumstances call for silence, turn your laugh into a smile.

Don't settle. Know what you want and reach for

it. And if you don't know what you want, be patient. The answers will come to you in time, and you may find that your heart's desire has been right under your nose all the while.

And remember, always remember that you have a mother and a father who love each other and love you.

I feel you growing restless. Your father is making strange gasping sounds and will surely lose his temper altogether if I do not move from my escritoire to my bed.

Welcome to the world, little one. We are all so delighted to make your acquaintance.

—*from Eloise, Lady Crane,*
to her daughter Penelope,
upon the occasion of her birth

Meet the Bridgertons . . .

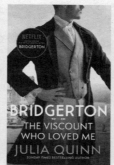
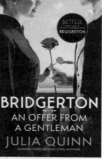

BRIDGERTON
THE DUKE & I

BRIDGERTON
THE VISCOUNT
WHO LOVED ME
JULIA QUINN

BRIDGERTON
AN OFFER FROM
A GENTLEMAN
JULIA QUINN

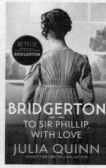
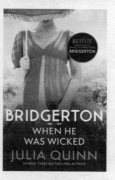

BRIDGERTON
ROMANCING
MR BRIDGERTON
JULIA QUINN

BRIDGERTON
TO SIR PHILLIP,
WITH LOVE
JULIA QUINN

BRIDGERTON
WHEN HE
WAS WICKED
JULIA QUINN

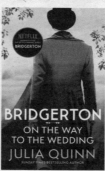
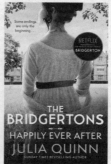

BRIDGERTON
IT'S IN HIS KISS
JULIA QUINN

BRIDGERTON
ON THE WAY
TO THE WEDDING
JULIA QUINN

THE
BRIDGERTONS
HAPPILY EVER AFTER
JULIA QUINN

Available from

PIATKUS

*Let the notorious Lady Whistledown
be your personal guide to the Bridgerton world,
offering new gossip and classic quotes from the most
beloved Regency romance series of all time!*

Available from

Do you love historical fiction?

Want the chance to hear news about your favourite authors (and the chance to win free books)?

Suzanne Allain
Mary Balogh
Lenora Bell
Charlotte Betts
Manda Collins
Joanna Courtney
Grace Burrowes
Evie Dunmore
Lynne Francis
Pamela Hart
Elizabeth Hoyt
Eloisa James
Lisa Kleypas
Jayne Ann Krentz
Sarah MacLean
Terri Nixon
Julia Quinn

Then visit the Piatkus website
www.yourswithlove.co.uk

And follow us on Facebook and Instagram
www.facebook.com/yourswithlovex | @yourswithlovex

PIATKUS